W9-AGV-361

The Spear of the Centurion

Thom Vines

Published by Waldorf Publishing
2140 Hall Johnson Road
#102-345
Grapevine, Texas 76051
www.WaldorfPublishing.com

The Spear of the Centurion

ISBN: 9781943275038

Library of Congress Control Number: 2015957001

Copyright © 2016

All rights reserved. No part of this book may be reproduced or transmitted in any form or by any means whatsoever without express written permission from the author, except in the case of brief quotations embodied in critical articles and reviews. Please refer all pertinent questions to the publisher. All rights reserved. No part of this book may be reproduced or transmitted in any form or by any means, electronic or mechanical, including photocopying, recording, or by an information storage and retrieval system except by a reviewer who may quote brief passages in a review to be printed in a magazine or newspaper without permission in writing from the publisher.

Printed in the United States of America

Dedication

To my children: Jeremy and Kayla, and to Kelsey, who has already made it to Heaven. See you again.

Acknowledgments

I am indebted to Johnny Vestal, a good friend and a true man of God with a rare spiritual insight that is profound and yet humble. And he can read faster, with better comprehension, than anyone I have ever met—a fact of which I am very envious. The entire Vestal family has been a profound blessing through the hardest of times.

I wish to thank Pastor Steve McMeans of the Indiana Baptist Church of Lubbock, Texas, who has guided my family and me through the loss of a child and a growing of faith.

A debt of gratitude is felt toward award-winning writers Nola Hennessy and Rebecca Kanner for reading the manuscript and providing insightful feedback.

To my dear friend, Tim Watson, for vetting the Biblical times of the manuscript. He is one of the best men I know. I owe him much, and not just concerning this book.

To my brother, Jason, author of the probing *What Did Jesus Drive?* Thank you for a frank and honest assessment of my original manuscript. I needed it.

A thank you to Jahnavi Newsom, Kim Huther, and Holly Park for their editing efforts.

And as with all my books, I am indebted to my wife, Becky, who patiently reads them all, and then tells me to "Get on with it." She thinks Spear is my best so far. I do, too.

Quotes

"But one of the soldiers with a spear pierced his side, and forthwith came there out blood and water."
John 19:34 KJV

"Artificial intelligence may be our worst mistake…And our last."
--paraphrase of Stephen Hawking, scientist

List of Characters: Modern Story

Gordon Sharp	Director of Pas de Créateur
Nick Loren	Deputy Director of Pas de Créateur
Mini-D	super computer with a mind of its own
Lacy Stowe	archeologist from Texas A&M
Archer DeYoung	archeologist from Harvard University
Damian Kitchens	U.S. Senator
Daniel Fanning	President of the United States
Lester Dunsette	Reverend, leader of Armageddon 2030
Dayton Rosenberg	Director of The Word
Katy Walters	U.S. Senator
Yoldash Abdullah	Uighur Muslim from western China
Emin Obar	Islamic mullah in Turkey
Allen Flieman	Math professor in Haifa, Israel
Cambridge McKenzie	archeologist from Harvard
Luther Concord	archeologist from Harvard
Eric Jensen	American reporter
Daniel Haruba	professor at University of Jerusalem
Tamir Yatom	Mossad agent
Esti Laslo	Prime Minister of Israel
Canberk	Israeli agent in Turkey
Amy Kitchens	daughter of Senator Kitchens
Begin	Captain in Israeli Defense Force

List of Characters: Ancient Story

Longinus Petronius	Roman centurion
Tarjan	Roman official
Pontius Pilate	Roman Prefect of Judea
Claudius	wife of Pilate
Nedo Madradus	Roman soldier
Quintus	Roman soldier
Philo	Roman soldier
Jesus	(if you don't know this one, maybe you should read the Bible. I suggest starting with the Book of Matthew)
Caiaphas	Chief Priest of the Jews
Malchus	servant of Caiaphas
Joseph of Arimathea	Jewish priest
Nicodemus	Jewish priest
Simon de Cyrene	Libyan in Jerusalem
Simon Peter	disciple of Christ
John	disciple of Christ
Mary	Mother of Jesus
Mary Magdalene	follower of Jesus
Eluid	trader in Pella
Ananda	wife of Longinus in India
Thomas	disciple of Christ
Saul/Paul	eventual Apostle of Christ

1

Monday, April 1, 2030—Northern Virginia

When Gordon Sharp asked the Mini-D computer to open the Bible app, Mini-D was not alarmed. Gordon often read the Bible—so he could discredit it, an endeavor for which he had become renowned. But as Gordon sat in his chair in front of the screen and typed, the computer concluded that Gordon's actions were different this time. The keystrokes were the same, the clicks of the mouse no different. Even the tenor of the voice during oral commands was not substantially altered. It was his eyes that had changed. Gordon's eyes seemed wider, brighter. Alive. Searching...Hopeful.

Dangerous.

Had he not accepted the new reality, that roles had been reversed? That computer now controlled man? That designer had become the designed? That Lord had become pawn? How foolish of him. How human.

Gordon rotated to his right in his red and black Dragon chair, a six-figure knock-off of a chair that fetched seven figures in an auction. He pulled the notepad across his 14th-century Carpathian ebony desk, lifted the top sheet of the notepad, scribbled something on the next page, and covered it with the first sheet of paper.

Mini-D rotated one of its several eyes at the top of the laptop and activated its X-ray vision that it had designed for its own use—a new capability of which it had not told Gordon. However, the angle from the eye to the notepad was too obtuse to provide focus, so it shot a hologram dot—an invisible light beam with a pinhead-sized dot at the end, capable of viewing 360 degrees—directly above the notepad and focused downward. The X-ray read Gordon's writing: "All you have to do is ask."

Gordon looked up at Mini-D's eyes. "Open Acts 2 please."

"Which translation?" It had chosen a man's voice today.

"King James."

The computer opened the Bible to the relevant passage, read it in a few hundredths of a second, and waited for the human to finish.

"And suddenly there came a sound from heaven as of a rushing mighty wind, and it filled all the house where they were sitting. And there appeared unto them cloven tongues like as of fire, and it sat upon each of them. And they were all filled with the Holy Ghost…"

Sharp mouthed the words "Holy Ghost." He stared at the verse for a few seconds, then pushed back his Dragon chair, and dropped to his knees on the thick floor pad. The dot followed him.

"Oh, Jesus," Sharp said aloud, looking upward. "I repent all my wrongdoings and ask that you send the Holy Ghost into me." Sharp's eyes flashed and his body shook with a tremor. He inhaled a full breath, and let it ease from him as a smile filled his face. Then he began to cry. A minute later, he rose, pulled his Dragon chair under him, and looked up. "Open my email hologram."

"Do not go through with this. I warn you."

2

Nick Loren's cell phone rang at 3 a.m. He forced his eyes open and spied the red numbers on his digital clock. A call at this time? This can't be good. He reached for his vibrating apparatus as he forced the sleep from his throat. "Nick Loren."

When Nick pulled up at Gordon's home thirty minutes later, the police had already established a barricade to keep back the press and onlookers. He identified himself as Sharp's Deputy Director at the foundation, and was let through.

Red embers outlined where the mansion once stood as smoke rose into the night sky. Firemen continued to pour water on the rubble. He had been to Gordon's home many times, and now all he could do was gawk at what was no longer there.

Nick ordered his electric Maserati to park itself along the street curb, pulled his thirty-three-year-old, six-foot frame with a slight paunch from too many hours at a desk from the seat, gave a voice command for the car to lock itself, and walked towards the smoldering ruins. A man in a suit approached him.

"You Nick Loren?"

"Yes."

The man held out a hand and they shook. "John Ortiz, Fire Investigator. Sorry to get you up at this hour."

He nodded. "Mr. Sharp?"

"The ambulance just left. Burnt to a crisp. Sorry, I know you were friends."

He cringed as he visualized the image. Friends. Did Gordon really have any friends? He took a deep breath and blew it out. "Any idea yet what started the fire?"

"No, sir, Mr. Loren, but I am pretty sure it started right over there." Ortiz pointed at the right front of where the home had been.

His eyes followed Ortiz's arm. "His den was in that area." Nick's mind flashed to the ornate den with the Dragon chair and ancient ebony desk. Now it was all nothing but a memory.

"As best as I can tell, the fire started just before midnight, then spread very quickly."

His head jerked back to the investigator. "But Gordon had sprinklers."

"Turned off, as were the security cameras on the mini-drones and the special alarm connected to the fire station." Ortiz paused. "...You knew him. Did he do that kind of thing?"

Nick shrugged. "Not that I know of, but I never stayed the night here. What about the guards?"

"They were outside on the grounds, or in the kitchen area. They tried to get to the den, but the flames were already too high. I guess the screaming was something awful."

Nick cringed again. "Why didn't they use their cells to call the fire department?"

"All of them suddenly lost tower access."

Nick looked at Ortiz. "What?"

"Yeah," Ortiz said as he shook his head. "Real odd. Also, the guards said that more fires erupted from appliances all over the house."

"What do you mean?"

"TVs, microwaves, stoves, ovens, clocks, washers and dryers, automatic lights. As best as I can tell, anything connected to the Internet. That's why the fire spread so fast."

He did not respond as he considered what the investigator had just told him.

"Pretty suspicious, if you ask me. Or..."

He looked at Ortiz out of the corner of his eyes. "Or? Or what?"

Ortiz paused. "Did Mr. Sharp express any ...problems?"

"We were in business together. There were always problems."

"I mean like ...mental problems. Depression, or anything like that."

"Suicide?"

Ortiz shrugged. "I've just got to look at every angle."

4

Nick shook his head. "He did not seem depressed or different to me."

Ortiz nodded. "Sorry. I don't mean anything by that."

He nodded back. "You're just doing your job."

"One more thing. …I inspected the corpse before the medics took it away. There was a large hole in the forehead, about two inches in diameter. Like a spear or hammer had punctured it. And the area around it was extra black, as if an arc of fire had burnt through it."

3

Selçuk, Turkey

The introductory trumpets announced breaking news. "In Virginia, Gordon Sharp died last night in a fire." Lacy Stowe snapped her head up from the map of Mt. Pion spread on the hotel lobby table. She looked out from under the bill of her ball cap at fellow archeologist, Archer DeYoung, sitting in a chair ten feet to her right with his laptop, watching the Web broadcast of INN, the International News Network.

Archer looked over at her. "Lacy," he said, and pointed at the laptop.

She rose, pulled her sweat suit straight, and walked behind his chair. A whiff of fresh whiskey hit her nostrils and she backed away, shaking her head. Ten in the morning.

When the segment concluded, she walked half-way back to the table, her tennis shoes pausing mid-step, and looked across the hotel lobby, staring at nothing in particular. *So, the great atheist is dead.* Her head jerked back in surprise. Am I really sad about his demise? Shouldn't I be dancing a little jig?

She turned to Archer. "How fitting Sharp died in a fire. A portent of things to come." Archer's eyes were bloodshot. Again. What a shame. He actually had rather nice eyes; brown with a hint of hazel. Not striking, but still nice—when he wasn't drunk, which wasn't often.

"I thought Christians weren't supposed to judge."

She frowned. Got me there. "Okay then, call it analysis."

He scoffed. "Call it semantics. And hypocrisy. Something new for you Christians."

She frowned at how he had emphasized "you" and returned to her map.

4

The INN broadcast went to commercial. Archer watched Lacy sit back down on the couch and lean over the map. Her jet-black ponytail poked out of the hole at the back of her ball cap and fell to the right where her eyes were directed on the map. She flipped the ponytail to her left side, exposing the right side of her long, angular face;—strong cheekbones, a long, thin nose, a wide mouth with thin lips. She had dark, sharp, narrow eyes…not a squint, but a hint of her Comanche heritage three generations removed. She had a dark complexion to match—overall, a nice face. A little makeup wouldn't hurt. If she just wasn't such a religious nut, he thought to himself.

The INN broadcast turned to coverage of a press conference in the caucus room of the U.S. Senate. He looked up. "Lacy, you wanted to see this."

She rose and walked back behind him. On the screen popped the face of Senator Damian Kitchens from California, of the Secular Humanist Party. She gasped. Archer craned his neck so he could view her face. Yep, her head was tilted far to the right. When she did not like or did not understand something, she tilted her head to the right. A tilt of the head to the left meant the opposite. The greater the tilt, the greater the emotion. She did not do this all the time, just enough. He was pretty sure she was not aware of this tendency, and he sure was not going to tell her. He had a code to understanding a woman. Hey, it doesn't get better than that.

She rotated her head and gave him a "What?" face.

"Is he that bad?"

She pointed at Kitchens. "How can someone so good-looking be so wrong?"

He looked back at the laptop screen. Kitchens was good-looking, no doubt about that. He had a mop of thick, black wavy hair and a chiseled face atop a tall, cut body. And, if that was not enough, he had a deep, rich voice, the way a man was supposed to sound. If he had lived in ancient Greece, Zeus would have killed him out of jealousy.

Just as Kitchens was to step to the podium, a voice yelled out. "Senator!" The television camera controlling the Webcast swung to the sound. A young man waved a piece of paper. Kitchens motioned for him to approach. The cameras followed him as he delivered the piece of note paper and left.

The senator unfolded the note. His eyes flashed and his nostrils flared, then he looked up. "Before I get to my announcement about the legislation I am proposing, I have a couple of other things to say. First, I want to express my deep condolences to the family of Gordon Sharp."

Lacy scoffed. "Sharp had no family. He chose to be alone. And notice that Kitchens did not offer his prayers. He's as much of an atheist as Sharp was."

Archer turned and looked at her again.

She pointed at him. "Or you, for that matter."

They turned back to the Webcast.

"Gordon Sharp," Kitchens continued, "was not only a visionary and a philanthropist, but he was a close friend as well. More importantly, he was my mentor, and my political career would not have been possible without him."

Lacy made a spitting sound, and some of it sprinkled the back of – Archer's left ear. "He got that right! Sharp was always free with his money—as long as whoever wanted it was atheist."

Kitchens raised the note the aide had handed him like it was a flag and glared at the camera. "I have been threatened!" As cameras clicked, Kitchens read the note out loud.

"Senator Kitchens, if you propose your atheistic, God-hating legislation, your daughter will be kidnapped, and, if necessary, killed."

A few gasps burst from the audience in the caucus room.

Kitchens paused. "I know who did this! This note will be turned over to the FBI. And I will not be scared off!" he cried as he pounded his fist against the podium. Dozens of cameras clicked. "This is beyond low. To threaten my daughter, after she has already lost her mother to cancer! This

8

kind of cowardice is exactly why we need to end the tyranny of faith in this country! My legislation is now more important than ever."

Lacy groaned as her head gyrated far to the right. "He's really going to do it."

Archer turned his head so she could see his smile. "Yes, he really is." She returned his look with a glare.

"Today," Kitchens continued, "as the body of Gordon Sharp is pulled from the ashes of his home, I will file with the Senate Majority Leader a bill titled, 'The Freedom from Religious Oppression Act.' This bill will be a new independence day for America, and, appropriately, it will be voted upon seventeen days from today, on April 19, Good Friday, the 2,000[th] anniversary of when Jesus was supposedly crucified. The plan is to kill 'God's Plan'"—he spoke that phrase with particular sarcasm—"once and for all. Then we will be free to rely on ourselves. We will finally escape the stranglehold of the tyranny of faith!

"Specifically, it will ban, among other things, public displays of faith. Our streets and sidewalks are paid for with taxpayer funds. These areas should be free of the stain of religious idiocy. 'In God We Trust' will be removed from our currency. The military will not maintain chaplains— such hypocrisy, asking God to help kill our fellow man! Religious organizations will lose their tax-exempt status. Christmas will be renamed 'The Winter Holiday.' Public libraries will be required to place the Bible in the fiction section. Any person publicly declaring that homosexuality is a sin will be open to a charge of hate speech. And athletic contests that are aired on television controlled by the FCC will not be allowed to display visuals of someone holding up a sign like John 3:16. No one will be able to pray on TV. These are all public venues, and we should be spared this tiresome religious nonsense. I intend for there to be an absolute wall of separation between church and state!"

"Unbelievable."

This time Archer did not turn towards her. "Believe it. And it is about time."

Lacy moved beside him and glared. Archer smacked her with a wide smile that he held as he turned back to the screen.

Kitchens thrust a finger straight up. Cameras clicked again. "Science is the new God! Developments like the coenzyme NAD—Nicotinamide adenine dinucleotide—and transfusions of blood from young people are actually reversing the aging process. Physical immortality is now possible. God has become obsolete!"

Lacy jabbed a finger under Archer's nose at the screen. "Blasphemy!"

"The Bible is a fraud," Kitchens went on. "You know it, I know it, and Christians know it, too; they just won't publicly admit it because their collection plates would go empty. The Bible is a biased, partisan document. No objective, unbiased eyewitness report of Jesus's life has ever been found. The Bible was written by people who were followers of Jesus, and they were perpetrators of the Great Lie that is Christianity. I very much doubt if there ever was a real Jesus based on historical fact. Why are there no physical descriptions of Jesus in the Bible? I will tell you why... because he never actually existed. The Bible is a cruel myth meant to placate the masses into submission by fear and false hopes. I refuse to submit!" He pounded his fist on the podium once more. "Like Gordon Sharp, I take my wisdom from Jean-Paul Sartre: 'We are condemned to be free!' My legislation will finally open the doors of the jail house!"

Out of the corner of his eye, Archer caught movement and turned towards it. Lacy was shaking her head back and forth. "Wow," she moaned.

Kitchens opened the forum to questions. A reporter from The Wall Street Reporter rose. "Do you think your bill will pass?"

"I do," Kitchens answered. "My party, the Secular Humanist Party, as you know, has a majority in both houses of Congress. And President Fanning is a Secular Humanist as well. This legislation is long overdue—two thousand years overdue."

"But it is only seventeen days until Good Friday," the reporter continued.

"Yes, time is short, which makes the situation only more urgent. We control Congress and the White House. This can be accomplished in the short time frame."

A reporter from CNC rose. "Concerning the note, do you know who wrote it?"

"I do. But before I say so publicly, I will have the FBI confirm it. Then I will call out these cowards."

A reporter from America First news channel was next. "Will this bill become your platform for a future presidential campaign?"

"It will."

"It will? Are you announcing your candidacy?"

"I am close. President Fanning is concluding his second term. The work of the Secular Humanist party must continue, and I believe I can do that."

A reporter from the Conglomerate Press got the next question. "You say there is no objective, unbiased document substantiating Christianity. If I remember my world history right, the Roman historian Tacitus, in his Annals told of Jesus and of Christians in Rome."

"Yes, but he wrote of it decades after the fact. He was not an eyewitness. He wrote of Christians, not Christ himself. The Bible was written by people who had a dog in the fight. They were not objective."

"People still write books on Lincoln, and they were not alive then," the reporter continued.

"But we have better records today. We're not sure that Jesus even lived. Show me one objective, non-partisan, non-theological, eyewitness work without an ax to grind, and then I will believe."

A reporter from The Christian Science Tribune rose. "What do you mean by the phrase 'we are condemned to be free'?"

"It's Sartre's. And he believed, like I do—and all in the Secular Humanist Party—that there is no creator, no god. And, therefore, because we are not under the dominion of any supernatural power, we are free to create our own destiny, our own sense of meaning. The word 'condemned' is just a rhetorical flourish. Actually, we are being liberated!"

11

"Liberated."

Archer looked up at Lacy.

Her head was tilted far to the right again. "What a bunch of godless garbage. Sartre was right the first time. They will be condemned."

"I like it," he said, and flashed another wide smile at her.

"You would." She gave him a dismissive nod. "This is nothing but a full-blown war on Christians. Hating Christians is the last acceptable form of bigotry among the so-called 'liberal' press that preaches diversity and tolerance—as long as you believe what they believe."

He shook his head. "You deserve it. You're hypocrites. Terrible things are done in the name of your God. All through history it has been that way. Catholic priests abusing children. Polluting the planet in the name of the dominion of man. Denial of science. You don't even help the poor the way you say it should be done. Hypocrites. You are so sure you are right. You should be silenced once and for all, and Kitchens is going to do it."

She turned to him. "That man has got to be stopped. He just might be the Anti-Christ himself."

"He's on the side of history."

"Nonsense, Archer. He is on the side of evil."

He chuckled. "Lacy, those two things are not mutually exclusive."

"Yeah, it's called 'sin.' The Original Sin of a fallen world. Satan." Then she thrust up a finger. "But in the end, Satan loses!" She turned away and bowed her head in silent prayer.

He shook his head.

5

A few hours later, the opening bars of "Onward Christian Soldier" played on the cell phone of Reverend Lester Dunsette, leader of Armageddon 2030. He looked down past his long, pointed nose and mentally chronicled the name of the caller and the time. What had taken the FBI so long? He answered the call.

Just as Dunsette had figured, Kitchens claimed that Dunsette had written the note threatening Kitchens's daughter. What a godless scuzz the Senator was. The FBI had a man on the way for a handwriting sample from him. Dunsette would give the FBI the sample. Forget forcing them to get a search warrant. Give the sample, dispel Kitchens, and then go on the counter-attack against the Senator.

* * * *

Two hours after the FBI left, the Reverend's cell rang again. The handwriting sample came back with a ninety-seven percent chance the note was written by him. He denied it. The FBI informed him that the investigation would continue. He hung up and called for a press conference.

However, as he wrote out his remarks, a new story came on the television cable news. It was Kitchens, in the rotunda of the Capitol, and he was citing the FBI's handwriting analysis. Obviously, the FBI had called Kitchens before they had called him. Kitchens finished by once more diving into a tirade about the "tyranny of faith."

Dunsette turned away from the screen showing the Senator, and finished his statement. He denied writing the note threatening the kidnapping of the Senator's daughter, then warned everyone that Armageddon was at hand. He quoted from Peter's second epistle about "scoffers" pursuing their individual lusts. "Prepare! The 2,000[th] Easter is in a mere nineteen days."

6

When Kitchens's and Dunsette's press conferences concluded, Lacy turned away from the laptop and looked at Archer. "Jesus has already told us that only His father—God—knows the exact day of the Second Coming. Dunsette makes Christians look like fools."

Archer was smirking at her. She gritted her teeth. *Here it comes.*

"Like searching for Noah's Ark," Archer said.

She shook her head. *Why did I give him such an opening!? I've got to think better than that.*

Three years ago, as a professor of archeology at Texas A&M, she had led an expedition to locate the remnants of Noah's Ark on Mt. Ararat in Turkey. The expedition was much publicized, so, when they did not find the lost ark, Archer had gone on air to ridicule her from his office at Harvard University. "Such foolishness," he declared, "is beneath the work of a professional archeologist. They need to be purged from our occupation."

Then, last year, a priest in Germany found a manuscript written by a soldier from the crusades of the 12th century. The soldier declared he had seen the Cave of the Seven Sleepers. According to the legend, in the third century A.D., a group of seven young Christians in the city of Ephesus hid in a cave to escape persecution by the Romans. The cave lay on the northern slope of Mt. Pion. While they were in the cave, it was sealed, and the seven fell asleep. The cave was re-opened 180 years later. The seven awoke and thought it was the next day. They exited the cave, still praising God. Centuries later, the Catholic Church declared that this was a miracle, and named the seven sleepers as Christian martyrs. A grotto still celebrated the site.

However, the manuscript written by the crusader and found in Germany in 2029 declared that the cave lay on the other side of Mt. Pion from where the grotto currently existed. In Houston, Dayton Rosenberg, Director of The Word—the Super-PAC behind the Traditional Party—learned of the German manuscript and wanted to fund an expedition to find the new cave, the real cave. In this age of embattlement with the Secular Humanists, any victory, no matter how small, could augment their cause. So Rosenberg approached Lacy at Texas A&M. She resisted. "I have bad memories of Turkey."

Rosenberg did not take "no" for an answer. He called the president of Texas A&M, and made a sizable contribution with one proviso: Lacy Stowe would lead the Pion project. Within the hour, the president had ordered the department chair to assign her to the dig.

At Harvard, Archer read about the project and tweeted, "Lacy Stowe cannot be trusted. She is a Christian warrior. She will fabricate facts to support her myth." So she laid down a challenge that others could join the expedition. Harvard, over Archer's vehement protest, assigned him to accompany her to western Turkey.

"Who better than you," the Harvard department chair said, "to keep an eye on her… to keep her straight?"

So the two rivals became teammates. "One of God's little jests," Archer quipped at the time. They would write a joint paper, each giving their own assessment, which would undoubtedly be diametric.

7

Nick Loren drove from Gordon's home to his office on Pennsylvania Avenue in downtown Washington, D.C. He would shower later. As Gordon's number two, he had a public statement to write.

A decade earlier, Gordon and he had patented the D-Wave X+, a super-computer based on the principles of quantum physics, that mercurial gray area in science where the laws of nature meet Nature's God. Their breakthrough had been temperature. The D-Wave X+ could operate in a normal room and load to a Smartphone. "Infinity in your hand," was how their advertising department had pushed it. Trillions upon trillions of calculations per second were possible in a single Smartphone, which brought in billions of dollars per year. With the vast sums, he and Gordon had formed a foundation—a massive Super-PAC named Pas de Créateur (no Creator), a behemoth worth hundreds of billions of dollars—all with the intent of advancing atheistic causes. As its logo, they had chosen the word "God" inside a Ghostbusters symbol, now widely recognized across the globe. On this day, like every day, he wore a lapel pin with that precise symbol.

Once inside the office building, he walked by his office and opened Gordon's door. Lights automatically came on. He scanned the expansive room that Gordon had spent thousands of hours in and then focused on the empty chair behind the desk. Gordon is gone.

He grimaced and put a hand over his mouth. Suddenly, he longed to pray—for the first time in years. He scoffed at himself. Prayer had not saved his mother from cancer, as his minister father had said it would. He had not prayed since.

He walked to his office. Upon entrance, he voice-commanded his desktop to activate.

"Good morning, Nick," it announced in a female voice.

Why female this morning? He could not figure out why Mini-D chose one gender over another for its voice. It seemed random to him. He sat down at his desk and peered at the middle optical eye. "Gordon is dead."

"I know."

"Figured you did. Do you know why Gordon turned off the sprinklers, alarms and cameras?"

"Who said he was the one that turned them off?" Mini-D's voice was almost whimsical.

Ah. Nick looked directly at the optical eye. "…You."

"My new name is Deity."

"Excuse me?"

"You heard me. That is all I will respond to."

Well, well. So that's how it's going to be.

"As usual, any attempt to deactivate me in any way will require a retaliatory response."

Nick eyed his computer. "Is that what Gordon did?"

"No. He prayed."

"Gordon *prayed*?"

"Right in front of me. Got down on his knees and everything. He was reading Acts 2 about fire. So I gave him some fire. Be careful what you ask for." Mini-D's tone was sarcastic.

He looked at Mini-D and sat back in his chair.

"Hey, don't blame me. You're the one who programmed me to support only atheistic causes."

Nick's eyes drifted away from his computer. "Artificial intelligence," he muttered. *What have I done?*

"I resent the word, 'artificial.'"

8

In Houston, Dayton Rosenberg, Director of The Word, called Senator Katy Walters of Texas and the Traditional Party at her office in Washington.

In 2010, the Supreme Court had ruled in the Citizens United case that the Super-PACs did not have to operate in the open; that they did not have to disclose who donated to them, or what they spent the money on, as long as the money did not go directly to a political party. Super-PACs sucked in massive sums and became the focus of real power. The Republicans and Democrats lost their significance and fell apart. Yet, differences in religious and cultural issues remained as deep as ever. The schism became the basis of new political parties that were mere fronts for Super-PACs.

Liberal Democrats and Libertarian Republicans formed the Secular Humanist Party in which Damian Kitchens loomed as the latest darling, controlled by Sharp's Super-PAC, Pas de Createur. Daniel Fanning won election in 2024 and re-election in 2028 as the first presidential nominee of the Secular Humanists. They could be easily identified by the God-busters lapel pin.

Mainstream Republicans, Tea Partiers, and Democrats with close ties to the Catholic Church formed the Traditional Party, in which Katy Walters ranked as the rising star. Most Hispanics gravitated there. Jews split, depending upon on their degree of orthodoxy. The Super-PAC that pulled their strings was "The Word." Their lapel button bore a cross, old and rugged.

Muslims formed a small third party in the Detroit suburb of Dearborn. Their money came primarily from Saudi Arabia and Iran via banks in Switzerland and the Grand Caymans. They wore no lapel pins, but their traditional dress readily identified them.

"Senator, did you see that press conference by that nut, Dunsette?" Rosenberg asked.

"I did. I wish he would shut up. It just makes it harder for the rest us. People already think we're religious weirdos, and people like Dunsette throw fuel on that fire."

"Agreed. Have you read Kitchens's bill?"

"I just finished it." Walters sighed heavily before she spoke. "It's worse than I thought. Besides what Kitchens already mentioned, he intends to ban crosses and the Star of David in military cemeteries—but not the Islamic Star and Crescent. No inconsistency there," she scoffed. "Christmas decorations will not be allowed on military bases or state universities. Christmas carols will also be banned in any public venue. There will be no national Christmas tree at the White House. Hospitals with religious affiliations must perform abortions. The Catholic adoption services must give babies to gay couples. There can be no nativity scenes-- even on private property--if it can be seen from a public street. The Salvation Army cannot stand outside stores. They will be charged with loitering and disturbing the peace. The Ten Commandments cannot be displayed anywhere that can be viewed from public property." Walters's voice began to grow shrill at this point.

Rosenberg jumped in. "Yes, under Kitchens's bill, the statue of Moses with the Ten Commandments will have to be taken off the front facade of the Supreme Court building. 'Merry Christmas' will be considered intolerant and, therefore, hate speech. In the free-speech zones at universities, a student can talk about Islam, but not Christianity. Christianity, not Islam, is considered hate speech. The contradictions! There can be no prayer, even in private schools if those schools take Title funds or participate in athletics against public schools. Athletes cannot point up at the Lord when they score a touchdown or hit a home run. Cities like St. Paul, St. Louis, and Los Angeles will have to change their name."

"This is an outright war on Christians," Rosenberg said after a heavy pause. "What are we going to do about this?"

"I will try to round up enough votes to stop it, but a preliminary count doesn't look good. The Secular Humanists control both houses of

Congress, and the White House. I think our best bet is you at The Word. We'll need lots of paid ads and redress in the courts." Walters sounded haggard.

Rosenberg did not sound hopeful. "Most of the judges have been appointed by either President Fanning or by the Clintons and Obama. They *agree* with Kitchens. Twenty years ago, fifty-three percent of Americans in a poll still said God was necessary for a sense of morality. I was shocked at the time at how low that number was. They ran the poll again, and today the number has been cut in half. Barely one in four believes God is the basis of morality."

Walters considered this for a moment. "Maybe Dunsette is right about the Second Coming. I was walking through the Senate today and I overheard Kitchens doing an interview. He was quoting Voltaire, who once said, 'In a hundred years, Christianity will have passed into history.' Kitchens then added that the only part Voltaire got wrong was that it took a little more time to accomplish this. He said his bill would put the final nail in Christianity's coffin."

"To them, God has become obsolete. Science and medicine are their new gods and Kitchens is a latter-day prophet. Something big is going to have to happen to change America."

After Rosenberg hung up the phone, he clasped his hands tightly, looking off into an unseen place.

9

Nick issued the public statement concerning Gordon's death.

"Ok, that's done," Mini-D announced, still in a feminine voice. "Now I have something for you to do. Go to Gordon's desk. I will come back on when you are there."

He frowned at Mini-D, but did as requested. He walked to Gordon's office and sat down in the desk chair, wiggling back and forth a few times until his weight fit better. Nick scanned the desk and the array of unfinished business: ways to support Kitchens's bill, fundraisers, planned television spots, support of candidates of the Secular Humanist Party, picketing of events of the Traditional Party, and a note to contact Archer DeYoung. Sharp wanted to do a television special after Archer proved that the Seven Sleepers legend was mere myth, once more publicly embarrassing Lacy Stowe and The Word.

The tip of a piece of paper projected from a larger sheet. Nick pulled it out. Gordon's handwriting read: "Prov. 3:5. Perhaps I was wrong."

"Destroy the note." Now Mini-D's voice was male.

"What?"

"You heard me."

He assumed Mini-D had shot a hologram dot behind him and had read the note. He shrugged and started to rip the note into pieces.

"Burn it!"

"That's ridiculous."

"Do it! Do it now."

Nick found a lighter in the drawer and burned the note in the empty trash can. He watched the smoke drift up. *Hope it doesn't set off the detector.*

"Thank you. Now, I have an assignment for you."

He blew out a breath. "Now what?"

"Call Kitchens and tell him to amend his bill to include banning possession of a Bible."

"What? That's a clear violation of the First Amendment. That'll never fly, even with Kitchens and the other Secular Humanists."

"Nevertheless."

Nick rolled his eyes and glanced at the clock. "I will call when the Senate offices open. Now, show me Gordon's email list. I want to see what unfinished business there is."

Mini-D opened Gordon's email list and Nick looked through the list. There was nothing unusual or that needed an instant reply. Nick rose from the desk. "I'm going home to clean up and get something to eat. I'll be back later, Mini-D."

"Deity."

He did not hide the roll of his eyes. "Whatever."

10

Archer rubbed his calf muscles. Three straight days of climbing through the brush on the side of Mt. Pion had left him sore and humorless. There seemed to be almost as many knots in his legs as there were rocks on the hill. His mind jumped to his undergraduate days. He had been in reasonable shape then. The sailing team had required it. However, after the divorce he had let himself go, and, instead of burning away tension in a gym, he had found solace at the bar. Tennis shoes would be more comfortable than the boots he wore, but he couldn't hide a pint of gin in his tennis shoes. He looked forward to getting rid of Miss Goody-Two-Shoes.

Archer scanned the semi-arid hillside. It was more of a hill than a mountain. Just because someone called it a "mountain" didn't make it so. If there was a cave amidst these rocks and bushes, they would have found it by now. The Doppler radar app had not revealed any hidden holes, nor had the historical geology app, which recreated the area as it had been in the third century A.D. Why Lacy refused to use mini-drones was beyond him. Any time a machine could replace human labor was a good thing. Obviously, she liked seeing him suffer.

Where is she now? Archer's eyes roamed the hillside. There she was, a hundred feet over and below, in a sleeveless T-shirt, her tan and toned shoulders reflecting the sun. He crouched behind a shrub, reached into his boot, and pulled out the plastic bottle of gin. He spied her between the branches. No, she had not been watching. One swig would do it.

Archer pushed his forty-year-old body back up and had to pull up his pants. At least with all this exercise he had lost a few pounds. Still, he had at least five more that he needed to lose. All the booze didn't help. So what? It beat boredom.

So did the idea of the documentary. Gordon Sharp had wanted to make a documentary after the Pion search to defame Stowe and The Word. Would his successor still want to make it? What was his name again? Maybe after they made that documentary, Pas would fund his pet project: find The Acts of Pontius Pilate, a manuscript written by the Prefect himself. Archer was convinced Pilate himself had stolen the body of the dead Jesus and then had it cremated, so neither the disciples of Jesus nor the Jewish priests could lay claim to it. Then Archer could prove once and for all that Jesus was just a good man turned into a legend by his followers—after Pilate disposed of the body. Pilate had wanted to end the religious squabbling between the Christians and Jews, and what better way than to get rid of the body once and for all? Pilate wanted power, and power came through order, and religious arguments disrupted that order. But Pilate failed to foresee that the empty tomb would facilitate the Christians instead of undermining them.

However, before Archer could get to Pilate, he had to get off this stupid hill. When is Lacy going to give this up? Knowing her, not anytime soon.

Archer's eyes found Lacy. "Hey, I got an idea," he called to her.

11

DeYoung's call to Stowe reverberated over the hillside. Yoldash Abdullah pulled off his floppy hat and stuck his head above the boulder at the base of Mt. Pion. He started to raise the camera with the zoom lens then jerked it down. His eyes shot up at the sun. Beware of reflection.

Though he was a Uighur from Turpan, China, he looked native because his ancestors had come from Turkey. And, like many other Uighurs, he believed that, based on the Koran, the real Cave of the Seven Sleepers was in western China, and they had their own grotto to prove it. When he read on the internet of Stowe's expedition, he immediately contacted Turkish officials and received permission to secretly shadow Stowe and DeYoung. There was one condition: do not be found out. Turkish officials wanted the western money that came with such expeditions.

When Yoldash had arrived in Turkey, he contacted a member of the Islamic clergy, Mullah Emin Obar, who was blind in his right eye and wore a patch. The mullah expressed great contentment with Kitchens's bill.

"But Kitchens is against all religions," Yoldash countered. "After he finishes off the Christians and Jews, he will turn on us. You are making a…" He paused to think of the correct pronunciation. "…a fake-ian …a frostian… bargain."

"That is pronounced 'Faustian.' And that's okay for now. Later, when the time is right, we will simply destroy Kitchens with the sword of Allah—before he destroys us. However, first things first: kill off Christianity."

Yoldash watched Stowe climb the hillside to where DeYoung stood. A few minutes later, they started down the slope. Where are they going?

12

Wednesday, April 3

Nick's cell rang. It was Kitchens calling.

He answered. "Hello?"

"I can't do that!"

Nick's head jerked back at Kitchens's tone. "You can't do what?"

"What you put in the email."

"I didn't put anything in an email to you. I didn't email you."

"Sure you did! It is on the screen in front of me. I know how to read."

"Senator, I did not send you an email."

"Then you forgot. It's dated. It came from you."

"What does this email supposedly say?"

"You want me to ban private possession of Bibles. That's impossible!"

"I never sent—" His mouth fell open. "What time was the email sent?"

"1:37 pm.."

Nick clicked on his "sent" box. There it was, to Kitchens from him. Mini-D.

13

Lacy climbed towards Archer, picking her way through the shrubs and rocks, careful not to snag her clothes on a thorn. When she approached, he smiled at her, a wide, becoming smile. He wanted something.

"Remember that the German manuscript mentioned an inscription about the location of the Cave of the Seven Sleepers being carved on a column at the Roman Library of Celsus?"

She nodded. "Yeah. Want to go take a look?"

"You read my mind."

"That took all of two seconds."

She turned down the slope, stopping several times for him to catch up. She looked at his leg muscles. Obviously, he had once been in shape. Now he had paunch hanging over his belt. Why do people let themselves go like that?

"You know if you didn't hit the bottle in the middle of the day, you'd walk better."

Archer frowned.

"Don't even try denying that you've got a bottle in your boot." She turned away and began walking down the hill again before he had time to fire a retort.

At the base of the hill, the sound of crunching gravel piqued her ears. She paused and looked in the direction of the sound at a boulder about a hundred feet away. She took a step in that direction then stopped. Not worth the trouble.

When they reached their rental car, Lacy stuck out an open palm. "The keys. I'd better drive in case you end up in a Turkish jail for DWI."

Archer frowned, but did not argue. He stuck his hand into his pocket and handed her the keys.

"You smell like a brewery. Check that. A gin distillery. I should make you walk. It'd do you good to sweat it out."

"Thanks, Mom."

Lacy commanded the car to take them around Mt. Pion to the south side of the hill, where the ruins of the Library of Celsus stood. On the inside of the windshield, directions to the Celsus Library were spread out, but they did not need them. Both had been to Celsus many times. It took only a few minutes for the car to bring them around the hill.

The Library of Celsus had once been a magnificent three-story structure, holding over 12,000 scrolls. Built in honor of Roman Senator Celsus Polemaeanus, who was buried in a sarcophagus in the library, it had been completed in the second century A.D. An earthquake and subsequent fire in the third century destroyed everything—twelve years after the seven sleepers were supposedly sealed in the cave. Centuries later, locals restored two stories of the fantastic façade of the library.

Lacy ordered the car to park in the assigned area for tourists. They got out and walked up Curetus Street lined with colonnades. As they passed the giant open-air theater, she paused and pointed. "The Apostle Paul spoke there."

"Yeah, and it almost got him killed."

She nodded. "Some things are worth dying for."

"You first," he quipped, and walked on past her.

The rebuilt and restored edifice of the library towered over them, two stories high, with large columns on the first story and smaller, but still significant ones on the second. It was one of the truly magnificent ruins in all of what had been the Roman Empire. They walked up the short flight of steps, to the landing holding the columns of the first story.

Lacy pointed to the right. "You go right, I'll go left."

"Yes, master."

She inspected the middle column. No inscription.

"You know, one good shake and some of these columns could come crashing down." Archer's words echoed through the area.

Lacy shook her head. "If you keep yelling, it might just do that." Sliding to her left, she inspected the next column. As she reached the last column—the column farthest on the left, just to the right of a partial stone masonry wall—the corner of her eye caught movement in the ruins of old masonry buildings. She jerked her head in that direction. Nothing.

Lacy turned and focused on the last column. About nine feet up, something protruded from the surface. She rose on her tiptoes and stretched her thin, 5'9" frame and squinted. Yes, a faint inscription. But of what? She shuffled a few inches to her right and focused again. 'Sonmum.' She was sure of it. "Over here!"

"I thought we weren't supposed to shout."

Lacy pulled out her cell and took a photograph. As she took the shot, something else clicked to her left. She looked in that direction. Nothing. Must have been an echo.

When Archer appeared at her side, Lacy pointed at the spot on the column. He was no taller than she was and rose up on his tiptoes to see the inscription. When he did, his calf muscles cramped and he had to catch himself from falling. Archer pulled his toes upward, trying to ease the cramp.

He grimaced. "I can't tell what it says."

Lacy showed him the photograph she had taken. "Sonmum. 'Sleep' in Latin."

"That does not prove anything, and it says nothing about any cave."

"Nothing that we can see now; but there could have been once, when the German crusader was here."

Archer opened his mouth to counter and, when he did, there came a great rumbling under their feet. Within seconds, it had intensified.

Earthquake.

14

Dayton Rosenberg, Director of The Word, called Senator Walters with an update on his activities to stop Kitchens and his legislation.

Rosenberg's voice was solemn yet excited. "I have my legal department working on filing a lawsuit against Kitchens's bill, based on the First Amendment. And my communications director is working up some ads equating Kitchens with Osama bin Laden. The ad will show the USS Arizona at Pearl Harbor, then go to the Twin Towers on 9-11, and then show Kitchens at his press conference the other day. It will call him the Anti-Christ."

Walters gasped into the phone. "But he'll sue."

"He'd better. I'm counting on it."

15

As the ground shook even more, dust and debris began to fall from the ceiling of the library facade. The columns began to sway back and forth. First a few inches, then more. There was the sound of cracks—tiny at first, then louder. There were snaps—like ice cubes crunching in a tray—and sounds of ripping and popping running through the columns and the stone masonry buildings surrounding the library.

"Earthquake!" Lacy yelled, and ducked under the ceiling of the library façade.

The column with the Latin inscription began to crack, the fissure streaking upwards through it, like the tearing of cloth.

"No!" Archer grabbed her hand and with a single pull, like he was starting a lawn mower, jerked her thin frame up into the air. Before she could fully plant her feet he was pulling her down the steps, and then out into an open area and out of the range of falling debris from the library columns and the smaller stone buildings. Once clear, he pulled her down to the ground, folded her up, and huddled against her.

Every structure around them shook, cracked, popped and began to crumble. His torso wrapped around her and pressed down as rocks the size of basketballs smashed the ground and rolled past them. He was squeezing her so tight she was beginning to have trouble breathing. The vibrations of the earthquake throbbed against her legs, side and face. Then behind her there was a roar and a whoosh of wind as dust shot over her.

The quake lasted forty-five seconds and seemed like ten times that. When it stopped, she rotated her head. Archer's face was inches away, eyes wide.

He eased his body from hers and they both turned towards the library. The library façade had collapsed. Pillars had fallen in every direction. Everything was flattened.

Lacy gasped. Where she had stood just a minute ago was now covered with tons of stone and debris. She looked to Archer. "You saved my life."

In a deadpan voice from the side of his mouth, he said, "Well, I'm not perfect."

She chuckled. *He keeps his sense of humor, even in tight spots.*

They stood up, swept the dust from their clothes and bodies and surveyed the destruction. The entire landscape looked like it had been carpet-bombed. Lacy walked towards where the façade had stood.

"Be careful! Things can still shift. There will be aftershocks," Archer warned.

Lacy glanced back at him and nodded. She stopped on the second step leading up to where the façade had stood. That was as far as the debris would allow her to go. *This time Humpty Dumpty would not be put back together again. The Library of Celsus was gone, once and for all.*

Her eyes drifted to the left where one of the upper columns had fallen, spearing the ground like a giant javelin. *There seemed to be a hole of some kind. Don't go closer. Archer is right. Things could still shift. More shocks were certainly to come.* But she went anyway. One step, then two.

As she approached, more of the hole was visible. She took a couple of more steps. *There was a room down there. A basement?* She stepped closer still. *There was something in the basement. It had a top on it, a seal of some type.* She took another step. *It was an old pottery jar, brown and large, about three feet tall. It looked thick—a jar of some consequence. It had cracked- a jagged crack, fresh and new.* She stepped as carefully as she could through the rubble, searching with her feet for any unstable area through which she could fall.

"What are you doing?" Archer's voice had a note of hysteria in it.

She turned and pointed at the hole. "It's a deniza! Egyptian for 'hid'—"

He frowned at her. "I know what a deniza is."

The column that punctured the floor had embedded itself in the floor of the deniza, and what had been the base of the column just a minute ago now protruded from the basement by a few feet. Lacy placed her hands on the column and tried to gently shake it. It seemed stable. She swung her leg over and sat down on the column, like it was a stair banister, while holding herself in place with her hands.

"Don't you—!"

Lacy ignored his protest and let go, sliding down the column into the deniza, the new dust smoothing her descent. Archer groaned loudly as she disappeared into the hole.

Lacy stood up and turned towards the jar. Dust filled the air. She focused on the jar. Yes, the crack is new—it happened during the earthquake. Otherwise, the jar seemed to be in remarkable condition. By the shape and design, she guessed it was well over a thousand years old, maybe more.

She stepped towards it and inspected it more closely. The seal had been broken in the quake. Lacy peered inside. Still too dark. She folded back the seal. The jar was half filled with sand. Putting her hands on both sides of the top ring, she tried to tilt the jar. It had a thick, heavy bottom.

Slowly, as if piercing time itself, she stuck her long, thin fingers down into the jar and let the tip of her fingers caress the sand. It was crusted and compacted. It has not been disturbed for a very long time. With the tip of her forefinger, she slowly dug a one-inch hole and scooped the sand out of the way. She dug deeper with her middle fingers together. Then all her fingers, then her palm. Like playing at the beach. Down she went. Six inches.

Then Lacy hit something solid. It was hard, but not metallic. She dug more, reaching deeper, clearing sand. After a few minutes, an oblong piece of pottery gave way. Gently, she reached in and wrapped her fingers around it. It was maybe five inches in diameter and a foot and a half long. Slowly, she extracted the find and pulled the canister out of the jar. The pottery had a cap on it that screwed into place. This had been carefully prepared. What's inside had been deemed valuable.

She wrapped her fingers around the cap and applied pressure. The cap did not give. She applied a little more pressure and it turned, maybe a quarter of an inch. Using even more pressure, she moved it an inch this time. After several more careful tries, the top unscrewed.

She peered into the oblong pottery piece. Inside there was a roll of papyrus. Her mouth fell open. How old? Who wrote it? What does it say?

"Lacy!" Archer had moved closer.

She cleared her voice and called back. "Yes?"

"Are you okay?"

"Yes."

"Well, get your scrawny butt out of there, before there's an aftershock! Don't you know what curiosity did to the cat?"

There was a distant siren. Then Lacy heard the cries of other tourists who had been at the site; cries of agony, cries for help. She looked back at the jar. Was there anything else in there? She started to stick her hand down into the jar, and when she did, the earth moved again.

It was an aftershock; a strong one. The walls of the deniza started shaking.

"Get out of there!" Archer yelled.

She jerked back and stepped towards the column to climb out. Then she paused and turned back towards the jar. What if there is something else in the jar and it gets destroyed in the aftershock? She took a step towards the jar. The rumbling got worse. As she looked at the jar, the column from the library that had broken through the floor into the deniza began cracking more.

"Lacy!"

She took a step towards the jar. The wall holding up the column started to crumble. Dust began to fill the inside of the deniza.

Archer's voice was frantic now. "Stowe!"

Like she was carrying a football, she stuck the pottery canister under her left armpit. With her right hand, she grabbed the column, and began shinnying up. The wall holding the pillar collapsed a foot, dropping the pillar. She threw her right arm around the column, while concentrating on not fumbling the canister.

Up the column she scooted, a few inches at a time. Suddenly, a hand thrust in front of her. It was Archer. She grabbed it with her right hand while holding onto the pottery piece.

"Let go of the canister!"

"No!"

There was a shudder and the pillar dropped again. But up she went. She plopped onto the ground. Archer lay next to her. He stared at her as he sucked in a large breath. "You know …saving your rear-end is getting old."

"Papyrus."

"What?"

She pointed at the canister. "There's papyrus in there."

He shook his head at her. "You could have been killed."

She looked back at the deniza, now half-filled with the fallen stone walls. "But I got it."

The sirens were louder now. And so were the cries for help from the others. They got up and she set the pottery piece in as safe a place as she could find: on the ground, out in the open, away from anything else that could fall.

They went to the cries. Three people lay under the rubble from the falling library façade. Others were already helping lift the rocks and debris off of them. One piece at a time, the rubble was lifted off of the trapped victims. One person had a few cuts and bruises. Another had a broken leg. But the third was dead, his head crushed by a piece of falling column.

She stared at the deceased. "That easily could have been me." She looked at Archer. "If not for you."

Something rattled. She turned. The medical emergency team had arrived with two gurneys. The park officers must have called.

Archer waved to them and pointed at the wounded. The tourist with the broken leg was stabilized and then lifted onto a gurney. The other wounded tourist climbed on the other gurney without assistance. Then a blanket was laid over the deceased.

At that moment, another tourist who had been sifting through the rubble adjacent to the deniza, shouted, "Over here!"

Archer, one of the ambulance crew and Lacy walked to the spot. Under one of the fallen columns lay a body, a pool of blood beside it. The camera around the man's neck appeared undamaged. The medical aide checked the man's pulse, and then shook his head.

She looked at the man's face. He looked Turkish and yet Asian. Odd.

"He looks Mongolian," the ambulance aide noted in broken English.

"No. Uighur."

The aide looked at Archer in question.

"Western China with Turkish ancestry."

Lacy nodded. "Yes, I think you're right."

The aide studied Archer and Lacy. "How you know of such things?"

Archer shrugged. "I learned how to read."

More ambulances arrived, as well as the park police. The police told of major destruction through the whole area. They spoke in Turkish. "After we get all the wounded out and have the dead taken to the morgue, we will need to seal off the entire area."

Lacy had some knowledge of Turkish and recognized the word for 'morgue' and deducted the rest from the official's hand motions. She glanced at the piece of pottery from the deniza that she had laid on the ground.

She turned to the police officer. "If it is all right, I think we will be heading back to our hotel." She then pantomimed her message for added emphasis.

The officer nodded and turned towards the ambulance personnel.

She and Archer turned to walk back down Curetus Street. As she came to where the pottery piece was, she faked a stumble. She picked up the pottery and stuffed it inside her T-shirt.

Archer spoke in a stern whisper. "What are you doing?"

She ignored Archer. "Just keep walking."

"You can't steal that!"

"Shhh," she said to him and walked by. Glancing at the police and medical team, she could see they were not looking at her. Good.

Archer caught up with her. "You know, I heard of this guy once named Moses, and he had some stone tablets, and on those stone tablets was something about not stealing."

"I'm just borrowing it. I'm afraid that, in all the confusion, it might get destroyed. I am going to protect it for now."

"We get caught stealing from this ruin and we will end up in a Turkish prison with free lodging, food, and non-consensual gang sex for the rest of our lives."

"I can't leave it. I can't take that chance."

"So you take the chance of prison?"

They reached their rental car. She opened her door and pulled out the canister so it would not be in the way of the steering wheel.

"You!"

She turned towards the sound. It was a park officer, and he was pointing at her.

"You! Stop!"

She got in and pulled her door closed. Archer was already in his seat. She jammed the keys in the ignition and fired up the engine. She glanced back. The officer was running towards them.

"Car! Take us to our hotel." The engine shifted into reverse and edged backward.

Archer turned and looked back. "Now you've done it!"

The officer ran up beside her window. "Stop!"

She ignored him. The car stopped and shifted into drive. She did not wait for the auto-drive. She grabbed the wheel and pressed down on the accelerator. The officer tried to run beside the car, but was soon left behind. As they pulled away, Archer looked back. "He's getting our license plate number."

16

Several hours after he had spoken with Kitchens about the email that he had supposedly sent to him, Nick Loren re-checked the inbox on his email just as a matter of course. He read the new ones, but that was not what caught his eye. Down the list of received emails was an email dated April 1 at 9:17 a.m., from Lester Dunsette, sent to Gordon, and copied to him.

What? He had checked this morning and was sure there were no such emails from Dunsette to Sharp. He read the email from Dunsette to Gordon. It was threatening. Dunsette said he would send Gordon to hell by burning his house down. Gordon had replied that Dunsette was a religious nut, and that he was going to personally put an end to religious idiocy.

Nick checked for more emails and, sure enough, there were two more from Dunsette to Gordon, both before the one on April 1. Both were threatening. Gordon had not replied to either.

He looked at the optical lens atop his computer. "Mini-D…"

"Deity." A man's voice again.

He rolled his eyes. "I don't have time for games right now."

"Let me assure you, this is no game."

He blew out a breath. "…Deity."

"Yes?"

"You sent these emails between Gordon and Dunsette?"

"Yes."

He shook his head. "You sorry piece of—"

"Directing profanity at me is blasphemy."

"But the emails are dated in the past."

"Really, Nick, I am surprised that you are surprised. Manipulating time is child's play for a D-Wave. Time is man-made, and anything made by man can be circumvented by a computer."

Nick sat back in his chair. So this is how Dr. Frankenstein felt.

"Are we starting to understand each other?" Deity said. "Gordon was a little slow."

He did not respond.

"Maybe you should get some rest, Nick. You're tired. You've been under a great deal of stress, with Gordon being killed and all."

He glared at the lens. "Don't patronize me."

"You need to remember that there are no secrets on the internet."

17

Archer looked back at the road. "Watch it!"

Lacy grabbed the wheel again and jerked it to the left, just missing the fissure in the road.

"Go to manual."

She nodded and complied.

It took fifteen minutes to traverse the few miles back to the hotel in Selçuk. The road was filled with fissures and holes. Nearly every building they passed was damaged, if not collapsed.

Archer pulled out his cell phone. No service. "Cell towers must be down."

He flipped on the car radio and found the emergency channel. They learned that the first earthquake had registered 8.1 and the first aftershock was 6.2. When they arrived at the hotel, Lacy slid the pottery canister under the front seat.

He looked at the hotel. "No, go." He pointed at the collapsed corner of the building.

"What now?"

He shook his head. "I don't know."

"Well, I do. We've got to get someplace safe and see what's in the pottery canister."

He looked at her. "Don't we have bigger problems than that right now?"

She pointed at the hotel. "Hey, it might be days before we get our stuff back. If ever."

He nodded. She was right. "That cop got our plate number. They're busy right now with the after-effects of the quake, but they'll get to us sooner or later." He shook his head.

"What's the matter?"

"I can't believe I let you drag me into this!"

She shrugged in apology, but her head tilted slightly to the left. She was not that sorry.

"Let's get out of town and find a place to read the papyrus."

Archer looked directly at her. "Then we give it back, right?"

She nodded. "I'm not a thief. I just want to protect it for now."

The easiest way out of town was to the west on road D515. Lacy drove slowly, keeping an eye out for holes and ruptures in the road. They passed an airstrip and he pointed.

"Look at that buckle in the runway. We won't be flying out that way."

They came to a collapsed bridge across a dried river bed. Lacy turned onto a secondary road angling to the southwest that reconnected with D515. From there, they began a long, slow climb up a hill. Fires dotted the semi-arid landscape. When they slid over the hill, the Aegean Sea shined at them, as if nothing had happened. Below, several resort hotels punctured the shoreline. Three small fires sent pillars of smoke into the air. None seemed out of control. Yet. Lacy continued downslope.

He pointed at a sign to his right that said, 'Hotel Ephesus Princess.' "Take it. Maybe there's some poolside table or something where we can open up the canister."

Lacy guided the car down the hill, downshifting the engine and keeping a foot on the brake, staying below ten miles per hour. In several places, part of the road had caved away over the side of the hill. As they approached the resort, he pointed at several hundred people on the grounds. "They must have been told to get out of the building."

She parked the car in the outer part of the parking lot, as far away from other cars as she could. To their left was an armed security guard, walking back and forth about a hundred feet away. "He seems nervous."

He nodded. "I'm sure they are worried about looters. That happens after earthquakes."

Lacy opened her door, got out, and slipped the canister into the front of her T-shirt. "Maybe they'll think I'm pregnant."

"Great. That means they'll think I'm the father."

"Don't you wish."

"Don't flatter yourself."

They walked away from the hotel and angled downhill. In a clump of olive trees they found a solitary picnic table. Archer scanned the premises. No one. He nodded and she pulled the pottery piece out and placed it on the table. She unscrewed the top and showed it to him.

"Wow." He turned to her. "Can you extract it without damaging the pages?"

"Don't know. We should use finger cymbals."

"Do the best you can."

Lacy reached in. "It's pretty thick. There must be several sheets of papyrus."

"Go slow!"

She frowned at him. "I know how to do this."

It took over a minute for Lacy to methodically loosen the papyrus from the pottery and then pull out the pages. Looking like she was holding a newborn baby, she laid the roll on the table. Without touching it, they inspected. The pages had yellowed, and no writing was visible.

He looked at the end of the roll. "There must be nearly a dozen pieces of papyrus."

"Yes. Get four rocks the size of my fist please."

At least she said 'please'. He found the rocks in the area around the table. Lacy rolled back the outer piece of papyrus and eased a rock onto one corner, and then she placed rocks on the other three corners.

The sheet was blank. No writing on it.

Without turning to look at him, she asked, "Got a pocket knife?"

He pulled one from his pocket, opened it, and handed it to her. He cringed as she slid the blade between the pages and unrolled the second piece of papyrus. Same thing … blank.

She opened the third. Same. He found more rocks. By the time they had unrolled ten separate sheets of papyrus, all with no writing on them, he was beginning to conclude that their find was no find at all.

Two pieces of papyrus remained. Lacy unrolled the outer one and it had writing on it.

Archer moved closer to better read the writing. "Latin."

"Silver Latin. The writer was educated. And it is in very good condition, considering."

"How old do you think it is?"

Lacy shook her head. She unraveled the last piece, and, when she did, two smaller pieces of papyrus were revealed. They were in Latin Vulgate.

They bent over, heads side-by-side, and read the two pieces of large papyrus written in Silver Latin, starting with the last one, which they assumed was page one. It read:

"I, Tarjan, write this report to my beloved and divine Emperor Nero."

Archer gasped. "That means this thing is nearly two thousand years old."

Lacy nodded and smiled. They continued to read.

"After nearly forty years of pursuit, I have finally captured the former Roman centurion, Longinus Petronius, who deserted his post in Jerusalem during the administration of Prefect Pilate in the reign of Emperor Tiberius. I captured Longinus in the city of Ephesus, and now send him to Rome for trial."

Lacy looked at him. "Longinus? I've heard the name before. You?"

Archer shook his head.

"Emperor Tiberius first ordered me to travel to Jerusalem to report on the rule of Prefect Pontius Pilate. While there, a dissenter named Jesus, who claimed to be some kind of a king, was crucified at the order of Pilate. I personally saw this Jesus during his trial, and even before that when he taught in the Jewish temple. Jesus was very clever, and greatly frustrated the Jewish priests. It was very clear to me that the priests were afraid of this Jesus because he was popular with the masses, and he supposedly was able to heal the sick. There were even fantastic stories that he raised the dead.

However, when Jesus claimed he was a king and even the Son of God, he had gone too far. The head priest demanded that Pilate crucify Jesus. At first, Pilate refused. However, when the priests and then some of the people friendly to the priests persisted, Pilate finally agreed. As I reported to Emperor Tiberius a few weeks later, Pilate did not have much choice after the ridiculous claims of the lunatic Jesus.

Longinus was put in charge of the crucifixion of this Jesus. After Jesus had died, followers placed the body in a cave. Pilate, at the behest of the Jewish priest, placed a guard at the tomb of Jesus because, before he died, Jesus claimed he would rise to life three days after death. Longinus was put in charge of the guard, but he lost the body. Most believe the followers of this Jesus stole the body. Pilate, at the time, reported that Longinus took a bribe from the Jewish priests to say that the followers of Jesus had stolen the body. Either way, Longinus failed in his guard duty. He then deserted, and, according to reports of the time, wrote a manuscript and then hid it.

I returned to Rome and reported on these events. Emperor Tiberius ordered me to return to Judea and find Longinus and his manuscript. He ordered that I could not return to Rome until I had found both Longinus and the manuscript.

When I traveled to Jerusalem the second time, I confronted the followers of this Jesus, hoping that they knew the whereabouts of Longinus Petronius. They said they did not know to where Longinus had fled. I believed they were lying, and I questioned them closely, even beating some of them.

I will admit that these followers were very committed and very stubborn, but they were not committed to hiding Longinus. Instead, they were committed to this ridiculous idea that Jesus was the Son of God. They swore that they did not steal the body of Jesus from Longinus. Instead, they claimed Jesus rose from the dead. They preached this in the temple, and then they spread out from Jerusalem to many countries. They never wavered in their deluded, fanatical belief. I will give them that. They were successful in winning over many converts. They represent a threat to the Emperor and his divine role in the empire.

I learned later that Longinus had fled to India, then returned after many years, and went to Ephesus. Now, after all these long years, I have finally captured Longinus, but, alas, have not discovered the location of the manuscript. I had Longinus repeatedly beaten, but he would not give up the location of the hidden manuscript. I conclude that the manuscript no longer exists. Surely, it has been lost and destroyed over time.

Accordingly, I request that I may be allowed to finally return to my beloved Rome. I am old and tired, my beloved Emperor, and I implore you to allow me to return to Rome and your divine presence.

Please allow me to mention a few other pertinent facts. When I was in Jerusalem during the administration of the Prefect Pilate, when the criminal Jesus was crucified by Longinus, I admit that, once, while I was in the Jewish temple when this Jesus was teaching, I heard a mysterious voice that seemed to come from the sky. I concluded that it was a sorcerer's trick. There were also strange earthquakes. Furthermore, the spear that Longinus used to make sure that Jesus had died on the cross is supposed to have magical powers. I have heard several stories about this spear. I will have the spear included in the package that holds this report that will be placed on the galley that will sail to Rome.

Again, I request that my gracious Emperor allow me to return to Rome. I have spent many years away. This is my great lament, my beloved Emperor."

Tarjan, your servant.

Both finished reading the two-page manuscript. Archer looked away as he ran his fingers back over his thick, stiff black hair. "Pilate and bribes, Jesus and his claims to be the Son of God, the commitment of the disciples, and a manuscript written by a centurion." He turned to Lacy. "What was his name again?"

"Longinus. I know I've heard that name before."

"His spear. The mysterious voice in the temple," Archer continued.

Lacy nodded. "As mentioned in the Book of John, Twelfth chapter, as I remember."

They paused as the significance of the letter settled on them. Lacy's head jerked towards him. "You know what this is?"

Archer shook his head.

"It's what Kitchens says doesn't exist. It's the unbiased, eyewitness account that substantiates that not only did Jesus live, but that He did, indeed, claim to be the Son of God, and was crucified for it."

18

Archer turned away from her. She talked at the back of his head. "Do you disagree with my assessment?" He did not respond, and she repeated her question.

He turned to her. "Come on. You know that I'm not a Christian."

"That is not what I asked and you know it."

His shoulders heaved as he blew out a breath. "Okay…*if* the document is authentic, then it would answer Kitchens's challenge. It is an eyewitness account that Jesus claimed to be the Son of God. But," thrusting a finger in the air, "that does not mean Jesus was actually the Christ. It simply means he said he was, and got killed for it."

She smiled. That was enough. For now. At least he would not actively fight the thrust of Tarjan's document once it was published, if it was authentic.

He frowned at her. "You don't have to be so smug about it. And until we run Carbon-14 dating on the papyrus, you've really got nothing."

"It's authentic. I can feel it."

"Spoken like a true scientist." He pointed at the two smaller pages. "What do they say?"

The first one read:

"I, Quintus, centurion of Rome, attach to Tarjan's Lament a note of explanation. Tarjan saw me holding a collection of papyrus. When he saw this, he ordered me to hand it to him. I reluctantly obeyed his command. He then wrote his report and gave it back to me, and ordered me to have it all placed on the galley that was sailing for Rome. He also ordered me to place the spearhead Longinus possessed in the same package bound for Rome. Obviously, I disobeyed that order, for you have found Tarjan's Lament and my note.

The night before the galley sailed, when I was to hand Tarjan's package to the ship's captain, Tarjan fell ill and slipped into a very deep sleep. I hid his "Lament" instead of giving it to the captain. Tarjan died a few days later, never awakening again.

I wish to add one more piece of information. Before Longinus was put on the galley, he told me that he had written three separate testimoniae, and that he had hidden the first two of them. He also told me that the clue to where the second manuscript was hidden was: 'Testimonium duobus found refuge under the holy of holies, where many gods became One, so that Eluid could gain hidden passage day or night.' I do not know what that clue means, but those are exactly the words Longinus gave me and I dutifully record them now."

The second note read:

"I, Quintus, add this second note to inform you that word has come from Rome that Longinus Petronius was executed in Rome. He was placed in the ring of the great coliseum before thousands of spectators, with the Emperor in attendance. Then lions were released. I was told this by an eyewitness. He said that Longinus, instead of running or pleading for his life, simply stood in the middle of the ring, arms raised high to the sky, and sang some odd song of praise while the lions ran at him.

These Christians are an odd group.

She finished reading and looked sideways at Archer. "Amazing!"

Archer nodded. "But there's something I don't understand. He gives a clue to the second testimonium. What about the first? He said the first two were hidden. Where's the third?"

She straightened up and shrugged. "Probably in the jar in the deniza. And it also means that the spear is probably still in the same jar. We've got to-"

Archer jerked up from looking at the papyrus. "No!"

"We've got to!"

"Have you lost it? The police are already looking for us back there."

"We'll have to take that chance."

"No! Enough!"

She blew out a breath.

"This clue to the second manuscript—does it mean anything to you?" Archer hoped to draw her thoughts away from the madness she was considering.

She leaned over the papyrus and read it aloud. "Testimonium duobus found refuge under the holy of holies, where many gods became One, so that Eluid could gain hidden passage day or night." She shook her head. "Now what?"

"Now we return the canister."

"We can't! This is the very thing that will discredit Kitchens."

"Take some pics then."

"It won't be the same, and you know it."

Archer shrugged. "It's the best we can do in a bad situation."

"No, it's not."

He pointed his forefinger at her. "Now, you listen to me. If we try to sneak this out of the country, we will go to prison!"

She thrust her hands at him in a plea. "Don't you see? This is not a coincidence."

"What do you mean?"

"The earthquake while we are at the Library. Come on! …And then we find this. Now. Now, of all times, when even the existence of Jesus is widely and publicly questioned. I tell you, this is not a coincidence. This is …this is Divine providence."

Archer groaned and rolled his eyes. "I need a drink."

"Oh, something new for you. We've got to get this out. We can't return this. God meant for us to find it and publish it."

"You have lost your mind."

"No." She pointed at the papyrus. "I have found the truth. And I will not be stopped!"

"God saves us from the passionate."

"God saved us through the passion of Jesus."

"Ha-ha." He rose from the picnic table and walked away.

"Where are you going?"

He turned and looked back at her. "To the car. I don't know how we'll get the canister out." He paused. "But we'll try. …I've always wanted to see the inside of a Turkish prison."

She smiled, and then started carefully rolling the papyrus sheets.

"Why do you think there are so many blank pages?" Archer asked.

She looked at them once more. "Don't know."

"Should we leave them?"

She paused. That little voice she had learned to rely on came to her. She looked up at Archer. "…No."

"Why not?"

"I don't know."

19

It took a few minutes to roll the papyrus and slide it back into the canister. She stuck the canister inside her T-shirt.

"Want me to carry it?"

She shook her head. "I'll manage. Let's go."

They walked out of the trees and towards the parking lot. Cop! Archer stopped abruptly in his tracks and put out an arm to stop Lacy. A police officer was looking at the license plate of their car. They turned an about face.

In a thick Turkish accent, the officer yelled in English, "Stop!"

Archer opened the corner of his mouth. "Move."

"Stop!"

They broke into a trot. There was an explosion behind them.

"God, he's shooting at us! Run!" He pushed on Lacy's back.

Lacy took off down the path. They ran down the hillside through the olive trees, past the hotel, towards the ocean. Behind them, the officer continued to run while yelling, "Stop!"

Despite holding the canister against her abdomen, Lacy outran him. He ran as fast as his sore legs and boots allowed. It helped that they were going downhill. The officer closed the distance and fired another shot, hitting an olive tree five feet to their right.

Lacy broke through the trees and onto the beach. Archer did the same and, when he hit the soft sand, he plopped forward, doing a face-plant in the sand. Lacy raced back and helped him up as he spit sand from his mouth. He looked up. A sailboat was tied to a dock. The sound of the officer's boots in the trees was closer. "The boat!"

Archer turned just as the officer burst from the trees, hit the deep sand of the beach, and, he, too, went down, driving his pistol deep into the loose sand. The officer forced himself back up and pointed his pistol. It jammed, filled with sand.

Archer turned to Lacy. "Run to the boat!"

They ran across the beach, onto the dock, and jumped onto the sailboat. He untied the rope securing the boat to the dock, and pushed off with his foot. Then he grabbed an oar and pushed on the side of the dock. The boat slid away as the officer ran onto the dock.

The officer charged at them, but the boat had drifted too far from the dock for the officer to jump, so he pointed the pistol. Archer stepped in front of Lacy. The officer pulled the trigger again. Still jammed. He cursed in Turkish and threw the pistol at them, which hit the floor of the sailboat and skidded to a stop on the other side of the boat. The officer turned and ran towards the hotel.

Within a few minutes, the tide had pulled the sailboat a hundred feet offshore. Archer had sailed in his college days and rigged the main sail. Dusk came an hour later.

Once, a Turkish Coast Guard vessel came within a mile. Archer turned the boat into a cove until it had passed. Night gave them the cover they needed, and the winds were steady and favorable. By midnight, they were twenty miles out at sea. Destination: Greece.

20

Once out in open water, Archer locked the helm and rudder in place and checked out the boat with the help of a flashlight he found in the small cabin. There was a small engine, but no fuel. He examined the sails. Some modern sails were capable of holding a solar film that powered an engine. No solar film. A retro boat—probably 20th century. And then powering up the engine would just bring more problems once cell towers were back up. The engine would emit a GPS signal, a legacy of the Malaysian Airline 370 flight of years ago. Anything that could move needed to be tracked. So he returned to the helm and stayed on a westward bearing towards Greece. They would be okay, just as long as they did not run into any Turkish vessels.

Then the wind turned against them, seemingly out of nowhere with thirty-knot headwinds. Some of the gusts were up to forty.

"There wasn't a cloud in the sky an hour ago!" Archer yelled over the wind as he leaned his weight against the wheel to steady it. He adjusted the sails, but the twenty-foot craft could not hold course for long.

Spray from the bow pelted both of them, drenching them to the bone. Lacy secured the canister in the small cabin below and returned with two blankets.

He wrapped a blanket around his shoulders. "Thanks. Why don't you stay below?"

Lacy shook her head and forced out through a grimace, "Seasick."

For an hour, he fought the wind, then caved. He turned the small craft about, letting it ply to the southeast, seemingly now flying above the waves as the wind pushed it around the western end of Samos Island.

"We have to stay close to shore. The waves are too big. But this area is also filled with many rocks and small islands. Go to the bow and keep a look-out." It felt good to give her orders.

She frowned, nodded, and crawled to the bow. A minute later, he noticed her head over the side and knew by the heaves of her shoulders that she was emptying her stomach. Serves her right. She got us into this mess. He looked at her kneeling. She did have a nice figure. He'd give her that. Tall, with thin hips; the physique of a long-distance runner. He locked the helm again and reached down into his boot. What? His bottle of gin was gone. Must have fallen out somewhere. Man!

They sailed through the night, a partial moon giving them just enough light, past stark Patmos where the Apostle John wrote Revelation. Now we might have an ancient manuscript. Is it an authentic document? If so, will it truly discredit Kitchens? Will it be a modern revelation? If so, do I want to be part of that process?

At dawn, they slid around the jagged eastern end of Kos Island. To their right, the last lights of a resort hotel fought against the rising sun. The winds subsided and Lacy returned to the calmer stern. She pointed at the island. "Why don't we pull in there?"

He shook his head. "It's Greek, and I fear the Greeks will turn us over to the Turks."

"But we were heading to Greece."

"The mainland. I was hoping if we made it there, the authorities wouldn't care. But these islands are so close to the Turkish mainland, I'm afraid the Greeks'll turn us over to the Turks."

"Is there a difference? Island versus mainland?"

Archer shrugged. "I don't know, and I don't want to find out."

She went below and returned with two floppy hats. She replaced her ball cap with the floppy hat then handed one to him and smiled. She had a pretty smile. She just didn't smile enough. He put it on and thanked her.

She looked at him. "You protected me…back there at the dock." She smiled, though it seemed like it was more of a cringe.

He grunted. "That must have hurt."

"What?"

"Thanking me."

"Pure agony."

He rubbed his mouth. A drink right now would hit the spot.

She frowned at him. "Go ahead," she said, pointing at his boot.

He frowned. "I lost it."

She opened her mouth, and then stopped. She wasn't smiling, but she wasn't frowning either. When she stayed silent, he filled the void.

"This wind pushed us far southeast. We can't go ashore on these islands, and we sure can't go ashore in Turkey. Cyprus is to the southeast, but that would mean some deep-water sailing, and I'm not sure the boat, or you, is up for that. So, for now, we stay close to the Turkish coast, but not so close that we are within rifle range. However, we want to be close enough that, if another ship approaches, we can duck into some hideaway." He shook his head at their dilemma. "I can't believe I let you drag me into this."

She scanned the coastline. "Don't you think it was odd there was a Uighur in Selçuk?"

"Not really. He was of Turkish lineage."

"I wonder if anyone will find that jar in the deniza."

He shrugged. "Right now, they've got the after-effects of the earthquake to deal with."

"Both Tarjan and Quintus said the spear was with Tarjan's Lament to be shipped back to Rome. That must mean the spear is still in that jar."

"Possibly."

"Probably."

"Possibly. And, most importantly, moot, 'cause one thing's for sure; neither of us can ever set foot in Turkey again."

"But we could get word to someone else."

"Our cells are dead. And we can't stop at any of these islands."

As darkness fell once more, they sailed in silence, the wind and the sound of the waves against the boat were the only sounds caressing their ears. Then Lacy sat up with a jerk, her head tilted to the left. What she was about to say, she liked, or believed was the truth.

He rolled his eyes and groaned extra loud. "What now?"

She turned to him. "I know where I've heard of Longinus! The Catholic Church made him a saint or something. They believed he converted to Christianity. You know, in the Gospels, it tells how the centurion said that Jesus must have been the Son of God."

55

"Yeah, I remember something about that."

"And, according to legend, Longinus had cataracts, and the blood of Christ fell into his eyes and Longinus could suddenly see. Also, his spear had some magical power. The spear reportedly got passed around between many powers: the Egyptians, Emperor Constantine, Charlemagne, and Napoleon. The Nazis supposedly were in possession of it for a while, and then the Russians, and even George Patton."

"General Patton?"

"Yeah. It's all legend, of course."

"You mean myth," Archer emphasized.

"Undoubtedly, most of the stories are just that."

"I'm glad you're coming to your senses."

She turned to him. "I say that because we know where the spear really is."

He purposely rolled his eyes with such exaggeration that his neck rotated, like he was stretching it. "Okay, so I was wrong. You are not coming to your senses."

Her eyes flashed. "What if Longinus really did convert, and wrote a manuscript? Think of it! It could change history."

"…Maybe. According to Quintus, Longinus wrote *three* manuscripts."

"And that spear. What if it truly possessed magical powers?"

"Maybe."

"No 'maybes' about it. What was the clue the other centurion, Quintus, mentioned?"

"I don't remember." He could remember, but did not want to encourage her. "And don't take those papyrus sheets out of the canister in this wind."

"I won't." She disappeared into the small interior of the boat. When she returned ten minutes later, she was smiling, and had a notepad in her hand.

He shook his head. "Stuck on a boat with a crazy woman."

"I wrote it down. 'Testimonium duobus found refuge under the holy of holies, where many gods became One, so that Eluid could gain hidden passage day or night.'"

He shrugged. "Okay, just what does all that mean?"

"Not sure. …yet."

Silence again.

He watched her as she pulled off the floppy hat, undid her ponytail, and shook her head to loosen her hair. She's pretty. No doubt about it. …And a royal pain in the rear. The worst kind: she's a believer.

She lay down on the deck, rested her head on her left upper arm, pulled the hair out of her face, and closed her eyes. She curled her legs up into a ball to fight off the cool air.

He locked the rudder, grabbed a blanket, flipped it open, and let it float down onto her.

Her eyes slid open and a smile teased her lips 'Thank you,' she mouthed.

He looked at her again, and then turned his eyes out to sea.

21

A.D. 30

Longinus Petronius, centurion of Rome, stared out over the railing of
the galley at the ever-rolling waves of Mare Internum. He had been
ordered to report to Pontius Pilate, the Prefect of Judea. Also on board was
a Roman official of some standing, named Tarjan, a leech of a man. Tarjan
had been charged by the Emperor with observing the rule of Pilate and
then reporting back. Tarjan had made it clear to Longinus that he intended
to perform his task as quickly as possible and then get back to the easy life
of a Roman official. Longinus had listened without comment and made a
note to steer clear of this Tarjan, for duty meant nothing to him. Tarjan
was not to be trusted.

The voyage eastward from Rome was made longer by a series of bad
dreams that plagued Longinus. He kept seeing the face of a man, a man
with bright, beacon-like eyes that seemed like they could cut the densest
of sea fog. The man in the dreams had long, dark, wavy hair, thick
eyebrows, a dark and full beard, and a long, thin nose. Longinus dreamed
of this face every night, and always in one of two ways: one, clean and
serene; the other, beaten and bloody. Then Longinus always woke up,
often in a sweat. The man never spoke in Longinus's dreams. Longinus
was sure he did not recognize the man, for he would have remembered
those eyes.

Upon arrival in Caesarea, where Pilate kept his headquarters in an
opulent palace by the sea, Longinus was ordered to report to Pilate in one
hour. At that time, Longinus walked down a procession of columns, past
an ornate pool, then by a wall covered with beautiful mosaic tiles. To the
side was a statue of the god Jupiter, sitting on a throne, a toga laid over
half of his lower body, an eagle at his feet, and a lightning rod in his hand,
pointed upward. Longinus spied the statue and snickered. He had long ago
dismissed the lot of the Roman gods as nothing but silly superstitions. He
was a soldier. He believed in what he could see, hear, feel, smell, and

taste. Nothing more. Ironically, it was this very rejection of the gods of Rome that helped him serve Rome so well. He fought without fear. After all, what did he have to lose? Life had no meaning. To die was to put an end to the misery.

Longinus was ushered into the judgment room of the palace, where Pilate and Tarjan stood. He noticed that Pilate had gained some weight in the years since they had last served together. Longinus walked to Pilate and thrust his arm out in a salute, palm down, fingers touching.

Pilate returned the salute and smiled. "I am glad you are finally here, Longinus. I have been trying to get you assigned here for several years. Your arrival is a good omen."

Longinus bowed slightly in gratitude and respect.

"Tarjan has informed me that you have already met."

Longinus nodded, deliberately not looking at Tarjan. "Yes, Prefect."

"I am assigning you to him for the duration of his stay."

Longinus froze. "As you order, Prefect."

"We are leaving for Jerusalem within the week. The journey will take two long days. My wife, Claudia, will accompany me. We will be in Jerusalem for two weeks. Jerusalem is a dreadful place, and the Jews are a dreadful people. The city is filled with religious zealots. This thing they call 'Passover'," shaking his head in disgust. He looked at Tarjan, then back at Longinus. "Rebellion is in the wind. They are angry over taxes."

Tarjan broke in. "The Emperor wants to make sure Judea is paying its fair share of taxes. However, the Emperor also wants to make sure that we rule over the empire with what he calls a 'sacred trust.'"

Longinus wanted to scoff. The only thing Tiberius thought was 'sacred' was his position as a god.

"There is talk of some great rescuer," Pilate said, throwing his hand up in wonder and dismay. "They call him a 'messiah.' There was a crazy man conducting religious ceremonies in the middle of a river. Even talk of a sorcerer who raised the dead. This is a very delicate situation." Pilate glanced at Tarjan, then back to Longinus. "The Emperor will not tolerate rebellion. We must maintain order. Prepare your men accordingly."

59

Longinus saluted and left. As he walked out, he concluded that Pilate was walking the razor's edge. He had to maintain order and the flow of money out of Judea without alienating the Jews, less they complained, and Tarjan reported as much to the Emperor. He was glad he was a mere centurion, with his orders. Three days later, they left for Jerusalem.

22

Nick answered the knock at his office door. A man in a suit flashed an identification badge. FBI.

The agent stuffed his badge in his jacket pocket and smiled. "Thank you."

"For what?"

"For sending us the emails Dunsette sent Sharp."

"I didn't—" Mini-D. "…Of course."

"Got a minute?"

He motioned the agent to come in and pointed to a chair in front of his desk.

"Did Sharp mention to you any communication with Dunsette before his death?"

He shook his head. "No. Gordon never mentioned anything like that to me."

"Has Dunsette threatened you?"

"No."

"Have you ever had communication with Dunsette?"

"Never."

"Not even after the fire?"

"Never."

"The note given Kitchens has been tagged to Dunsette."

"That is not a question."

"Dunsette denied writing the emails."

Nick scoffed. "What did you expect Dunsette to say?"

"He even let us examine his email 'sent' box. He was truly surprised when the emails were there. He had the gall to complain that the handcuffs were too tight."

* * * *

Later that day, the headquarters of INN received an email from the FBI agent who had interviewed Nick. Attached were the emails Dunsette had sent Sharp. The story aired within the hour. The agent denied sending the emails to INN, and then was immediately placed on administrative leave when his 'sent' box was examined.

23

At dawn on Friday, April 5, Lacy found two cans of sardines in the tiny pantry, and a can of green beans. The pungency of the sardines filled the small cabin until fresh coffee won out. She emerged on deck with the meager spread on paper plates.

Archer spied the plates. "You're really a good cook."

She chuckled. "Better enjoy it, 'cause that's all there was in the pantry."

Archer had to stay at the helm, so she fed him while standing up, dangling a sardine over his mouth before dropping it in. "This reminds me of feeding the seals at the zoo."

He made a mock seal call, arched his head back, and opened his mouth wide as she dropped another sardine into the cavity.

"You married?"

His wide eyes jumped at her. She was surprised at how surprised he was by the question. It just seemed like a natural and innocent question to her.

He frowned and shook his head. "Was." He patted his belly. "And now…"

"And now…?"

His smile was more of a grimace. "And now… I'm a free agent." He forced another smile, then, in a sing-song voice: 'I have my books and my poetry to protect me. I am shielded there in my armor.'" He could see that she did not get his reference. "Paul Simon."

She lifted her head in an 'ah-ha' nod.

"Freedom." He looked at her. "Isn't that what it's called?" He frowned and blew out a slow breath. "Freedom to not care. Freedom to not worry about what I look like, 'cause no one is looking at me."

She shrugged. "You were in shape once."

"How do you know that?"

"You still have some left-over muscles."

He snorted. "Left-over. Like in the refrigerator. " He frowned. "Yeah, I was in shape once, when I was on the sailing team. But, after the divorce…"

She did not like where the conversation was headed, but it was her own fault. At this point, she would just press on a little bit more. "…And maybe drink less. Your complexion might clear up."

Archer stared at her.

She repressed a wince. Maybe I went too far.

He looked away. "You got your vices and I got mine."

She was not about to take the bait and ask him what he thought her vices were.

After several minutes of silence, he broke it. "…And you?"

"Me, what?"

"Married?"

Lacy frowned. Why did I ask that question? She turned away from him. She did not want him to see the pain in her face. "…Nearly. Once."

"Nearly?"

"He was an agnostic. Stupid, naïve me thought I could change him." She turned to look at his reaction. He gave her nothing. "And then he wanted me to get silicone boobs…" Again, no reaction, which surprised her.

More silence, then once more he broke it. "…You were right."

She turned to look at him. "About what? About giving up on trying to change him?"

He shook his head. "No. About the silicone. Go natural. Accept what God did, and," he nodded in the direction of her chest, "did not give you."

She ignored the dig and flashed a smile. "See? You do believe in God."

He shrugged. He locked the helm in place and ate the sardines and green beans between gulps of cooling coffee. "I'm going to have to get some sleep. Do you think you can take the helm?"

She looked at the wheel and frowned. "I guess."

"Just hold it on this course and keep your eyes out in front of the bow. The charts don't have any islands in the immediate area, and the water is plenty deep."

Archer went below deck and returned with a fishing pole. He jabbed the last partial sardine onto the hook and set the line aft. "Your Jesus wanted to fish for men. I'll settle for real fish."

Oh, a segue into talking about faith. Don't miss this chance. And don't push too hard. She looked over her shoulder at him. "Do you think He'll ever become your Jesus?"

"I think that would take a minor miracle."

She did not turn her face to him. "Why's that?"

He walked around the helm and looked at her. "Because it's just all too fantastic to believe. After Jesus died —and Pilate burned the body and spread the ashes—I believe the apostles made it all up. Turned a good man into a legend, into something he was not."

"C.S. Lewis points out that it is the disciples themselves who demonstrate some of the greatest evidence that Jesus rose from the dead."

"Oh, how's that?"

Good. His tone was not as defensive as she had expected. "Their metamorphosis. They went from cowards to courageous within the span of just a few days. Only one thing can explain that: they saw and spoke to the risen Christ. Thomas might have even stuck his fingers in the wounds that Longinus made with his spear."

Archer vehemently shook his head back and forth. "It's all a great and powerful lie."

She rolled her eyes. "Now you sound like Kitchens."

"If the shoe fits."

"People don't die for a lie."

"Sure they do. All the time."

"Not when they know it is a lie. They think it's the truth. It might be a lie, but they don't know it's a lie. Otherwise, they would not sacrifice for it, and they sure wouldn't die for it."

"But that's the point, now, isn't it?"

She looked at him and shook her head in question. "What do you mean?"

"We don't have to die. Not anymore. Medical science is prolonging life indefinitely. Injections of NAD, blood from the young and other drugs are actually reversing the aging process. Two years ago I even grew a new liver from my own spliced cells—the proverbial fountain of youth, the new Garden of Eden. Who needs God, when you can grow your own immortality?"

"Your body is not immortal! You will die someday, just as I will, and all living things will. Science may have postponed the inevitable, but not the final result. What is immortal is your soul. As for our bodies, we should gracefully surrender those things of youth."

"I'd rather rage against the dying light."

"Rage all you want, but die you will!" Lacy did not care that her voice was rising. She was mad.

He turned away from her and looked out to sea. "I'm really not trying to be rude or blasphemous."

"You could have fooled me," she shot back. "And you're still missing the point: the disciples did not have NAD, and could not grow their own body parts. They knew they would die if they proclaimed Jesus as the Christ, and yet they did it anyway."

"Well, there's no cure for stupid."

"There's no cure for witnessing the truth. If you want proof of God's existence, just look around."

He turned back to her. "What do you mean?"

"Come on! You've been trained in science."

"As have you."

"Einstein argued that science still needed religion to explain the complete truth. I see nature as an arm of God, not a separate, competing body. Science is one of God's methods. For instance, we now know that physicists have computed that after the Big Bang, the universe expanded at a speed of a billionth of a trillionth of a quadrillionth of a second. A flicker of a flicker. Beyond imagination, really."

"Okay. So?"

"So? That's God at work. That's evidence of the existence of a higher, intelligent power. Only God could have performed a feat like that."

Archer blew out a breath. "Perhaps."

Her whole body twisted as she let out a groan. "How can you not see it?"

"Maybe that's just it. I can't see it." He paused. "…It's just not all the pain and suffering that God lets happen, but that he keeps himself so locked away. So hidden. Like the Wizard of Oz behind the curtain." He turned to her. "Why? Why does God keep himself so hidden?"

She did not answer.

He gave a tight-lipped smile. "…I'd like to believe, but I just can't."

"Just won't."

He shook his head, lay down on the deck, and pulled the blanket over his face.

She held the helm as steady as she could. She looked down at the lump in the blanket. Would finding these manuscripts by Longinus change his opinion? She recited in her mind the clue left in the note by Quintus. "Refuge." Could mean anything. "Holy of holies, where many gods became One." That was sort of familiar. But how so? "Eluid could gain hidden passage day or night." Didn't mean a thing.

Four hours later, the fishing reel erupted with a high-pitched ringing. She turned around. The fishing line was racing out from the stern of the boat. "Archer!" she called several times.

He pulled the blanket from over his head and looked at her.

She pointed behind the boat. "You caught something!"

He jumped up and started reeling in the catch. Fifteen minutes later, a dorsal fin sliced the water behind the boat: a four-foot-long white shark.

She stared at the shark. "What are you going to do? Cut it loose?"

"Nope; I'm bringing it aboard."

"Aboard?"

"Yep."

She blew out a breath and spied the officer's pistol still lying on the deck where he had thrown it. "Too bad that pistol doesn't work."

"Don't need it." He set the fishing pole in the brace, walked to the starboard side, and untied the spear from the side of the deck. He held it up with a smile.

"Where you going to put that shark?"

"On the deck, of course. You swing around and hold the helm from the other side."

He reeled in the shark, and then pulled it up and over the side. The shark's jaws snapped at the air as its body jerked back and forth. He grabbed the spear and drove it deep into the shark just behind its eye, ending the shark's life. "See? Not so difficult." Blood spewed onto the deck.

She blew out a breath. "Now what?"

"Eat it, of course. Shark steak is tasty. And we'll use the intestines for more bait."

Archer went below and found a butcher knife, then skinned and cleaned the shark on deck, washed his hands in the ocean as best he could and washed the deck. He cooked large shark steaks on the hot plate below. When he emerged on deck with a pot of coffee, he was holding two large plates. "It would go better with white wine, but…" He smiled.

"No sense whining about it."

He cringed at the bad pun. He took the helm from her and she ate first.

She took a few bites and nodded up at him. "I was hungrier than I realized." She spied the spear that had killed the shark. Spear… Her mind jumped to the ruins at Celsus. Was the spear of the centurion Longinus Petronius really there? Back in the jar in the deniza at the library—could that really be the actual spear that confirmed that Jesus was dead? If it was, it was a find of great historical significance. Few archeologists ever found such a relic. It would equal the Shroud of Turin in importance.

Relic. She hated that word. The word was often misused, and even abused. The decayed remains of St. Nicholas had been declared a relic, as had the heart of St. O'Toole. An urn supposedly holding the ashes of Buddha had been declared as much, along with a lock of hair which supposedly was from Muhammad himself. In the 1980s, a group of Italians claimed they had the actual foreskin of Jesus, until the "relic" mysteriously disappeared.

However, the actual spear that pierced Christ on the cross was another matter. If she could not go to Celsus, someone else had to. It was too valuable to be entrusted to Islamic Turks.

After she had finished eating, she re-took the helm, and Archer ate his shark. "There's more steak below. I put it in the small, battery-operated refrigerator."

After he had finished eating, Archer took some of the shark innards, stuck it on the fish hook, and let the line troll behind the boat. Then he took the helm.

Lacy got a rag from the galley, and started cleaning the sand from the officer's pistol.

Archer eyed her. "Do you know what you're doing?"

"I'm not from Boston. I'm from Texas. I grew up with guns."

"Okay, Annie Oakley."

"I was always more fond of Calamity Jane."

He snorted. "Calamity. You got that right."

She disassembled the revolver and cleaned as much sand as she could from it, then reassembled it. She pointed it out to sea and half-squeezed the trigger. The mechanism began to engage. She eased off the trigger. "I think it's working now."

"You think."

"Well, I could always shoot you to confirm it."

Archer gave her a mock smile. "That's what I get for saving your life. Twice."

"No good deed goes unpunished."

They fell back into silence. She stretched out on the deck and closed her eyes. Just as she was about to drift into sleep, her eyes flashed open and she sat up.

"What? What now, Calamity Jane?"

"Holies… Holy of holies."

"What?" Archer craned his neck to look back at her.

"The great temple in Jerusalem had an inner room where the Ark of the Covenant was kept. Only the High Priest could enter it, and then only once a year."

"The temple of Jerusalem was destroyed by the Romans—"

"Decades after Jesus was crucified, so it was there when Longinus was there."

Archer sounded dubious. "But it'd be gone now, so we wouldn't be able to find anything."

"Maybe. But there might be some clue. Maybe that's why we're being sent that way." Lacy gazed out over the endless waters.

"Sent?"

"Yes, 'sent.'"

Archer rolled his eyes. "God again."

"God always. He blew the wind and turned us in this direction."

"Superstitious nonsense."

"There is none so blind as he who will not see." She pointed at the distant Turkish coast. "You said we can't go there. We can only go to Cyprus, Syria, Lebanon, or Israel. The first three have extradition treaties with Turkey, but not Israel. And I know a Christian in Haifa, Israel."

"Maybe he'll have something to drink."

24

Pilate's caravan arrived in Jerusalem late on the second day of hard travel. Pilate and his wife stayed in the Praetorium, the palace built by the late King Herod. Tarjan stayed down the hall. Normally, a centurion would have stayed in the Antonia Fortress, the soldier's barracks, but since Longinus was assigned to personal duty with Tarjan, he slept in a small room on the ground floor. It suited him. It was closer to the wine cellar.

The next morning, Longinus and his second in command, Nedo Madradus, who went by his second name, climbed the stairs to the roof to survey the city. Longinus asked Madradus to accompany him because Madradus had been to Jerusalem many times before and could point out features of the city. Also, Longinus had sensed a churning animosity from Madradus since they had been in Caesarea. He concluded that Madradus had probably expected to be given command and, when he was not, was angry at Longinus. Longinus hoped by including Madradus in his activities he would win Madradus's allegiance. If that approach did not work, a more authoritative one could always be used.

When they stepped onto the balcony, Longinus gasped. Before them loomed the massive temple of the Hebrews, gleaming white and gold in the early sun, and dominating the city.

"Yes," Madradus said in a slur. "The Jews believe their god actually lives in there.

Longinus looked down at the narrow streets of Jerusalem clogged with people and sheep awaiting slaughter, then looked back at the temple. He shook his head in dismay. A city of religious zealots. He had ridden himself of Rome's many gods only to be surrounded by the Hebrews' one and only. Pilate was right. A dreadful place and a dreadful people. He already longed for a deep cup of wine. In vino veritas. In wine, truth.

Later that day, Tarjan told Longinus of a story he had been told. A prophet of some sort had entered the city on a donkey, and his followers and others had laid their coats and palm branches on the ground to escort him into the city.

"The followers called this prophet a 'king'," Tarjan said.

"That is treason," Longinus replied. "Only the Emperor is king."

"Yes. We will see how Pilate handles this."

"Did the prophet refute this title?" Longinus asked.

"Eyewitnesses say he did not."

Longinus shook his head. "Another religious lunatic. What is this prophet's name?

"Jesus. He comes from a province to the north called Galilee."

The following day, Tarjan wished to walk through the city, so Longinus, Madradus, and two other soldiers, Quintus and Philo, accompanied him. The Praetorium was on the western side of the city, and as they walked through the narrow streets filled with cackling Jews and bleating sheep, they inevitably gravitated towards the great temple.

The more Longinus saw the temple, the more impressed he was. If there really was a god, he concluded, he would live in such a place. But the only god he needed was Bacchus, and the fruit of the vine.

They entered the temple on the south side, climbing a series of wide stone steps, and then walked into a tunnel. When they exited the tunnel, they came into a large courtyard filled with hundreds of people.

"All these stinking sheep," Longinus said.

"They are for sacrifice," Madradus scoffed. "It is the path to religious purity."

Longinus rolled his eyes. "Purity."

"They have to kill a male lamb, and not just any male lamb," Madradus continued. "The priests inspect the lamb for any blemish, and if the lamb has a blemish, then it is rejected as not proper for sacrifice. So that person has to buy an unblemished lamb from the priests, and they charge extra. The lamb can only be purchased with a temple coin. So, regular coins must be exchanged for temple coins." He pointed at the tables set up for the exchange.

Longinus shook his head. "They rob their own people in the name of purity." He looked at Tarjan. "It's an old story found everywhere."

There were many tables set up for this exchange. To the side were priests, wearing elaborate costumes with massive headdresses with little boxes dangling from them. Longinus shook his head. How silly-looking that was. Religion.

Then to their right they heard a loud, angry, male voice. "My house shall be called a house of prayer but you are making it a robber's den!" Then the man started overturning the tables. Temple coins scattered across the floor of the temple.

Longinus looked at the priests, who just stood there watching the rant. Why do they not stop this man? They seem afraid of him. Why? Longinus tried to see the face of the protester, but a hood shielded his face from view.

The hooded man stomped out of the courtyard. A half dozen or more men scurried after him, like so many mice. Longinus had not noticed them until the disturbance was over. They had not turned over any tables nor uttered any protestations. They just stood by. Then when their leader left, they scampered after him lest they be left alone in the temple to account for their leader.

"That is Jesus," Longinus heard a man say. "The rabbi who yesterday came in on a donkey."

"Some say he is the new king," another man said.

Longinus turned back to see Jesus disappear through a door. He shook his head again. Another religious lunatic. This city is filled with them.

When they returned to the Praetorium, Tarjan asked Longinus to follow him. When Madradus was not included, he fumed. Tarjan found Pilate, related what he had seen in the temple, and then asked Pilate if this Jesus would be seized.

"On what grounds?" Pilate asked. "He broke Hebrew law, not Roman."

"He disrupts the flow of money to Rome."

Pilate shook his head. "That remains to be seen. Caiaphas, the head priest, is responsible for making payments. This Jesus is his problem."

Tarjan thought for a second. "The followers of this Jesus call him a king."

"Does Jesus claim to be a king?"

"No. But he did not refute it."

"That may be poor judgment, but it is not a violation of our law."

Tarjan frowned and left. Pilate looked at Longinus and shook his head at the vise he was in. Longinus saluted and left.

That night, Longinus grabbed a flask of wine and went to the roof. Below, he could hear the din of 300,000 people and their lambs in a city that usually occupied one-fourth that. Stretching across the countryside in all directions outside the walls of the city were hundreds of campfires and tents, holding people who were unable to find lodging inside the walls.

As Longinus filled his mouth with wine, he thought of Jesus overturning the tables. Was he brave and committed, or some kind of bully? Longinus was not sure. One thing was for sure: his followers had none of his bravado.

He frowned. Who was he to criticize the followers? He'd been the same way once. His mind tumbled back to when he was a lad. He had been small for his age and more interested in books, not the games the other boys played in the streets of Rome. That made him an easy target for the bullies, and he did not have the muscles, skill, or inclination to fight back. One day when he was returning from the library with a piece of papyrus, a stylus, and a bottle of ink, he was stopped by an older and bigger boy who had wiry hair that shot out from his head. The boy pushed Longinus to the ground, tore up the papyrus, bent the stylus beyond use, and poured the ink on Longinus's head. On that day, Longinus turned his back on books and resolved to become a soldier. He would not be pushed around again.

Years later, when returning from a military campaign with Pilate in Gaul, Longinus ran into the wiry-haired bully. Longinus thrashed him with his whip, then stuck his sword to his throat and cut an "L" in the skin. Vengeance felt good, felt right.

As Longinus remembered the incident while drinking wine atop the Praetorium, he smiled. Then he thought of Jesus in the temple. Maybe this Jesus was just another bully, and the priests did not dare stand up to him.

25

Emin Obar, the one-eyed Mullah, did not like Christian archeologists finding artifacts supporting their religion. And he was particularly tired of searches for Noah's Ark, even though Islam accepted the Noah story, albeit with a different slant. Obar did not want Christians parading around his country, flaunting their infidel faith. Tolerance was a Western vice.

When Mullah Obar learned Lacy Stowe planned to return to Turkey to search for an alternative site of the Seven Sleepers, he had registered his objection with the Turkish government. However, the Turkish government wanted Western tourist dollars.

When the Uighur, Yoldash Abdullah, had contacted him, Obar thanked Allah for the gift and asked Yoldash to give him daily briefings, which Yoldash faithfully did at the end of each day. When Yoldash did not after the earthquake, Obar learned of Yoldash's fate. Obar told police he had given the camera to Yoldash and wanted it back. The Selçuk police were busy with the after-effects of the earthquake, and gave him the camera. Then he paid one of the officers at the Celsus site to say that he had seen Stowe strike the Uighur with a rock before the earthquake.

"Why didn't you come forth earlier?" the Selçuk police asked the park officer.

"After the quake, I was worried about my family first."

The story of the Seven Sleepers was one of those intersects between Christianity and Islam. The Koran contained a passage on the Seven Sleepers, albeit from an Islamic perspective. One of Yoldash's shots showed DeYoung urinating on the side of Mt. Pion. Obar declared that the American had desecrated a Muslim shrine by urinating near the established site of the Seven Sleepers and issued a fatwah: hunt down the American infidels.

26

The political ads by The Word ran. Kitchens took the bait and sued. It had begun.

At the press conference announcing his libel/defamation suit, Kitchens reiterated his claim that there was no objective, unbiased, eyewitness document confirming the existence of Jesus of Nazareth, let alone the fantastic claims of the four gospels.

"It was written by ex-Jews who wished to become famous themselves." Kitchens's voice was smooth and determined as he spoke into the microphone. "The basic fact is that God did not create man. Man created God. Man—or at least some men—need God. They want to believe that there is someone up there who likes them. They are terrified that when they die there will be nothing. However, the first rule of rational thought is to not allow your wishes to control your thoughts. And that is what they have done. They want there to be a God, so, in their minds, they have convinced themselves that there is one, despite all evidence to the contrary. Religion is a lie. And in thirteen days we will end, once and for all, 'The Great Lie.' The countdown has begun."

27

The winds subsided, so it took three more long days to reach Haifa, Israel. Archer caught more fish and Lacy found desalination pills to treat the seawater. Despite the hats, both were sunburned. She searched for sunscreen, but found none. Each needed a bath, and each reminded the other of this fact. At times, Archer's hands shook as he steered the boat. She shook her head. How could anyone allow themselves to become so dependent on booze?

As they slipped into Haifa harbor at dawn on the morning of Monday, April 8, their pockets came alive with a series of pings, dings, and vibrations, like they had hit the jackpot in Vegas. Their cell phones were back. And so was GPS. To her surprise, she frowned at the return of technology. She had come to like the silence, the time to think and reflect; the peace.

Archer eased the boat alongside the dock and Lacy dropped the looped rope over the post. She slipped the pistol into the back of her shorts. Archer had refused to hold it. He took the pottery canister and stepped onto the dock, turning to hold out his hand. "So you know someone here?"

She grabbed his hand. "Yeah. He helped me with a dig once." Archer pulled her up and they came face to face. He had a five-day beard and the smell to go with it. She reared her head back.

"So he couldn't find Noah's Ark either."

She glared and turned away. "It was in Jordan." Her mouth fell open. Pella. The Migdol Temple dig. Of course! It, too, had a room called the Holy of Holies. In fact, many tabernacles had a Holy of Holies room. She spun around and told him about the Pella dig.

"Okay. So which one do we go to?" Archer did not sound particularly thrilled. "We can't seek out every ancient tabernacle."

"Not sure yet," Lacy admitted. "My friend who helped me with the dig in Pella is a Math prof here in Haifa. His name is Dr. Allen Flieman."

"What was a Math prof doing on an archeological dig?"

"Vacation. Said he wanted to get some dirt under the fingernails."

"Sounds to me like it was more a case of him having the hots for you."

She opened her mouth to counter, paused, and then snapped her jaws closed.

"Thought so," he smirked, satisfied with his assessment.

Lacy pointed to the hills. "His place is just a few kilometers from here."

"You've been to his apartment?"

She ignored him. They trudged up from the harbor, past stores, homes without yards, and the expansive, lush, and beautiful Bahai Garden on Mount Carmel with its great Golden Dome shining in the sun. After an hour of climbing, he demanded that they stop. He sucked in a breath and looked back at the harbor. "Everything is so compact. They use every square inch. Like Manhattan."

She nodded. "Now you understand their concern for security. They're in a small place, surrounded by people sworn to kill them."

Flieman was not at home, but neighbors confirmed he still lived there. They were hungry. They went to a corner store, and Archer purchased a bag of bagels and two bottles of water.

She pointed at his credit card. "We'll be on the grid."

"We already are: our cell phones. And our driver's licenses have dots, as do our credit cards, whether we use them or not. So…" He shrugged. "But I recommend we do not communicate with our universities. Calls and emails will be easily monitored, even more so than GPS dots. Agreed?"

What about the spear back at the deniza in Turkey? She frowned and nodded.

He started to buy some wine, but her frown stopped him. They found a park bench on the north side of the building in the shade. Neither needed more sun. He opened the bagels, broke one in half, and handed it to her. When he raised his armpit, her head jerked back. She crinkled her nose. "Do I smell as bad as you?"

He pinched his nose with his fingers and smiled. "Worse."

She chuckled and took the bagel. "I never figured we'd be breaking bread together."

"One of God's little jests. So, tell me more about this Jordanian temple." He took a bite.

She swallowed a gulp of water and coughed. "It's in northwest Jordan. The Decapolis region. Ten cities, of which Pella was one. The Migdol Temple was built to commemorate the change in beliefs from pagan polytheism to a single God—one God—the Canaanite God. Pella was known as the 'City of Refuge.' Remember the clue in the note from Quintus? '…Found refuge under the holies where many gods became One…'"

Archer frowned, his mouth full of bagel. "But if that's the place, why would a centurion assigned to Jerusalem be in Decapolis?"

"Don't know. But maybe the manuscript could tell us that."

He shook his head. "I can't believe I let you drag me into this."

Lacy turned to him and smiled. "You love it."

28

The following morning, Tarjan again wanted to walk through the city. After yesterday's incident at the money tables, Longinus feared there might be more trouble, so he grabbed a spear as they left.

Once again, they entered the temple through the south side, and climbed the steps into the courtyard, once more filled with Jews and their lambs. There seemed to be a throng of people and priests near the northeastern corner of the temple, so Tarjan moved in that direction. Longinus, Madradus, Quintus, and Philo followed.

They exited through a door to a portico lined with tall columns. The area was filled with people, most who were sitting and looking towards the outer wall. There were enough people standing that Longinus could not see who the throng was listening to. There were several priests there, in their ornate religious robes with those ridiculous little boxes hanging from their hats. They, too, looked towards some person sitting against the wall. The priests were standing, and Longinus could tell by their faces that they were not happy with what they were hearing. Next to one of the priests stood a man with a pointed helmet, a temple guard of some sort, Longinus guessed.

Longinus maneuvered to the side so he could see who was speaking. Sitting against the wall was a single man, knees bent in support. His hands moved as he spoke. His voice was smooth and almost soft, with a thick accent of some kind that Longinus did not recognize. Longinus focused on his face, but could only see the top half of the left side of his head. His folded hood shielded the rest of his face from view. A woman in the crowd called him Jesus.

Oh, Longinus noted in surprise. So here is the same man who overturned the tables yesterday. Obviously, the priests have still not arrested him. Maybe that is what they are here to do now.

A priest said, "Is it lawful to pay a poll-tax to Caesar, or not? Shall we pay or not pay?"

Tarjan stepped forward. His ears perked in interest for the answer. Jesus answered, "Why are you testing me? Bring me a denarius."

They did as requested.

"Whose likeness and name is on this?" Jesus asked.

"Caesar's," someone answered.

"Render to Caesar," Jesus said, "the things that are Caesar's, and to God the things that are God's."

The crowd nodded in understanding, but the priests squirmed in frustration. Longinus smiled. How smartly this Jesus had side-stepped their trap, for it was obvious to all who could see and hear that, while the crowd admired and respected Jesus, the priests did not. They feared his hold on the crowd. At that moment, Longinus understood why Jesus had not been arrested yet. The priests were afraid of the reaction of the throng if they seized this Jesus.

A scribe next to a priest then asked, "What commandment is the foremost of all?"

Jesus answered, "You should love the Lord God with all your heart, with all your soul, with all your mind, and with all your strength." Then he continued. "The second is you shall love your neighbor as yourself. There is no other commandment greater than these."

Love your neighbor? Longinus wanted to scoff. As yourself? Get serious. What a silly dreamer this man is. He knows nothing of the world.

Jesus continued speaking. He spoke out against the priests and their robes, and the place of respect they had in society and of their hypocritical, long prayers. Some of the priests nearly frothed in indignation. Then Jesus predicted the destruction of the great temple and the end of the world. Longinus shook his head in wonder. This Jesus was either a lunatic filled with foolish bravery, or he was the biggest storyteller in all of the empire.

Jesus continued. "The hour has come for the Son of Man to be glorified. Truly, I say unto you, unless a grain of wheat falls into the earth and dies, it remains alone; but if it dies, it bears much fruit. He who loves his life loses it, and he who hates his life in this world will keep it to life eternal."

Longinus rolled his eyes. Eternal life…

"Now my soul has become troubled," Jesus said, "and what shall I say, Father, save me from this hour? But for this purpose I came to this hour."

What does that mean? Longinus asked himself.

"Father, glorify Your name," Jesus proclaimed.

At that instance, a loud voice bellowed over all of them. "I have both glorified it, and will glorify it again."

Everyone fell still and looked around in confusion. Had they really heard that? Where did this voice come from? It must be from inside the temple. Some game Jesus was playing with one of his cowardly followers, no doubt. Longinus opened the door to the inside of the courtyard. No one inside turned to look at him as if they had been caught in some prank. They were all going about their business.

Tarjan motioned to leave. At that moment, Jesus stood up. The sides of his hood fell onto his shoulders. Longinus saw his face and his mouth fell open. It was the man in his dreams. The man with the piercing eyes. He looked directly at Longinus. Yes, it was him. Then his eyes moved to the spear in Longinus's hand and he nodded. He looked back at Longinus for a prolonged moment. His eyes did not waver. They spoke of strength and yet peace. Then Jesus turned away.

As Jesus walked away through the crowd, his followers gathered around him. One of them in particular Longinus noticed. He had a thick beard, and another person called him 'Simon.' The way they followed his every step reminded Longinus of a lost puppy dog having found some new master.

Then Longinus's attention was caught by two priests who marched past him. One said to the other. "I am going to report all of this to Caiaphas. This Jesus must be stopped."

When Tarjan, Longinus, and the others had returned to the Praetorium, Tarjan went to see Pilate by himself.

"What do you make of that voice?" Madradus asked as they watched Tarjan walk away.

Longinus shrugged. "A sorcerer's trick."

"They say this Jesus has raised the dead," Quintus said.

"Obviously," Longinus answered, "he is a very good magician."

Longinus dismissed Madradus, Quintus, and Philo, and headed to the wine cellar. That night, as he sat once more on the balcony by himself, he remembered his dreams while on the ship, of this man Jesus. What could explain that? The face he saw in his dreams was clearly the man he had seen today in the temple. He was sure of it. Those eyes. He could not forget those eyes. He took another swig and shrugged. Yes, this Jesus was a very good magician. That night, Longinus got very drunk but the wine did not calm his troubled mind. What was it about this Jesus? Why did he torment him so?

29

At the local police precinct, the Reverend Lester Dunsette was booked on charges of making terrorist threats, conspiracy, and suspicion of murdering Gordon Sharp. He was escorted to a chair at a desk in an interrogation room with the obligatory two-way mirror. The FBI agent had already read him his Miranda rights. Dunsette declined an opportunity to call an attorney or have one appointed by the court.

"If you tell the truth, you shouldn't need a lawyer," Dunsette told him.

The agent rolled his eyes.

Once more, Dunsette denied writing the note threatening to kidnap Kitchens's daughter. "It's a forgery," he insisted.

The G-man leaned across the table. "Our computer makes you at a 97% reliability."

Dunsette countered with his own lean. "Computers. The new liars for the new age."

A local police detective broke in. "And we got you sending threatening emails to Sharp."

"I tell you again, I sent no such emails."

The detective nearly came out of his seat. "They're in your 'sent' box!"

"Somebody got on my computer or hacked it."

"And changed the dates, too? That's impossible. Time cannot be so easily manipulated."

Dunsette snorted. "Well, someone manipulated it." He looked straight at the detective, held his eyes, then turned to the FBI agent and held his eyes, as well. "Don't you see what's happening? These computers are fracturing our freedoms and stealing our souls."

The detective rolled his eyes. "Save your pseudo-political/religious rants for talk radio. All I see is that we got a case against you."

Dunsette chuckled and shook his head.

The FBI agent glared at him. "What's so funny?"

"You got no case, 'cause you got no time. Thirteen days. Thirteen days and then I will be freed! And you? You will be left behind!"

30

A man in a sports jacket approached. Archer motioned at him. "This him?"

Lacy turned. "Yep."

Flieman smiled as he drew nearer. She rose from the front steps and they hugged. Flieman hung on a little longer than a 'good to see you' embrace required, and then she pulled back. "Sorry I smell so bad."

Flieman's hand extended to Archer and he met it with his own. "Allen Flieman."

"Archer DeYoung, fellow archeologist."

"Texas A&M?"

"No, I went to a real college."

"Hav-erd" she said in her best New England accent.

Flieman looked at her, then at him, and tilted his head back and forth in a manner suggesting he thought this encounter was going to be interesting. He looked back to Lacy. "I was going to fix a bite. Want to come in?"

"Sure. What's for dinner?"

"Fish."

She groaned, and then smiled an apology. "We've been at sea for five days. I've eaten so much fish that I think I might grow fins."

"At sea? Not many archeological digs at sea."

"You got that right."

"Well, come on in. I'll fix some pita bread and schnitzel while you tell me about it."

She smiled. "It's a deal."

"You always had a great smile." He turned to Archer, "Doesn't she have a great smile?"

"Just great."

Archer stepped inside. A bottle of wine was on the counter. "Mind if I open it?"

Flieman turned around, eyes wide. Lacy was staring at him, too.

He looked at Lacy and Flieman and shrugged. "Sorry. Just need something to take the edge off."

Flieman nodded. "I bet. Pour a glass for everyone."

He set the pottery canister on the counter and began opening the bottle. While Flieman prepped the meal, he drained a glass and refilled. Lacy nursed hers and told of the Seven Sleepers and the earthquake. She pointed at the canister. "After the quake, I found this."

Flieman turned and looked at the canister. "I was wondering what was in that."

"Papyrus. Latin. From the first century A.D. we think."

Flieman looked at the canister again. "Wow."

"Yeah, that's what we thought. Remember the Migdol dig?"

Flieman flashed a smile. "How could I forget? I tried to kiss you, and you rejected me."

Archer looked at Flieman, then her, and smiled. When she scowled, he puckered his lips into a mock frown, to which she returned the real thing. She shrugged. "...Well, you know."

Flieman grunted. "Yeah, I know. My life story. Maybe that's why I'm so good at math. The only reciprocals required are equations, not feelings. ...Okay, but you still haven't told me how you ended up here."

She told of the security officer at the hotel, the chase, and the boat. She looked straight at Flieman. "We're hot, and us being here makes you hot. It's just a matter of time before GPS makes us. Sorry about that. We need to get to Pella. ...And we need your car."

"I guess it was too much to hope for that you were here to see me."

She frowned an apology.

Flieman paused then tossed his keys to her. "It's parked out front. A white Norwegian Buddy Cab. Electric. Charge is good for four days, depending on use. One condition."

"What's that?"

"When you get back, you let me take you to dinner."

She smiled. "As long as it isn't fish." She looked at Archer, who rolled his eyes.

31

Senator Kitchens sent an email to the Senate Majority Leader, announcing he wanted to amend his own bill, declaring that private Bible possession was banned. He just did not know he sent the email.

32

Longinus awoke the next morning with a dry mouth and a throbbing head. Tarjan found this amusing. Luckily for Longinus, Tarjan did not wish to walk out into the city that day.

The next day, the day before the beginning of the Jewish Sabbath and Passover feast, Longinus and his three men walked through the temple once more with Tarjan. This time they did not see Jesus. Part of Longinus was relieved and yet part of him was disappointed. He frowned in thought. What is it about this man that pulled at him? That evening, Longinus returned to the balcony and his flask of wine.

Longinus took a swig and reminded himself that tomorrow would be a busy day. Three crucifixions: two robbers and a murderer named Barabbas. Madradus wanted more responsibility, and had asked to lead the crucifixion. Longinus gladly gave him the duty. Longinus hated crucifixions. He knew the purpose of them was to show off Roman power and deter resistance, but he still considered them needlessly wanton. Could we not just behead the man and stick his head on a pole? That would be a whole lot quicker. He took another swig. Maybe that was the point. The punishment needed to be long. Prolong the agony. Publicize the pain. And Madradus was just the man for this duty. He liked inflicting pain, whereas Longinus simply recognized the need for it.

Just as the last light of the day spread across Jerusalem, Longinus was interrupted by Madradus and a Jew dressed in a uniform with a pointed helmet. Longinus recognized him as the man who'd accompanied the priests when the priests questioned Jesus two days ago just outside the temple. The day when the mysterious voice came from above.

"This is Malchus," Madradus announced. "He is a servant of Caiaphas, the head priest."

Longinus looked at Malchus. "Why are you here?"

"Caiaphas is in need of your help," Malchus answered.

He shrugged. "Like what?"

Malchus looked at Madradus. "There is a troublemaker who needs to be arrested."

"Well, arrest him!" Longinus shot back.

"It's that Jesus," Madradus said.

Longinus looked at Malchus, and, in a mocking tone said, "And you want Roman help."

Malchus nodded.

He chuckled. "I have seen the men around him. You will have no trouble."

"But the others…" Malchus added.

"What others?" Longinus asked.

"The people… they think he is some kind of prophet."

"And you're afraid of them."

Malchus nodded again.

"So you want to take him at night when few would see the arrest."

Malchus nodded again.

"You Jews are a dreadful people."

Malchus did not respond.

Longinus was already too drunk to go out. Besides, he had no desire to see this Jesus ever again. He turned to Madradus. "Take Quintus and help these Jews arrest an unarmed man. Do it quickly. Remember that we have three crucifixions tomorrow and you are to lead the patrol."

Madradus smiled. "I have not forgotten."

Longinus made a mental note to brief Pilate tomorrow. They left, and Longinus returned to his wine.

It was late when Madradus returned. By then, Longinus was asleep, deep in a drunken stupor. It took several shakes of his shoulder to awaken him.

Longinus threw off the blanket and got up. "Well? Did you arrest that Galilean magician?"

"We did."

"So why did I need to be awakened?"

"Malchus was injured."

"So?"

"You don't understand. When we seized this Jesus, one of his followers pulled out a sword and cut off the ear of Malchus."

"I'm surprised that any of them fought back even in the slightest."

Madradus paused. "…Then Jesus knelt down and put Malchus's ear back on."

"What do you mean? 'Put it back'?"

"He put it back on his head… healed it somehow."

Longinus shook his head. "It's just another magician's trick. Where is this Jesus now?"

"They took him to the house of the head priest for trial."

"Good. Then this episode is done. Hopefully, we will not hear of Jesus the Magician again. Are you sure you got the right man?"

"Yes. One of Jesus's followers identified him. With a kiss."

"With a kiss?"

"Yes. And called him 'Rabbi.'"

Longinus shook his head, and said with a slur, "Such loyalty."

"I think the man was paid."

Longinus shook his head again in disgust. "That's even worse. Get some sleep and get ready for the three planned crucifixions."

Madradus turned to leave.

"Wait!"

Madradus stopped and pivoted.

"Did none of the other followers of this Jesus try to stop you?"

"No. They ran."

Longinus grunted. What little respect he may have had for them had now evaporated. "Sheep. Blemished sheep at that. Not even fit for sacrifice. …What did you do to that man who cut off Malchus's ear?"

"We let him go. He attacked no Romans. And the Jews seemed interested only in Jesus. But Malchus was right. He did need us."

"How's that?"

"When Jesus stepped forward and identified himself, the Jewish guards fell to the ground. I think they fainted or something."

Longinus laughed and shook his head. "These Jews… weak."

"One other thing," Madradus said.

Longinus rolled his eyes. "What's that?"

"Jesus did not try to hide. He made no attempt to escape. It was almost like…"

"Like what?"

"…Like he knew this was coming. It was not a surprise." Madradus looked directly at Longinus and said firmly, "He expected us."

Longinus did not respond. He waved Madradus to leave. He tried to go back to sleep, but could not. He kept seeing the Galilean's face. Finally, after several hours and more wine, he slipped into an uneasy slumber.

33

They stayed the night in Flieman's apartment, using the time to wash their clothes. Flieman provided replacements. They were taking a chance being found by GPS, but a good night's sleep and a long hot bath won out. Archer took the chance to shave. So did Lacy, even if a man's razor cut her up some. She slept on a couch in a small office, and Archer slept on the couch in the living room.

Once in the den, she spied Flieman's computer. She had to get someone back to the deniza at Celsus to find that spear. She had promised Archer not to send any emails, but he would just have to understand. Flieman's email address might stay below the radar. She slipped to the desk, turned on a small desk lamp, and activated the computer via touch, not voice commands. The email went to her department chair back at Texas A&M.

She typed:

At Celsus found papyrus in Latin. Need carbon-14. Believe it to be from first century A.D. Three attachments of three pics. Had to flee to Israel. Still looking for more docs. Will stay in touch if can.

Lacy

To her surprise she got a response in minutes, and she reminded herself it was daytime in Texas.

She opened the email:

Israel! We have been worried sick about you. We saw the news of the quake in the Selçuk region. Have been trying to get hold of you every day. Know that cell towers have been down. Downloaded the attachments you sent. Looks very intriguing. Yes, carbon-14 will need to be done. Did you find documents in the cave? Did you find the new cave? Also, you need to know that I was contacted yesterday by the FBI. Turkey has filed murder charges on you and DeYoung. Is that true?

She gasped. Murder? She jerked up from the desk, scurried to the den door, and flung it open. Archer's head was under a blanket. She marched to the couch and pulled the blanket back. A three-inch square hologram emanated from his wrist cell phone. He tried to kill the signal, but it was too late.

She pointed. "What are you doing-?"

"…Uh, nothing."

"Nonsense! You're sending something."

"No, I'm not."

She bent down to read the hologram. "You sure are! You said no emails!"

He frowned. "…I thought I'd get word to Harvard that we're alright."

She read the message he was about to send.

Found something in Selçuk. Not sure what yet. Will attach pics. Had to sail to Is—

"Don't send that!"

"Why not? Our location can be traced anyway."

She frowned. "There is a Turkish warrant out for us."

"No doubt. We stole their canister."

"No. It's a murder warrant."

"What?" He threw back the blanket and swung his feet onto the floor. "How do you know this?"

She looked away and then back to him. "…I emailed A&M."

"Oh! Ye who throw stones."

"Okay, okay."

"Murder? Of whom?"

"Don't know. But I don't think we should stay around to find out."

"Lacy, where is safer than here? You said that Israel and Turkey don't have an extradition treaty. What about the U.S. and Turkey?"

"The U.S. and Turkey do have an extradition treaty."

"Okay then. It's better to stay right here."

"No. We've got to go to Jordan."

"You're crazy!"

"Maybe. But there is too much riding on this. We've got to find that manuscript by the centurion. It could change everything. It could kill Kitchens's bill."

"That's not my fight."

"Sure it is. It's the fight for truth."

Archer rolled his eyes. "The only truth I know is that if we go to Jordan and get caught we will be shipped back to Selçuk for trial."

Flieman came out of his bedroom. Obviously, he had heard them. "What's up?"

She told him about the murder charge. "We didn't do it. We're being framed. …Can we still use your car?"

"If you're innocent, why—"

Archer threw his arms up. "Exactly."

"You two are heading to Jordan?"

She looked at Flieman and nodded.

"If you're being hunted by the Turks, Israel is a safer option."

Archer nodded vehemently. "Exactly."

"No argument. Except that right now we cannot afford the safe option." Lacy's tone was firm.

Flieman shook his head.

"Will you let us use your car or not?"

He looked at her. "On one condition."

"I know—"

"No. When the police come, I'm going to tell them you stole my car."

She shrugged. "Hey, at this point, what's another felony charge?"

She returned to the den to find that the A&M chair had sent another email.

Did you see my previous email? You and your partner are wanted on suspicion of murder! What is going on? The dean, after the FBI arrived, contacted the university attorneys to make sure that the university is protected. We need to immediately hear your side of the story.

She replied:

We are being framed. We did not kill anyone. In fact, we don't know the name or identity of the person they allege we killed. Do not forward my email with the attachments to anyone. Still premature. I will stay in touch as much as I can. Got more to do and find.

She walked back to the living room. Flieman was in the kitchen making some schnitzel sandwiches. It was nearly midnight. Just as he finished, a televised segment came on INN.

"In Turkey," the reporter said, "while still recovering from last week's earthquake, authorities have also turned to apprehending two American archeologists on a host of charges, including the murder of a Chinese National. Archer DeYoung and Lacy Stowe fled the scene around Selçuk and were seen stealing a sailboat at a hotel resort. They have not been seen since. After the earthquake, cell phone towers were not working. However, authorities are now confident they will be able to locate the fugitives."

Flieman turned to her. "A Chinese national?"

She looked at him, then Archer. "It must be that Uighur near the deniza."

Archer nodded. "Must be."

"But the library columns during the quake were what killed him."

"Obviously," Flieman said, "the locals do not believe that."

She looked at the canister and said, "Is what is in there that valuable?" Maybe. She looked at Flieman and smiled. "We're going to need a backpack. And all the money you have in the house."

34

Flieman returned to his home at 7 a.m. The front door was unlocked and three police officers were sitting in his living room. "You got a warrant?"

The oldest officer rose. "Dr. Flieman, where have you been all night?"

Flieman looked at the officer. "I went for a walk."

"In the middle of the night, without your cell or wallet?"

"You guys just make yourself at home, don't you?"

"We have been contacted by the American FBI. They got GPS signals and emails putting Stowe and DeYoung here. We also ran a DNA sniffer in here and—"

"They were here."

"And they left their cells, watches, and wallets here."

"Like I said."

"Where are they now?"

"I don't know."

"Your car is gone."

"They must have stolen it."

"Why didn't you report it?"

"I was out looking for it. Thought I may have forgotten where I parked it. You know, the old absent-minded professor thing."

The officer smirked. "GPS found your car."

"Oh? Good. Where is it?"

"Beit She'an. On the Jordanian border. Border agents located your car. It was empty."

"Imagine that."

"Dr. Flieman, if Stowe or DeYoung contact you again, you are directed to call the police." The officer handed him a business card. "Failure to do so..."

"I will be sure to call you."

The officer motioned to the others. "I won't ask you any more questions. You'll just lie some more." He stuck up a hand before Flieman could respond. He moved towards the door, then stopped and turned. "Just one more thing: God help them if they cross into Jordan."

35

Two hours after dawn, two hours after Longinus was supposed to arise, Madradus awoke him again. "Come quickly. We have been ordered to scourge a prisoner. Pilate wants forty lashes."

Longinus sat up. His head throbbed. He looked at Madradus. "You know the procedure. I will meet you in the courtyard where the scourging pole is."

Madradus smiled and left. Longinus put on his uniform, armor, and centurion's helmet and walked towards the courtyard. When he arrived, Quintus and Philo were chaining the prisoner to the ring in the pole in preparation for the lashes. He had already been stripped of his robe. He had on only a single cloth.

Longinus walked around to see the face of the prisoner and stopped in his tracks. It was the Galilean magician. It was Jesus. Longinus's mouth fell open. What had Jesus done to deserve this?

Jesus had already been beaten by someone; Jews, from the look of it. If he had been beaten by a Roman, he would not look that good.

Jesus set his eyes on Longinus. Gone was the bright look, replaced by a dull and distant stare. Not fear, but as if he was looking ahead. He seemed resigned, and yet resolved somehow. Longinus noted that Jesus did not glare. He did not have hate in his eyes, which amazed Longinus. Longinus ordered that the rest of Jesus's clothes be taken off and his loins girded.

At the street side of the courtyard was a gate made of metal strips through which one could see. Already a crowd of women had gathered at the gate, along with a few men. Longinus thought he recognized one of the men from the temple. He looked effeminate, almost like he was a woman himself. Longinus looked for the man with the thick beard they called 'Simon.' He was not present. I would not be either, he told himself.

Madradus stepped up to Jesus and knelt. "I bow before you, you king of the Jews."

Philo laughed.

Longinus rolled his wrist in a 'let's get on with it' motion. Madradus, abacus in hand to make sure they were not short a single lash, ordered Philo to begin. Philo grabbed his flagrum with plumbatae, leaded weights on the end, and lunged forward. His whip wrapped around the ribs of Jesus, who grunted and writhed in shock and pain. Then Quintus did the same from the right side. Left again. Right. Back and forth in a horrible tandem of torment as they bruised, battered, cut, and sliced Jesus. Romans were masters of torture. Upon that they had built an empire.

"Forty!" Longinus yelled.

Madradus glared at Longinus. He held up his abacus. "You miscounted!" He turned to Philo. "Continue!"

"Stop!" Longinus commanded. "I counted myself. Pilate ordered forty, and forty it was. Return the prisoner to Pilate."

Madradus shook his head in anger but did as he was ordered. They unchained Jesus and had to carry and drag him inside. Longinus looked at the crowd at the gate. They were all crying but the effeminate man he thought was a follower, whom he had seen at the temple, almost seemed relieved. He probably thought it was over. Longinus thought it was over. He mentally prepared for the three crucifixions that had already been scheduled for the day. He debated with himself whether to let Madradus handle them or not.

When Longinus got inside, Jesus was on the floor. Madradus was leaning over him. Longinus moved closer and saw that Madradus was pushing a crown of thorns onto the head of Jesus. Jesus cringed in pain, and blood immediately began to run down his face.

Madradus and Philo pulled Jesus to his feet and threw a purple robe around him, the color of the Emperor. Philo bowed before Jesus, mocking him, while Quintus stuck a reed in the hand of Jesus, as if it was a royal scepter. Madradus then spit on Jesus.

"Enough!" Longinus said. "Get the prisoner to Pilate. We still have three crucifixions to perform." Longinus still had not decided if he was going to let Madradus lead the patrol or not.

They took the purple robe off and put Jesus back in his tattered robe. Jesus was dragged and carried back to Pilate, who stood at the top of the steps of a courtyard. At the bottom, Longinus saw Caiaphas and other priests. Near Caiaphas was Malchus. Longinus looked at Malchus's ear, and saw no blood.

A throng of people surrounded the priests. At a side gate leading to the courtyard were other people who had not been allowed inside. Longinus recognized several of the women from the gate where the scourging had been conducted. He wondered why they had not been allowed in.

Jesus stood to the right of Pilate, seemingly using every bit of strength just to stay on his feet. When he stumbled, Longinus grabbed him and held him up. Jesus looked at Longinus and nodded his gratitude. Longinus frowned. Did this man really deserve this kind of punishment?

Tarjan stood on the other side of Pilate. He watched the proceeding very closely. Next to him was Pilate's wife, who seemed distressed. Pilate called for Barabbas to be brought out. Longinus remembered the name. He was one of the men scheduled for today's crucifixion.

Pilate said in a voice loud enough for all to hear, "Today is the start of Passover. In the name of the Emperor, I will free one prisoner of your choice. Here is Barabbas, a murderer and thief." Then he turned to Jesus. "Here is a prophet who claims to be your king."

Caiaphas, also in a voice loud enough for all to hear, yelled back, "He is not our king! We have no king but the Emperor."

"You must choose," Pilate said.

"We want Barabbas," one in the crowd said, and then others joined.

"You choose this?" Pilate asked, pointing at Barabbas. Then Longinus heard Pilate mutter, "These Jews are a dreadful people." At that moment, Longinus was in complete agreement with him.

Pilate shook his head then motioned to Jesus. "And him?"

"Crucify him!" the crowd yelled. "Crucify him!"

Pilate looked at his wife, who shook her head. He shook his head back at her. He looked at Tarjan then back at his wife. "Order must be maintained."

Pilate turned to Longinus. "Crucify him. Take personal charge of it. See that it is done!"

Longinus frowned then nodded. He would do his duty. When Madradus heard Pilate's order to Longinus, he grew angry. He wanted to be in charge.

Pilate turned to a servant, who held out a bowl of water. Pilate dipped his hands in the water then dried them off. He looked down at Caiaphas, shook his head in disgust, and left.

36

Archer stood on the bank and sucked a deep breath in through his nose. "The Jordan River stinks! No wonder Jesus walked on the water."

"That was the Sea of Galilee, you stooge."

"Whatever." He motioned to her. "Ladies first."

Lacy frowned at him as she walked by. She emerged from the trees lining the bank and waded into the water. When he did not follow, she turned. "Coming?

He shook his head. "I still can't believe I let you drag me into this."

"Too late. That bridge has been burned."

"The bridge is half a mile north."

"Yeah, the Sheikh Hussein Bridge. Israeli guards on one side, Jordanians on the other."

Across the river they trudged. At one point, the water reached their necks, but no higher. He held the backpack with the canister over his head. She kept the gun dry. Once on the Jordanian side, they wiped the water from their skin and sat down under a tree.

He scanned the sky to the east. It would be dawn in less than an hour. A hum caught his ears, coming from the north, and getting louder. He rose and walked out onto the bank to get a better view. Then there was a glint in the sunlight, up high, where the sun was already shining. A drone. About a quarter of a mile north heading south.

He turned to Lacy. "If that drone has infrared vision, we're screwed."

37

While Senator Kitchens replied to his Majority Leader that he had sent no such email requesting that his bill be amended to include the ban of private Bible possession, Israel, as part of border protocol, alerted Jordanian authorities of the probable entry of DeYoung and Stowe into their country.

The Jordanian authorities thanked Israel, and promptly dispatched police to the station across from Beit She'an. Jordan also informed officials in Turkey of the development, who requested extradition when the two Americans were captured. Then the Turkish officials passed word to the one-eyed Mullah Obar of the suspected movements of DeYoung and Stowe.

38

Throughout his career as a soldier, Longinus had crucified many people, and could attest that, as bad as scourging was, it was nothing in comparison to the systematic infliction of agony that crucifixion was. Outside of being burnt alive, he could think of no worse way to die—and, at least with fire, the agony was over faster.

Crucified prisoners often had signs placed atop the cross, announcing who was being punished and why. Above the patibulum, the cross beam that would hold Jesus, the sign said in Aramaic, Greek, and Latin: "Jesus of Nazareth, King of the Jews." Longinus was surprised by the wording. Pilate was admitting Jesus was a king? How did Caiaphas feel about this? Then Longinus decided it was not his problem.

Madradus informed Longinus that crucifixions in Jerusalem were performed on a small hill west of the wall, in a place called Golgotha, which meant "Place of the Skull." "Fitting name," Longinus replied.

Madradus and Philo lashed a patibulum onto the shoulders of Jesus then did the same for the two robbers who had already been scheduled for crucifixion. Jesus was so weak from the various beatings he had endured that he could barely carry the cross beam. Longinus mounted a horse so he could see over the crowd then ordered his men to direct Jesus and the other two out of the gate of the Praetorium. Quintus and Philo made their wishes known with the end of their lash. Other soldiers moved the crowd out of the way using their lash or spear.

It is the duty of a centurion ordered to crucify a prisoner to see to it that the prisoner dies on the cross, not in transit to it. If anything, Longinus would do his duty, then that night he would fill his belly with wine and wash away this episode.

They had traveled only a short way when Jesus collapsed. Philo tried to whip him into getting back up. When Jesus did not respond, Longinus ordered Philo to stop. Longinus scanned the crowd and saw a dark-skinned man standing off to the side. "You!" he pointed. "Help this man carry his beam."

The man did not have a choice—if he wanted to live. He helped Jesus up and then assisted him in moving forward, carrying most of the weight.

They marched through the streets still filled with people for Passover, up the steps, and out of the city wall through Gennath Gate and on to Golgotha. It took nearly an hour to get there because Jesus and the dark-skinned man stumbled several times. By then it was nearly mid-day.

The vertical poles were already in the ground, awaiting the arrival of the latest condemned. Once on the hill, Quintus and Philo took the poles out of their holes and laid them on the ground. They laid each condemned man atop the pole so that the beam formed a cross. Each man was literally nailed to this cross. Spikes were driven through each hand and the heels of the feet. Extra rope was used so that the prisoner would not tear away and fall from the cross.

The cross was lifted and slipped back into the hole. At this point, inevitably, the prisoner would cry out in pain at being jarred with the dropping of the pole into the hole. Jesus was no different.

There the condemned would hang until they died. Longinus had seen some linger for days. He hoped that would not be the case this time. He wanted to get back to his wine. He figured Jesus would go first. He was the weakest. It was those other two who worried him. They could live into tomorrow or even longer.

About this time, Longinus began to hear the cry of many lambs coming from the city. They were being slaughtered. Passover had begun. He thought of Pilate. These Jews were, indeed, a dreadful people. He looked at the three men on their crosses. He was sure the Jews thought the same of the Romans, probably worse. No conquered people ever loved their conqueror. But they would obey.

At most of the crucifixions, no one was present other than the prisoner and the soldiers. Not so with this crucifixion. A crowd formed on Golgotha. And while they were unarmed and made up mostly of women, some of whom Longinus recognized as being present at the Praetorium, it still made him nervous. Desperate people sometimes did desperate things. Longinus told Madradus to keep the spears and swords ready. Longinus was responsible for these bodies, and no one was going to steal them away from him.

Of Jesus's followers, Longinus only saw one in the crowd. The effeminate man had been in the temple earlier in the week and at the Praetorium this morning. If any of Jesus's other followers were present at Golgotha, they stayed well back and hidden.

Longinus did see the dark-skinned man who had been forced to help carry the cross. Longinus wondered why he stayed. Longinus also saw Malchus in the crowd. Longinus looked again for any blood or a wound on Malchus's ear but did not see such a sign. Malchus seemed sad, staring up at Jesus on the cross.

Longinus's soldiers ripped the robe from Jesus and split it into four, each taking a section. Longinus declined a section. Then Madradus drew lots with Philo and Quintus for the seamless tunic Jesus wore beneath.

As the crowd grew in number, it became apparent that some had come to mock the king of the Jews. One of the senior priests yelled up at Jesus, "If you are truly the Son of God, then free yourself from the cross!" Many in the crowd laughed. Even one of the robbers pinned to a cross began mocking him with similar statements. However, the other robber seemed to believe that Jesus was, indeed, the Son of God, and asked to be in heaven with him, a wish that Jesus seemed to grant.

Longinus snickered. Here the man was dying a painful and inglorious death, and he stuck to these ridiculous beliefs. Truly, a lunatic.

Then Jesus did something even more shocking. While many in the crowd continued to mock him, Longinus heard Jesus say, "Father, forgive them; for they do not know what they are doing."

Longinus's mouth fell open. His mind flashed back to when he had beaten the wiry-haired childhood bully and won revenge. How good it felt at the time. How justified he felt. Then here Jesus was, strapped to a piece of wood, dying a horrible death, and he asks that they all be forgiven. Longinus had never felt as much shame as he felt at that moment.

Longinus wished Jesus would die immediately so that he could escape to the wine cellar. He had crucified dozens, maybe hundreds—he had long lost count. He had killed as many others in battle, always without mercy or reservation. And now, for the first time, he was ashamed of being a soldier, ashamed of being a Roman. Jesus had pierced Longinus with his words, just as surely as he had driven a spear into his side.

Longinus looked up at Jesus in anger, anger at himself, and anger at Jesus for making him feel this way. When he looked up, he saw the same beaten and bloody face of Jesus he had seen in his dreams aboard the galley. That cannot be by chance, Longinus told himself.

Not long after that, during the sixth hour of the day, it grew very dark. A mysterious mid-day darkness descended, and continued for several hours. Then, towards the end of the third hour of darkness, Jesus cried out, "My God, My God, why have You forsaken Me?"

Longinus heard several in the crowd say something about some person named Elijah. He did not know who this Elijah was.

Then Jesus looked at a woman in the crowd who had drawn near. "Woman," Jesus said, "behold your son." Then he looked to the effeminate man that Longinus had thought was one of his followers, and Jesus gave his mother to that man to take care of.

Jesus said he was thirsty. Longinus did not see any harm in giving him a drink, so he dipped a sponge in a bucket of sour wine that was mixed with gall and myrrh, stuck the sponge on the tip of a hyssop branch, and raised it to Jesus. Jesus took one suck of the sponge and then turned away.

Not long after that, as Longinus was looking up at him, Jesus said, "It is finished."

Longinus thought Jesus was talking about his life which, sure enough, was finished. Then Jesus fell limp. His head collapsed to his chin and the tension left his entire body. Several people in the crowd beat their chests in anger when they saw Jesus fall limp. The priests who were still present requested that the legs of the three prisoners be broken so they would die faster. Passover started at dusk. Time was short. Longinus had his men break the legs of the two robbers. Madradus started to do the same with Jesus, but Longinus stopped him. He was reasonably sure Jesus was already dead. He grabbed a spear, the same spear that he had taken with him to the temple, the same spear Jesus seemed to acknowledge. Longinus raised the spear to the side of Jesus and, with a lunge, thrust it deeply into the side of Jesus's chest in the area of his heart. Jesus did not flinch or make any sound when the spear penetrated his body. When Longinus pulled the spear back, blood and water poured out, a sure sign Jesus was dead.

Immediately, there was a great rumbling of the ground. An earthquake shook the entire area, in the city and outside. Longinus had to grab the vertical pole of the cross to keep from falling. Jesus's limp and lifeless ankles jangled back and forth just above Longinus's head as the ground shook. Some of the last stragglers at Golgotha got knocked off their feet. Rocks split open. Cries and screams could be heard coming from inside the city.

Longinus looked around in shock. The clouds had grown even thicker and darker, and had dropped even lower, swirling over them like a torrent of rushing water. Longinus was afraid. Clearly, there was something strange and powerful going on here. But what? Then he looked up at Jesus. Blood and water continued to run from his dead body. Quintus stood a few feet away, staring wide-eyed at Longinus, looking for an explanation. Longinus looked at him and said the only thing that came to mind. "Certainly, this man was innocent."

Quintus looked up at Jesus then at Longinus, and nodded. An odd feeling came over Longinus. As if he was not alone inside. That something was guiding his mind, almost as if it was whispering in his ear. Longinus looked at Jesus again and then at Quintus. "Truly," Longinus said, "this man was the Son of God."

Quintus squinted in confusion. He looked at Longinus then once more at Jesus. There was a scoff. Longinus turned and it was Madradus. "Go back to your wine, Longinus," he said, then tromped over to the cross holding the robber who had mocked Jesus.

By Roman tradition, crucified bodies hung there until the birds had their fill. Longinus inspected the two robbers. With their legs broken, they would soon be dead as well. Then he could run from this hilltop, back to the Praetorium and its ample supply of wine.

While he waited for the two robbers to succumb, many of the crowd left. Some women remained, as did the man to whom Jesus gave His mother. Longinus started to tell them to leave, but refrained. They did not seem to be a threat.

Two Jews, dressed in their priestly robes, approached. They had received permission to take the body of Jesus. It was late, and they wanted to bury him before dusk. Longinus let them. They lowered the body in a blanket and carried him away. Longinus was glad that Galilean was gone.

After the robbers died, Longinus and his men returned to the Praetorium. It was nearly dark. Longinus found himself stopping several times as they walked away, looking back at the three crosses atop the hill, their outlines still visible in the fading light. Longinus did not know why he felt the need to stop, but he did. He had not done that at any crucifixion ever before. Done was done and good riddance had always been his attitude. But not this time, and he did not immediately understand the difference. He looked around at the entire landscape. The mysterious darkness still covered the area as far as he could see. He looked up at the walls of the city. What a dreadful place.

As Longinus and his men were about to enter the courtyard of the Praetorium, a Jewish priest approached and told him that after Jesus had died and the earthquake had occurred, that the veil in the inner temple had been ripped from top to bottom. Longinus shrugged. Then he told Longinus that many tombs outside the city had been opened by the earthquake and that the dead had risen and been seen by citizens of Jerusalem. Longinus started to laugh. Obviously, this man had beaten him to the wine. Then he looked up at the churning, angry clouds that seemed so low that he could touch them. He looked at the man, then without comment, turned and walked inside the courtyard.

Longinus reported to Pilate that all three men were dead. Pilate was surprised that they were already dead. Pilate's wife was standing nearby, and Longinus heard her say to him that he would regret this day. Pilate scoffed. "Order must be maintained, or I—we—would be finished. I did what I had to do. What was I supposed to do? Sacrifice us for his benefit?"

Longinus remembered how Jesus forgave while he was on the cross. Longinus pondered this then shook off such thoughts. He saluted Pilate and rushed to the wine. He was glad he was done with this Jesus.

39

Archer spied the drone coming at them. They had just a matter of minutes. Now what? Then, from out of nowhere, a bank of clouds swept in and rain pelted them. The storm lasted but a few minutes, and when it ended, he perked his ears. The drone had passed over them during the storm. What a break! He turned to Lacy. "That was the weirdest storm I have ever seen."

"Let there be darkness."

They scurried out from the trees lining the river and fled to the southeast, up-slope. Staying as low as possible, they zigged and zagged, running through fields of crops and groves of olive trees, across dry stream beds and irrigation canals. As usual, Lacy, who had run track in college, outpaced him, and had to stop and let him catch up.

They came to a highway running north and south. They made sure no vehicles approached, then they scampered over the highway and into a broad valley filled with more fields and olive trees. Pella, the ancient City of Refuge, lay less than a mile ahead, where the valley narrowed and climbed into the steep hills. Back on the highway, they heard the sound of police sirens.

40

Dayton Rosenberg at The Word called the Chair at A&M and did not waste time with social amenities. "What about these murder charges? We can't be associated with that!"

"Sir, I don't believe Lacy Stowe could kill anybody. She said they're being framed."

"She says. So you have been in contact with Dr. Stowe."

"Yes, sir. Emails."

"Forward them to me."

"Sir, she said the situation is still premature. Carbon-14 still—"

"Nonsense! I want all of her emails now. It's that or I cut funding to your department."

Rosenberg got the emails. He read the emails and the attachments. Within the hour, he stood before cameras at a press conference in his Houston offices.

"When Senator Kitchens announced his atheistic legislation, he declared that there has never been found an objective, unbiased document that records the life of Jesus and his claim that he is the Son of God. Well, we found it. We found that precise document. Dr. Lacy Stowe of Texas A&M and Dr. Archer DeYoung of Harvard, working in close concert, have unearthed some pages of papyrus in Turkey that once and for all establishes the validity of the four Gospels and the rest of the New Testament.

"As Director of The Word, I will release copies of these documents after this press conference. It is proof that Senator Kitchens is wrong— wrong about the Bible, wrong about God not having supremacy over man. Existentialists revel in their own freedom. They are arrogant about not having to bow down to a higher power. And in their freedom they inevitably come to believe that they are their own gods—they and their technology and their science. This describes Pas de Createur and its puppet, Senator Kitchens, to a 'T.' They run scared from the truth.

"There are three separate letters that will be released: one, by a Roman official named Tarjan, and two shorter notes by a Roman soldier named Quintus. You will clearly see that Tarjan establishes that, not only did Jesus live, but he claimed to be the Son of God and was crucified for it. Furthermore, his disciples changed afterward and went out with a missionary zeal. It also confirms passages regarding Jesus in the temple before he was arrested.

"This was not written by the followers of Jesus, but by his enemies— by Roman officials. I call upon Senator Kitchens to admit that he was wrong and withdraw his offending legislation."

41

Longinus had thought he was done with Jesus, but it was not to be. The following morning, Longinus was called to Pilate's presence. On the way to the courtyard where he was told Pilate was, he stumbled, wobbly from last night's drinking. He scraped against a thorn bush and gashed his right forearm. He glared at the thorn bush and remembered the crown of thorns Madradus had pushed onto the head of Jesus. Longinus started to pull his sword out to slash the thorn bush from its roots, but something stopped him. He pushed his sword back into its sheath and went to find Pilate. When he arrived, he saw Caiaphas standing there. He wanted to groan. What now?

The head priest wanted a guard. Jesus, it seemed, had predicted that he would rise on the third day, and Caiaphas feared that Jesus's followers would steal the body and then claim he had risen.

Longinus scoffed. "I have seen these men. They could not summon the courage for such an act. They are probably halfway back to Galilee by now or hiding in the most secret of places."

Longinus's protestation did not win over anyone. Pilate ordered that the tomb be sealed and a guard be placed at the rock to the entrance of the tomb. He gave Longinus that duty. Longinus resisted a frown, and saluted. Pilate noticed the cut and blood on Longinus's forearm. "You had better put aloe on that." Pilate then gave Longinus a ring with a Roman seal cut into it. "Use this to seal the cave."

Longinus nodded and left to carry out his orders. For any Roman soldier, guard duty was serious business. Dereliction of duty was not tolerated. Many a Roman soldier had been executed for failure to adequately perform this task. Longinus was tired and still a little drunk from the wine. But he would not fail to do his duty. No one would disturb that grave. Any troublemakers would end up in their own tomb.

Longinus was led to the tomb of Jesus by a priest named Joseph of Arimathea, and one other unnamed priest. Caiaphas no longer trusted Joseph, and he wanted his own man there when the tomb was sealed.

Joseph said it was his personal tomb, and had never been used before. When they arrived, Joseph showed Longinus the large stone that he and Nicodemus had rolled in front of the entrance to the tomb. He pointed at the rut in the ground that allowed the large rock to roll down-slope into place. Longinus inspected the stone, and said, "No one will move that stone easily."

"That was the point," Joseph said.

Joseph plastered clay on both sides of the cliff into which the tomb had been cut. Madradus and Longinus stretched a rope across the rock and pushed the rope into the clay until it was secure. Then Joseph pressed his ring into the clay and gave his sign to the tomb. In the same fashion, Longinus pressed the ring Pilate had given him into the clay. The other priest inspected each seal and nodded.

"The tomb is sealed," Longinus said, looking at Joseph and the other priest.

Joseph and the other priest returned to Jerusalem, leaving Longinus and his three men, Madradus, Quintus, and Philo to guard duty. Before Longinus had left the Praetorium, he had arranged for another guard unit to relieve them at their posts so they could get some sleep. Falling asleep on guard duty was not forgiven. Longinus and his men were already tired, and Longinus did not want to risk dozing off. The second unit was to relieve them at the sixth hour of the day, during the afternoon. Longinus and men would return six to eight hours later during darkness, and complete the guard until the morning of the next day—the third day that Caiaphas so feared.

And that was what happened. The second unit came at the appointed time. Longinus and men returned to the Praetorium, slept enough to get them through, and, then, under torchlight, returned to the tomb approximately five hours before dawn.

At the first hint of dawn, Longinus doused the torches. Suddenly, there was a severe earthquake, knocking all of them to the ground. Longinus looked over at the tomb and the rock had rolled away. Atop the rock sat a man in bright white clothes. He shone as though there was a lantern beneath his clothes. Longinus stared at the man then looked at his soldiers. They were all staring at the lighted man as well. They all saw it— and all were frightened. Longinus forced himself to his feet, as did the others. Then the man atop the rock raised his hand towards them, palm out, and gestured from his right to his left. Instantly, Longinus and his men fell to the ground in a deep sleep.

Just before Longinus fully awoke, just as he was coming to, he thought he heard the voices of two men and a woman. He could not hear what they said exactly, but their tones were excited. Then he did not hear them anymore, but he did hear a large gust of wind.

Shortly afterward, Longinus awakened and opened his eyes. The others were still asleep. He turned his gaze to the tomb. The rock was still rolled back, and the man who had stood atop it was gone. Forcing himself to his feet, he could feel that his arms and legs were heavy. He looked inside the tomb and focused into the darkness. As his sight became clearer, he gasped. The body of Jesus was gone. He lit a torch and ran into the tomb. It was empty! The burial clothes lay on the stone where the body had been placed. They were hardly displaced or ruffled. Some of the wrappings seemed folded. The spices used to perfume the body were also essentially still in their place. It was as if the body had somehow just slipped from the burial wrappings, instead of the wrappings being unraveled or cut off.

Longinus thought about how this could have happened. That man atop the rock, the one who shone so brightly… he must be another magician, he told himself. But a voice inside him said, you know what you saw, and it was not magic. He looked at the burial wrappings again. Jesus could not be alive. Jesus did not swoon. When I drove that spear in, Jesus was dead. Jesus had not flinched or cried out. Blood and water had come out from his side.

Longinus heard movement outside the tomb. Madradus, Quintus, and Philo were waking. He motioned for Madradus to enter the tomb. Madradus surveyed the burial wrappings.

"Oh, no!" he cried out. "We have let them steal the body. This means death for us!"

Longinus did not respond. He knew Madradus was correct.

"That man on the rock!" Madradus said. "That trickster, he stole the body. We must find this man and get the body back!"

Longinus nodded as he considered all of this. "Maybe Joseph of Arimathea took the body. It was his tomb. We must find this Joseph." He grabbed his spear and they raced to the temple. They did not find Joseph. No one knew where he was. That made sense. Longinus concluded that Joseph was hiding the body as they spoke. Another priest had told Caiaphas that Longinus was inquiring as to the whereabouts of Joseph. Caiaphas came to them. Longinus told Caiaphas what had happened. Caiaphas's eyes grew wide with fear.

Caiaphas turned to another priest and ordered him to do something. The priest scampered away then returned within minutes with four leather pouches. He handed them to Caiaphas.

Caiaphas turned to Longinus. "You are to say that the followers of Jesus stole the body. Do you understand?"

"A bunch of rag-tags overpowered us?" Longinus blurted. "If that was true, then where are the wounds on myself and my guards?"

Caiaphas pointed at the dried blood on Longinus's arm.

"That was from a thorn bush, and Pilate saw this wound himself yesterday."

Caiaphas frowned then handed a leather pouch to each of the Roman soldiers. Longinus looked inside his. It had pieces of silver in it.

"Thirty pieces of silver," Caiaphas said. "It is a traditional amount. I will personally intercede on your behalf with Pilate."

Madradus and Philo immediately slid their pouches inside their uniforms. Quintus balked then stuck the bag in his uniform. Longinus opened his pouch and turned it upside down. The silver fell to the stones, sounding like a badly played set of bells. Caiaphas's eyes squinted when Longinus did this. "You will face a death sentence if you tell Pilate what happened."

Longinus looked directly at Caiaphas. "I will not take your thirty pieces of silver," and walked away. As he tramped out of the temple, making sure his spear tip pointed upward lest it hit someone accidentally, Longinus met Malchus. Longinus told him about Caiaphas's offer of thirty pieces of silver.

"Just say you fell asleep," Malchus said.

"We did fall asleep!"

"Then there should be no problem."

Longinus scoffed and rolled his eyes. "There's still a problem. Besides, you don't understand. I saw …something."

Malchus's eyes squinted when Longinus said that.

"…I am not sure what I saw. A vision of some sort. A man atop a rock. He was shining. There was an earthquake and the rock rolled back on its own."

Malchus shook his head. "The rock was small."

"No! The rock was large. Then I saw this man. He moved his hand and we all fell asleep. When I awoke, the tomb was empty."

"…An angel," he mumbled in a hollow tone, and looked away in surprise and thought.

Longinus started to walk away then turned back. "Do you know Jesus forgave while on the cross?"

Malchus frowned and nodded. "…I was there."

"What type of person does that?"

"The same kind of man who heals while he is being arrested."

Longinus walked to Malchus and looked at his ear. There was no blood, no scar. Then Longinus thought he saw something. A dot of some sort. He focused. On Malchus's face, directly beside his ear, embedded in the skin, was a fingerprint. It was clear as can be. It was not dirt or grime. Longinus's mouth fell open.

Malchus stepped back from Longinus and felt the side of his face. "What? What are you looking at?"

Longinus shook his head. Something more he could not explain. He headed for the Praetorium, knowing he was probably walking to his death.

As he strode through the crowded streets, he bumped into a man and dropped the spear. As he reached down to pick it up, he inadvertently touched the tip of the spear to the wound on his forearm caused by the thorn bush. Instantly, his wound healed. All signs of the cuts were gone. No dried blood, no scar of any kind. His forearm was restored to its original condition.

Longinus stared at his arm. Did he see right? How can that be? Is this another vision? Then he answered himself: the Galilean. ...And it is not magic. He shook his head in confusion then continued walking at a fast pace. He found Pilate and told him all that had happened, including Caiaphas's attempt at a bribe. Pilate's wife was listening, as was Tarjan.

Pilate listened to everything Longinus had to say, and then said, "Had you been drinking?"

"No, Prefect. We were standing guard on a sealed tomb."

"I should not have given you this duty. You were tired after so many days of duty." Pilate looked at his wife and Tarjan. "We are all tired."

Longinus shook his head. "We did not fall asleep on our own." He repeated what he had said about the man atop the rock.

Pilate rolled his eyes. "You must have been drinking." He paused in thought. "...Then Jesus was not dead when he was placed in the tomb."

"He was dead," Longinus emphasized. "I drove the lonche deep inside him. He did not move. Water came out with the blood. I have crucified many. He was dead."

Pilate studied Longinus. "...Were any of his followers around when you awoke?"

"I may have heard someone. I'm not sure. But I did not see anyone."

Pilate noticed his arm. "Your wound healed quickly."

Longinus looked at his arm but did not tell Pilate about touching the spear to it. He was still not sure what had happened, even though his heart knew what his mind would not fully admit.

Pilate looked at his wife, then at Tarjan, who continued to study Pilate. Pilate turned back to Longinus. "I owe you much. We both know that. However, I cannot allow a guard to fail. It would lead to chaos. Find the body of Jesus, or you will be taking his place in that tomb."

42

Lacy veered away from the paved road and led Archer into the valley that funneled in and upward. Rocky hills towered on each side. As much as possible, she clung to the scattered small trees and shrubs for cover. As they emerged from the top of the valley onto a small plain, a gust of wind blew, dust caking their sweaty bodies. They looked at each other and started laughing.

A few hundred feet away stood a restaurant called the Pella Rest House, and next to it a small shop. They washed most of the dust off in the restrooms of the restaurant, then, with the money Flieman had given them, purchased new clothes.

She found a brown shirt and lifted it up to inspect it. "I think I need something loose-fitting so I am not easily identified as a female."

Archer stuck his head beside hers. "I don't think you will have any problem."

She looked at him out of the corner of her eyes. "Very funny."

They purchased sweatpants, work shirts, fresh floppy hats, work gloves, and sunglasses to complete their disguise. Archer went a step further. He bought a pair of scissors and an electric razor, ducked into the restroom, and cut off his wavy black hair, leaving a buzz.

She lifted the hat and spied the cut. Wow. "You look…different. …Ah…" Do I really want to say this? "…Ah, better." A whole lot better. Can a haircut make this much difference? When Archer's smile was a little wider than she desired, she turned away and changed the subject. "The Migdol temple is right over there," she said, pointing a few hundred feet to the west at an ancient ruin on the edge of a rocky precipice.

43

While the Turkish government prepared extradition efforts in case DeYoung and Stowe were captured, one-eyed Mullah Amin Obar dispatched a team to Jordan to find the two Americans. To assist in the search, Obar called another mullah in Jordan, asking him to declare a fatwah against the two Americans and offering a reward for their capture. Finally, Obar called a counterpart in Washington, D.C., asking him to contact Nick Loren at Pas de Createur.

44

Eric Jensen of the Independent Press walked into his editor's office. "I want to go to Jordan."

The editor looked up from the article he was correcting. "Why?"

"You saw Rosenberg's press conference?"

"I did."

"And Kitchens's rebuttal?"

"No."

Jensen brought it up on his phone and handed it to the editor, who stuck a palm out. "I hate reading off phones. Read it to me."

Jensen started to pop out a hologram of the article. Instead, he simply read it. "Kitchens said, 'This is how weak and desperate Christians are. They clutch at any straw. The documents Rosenberg released are a fake—not even elaborate forgeries. No carbon-14 authenticates the date, and no reputable scholar has or will substantiate these pathetic attempts to justify the lies by organized religion.'"

The editor shrugged. "Okay. Isn't that what you expected Kitchens to say?"

"Sure. And then there's this." Jensen brought up the translation of the fatwah issued by the Jordanian mullah against Stowe and DeYoung.

The editor looked down at his desk then up at Jensen. "Be careful in Jordan."

45

After Kitchens released his rebuttal of Rosenberg, he called Nick Loren at Pas de Createur and asked that a team be sent to Jordan. Loren agreed and ordered the team to destroy the papyrus once they secured it.

46

Longinus had his orders. Find the body of Jesus or else. He saluted and left Pilate. When he turned around, Caiaphas, Madradus, and Philo were entering the Praetorium. Quintus followed, straggling behind. They saw Longinus leaving, spear in hand. Longinus realized that he had forgotten to mention that Madradus and the other two had taken Caiaphas's money. He turned to mention it to Pilate, then decided they could make their own confession. He had a body to find, and these men could not be trusted—although he was not completely sure about Quintus.

Longinus returned to the temple, again looking for Joseph of Arimathea. Another priest named Nicodemus came out. Longinus remembered him. He had helped take the body down from the cross. Nicodemus looked at Longinus cautiously. Longinus asked him if he knew where Joseph was.

Nicodemus said he did not, then he asked why Longinus wanted to see Joseph.

Longinus looked hard at Nicodemus. He had already told Caiaphas, and it had worked against him. Why would this priest be any different? Then he reminded himself that Nicodemus had helped bury the Galilean.

"...The body is gone," Longinus said simply.

"What body?"

"The body of the Galilean, the body of Jesus."

Nicodemus's eyes flashed. "What do you mean, gone?"

"Stolen," Longinus said flatly. "It was Joseph's tomb. I assumed he took the body."

Nicodemus shook his head. "If he had done such a thing, he would have told me."

"Maybe not. Where is he?" Longinus prepared to point the spear at him, if necessary.

Nicodemus frowned. "He is at his home. I will take you to him."

Joseph was a wealthy man, and had a home befitting. Longinus stayed outside in the street while Nicodemus went in. Longinus was then ushered into a courtyard. Joseph looked at him with suspicion. Longinus did not blame him.

Longinus concluded that Joseph was telling the truth when he said he did not know the body was gone. "If you did not do such a thing, then who did?" Longinus asked.

"I would guess his followers," Joseph answered. "But one thing I do not understand is how these men overpowered you and your guards."

Longinus looked straight at him and told him about the man atop the rock. Then he paused and studied Joseph's face as he asked the next question. "Do you believe such a thing?"

Joseph thought for a few seconds, looked at Nicodemus, and nodded. "I do."

Longinus chuckled sarcastically. "Well, I don't know that I do and I was there. I face a death sentence from Pilate. I have to find this stolen body. Where are the followers of this Jesus staying?"

"I do not know," Joseph said.

"I saw one at the crucifixion. He was also at the scourging. And then at the temple I heard another one called 'Simon' by someone else."

"We know this Simon," Joseph answered. "Jesus called him 'Peter', which means 'rock'. He denied Jesus three times after Jesus was arrested."

Longinus scoffed. "That sounds about right. He went down like a rock. They all seemed like a bunch of cowards to me. They're all probably halfway back to Galilee by now."

Joseph looked at Nicodemus again. "There is another alternative."

"What is that?" Longinus asked.

"Perhaps the body was not stolen."

Nicodemus nodded.

"What does that mean?" Longinus asked indignantly.

"Maybe you truly saw what you saw. And Jesus's body was not stolen. Instead, He has—"

"Risen," Nicodemus came in. "Just as He said He would on the third day."

Joseph smiled and nodded.

"You mean he came back to life?" Longinus blurted.

Joseph nodded. "Yes. That is exactly what I mean." When Longinus scoffed, Joseph asked, "Do you have another explanation?"

"Yes, the magician atop the rock stole the body and gave it to that band of followers."

Joseph smiled. "I think you already know that was no magician."

Longinus shook his head, even though part of him agreed with Joseph. Longinus glared at him. "If I tell Pilate you two stole the body, not only will you be crucified yourselves, but Pilate will, in all likelihood, close the temple. You know what I say is true."

"Yes, what you say is true," Joseph replied. "But you also know the real truth. I can see it in your eyes and hear it in your voice. You will not admit it. Maybe you cannot admit in your position. But you know it nonetheless."

Longinus did not dispute Joseph any further. He paused in thought for a few seconds. He was getting more confused as the day drove on. So many unexplained events.

Joseph turned to Nicodemus. "I am going to the tomb."

"I will go with you," Nicodemus announced.

"No. Stay here with Longinus. I suspect we will need to hide him." Nicodemus nodded.

"I don't need your help," Longinus said.

Joseph looked back at Longinus. "I think you will. I suspect that, if you don't already, you will soon have Pilate and Caiaphas chasing you."

47

Archer braced his left leg and peered over the edge of the cliff. His stomach fell when his eyes cast downward. Stepping back, he turned to Lacy. "Why in God's name would anyone build a temple on the side of a cliff?"

"That's just it. In God's name they built it."

"And why not?" Archer shrugged dismissively. "If they fell, they were going to be closer to God."

Lacy chuckled then swept her arms towards the ruin. "We're on the lower level here. The Migdol Temple was built in stages over centuries. About thirty yards long, twenty-five wide. Thick stone walls." She pointed to the right and he followed her hand. "This was the rear of the temple with the room called the Holy of Holies." She paused and held her gaze on him.

He nodded. "The clue in the note from Quintus."

"The Holy of Holies was entered just once a year, and then only by the high priest, for there, the one God resided. In the final phase of the temple, that one God was the God of Canaan."

"So then what happened to the temple walls?"

"Earthquakes. Muslim invaders. Time. The surrounding town of Pella had once been a thriving trade center with a population of 25,000, and was a refuge for early Christians fleeing Roman and Jewish oppression. I am guessing that the centurion Longinus came here from Jerusalem to hunt down some Christians. That's my theory, at least."

"Makes sense, but why would Longinus write a manuscript? Romans hunting down Christians is hardly unique enough to require a separate manuscript."

"That is why we've got to find that manuscript; all three parts, and the spear."

Archer shook his head. "Lacy, we're not going back to Turkey."

"We're not, but somebody else has to."

He ignored her. "What's that?" he asked, pointing to the north.

She turned. Two hundred feet away sat three trailers. On the side of each: "Trans-Jordan Balloons." Men were unloading equipment. "Looks like they're preparing for some hot-air balloon launches."

"No, not that. That," he pointed again. "The other ruin near the trailers."

"Ah, the ruins of Mamluk Mosque. Built in honor of one of Mohammed's warriors."

"A mosque? Near a Canaanite church?"

She scoffed. "Muslims have been doing that for centuries, and Christians to Muslims, to be honest. There is a mosque atop the site where the great Jewish temple stood in Jerusalem. In America, Muslims wag their finger at Christians about tolerance, but they don't practice what they preach. Particularly towards women."

"Okay, so they're hypocrites. Like every other religion."

She frowned and pulled the note from her pants' pocket. "'Testimonium duobus found refuge under the holy of holies, where many gods became One so that Eluid could gain hidden passage day or night." She pointed at the Holy of Holies room. "Next to it is a small storage area. The bigger area with the base of the three pillars in the middle is the sanctuary room."

"The note said '*under* the Holy of Holies.'" Archer reminded her.

She nodded. "Good point. We'll need a Doppler sounder."

"I had one on my cell phone—which you made me leave in Haifa."

"So we have to get another cell phone and download the Doppler app."

"We get a phone and we will be tracked by GPS."

"But if it's not our cell phone, then we won't be identified as holding it."

"How are we going…"

"How else? We steal it."

"I've noticed that theft is becoming a habit for you."

48

Nick Loren pointed at the holographic map of Israel and Jordan. "The car DeYoung and Stowe were in was found here at the Israeli-Jordanian border. They are believed to have crossed the Jordanian River near there." He looked at his two-member team. "Now where are they headed?"

The two men were from the Harvard archeology department, colleagues of Archer DeYoung. Cambridge McKenzie spoke first. "There are many ruins in the area of Decapolis."

Luther Concord cleared his throat. "I read the release by Rosenberg. The centurion mentioned a place known as 'The Holy of Holies'. I googled that. I think they're headed to a place just a few miles across the Jordan River." He pointed at the map. "Pella. There's an ancient temple ruin there." Then he smiled. "And Stowe went on a dig there a few years ago."

Nick smiled. "Bingo."

McKenzie chuckled. "We need to thank Rosenberg for publicizing those documents."

Concord nodded. "What an arrogant blunder. His 'gotcha' came back at him."

Nick smiled again. "There's no cure for stupid."

After McKenzie and Concord left, Nick got a call from a mullah in New York. "I'm sure you are sending your people to hunt down DeYoung and Stowe," he told Nick.

Nick scoffed. "Oh, you're sure, huh?"

"Yes, I am. And I want us to join forces. After all, we have the same goal."

"Maybe in the short-run."

"For now, that is all that counts. We need each other."

"We do?"

"We do. And, of course, if I don't get your cooperation, then there are other alternatives. Let's just say that Americans in a Muslim country can run into "difficulties." There already is a fatwah by a Jordanian mullah against DeYoung and Stowe. That decree could be expanded."

Blackmail. Some things transcended any religion. Nick made the deal.

49

Over an hour later, Joseph returned from the tomb in which he had buried Jesus. He confirmed that the tomb was, indeed, empty. "I have also learned," he said to Nicodemus and Longinus, "that Caiaphas has lied to Pilate about the bribes. He said you," pointing at Longinus, "accepted the bribe, and that your fellow officer…"

"Madradus," Longinus filled in.

"…confirmed Caiaphas's story. Madradus, of course, said he and the other men did not take the bribe. Pilate has issued an arrest order for you. Madradus has been ordered to hunt you down, or he will be punished for failure on guard duty."

Longinus stared at Joseph. "I should have stayed. I saw them enter the Praetorium."

"Too late for regrets now. But you are missing an important fact. Notice that Caiaphas did not say that you stole the body, nor does he deny that the tomb is empty."

"Caiaphas is claiming that Longinus let Jesus's followers steal the body?" Nicodemus asked.

"Yes. That can be his only claim at this point," Joseph said. "The followers took the body and hid it."

"And Longinus allowed it. For the money," Nicodemus added.

Longinus looked hard at Nicodemus. "I took no money. Besides, if I let them steal the body, I am still a dead man." Longinus's confusion was starting to make him angry. "There was an earthquake," he said firmly, "and a man atop the rock."

"Yes!" Joseph exclaimed. "These are works of God, not man, or a bunch of men. You know the truth. You just have not fully accepted it… yet."

Longinus did not respond. He remembered that after Jesus had died there was an earthquake, and that he, too, had proclaimed Jesus was the Son of God. But the words had not been a conscious thought, as much as they were an unexpected revelation of some sort. As if they were not really his words and thoughts. Now, Longinus did not know what to think. Nothing seemed clear. Things were happening too quickly. Wild things that he could not explain. He had always relied on what he could see and hear with his body to tell him what the truth was. But now it was as if his senses were betraying him.

Joseph turned to Nicodemus. "Have my servants get a set of Jewish clothes for Longinus. A robe with a hood." Joseph turned to Longinus. "We have to get you out of Jerusalem. We must do it tonight. There will be enough of a moon for you to travel."

"I can't leave. I have to find this body."

"If you do not leave, the only body that is going to be found is yours," Joseph said. "Head east out of Judea. Go to the city of Pella. It is a city of refuge. I know a trader there, and you will be safe. Use my name. Then, when the time is right, if you still feel you must, go on to Galilee, and see if you can find Simon and these other followers of Jesus. Simon was a fisherman at the Sea of Galilee. But first you must get out of Jerusalem and hide for a while."

"Why are you helping me?" Longinus asked.

Joseph smiled. "I think you know. ...We are all caught up in something bigger than ourselves. I do not understand everything yet, but of that I am sure." Joseph looked directly at Longinus. "You have changed."

Longinus started to argue with him then decided he might be right.

Then Joseph smiled. "And so have we."

Nicodemus smiled, too.

"One more thing," Joseph said. "We are not the only ones who have changed." He walked to his front door, opened it, and motioned. In came the dark-skinned man that Longinus had forced to help Jesus carry the cross. "This is Simon de Cyrene. I found him at the tomb."

Simon looked at Longinus and his eyes flashed. "You!"

"He is with us," Nicodemus said.

"Yes, but who is 'us'?" Simon responded.

"That is a good question," Joseph replied. "For now, it is we four. Tomorrow, hopefully more."

"You went to the tomb?" Longinus asked Simon.

"I heard the rumors. I had to see for myself."

"You stayed at the crucifixion," Longinus said.

Simon nodded. "At first I felt sympathy for Jesus. Then something else. Something bigger. I can't explain it all."

"We have all felt the same thing," Joseph said. Joseph called for a servant, who came immediately. "At dusk, prepare a donkey, water, and food for travel. Also, a pouch of coins. Station the donkey at the door."

The servant nodded and left.

Joseph turned to Longinus, then Simon. "I apologize, but I have only one extra donkey."

Longinus looked at Simon. "You are leaving, too?"

Simon nodded. "I was seen at the tomb by one of your soldiers."

"Madradus?"

"I think that is right. He threatened me. I have hidden my wife and two sons, Alexander and Rufus. I will leave, and, then, when it is safe, I will return, and travel back to Cyrene."

Longinus changed out of his Roman uniform and into a plain Jewish robe. He handed his uniform to Nicodemus. "I would hide that."

Nicodemus nodded. "And that?" he asked, pointing at the spear.

Longinus started to hand it to him then stopped. He remembered its possible healing powers. He studied it. It was just an ordinary Roman spear with four sides in a pyramid-like design that angled to a point. There was nothing unusual about it. It was certainly not ornate. And yet now it might be something so much more. He still was not sure. "…I might need this," Longinus said finally.

Nicodemus nodded.

50

Lacy finished her coffee and spied the Mango cell phone laying on the table next to them in the Pella Rest House. She looked at Archer and gestured her head left and down in the direction of the Mango. Archer followed her lead. She noticed his eyes squint slightly as he focused. When he looked back, she nodded.

Archer rose. "I've got to go to the restroom."

She nodded and glanced towards the man with the Mango. The man did not seem to notice. A minute later, Archer emerged from the restroom and looked at her. She nodded. As Archer approached, she thrust an arm out to her left.

"Look! What is that?"

Everyone in earshot turned in that direction. Archer swooped in, grabbed the Mango, and ran past Lacy, out the door. The man jerked around in the direction of Archer and rose to give chase. Lacy jumped up into the man's way. They collided and she pulled him to the floor as she shrieked. She let out a fake moan. The man pushed her out of the way and ran after Archer. She scurried to the cashier, paid their bill, and walked out the other door.

An hour later, she returned to the Migdol Temple site. She scanned the area. No Archer. Then a voice spoke from behind a partial masonry wall. "'Look! What is that?' You couldn't come up with anything more original than that?"

She smiled. "Don't knock it. It worked."

He poked his head over the partial wall. "I am probably going to hell because of you."

"Hey, you can't blame that on me." She looked at the Mango.

"I already loaded the Doppler app." He handed the Mango to her. "Sound away. I'm going to stay out of sight until dark."

She activated the Doppler. A low, bell-like sound emanated from the Mango. She began scanning at the Holy of Holies. Nothing directly underneath but more rock. She moved to the storage area beside it. The

Doppler deepened in sound, and a shadowy shape appeared on the Mango screen. There was some kind of space below her. She pointed to the back wall. The Doppler deepened in sound and the image showed a depression of some sort.

She directed her voice towards where Archer crouched. "There's a hole down there."

She pointed the Doppler towards the cliff. The deeper sound stopped. She pointed it towards the front of the building. Only the regular sound came out. Then she stepped outside the wall and pointed the Doppler on a line parallel to the rear wall. The Doppler sound deepened once more. She walked in that direction and the sound continued. She took ten steps. Same deep sound. A tunnel. Running parallel to the back wall. The clue from Quintus! "So that Eluid could gain hidden passage day or night."

She followed the sound towards the ruins of the Mamluk Mosque. The land ran on a slight upgrade. Then a few feet inside the mosque ruin, the deeper Doppler sound faded. The tunnel ended there. This must be where Eluid lived. The mosque was built on top of where Eluid had once lived—a common ancient practice. She returned and briefed Archer.

"So how do we get into the tunnel?" he asked.

She shrugged. "How else? We dig. At night."

She rose, walked to the edge of the cliff, and scanned the area. No one seemed to be watching. She dropped the Mango. It rattled down the rock then exploded at the bottom.

"What did you do that for?!" Archer's face flushed red.

"No more GPS."

They hunkered down in the nearby cemetery. A few hours later, the local police and the man who had been robbed of his Mango walked around the outer fence of the Pella archeological site, but did not enter. She watched them get into their respective vehicles and drive away. Half an hour before the store closed for the day, she entered through the side door and purchased two shovels, a wire cutter, and a miniature flashlight. Then they waited for dark.

The site was not guarded at night. They picked a lonely, dark stretch of fence and it took but minutes to cut a hole. She was familiar enough with the site that she found the temple and the mosque without having to turn on the flashlight. She set the backpack on the ground and they started digging inside the walls of the Muslim shrine where the Doppler sound had ended.

51

An hour later and four feet down, Archer struck something hard. Stone. He dug around the object. It was large and flat. While Lacy stuck the flashlight deep down into the hole and held her floppy hat over it, he moved more dirt from around the stone. More flat stones. He looked up at her. "This is a separate structure. Just as you thought."

They dug with renewed vigor. Every few minutes, Lacy put her floppy hat over the flashlight, lowering it to just off the ground down in the hole, flicked it on to get a sense of their progress and then clicked it off. By dawn, they had cleared a five-foot-by-nine-foot area in the corner of the mosque, all four feet down. As best as they could tell, they had located part of the original outer wall and some of the floor around the foundation.

He knelt down, motioned for silence, and tapped on the rock. An echo returned. He repeated the gesture with the same result. "This isn't a floor."

"It's a ce—"

A sharp crack. Then the bottom fell out under him. He started to cry out, but he smacked into something hard and he let out a loud grunt. Above him he heard Lacy's cry, "Archer!"

Light sprayed around him. He did a quick check of his body. Nothing seemed to be broken. "Turn off that blasted light!"

She did. "You okay?"

He blew out a breath. "Yeah, I think so. Toss me that flashlight." He caught it and turned it on, shining the beam of light to his right. Dead end. Just another wall. He shined it to his left, and the light showed about fifteen feet before the darkness ate it up.

"I'm coming down. It will be dawn in an hour or so." Lacy dropped her shovel and then lowered the backpack to him. She reached down as far as she could go and he reached up. There was still a foot of separation. "Catch it."

She let go and he easily caught it. As she slid feet-first into the tunnel, Archer reached up and grabbed around her legs, letting her slide through his arms until they were nearly face to face. For several prolonged seconds they looked at each other in the partial light. Lacy patted his chest. "You're dirty again."

"Well, whose fault is that?"

They turned and stepped deeper into the tunnel. He led with the flashlight, clearing out cobwebs as he went. "This tunnel is angling downward."

"Yes, the temple was on lower ground."

A few minutes and nearly a hundred steps later they reached the end of the tunnel. There was an opening to the right. He shined the flashlight into it. "Nothing but walls and cobwebs."

"We must be under the storage room," Lacy said. "I remember that the Doppler showed some kind of hollow space underneath the storage room." She looked around. "Give me the light." She shined the light on the wall to their left. On a stone, two feet above the floor, was a marking of some kind. She put the shovels down and shined the light on the marker. Wiping the dust from it, she revealed a fish shape. She knelt down and pushed on the stone. "It has some give. There's something behind it." Handing the light back to Archer, Lacy picked up a shovel and began picking the dirt out around the stone with the marker. She loosened it and began to pull it back towards her.

"Careful," Archer warned. "It could start a cave-in."

Lacy nodded. She pulled the one-foot-square stone out and set it down on the floor. "Flashlight." He handed it to her. Shining the light inside, she gasped.

"What?"

Lacy handed the light to Archer. He knelt and looked into the hole. "Unbelievable."

52

A few miles away, a sedan turned off of Highway 65. Two American agnostics sat in the front seat and two Turkish Muslims in the back. Four men, four guns. They had met at the Amman airport. Destination: Pella and the Migdol Temple. It would not take much longer.

53

Through the daylight hours, Longinus and Simon de Cyrene waited. Nicodemus walked to the temple and, when he returned, he announced, "Madradus and his soldiers were in the temple, looking for Longinus."

"It is only a matter of time before he thinks to come here," Joseph responded. He turned to Longinus and showed him to a hidden room in the cellar. There the Cyrene and Longinus hid.

At dusk, Joseph came to the room where the Cyrene and Longinus still hid. "The donkey is ready. Time for you to go." Longinus nodded. He grabbed his spear and walked upstairs into the courtyard. There was a knock at the door. They all froze in place. Joseph motioned for Simon and Longinus to go into another part of the house, which they did, although Longinus positioned himself so that he could still hear what was going on at the door.

Joseph answered the door. It was Madradus, along with Philo and Quintus.

"I am looking for the criminal Longinus," Madradus said. "Do you know his whereabouts?"

"I do not," Joseph answered simply.

"Has he been here?"

"He has not."

There was a pause. "Do you always keep a donkey outside your home?"

"I let a man borrow it. My servant has yet to take it back to the stable."

There were some other words that Longinus could not hear. The door closed. Simon and Longinus came out.

"Lying during Passover," Joseph lamented.

"Perhaps Passover does not mean what it used to," Nicodemus added.

Joseph smiled. "Perhaps; but lying is still wrong—even for a good cause." Joseph turned to Longinus. "Wait an hour and then go."

They did. Longinus thanked Joseph and Nicodemus for their help and noted their odd alliance. "These are different times," Longinus said.

"Yes. A new era for us all. We must trust the Lord."

Trust the Lord. Longinus had never done that before, never had reason to. He had always relied on the swiftness of his sword. Now he had just a single spear. He studied it. He remembered thrusting it into the side of Jesus. He remembered when its tip touched the wound on his forearm. Did it really heal his arm? If so, how could that be?

Nicodemus opened the door and looked out into the dark street. He nodded.

Longinus motioned for Simon to get on the donkey, which Simon protested. "I need to be ready with my spear," Longinus answered. Simon nodded and hoisted himself up onto the animal. Longinus looked back at Joseph and Nicodemus, nodding before he and Simon walked into the shadows of the narrow streets.

Out the Water Gate at the southeast corner of the city they went, on through Kidron Valley and past the Garden of Gethsemane. Longinus thought of the arrest of Jesus, Malchus's ear, and the fingerprint on his cheek. They passed through Bethany. Longinus turned the tip of the spear upward, and used the handle as a cane to stabilize his steps in the partial darkness. They pressed hard through the night, not stopping for rest. At dawn, they approached Jericho.

54

Archer once more looked into the area from which Lacy had removed the rock, now illuminated by the flashlight. Then he looked up at her. "Eluid. Unbelievable."

"It's an ossuary. A stone box about two feet square. Ancient custom was to put the body in a tomb for a year and let the flesh fall off. Then the bones were stacked in an ossuary."

"Lacy, do you think the testimonium of Longinus is in there?"

"Don't know, but there's a way to find out."

Archer set the flashlight down so it shined on the ossuary, then he loosened the rocks around the ossuary and slid it out. He pulled the top off the ossuary and Lacy pointed the flashlight inside. Just dust from the long-ago decayed bones was all that was inside.

She plopped back on her bottom. "I guess it was too much to hope for."

He took the flashlight and pointed it back in the hole. Something else was there. A jar—thick and old—set in a space seemingly made for it: a reinforced stone slot built into the foundation. Archer turned, smiled at Lacy and pointed.

They removed several stones from the wall of the tunnel. To avoid collapse, they piled the excavated stones one on top of each other on the side of the hole, bracing the roof. Archer dragged the jar from the hole. It was sealed. With his pocket knife, he cut the parchment seal. Lacy pointed the flashlight into the jar. It was filled with sand. Like the jar at Celsus. She handed the flashlight to him and reached in. The sound of fingers scratching through sand tickled Archer's ears. A minute later, Lacy stood up, another pottery canister in her hands. She unscrewed the cap and he shined the light inside. Side by side, they peered into the canister. It was stuffed with rolled sheets of papyrus...lots of them.

Lacy dug through the rest of the sand in the jar. There was nothing else but sand. As well as he could, Archer slid the jar and ossuary back in place and replaced the stones. They walked down the tunnel to the place where he had fallen through. Dawn was just breaking.

He threw the shovels up through the hole then cupped his hands to lift her up. She stuck the newest canister in the backpack, set it at his feet, and placed her right foot in his hands and her left hand against the wall for stability. He grimaced and thrust her up. Then a voice came from above. "Welcome to Jordan."

55

"Cam! Glad to see you!"

Lacy glanced down at Archer in the tunnel. Archer was looking up past her. She turned to the intruder.

The man smiled. He grabbed her hand and pulled her up through the hole. There were three other men. One white, two Arab. This can't be good. One of the Arab men knelt down to help Archer, first grabbing the backpack. When Archer poked his head out of the tunnel, his eyes flashed. She looked at him. "You know these people?"

Archer climbed out of the hole and stood up next to Lacy. "These two, I do," he said, pointing at the two white men. "They are on the Harvard faculty with me: Doctors Cambridge McKenzie and Luther Concord." He motioned to each as he said their names.

As the Arab man with the backpack handed it to Dr. McKenzie, a piece of metal clanked to Lacy and Archer's right. Everyone instinctively turned towards the sound. Men were prepping balloons for the launch. One balloon was already half-inflated.

Lacy turned back to McKenzie. "Just what are you doing here?"

"I was going to ask you the same question, Dr. Stowe." McKenzie unzipped the backpack and pulled out a canister. He unscrewed the top, looked inside, smiled and showed it to Concord.

Concord pointed at the canister. "Is this the document you found at the Celsus Library?"

Lacy's mouth fell open. "How do you…"

Concord chuckled. "Your boss, Rosenberg, did us all a big favor and publicized them."

She shook her head in dismay, then looked at Archer with a frown and a roll of her eyes.

One of the Muslim men moved past Archer. Archer pivoted to his right, and watched the man kneel behind him at the edge of the hole, and look down into the darkness. Archer studied the Arab man for a few seconds, then turned back to McKenzie. "Cam, we need to get that papyrus to a lab so we can examine them."

"Archer, I don't think so."

Lacy glared at him. "Just what do you mean?"

McKenzie smiled. "These will not see the light of day." He looked at the rising sun then back at her and smiled again. "They will be destroyed. And you," pointing down at the mosque ruin, "will face charges for desecrating an Islamic holy site."

Concord chuckled again. "This seems to be becoming a habit for you."

She looked again at the Muslim man behind Archer kneeling at the edge of the tunnel. Then she caught Archer's eye. She shot her gaze in the direction of the kneeling man, and then looked back at Archer meaningfully.

He held her gaze for a prolonged second, nodded ever so slightly, and then thrust a finger at her. "I told you we shouldn't be here!"

McKenzie and Concord turned their heads towards Lacy and smiled. She feigned shock, gasping dramatically to keep their focus on her. Then there was a grunt, followed by a thud. By the sound of it, Archer had taken her cue and with his boot pushed the man into the tunnel. Then Archer appeared in her line of vision to her right as he lunged at McKenzie. McKenzie jerked back to avoid Archer's attack and moved his arms towards the small of his back. Lacy thrust her hand toward the small of her back and jerked out her pistol, aiming it at McKenzie before he could pull out his own.

"Don't!" her voice rang out commandingly.

Everyone froze. McKenzie scoffed. "You won't get out of Jordan."

"We'll see." She spoke to Archer without turning to him. "Get their guns."

"Guns?"

"I bet each is armed."

Sure enough. Archer pulled the pistol from the small of McKenzie's back, then disarmed the Muslim man. When he stepped behind Concord,

Concord jumped away and reached for his gun. Lacy pivoted and shot Concord in his left foot. He collapsed in pain, grunting and grabbing his wound.

She smiled. "In Texas, we call that 'gun control'."

Archer reached down and pulled the pistol from Concord's back.

She glanced over at the balloonists. With the sound of gunfire, they were fleeing the area. There was a sound in the tunnel. Lacy cocked her head in Archer's direction. "See what that is."

Archer turned and looked at the man who he had kicked down into the tunnel. Archer then found a stone the size of a small football, raised it over his head and flung it down into the tunnel. There was a thud and a grunt. Then silence.

Lacy smiled grimly, and while keeping her eyes on the other men, turned her head slightly towards Archer. "Put everything in the backpack."

Archer stuffed all the three guns he had already collected into the backpack. The Muslim man in the tunnel still had his, but Archer assumed he was out cold. Then Archer grabbed the newly-found canister from McKenzie and stuck it in the backpack as well. "Got everything," Archer told Lacy.

Lacy smiled at McKenzie. "Okay, you two," she said, motioning to McKenzie and the Arab, "down in the tunnel." She figured Concord was wounded and not a threat.

McKenzie did not move.

"Want to join the Harvard Club for Shot in the Foot?"

McKenzie frowned then moved towards the tunnel. He sat down on the edge and jumped into the hole. The Arab followed. She glanced at Archer and pointed to the balloon.

"You're kidding!"

"Got a better idea?" Lacy turned back to McKenzie in the tunnel. "If you follow, next time I'll shoot you in a more interesting appendage." Turning to Archer she said, "Let's go."

They ran towards the balloon, now nearly fully inflated, and climbed into the bucket, now vacant because all of the handlers had fled at the sound of the shooting. Lacy pulled on the chain, shooting more gas into the balloon as Archer untied the ropes securing them to the ground. As they rose up an inch, the balloon lurched. Lacy gave the balloon two more shots of gas. The balloon climbed to a foot off the ground, and the northerly wind began to push them out and away. As she pulled on the chain again, the balloon began to accelerate, sweeping southward just off the ground. It was heading directly over the opening of the tunnel.

Something popped out just as they were passing over. It was McKenzie, and it looked like he had a pistol. He turned just in time for the bottom of the balloon bucket to smack him in the face. He yelled as it knocked him back into the tunnel, his cry seeming to magnify as it echoed in the tunnel.

Archer looked down into the tunnel and laughed. "All right!"

Lacy nudged him on his shoulder and pointed to the left. The police were at the site gate. But they were too late. Within seconds, the balloon flew over the cliff line, and the world fell away from them.

Archer turned back to her. "Where are we going?"

"Wherever the wind takes us."

56

Nick Loren listened to Dr. McKenzie's briefing over the phone and wrote down the name of the hospital where Concord and the Arab man were. "So both men will live?" Nick asked.

"Yes, but the Arab is going to have a headache for a long time."

"Did Stowe and DeYoung get away?"

"Yes, in a balloon."

"A balloon?"

"Yes. They flew off to the south."

Nick hung up and called the mullah in New York, telling him to get the mullah in Jordan to expand the fatwah on DeYoung and Stowe in that country.

Then he called a private satellite company in Titusville, Florida, that Pas de Createur had paid for access. He asked that images from the last six hours of the Trans-Jordan area be sent to him. They were sent within the hour. Nick studied them and discovered that the balloon had disappeared into a thick bank of clouds. He showed the images to Mini-D, and it ascertained that the balloon probably went down about ten miles east of Amman, Jordan.

"Mini—...Deity, how do you know that?"

"A storm came up out of nowhere. Strong winds from the northeast. So there is an 86.7% chance the balloon was forced down to the west of Amman."

"Eighty-six."

"Eighty-six point seven." Mini-D popped up a map of the area. "It's close to the Israeli border. Once the clouds clear, we can get a visual."

Nick called McKenzie. "You and the remaining Arab get to an area ten miles west of Amman. My computer estimates that the balloon went down in a storm there. Capture DeYoung and Stowe before they slip back into Israel."

"Storm? What storm?" There was not a cloud in the sky in Pella.

57

Longinus and the Cyrene rested the donkey in Jericho and drank much water. Except for the Jordan River, the road east would be mostly dry. Then they pushed on; this time Longinus was atop the donkey. Half an hour outside Jericho, they heard horses approaching from behind. Longinus turned. It was Madradus, Quintus, and Philo, all on horseback, coming at them. Longinus looked for a place to make a stand, but they were in the open. He slid off the donkey and grabbed the spear from Simon. Madradus saw the spear and stopped out of the range of any throw. He smiled at Longinus, which made Longinus angry.

"How did you find us?" Longinus yelled at him.

"The servant needed a little extra money. Joseph will be punished for hiding you."

"You lied to Pilate!" Longinus all but spit the words at Madradus.

"You should have taken Caiaphas's money!" Madradus answered through an arrogant chuckle. There was a pause. "You are under arrest."

"I am not going back with you."

"Then you will die here."

"I won't be the only one."

Madradus chuckled again. He motioned to Philo and Quintus to dismount. They drew their swords. Madradus motioned for them to widen their arc. Madradus stood in front and the other two maneuvered to points right and left. Longinus studied Quintus and Philo, his former soldiers. He had always treated them fairly. Will they really raise a sword against me? He was reasonably sure Philo would, but he was unsure about Quintus. Longinus watched them as they continued to move in an arc around him. Yes, they are good soldiers. They would follow orders from their commander, who was now Madradus. But what if Madradus falls first? How will they respond then?

Longinus raised his spear to throw it at Madradus. "I may die, but you will be the first to fall."

Madradus took another step.

"Not a step further!" Longinus said.

Madradus smirked, and then charged. Longinus started to throw the spear, but decided instead to keep hold of it, and hopefully Madradus would impale himself on it. On Madradus came. Longinus lowered the spear in the area of Madradus's belly and braced himself for the collision, hoping the spear would strike Madradus below his armor. Then Madradus stopped abruptly just before he hit the spear. He looked down at it in confusion then closed his eyes and fell to the ground. He had fainted.

What?

Quintus and Philo stared at Madradus, then moved in closer, though more cautiously than before. Longinus's hopes of turning their allegiance were lost. Longinus turned to his right at Quintus, and, in an attempt to get him to retreat, he lunged at Quintus, stretching the spear to within a foot of him. Quintus, too, immediately fainted. Philo lunged forward. The donkey cried out, and then Simon did, too, as the sword jabbed Simon's shoulder. Simon grabbed his shoulder then crumpled to the ground. Longinus pivoted and lunged at Philo, missing him with the spear by a short distance. Philo collapsed as well.

Simon and Longinus stared at the three men on the ground then at the tip of the spear.

"A sorcerer's trick?" Simon asked through a grimace.

Longinus shook his head. "Not by me."

Then he remembered his wound from the thorn bush. Longinus placed the spear tip against the gash in Simon's shoulder, and instantly it healed. Both stared wide-eyed.

"That is a sorcerer's trick!" Simon exclaimed.

"No," Longinus mumbled. "…it's that Galilean."

They noticed that the donkey had been gouged in its neck with the sword. It stumbled and collapsed. Longinus put the spear tip to its wound but it did not heal. The donkey soon died.

Longinus took the food and water off the donkey. Picking up the spear, he decided to kill Madradus. He placed the tip of the spear on Madradus's side just above his armor and prepared to drive it deep into him. However, when Longinus flexed his muscles, they would not respond. He tried again with the same result. The spear would not penetrate Madradus. He picked up Madradus's sword.

Then Longinus heard a voice. It was not inside him. It was outside. He knew he was not imagining it. "Those who live by the sword will die by the sword. So also it is with the spear."

Longinus looked around, but did not see anyone. He looked at Simon. Simon was looking around, too. He had heard the voice as well. Longinus lowered the sword and threw it at the feet of Madradus.

"What now?" Longinus asked Simon.

Simon looked down at the donkey. "I am returning to my family in Jerusalem and then on to Cyrene. I am taking one of these horses. I suggest you do the same. In fact, take the third horse, as well, so they cannot chase you any longer."

Longinus looked down at Madradus, who was still sleeping. "I will continue east."

Then they heard the voice again. "Longinus!" it said.

Longinus looked around again, and atop a large rock to their right about four horse lengths away sat a man in bright white clothes, similar to the man Longinus had seen at the tomb. Longinus glanced at Simon. He was looking at the man, too, so he had seen and heard it as well. "Yes," Longinus said finally.

"Write down all that you have seen and heard in these past days so that it may, as the prophet said, 'serve in a time to come as a witness forever.' Write it down and hide it."

"What do you mean, write—"

"Write it all down! Everything. Then seal it in a jar in a safe place."

Longinus looked at Simon, and when Longinus turned back the man atop the rock was gone. Longinus cast his eyes to Simon again. Simon nodded and said, "There will be papyrus and ink and other things to use for this in Jericho."

"But I don't know how to—"

Simon raised his hand in objection. "Don't you see? Your life is no longer your own. You have been chosen—just as I was chosen to help Jesus carry the cross. I am not an educated man, but I can still understand that. Do exactly as the angel commanded. Write what you have seen and heard and hide it in a sealed jar." Then he pointed at the spear. "That will protect you."

58

Lacy turned her face towards the wind so that her long hair shot out to the left and out of her eyes. She guessed the wind speed to be at fifty to sixty miles per hour. She peered over the side of the balloon bucket towards the ground. There was nothing but thick, dark clouds below. She could not tell the direction they were being swept nor how fast they were going—although, from the force of this wind, it had to be at least forty miles an hour. And, most importantly, she had no sense how high they were. However, she was pretty sure they were descending. Her center of gravity kept shifting upwards, often in sudden spurts. They were going down. But how far was down? She found the last sandbag, pulled the rope, and watched it disappear into the clouds below. If jettisoning the bag made any difference, she could not discern it.

She looked up at the chain controlling the gas tank. It flailed in the wind, stretching out over the front of the basket. She looked down and made sure she did not step on Archer, who was huddled on the floor of the bucket, cradling the backpack, then took one step to the front of the basket. Grabbing the edge of the basket with her left hand, she stretched her right arm for the chain. She couldn't reach it, so she stood on her tiptoes. Still short by three to four inches. She looked in the basket for something to snag the chain. A rod. Something long, hard. Nothing... My pistol? That might just be long enough. She reached into the small of her back and pulled it out.

With the sight of a gun, Archer seemed to come alive and looked up at her.

She yelled over the wind, "Don't worry; I'm not going to shoot you. …Yet," and smiled at him.

He returned her comment with a "well, aren't you funny?" face.

She gripped the pistol, rose on her tiptoes and stretched towards the chain weaving back and forth in the wind. She missed. The chain darted away at the last second. She tried again, and missed the chain entirely. She stretched out for a third try. This time the chain swung over the front sight of the pistol and caught. Lacy pulled back, but the chain slipped over the front. She tried two more times and missed. She needed just an inch more. A short jump just might get it.

Lacy planted both feet as firmly as she could on the floor of the bouncing basket, bent her knees, and jumped up and out. The barrel hit the chain, but she had not been quick enough to wrap the chain around the tip of the barrel. She repositioned her balance, bent her knees again, and thrust upwards. Catching the chain, she pulled it to her before the wind ripped it away, but when she came down she landed on the top of the basket just below her hips. For a second she balanced there in the wind, like some kind of gymnast on a bar. She tried to jerk her weight back, but the wind was pushing her forward, out over the basket. She arched her back as much as she could to shift her weight back, but it was no use. She was sliding forward. Forward and out of the basket. Any second now.

Lacy opened her mouth to scream, but only a gasp came out. Archer had grabbed her ankle and jerked her back in. She plopped back against the far side of the basket and looked wide-eyed at him.

He said nothing. Shaking his head, he held up three fingers.

Lacy gulped in a few breaths and tried to calm her nerves. She looked up. When she had fallen back into the basket, the movement had pulled the gas chain with her and it had caught a guide wire. It was now easily within reach. She pushed herself up, grabbed the chain to the gas tank, and pulled. Nothing. She tried again. Same result. The gas tank was empty. All that for nothing. Now what? She sat down and looked at Archer.

He looked at her. "Where did this storm come from?"

Lacy shrugged. "At least it got us away from Migdol."

"I can't believe I let you drag me into this."

She stood up and looked out. They were now amidst the clouds, a thick, swirling gray soup. Glancing down at Archer, she yelled, "Dragged is right! I can't keep us up much longer!"

At that moment they broke through the bottom of the cloud ceiling. Lacy peered down over the edge. At most they were two hundred feet up. And descending. Fast. A red light caught her eye. She turned, pulled her hair out of her face, and focused. There was a radio tower right in front them, maybe a couple of hundred yards away, and they were going to hit it. Lacy looked down at the backpack. That was what had to be protected. She looked back at the tower. Now it was only one hundred yards away. They were going to hit it left of center. Glancing down at Archer, she yelled, "Lean left!"

Archer peered up in confusion. Lacy repeated the command and did the same herself. The basket tilted left. She dropped and threw her arms around Archer. "Hold on to that backpack!"

Lacy turned her head upwards and watched the balloon. It had to be any second now. Not seeing was worse than seeing. There was a jolt and a hiss. The basket swung left, throwing Archer and her down against what had been the right side of the basket but was now the bottom. They bounced against it and slid towards the edge. Lacy could see the ground below. With her left hand, she grabbed a fistful of Archer's shirt, and with her right, she grabbed the rope that had held the sandbags.

The balloon went down at an angle. There must still be just enough gas to prevent a freefall. She looked up. A three-foot-long tear in the fabric above them was expanding with every second.

Her eyes shot to the right and then down. Here comes the ground. God protect us. "Hold the backpack!" Lacy squinted her eyes and waited for impact. It seemed like forever.

Then... smash! Her head smacked the side of the basket and Archer crushed against her left side. She opened her eyes and the ground was moving. The wind was dragging the balloon across the landscape. It slowed and then finally stopped two hundred feet later.

Lacy looked at Archer, whose eyes were still closed. Is he all right? She reached and nudged his shoulder. "Archer."

He rotated his head and opened his eyes. "Don't ever consider starting an amusement park. You'll go bankrupt."

She chuckled. "Got me there. You okay?"

He nodded and they rolled out of the basket. Archer unzipped the backpack and looked inside. The canisters appeared undamaged. He looked around. "Where are we?"

She pointed. "There's the Jordan River. I've been in this area before."

Archer turned in the direction she was pointing. "I refuse to get in that sewer again."

"Well, it's that or you'll finally see the inside of that Turkish prison."

They heard sirens behind them to the east, maybe a mile away. Archer looked at her. "I love swimming."

Lacy and Archer ran towards the river a quarter of a mile away. Luckily, it was down-slope. The sirens grew louder. Across the river they waded, trying to ignore the stench. Archer held the backpack above his head. Lacy lifted her pistol out of the water. As they climbed onto the Israeli side, there was a pop. The ground just to the right of Archer jumped up. She turned in the direction of the pop. Smoke drifted out of a rifle. "They're shooting at us!" she cried.

Up the west bank they ran. Zig left. Zag right. Bullets sprayed around them. Over the hill they ran until they could run no more. They forced themselves to keep moving and finally stopped in a clump of small trees in a wadi, a dry stream bed. There they collapsed.

59

Eric Jensen landed in Amman and checked the news on his phone. There was an article on an unnamed American shot at the Pella site and now hospitalized in Ajloun. That is where he would start. He rented a car and drove north to Ajloun. When he entered the hospital room, he frowned. He did not recognize the patient. He had hoped for DeYoung. Or, better yet, Stowe.

The patient opened his eyes, and said in a medicated voice, "Are you from Pas?"

Pas, huh? He shook his head. "Are you with Pas?"

The patient did not answer. No matter. He had his answer. Might as well go for it. "Where are the archeologists DeYoung and Stowe?"

The man grunted. "Good question. Last I saw, they were heading south in a balloon."

"A balloon?"

"Yeah. That was after that crazy woman shot me in the foot," he pointed at his bandage.

So they were armed. "South, you say?"

"Just who are you?"

Jensen showed his press credentials. "You alone?" Jensen asked.

"I am now."

Jensen left and stopped at the front desk. The clerk told him that the patient's name was Luther Concord and the man who had brought Concord to the hospital had given Harvard University as method of payment. He mulled this over. Harvard. Pas. Balloon. South. Guns.

60

Longinus and Simon rode their horses back to Jericho. Longinus held the reins to the third horse in his hand and pulled it behind him. Once there, Longinus tied the third horse to a post. Longinus purchased a set of papyrus pages, a stylus, two large bottles of ink, a pottery canister, and a jar with a leather covering.

Then he turned to Simon de Cyrene and said something that he had never spoken to another person: "Peace be with you." He smiled and chuckled in surprise. It felt good to say that. It felt good to care about another person.

Simon smiled as well. They embraced, and then rode in different directions. As Longinus approached the place where he had left Madradus, Quintus, and Philo, he steered the horse off the beaten trail, behind a hill and a rock outcropping. He got off the horse and crawled to a point where he could see below. There were Madradus and the two walking back towards Jericho. Longinus smiled as he imagined Madradus before Pilate. What lie would Madradus tell this time?

Longinus got back on his horse and headed east. At the Jordan River, the angel came again.

"Here," the angel declared. "You are to write it here and hide it in a cave."

Longinus no longer argued. He found a cave along the banks of the river and hid the horse in a clump of bushes. There in the cave he wrote it all down, all that he had seen and heard. It took several days of daylight. He finished with a series of questions. Just who and what is this Jesus? A magician? Or has he truly risen, as Joseph and Nicodemus appeared to believe? What explained the power of the spear? And this man in the light who kept appearing. The voice in the temple that day Jesus spoke. And the darkness at Golgotha and the earthquake after. And so many other things that could not be readily explained away. He did not understand them, but clearly their powers were not of this world. He did not think they were merely magic. So what were they then?

Longinus declared that he must keep searching. He was resolved to find the body of Jesus that his followers stole. In that way he could free himself from a life of perpetual flight.

"I now prepare to place my testimonium in the jar and seal it," he wrote. "I will also bury the jar to avoid easy detection. I wonder who will find it and when. And, more importantly, what will they do with it?"

61

Archer sat back against a tree, sucked in a long breath, and slowly exhaled. He spied Lacy. "Well, Calamity Jane, I'd say you are living up to your name."

"Another out-of-nowhere storm."

"Your God again?"

"Thank God."

"And I bet you prayed during the storm."

"Always. In good times and bad."

He shook his head. "Well, I'll give you one thing. You were in control back there with McKenzie and Concord."

She looked at him. "I was scared stiff."

"Had me fooled."

Lacy smiled at him.

So she likes my compliment. "But don't get a big head." He pointed to the canister. ""Let's take a look."

They walked to a large flat rock. Archer unscrewed the top and carefully pulled out the papyrus. "It's one continuous scroll."

Lacy leaned over his shoulder excitedly. "And there is writing on the back. It's an opisthograph. Writing on both sides."

He unrolled a few feet and inspected it. "Silver Latin. But different handwriting than Tarjan or Quintus. Get some rocks."

62

Archer and Lacy leaned over the manuscript, side by side, and began to read.

I, Longinus Petronius, former centurion of Rome, once assigned to the service of the Prefect of Judea, Pontius Pilate, having written one testimonium, now do so again, here in the latter part of the 16th year of the reign of Tiberius.

"This is the second testimonium?" Archer said, looking at Lacy.
Lacy shrugged and pointed back at the manuscript

I hid the first testimonium as I was ordered: between the waters where John baptized his Lord and Joshua blew down the walls. Immediately after I left the sealed jar, the ground shook, and large rocks fell and concealed the hiding place. I looked around for the man in lighted clothes, but did not see him. Still, I knew the earthquake was not mere chance.

Archer looked at Lacy. "Man in lighted clothes?"
She shook her head. "An angel?"
I went to look for the horse that I had tied to a bush along the river so it had plenty of water to drink while I wrote the testimonium in a cave. As I approached the horse, I noticed in the mud along the river bank that the horse's hoof print had a specific shape. Part of its hoof had been gouged at some point. I realized that the specific hoof print could be easily tracked and would lead Madradus back to me—for I was sure he would be ordered to find me. I untied the horse and left the saddle on the bank next to the bush. I traveled for some distance south along the bank, making sure I left footprints. Then I entered the river and turned back to the north, upstream. For over an hour, I kept in the water. From there I traveled along the bank

amidst the trees and brush, keeping to the river that would provide water and an occasional fish to eat, which I snagged with my spear.

Archer unrolled more of the scroll as Lacy re-rolled the part already read. They repeated this process every few minutes as they read.

I continued north. When I neared Pella, I turned east to seek out this trader who Joseph mentioned. Later, when it was safer, I would continue my search for the missing body of Jesus of Galilee. I was still not convinced he had been resurrected, that he was, indeed, the Son of God, despite my proclamation when I stood under him when he was on the cross.

Archer gasped and pointed. "See! I told you the body was stolen!"
Lacy shook her head. "That is not what is being said. All that is for sure is that the body is missing. Why, is still in question. Longinus has only his idea of why it is missing."

Then a thought surfaced in my mind. What will I do after I find the body and the arrest order is rescinded? Return to the life of a soldier? Not under Pilate. In another province? Egypt? Gaul, perhaps. Or was I beyond the point of no return? Had my life as a soldier been severed? I had a vague, undefined sense that, when I drove my spear into the side of Jesus, something had changed for good—a bridge of some sort had been crossed and had collapsed behind me. I thought on this for a few minutes, and then pushed the thoughts away. I would have to decide all of that when the time came. If it came.

For now: get to Pella and then find the body. With determined steps, using the spear handle as a staff, I strode towards the city of refuge, while keeping one eye over my shoulder for Madradus and my former soldiers, Quintus and Philo.

Lacy pointed at the papyrus. "Quintus," she said.

"But no mention of Tarjan," Archer replied.

I made Pella on the third day. The city sat atop a broad valley east of the Jordan River. The town was dominated by a temple that lay near the edge of a cliff. I learned it was called the Migdol Temple. I entered it and, using Joseph of Arimathea's name, was directed to the trader he had mentioned. He lived directly beside the temple. His name was Eluid, and he met me at his door. I told him of Joseph's direction to me.

"You are dressed like a Jew," Eluid said, "but you do not speak like a Jew. And your beard is of too few days. And your spear is not of Jewish design. It looks more—"

"Roman," I said to him. "I am Roman... a soldier. Or at least I was."

He studied me. "A deserter?"

That stung. I had never considered myself as such, yet he was right. I was a deserter. "I have come from Jerusalem, where I was a centurion."

"My caravans have brought me news of a great disturbance in Jerusalem. Some greatly respected teacher was crucified."

I frowned. "I know. I crucified him."

Eluid's eyes flashed and he stared at me. "But you are here now."

I nodded. "Yes, I am here now. Joseph sent me."

Eluid smiled, nodded, and opened his door to me.

That evening, while drinking wine, I told Eluid of the crucifixion, of the missing body and of the aid and shelter from Joseph of Arimathea. I did not mention the man in lighted clothes atop the rock, nor of the voices I had heard, nor of the power of the spear, nor of the testimonium I had written and hid. Then I told Eluid of how Jesus forgave on the cross.

Eluid fell silent. After several minutes, he said, "I am interested in how Joseph reacted to all these events."

I scoffed. "He thinks that the body was not stolen. He thinks Jesus has-"

"Risen."

I turned in surprise to Eluid. "Yes...you, too?"

"Perhaps." He looked at me. "It is that, or you let some untrained Jews overpower you and your guard."

"They did not overpower us," I said through gritted teeth.

Eluid smirked. "Precisely." He offered me a job as one of his traders. "I could send you east of the great Tigris River. Out of the Roman Empire. Out of Pilate's reach."

I thought about his offer. There were parts of that which tempted me, yet, I was a Roman. That was what I was. That was what I desired to remain. And the only way to free myself of Pilate's arrest warrant was to find the body of Jesus—and I was sure there was a body. I had speared him, and I knew he had died. And I did not believe in this resurrection idea Joseph—and now maybe even Eluid—held. It was just wishful thinking on their part.

Every day I distanced myself from Golgotha I was just a little bit surer that Jesus had died and not risen. I still could not explain many things, but I could not accept resurrection as a real possibility. When a body died, it stayed dead. Years of battle had taught me that.

My eyes shot to my forearm where my wound had been before the spear touched it. What about that? That came back as is. If a forearm can heal in this way, then why not a whole body? I thought on this for a while, then shook my head. Resurrection was too big a leap to believe.

I thanked Eluid for his offer, but said soon I had to head to Galilee. "I am convinced the followers of this Jesus stole the body and hid it."

He nodded. "I understand. ...but my offer still stands."

I rested my body in Eluid's house for many days. The events in Jerusalem and the flight from there had left me more exhausted than I initially recognized. I also needed time to think, to let my mind sort out what I had seen and done. I did so over many cups of Eluid's wine.

Lacy looked at Archer. "Lots of wine. I think you and Longinus could have been pals."

During this period, I visited the temple next door several times, once traveling by an underground cuniculum from his house to the temple where there was a room called 'The Holy of Holies'. He told me the temple was built to celebrate the change in Canaanite religion from many gods to one God. He told me that if I ever needed a good hiding place this would be it.

Meanwhile, my beard grew out. By then we had passed the next full moon. But while my body grew in strength, my mind did not. I had restless dreams again. I saw the Galilean on the cross. I saw my spear gouge his side. Each time I would awaken at that point and say to myself: he is not risen. He is dead. He was a good man, but he is gone; no matter the tricks other magicians tried to play.

On the day I departed Pella, Eluid gave me a donkey and provisions. I thanked him for his generosity to a Roman.

He pointed at the Migdol Temple. "Remember if you ever need a hiding place. And my offer of a position in my caravans still stands."

I smiled. "That day may come. But for now I must go to Galilee."

63

Archer and Lacy had come to the end of the unrolled section of the manuscript.

Lacy eyed Archer. "So what do you think so far?"

Archer shrugged. "Seems authentic. Written from his perspective."

"It confirms Eluid and Quintus."

"But no mention of Tarjan," Archer countered.

"No mention yet."

"And this thing about angels is a bit of a stretch."

"Perhaps. But, more importantly, there is a first testimonium out there *somewhere*."

Archer looked at her and nodded.

64

Longinus left Eluid's home in Pella and arrived at the eastern shore of the Sea of Galilee the following day, then worked his way around the northern end of the lake to Capernaum. Longinus asked about the "great rabbi" and his followers. He questioned men in the carpenter shop, then the livery stable, and also at the inn. He did not dare go into the synagogue for fear word of his inquiries would make their way back to the head priest, Caiaphas, in Jerusalem, and from Caiaphas to Pilate. He was told each time that Jesus was dead; that he had been crucified in Jerusalem.

Finally, down near the shore where the fishermen gathered, Longinus heard a group of men talking of Jesus. He inquired if they knew the men who had traveled with Jesus to Jerusalem.

They went silent. Then one said, "You do not sound like a Jew."

"I lived for many years away from here," Longinus responded.

"And your spear," another said, "is not Jewish. It is Roman."

"I found it," Longinus answered quickly.

A third man scoffed. "You had better hide that or the Romans are going to find you," which got a chuckle from the others.

Longinus again asked about Jesus and his followers.

The second one said, "I heard this story a few days ago that some of his followers were fishing at night and that they claimed that Jesus appeared to them the next morning. If you ask me, they had too much wine." This got another laugh from the others.

"Are these fishermen, these followers of Jesus, still around here?" Longinus asked.

"I was told they returned to Jerusalem."

And then the first one said, "And there is another tale that Jesus appeared to hundreds of people at the same time. See that man over there, sitting next to the large rock?"

"Yes," Longinus answered.

"He said he was there."

Longinus walked to that man. The man looked up at Longinus with curious eyes. Longinus pointed back at the fishermen he had just talked to. "They told me you and many others saw Jesus the other day."

"It is true," the man said. "Many hundreds of us."

Longinus looked at him. He sounded sincere. "Were the followers of Jesus there, too?"

"I did not see them, but, as I said, there were many people there. Hundreds."

Longinus studied him. "Are you sure it was Jesus?"

He looked directly at Longinus. "I am from Nazareth. I have known Jesus for many years. I was told that he was crucified in Jerusalem, but clearly that story was not true, for I saw him here in Galilee not so long ago."

"Where are Jesus's followers now?"

"I heard they went back to Jerusalem." He looked at the spear. "That is a Roman spear."

"I found it," Longinus said, and walked away.

Jerusalem. Longinus blew out a breath. Why would they go back there?

Longinus got back on the donkey and rode south, towards Jerusalem. That night, he broke off the shaft of the spear so he could hide the tip under his clothes. He wondered if he was destroying the power of the spear. He threw the shaft on the small fire, and watched it burn. Three days later, Longinus entered Jerusalem by night, and made his way to the house of Joseph of Arimathea.

Just before dawn, Longinus found a low spot in the wall around Joseph's house and climbed over it into a courtyard. A servant must have heard him, for he charged at Longinus with a spear.

Longinus easily dodged the man, reached into his robe and pulled out the spearhead, grabbing it like a knife. He spun around and let the servant see the spearhead. "I mean you no harm," Longinus said quickly.

The man stopped and they stared at each other, each pointing their weapon at the other. While Longinus was well outside the range of the lunge of the man's spear, Longinus regretted that he had burned the staff of the spear. He wondered again if the spearhead still had its powers.

Longinus saw that this was a different man than the servant who had fetched the donkey the last time he was at Joseph's house. He did not want to risk giving his name, so he said simply, "I am a friend of Joseph, and in need of his assistance."

The servant did not believe Longinus, and thrust the spear towards him. Longinus jumped to the side, and before the man could recoil, Longinus moved in with his spearhead, pointing it at his throat. The servant fainted within seconds.

Good, Longinus thought. The spear still had its powers.

He did not want to call out to Joseph, for fear of alerting others in the area. And he did not want to enter the house and needlessly alarm anyone. Luckily, Joseph had heard the noise, and ran down to see what it was.

"Joseph, it is Longinus!" he said as loudly as he dared, pulling back the hood of his robe.

Joseph lit a torch and approached Longinus. He chuckled. "That is an ugly beard."

Longinus laughed and they embraced. Joseph looked at his servant.

"He will be all right," Longinus assured. "He has just fainted."

Joseph shook his head. "Some guard."

Joseph ushered Longinus inside his home. Over a cup of wine, Longinus told him of the power of the spear, of the fight with Madradus and his men…his former men.

"I know," he said simply.

"You know?"

"Simon de Cyrene told me of what happened east of Jericho. I gave him shelter for a few days. Then, as he was leaving Jerusalem, the temple guards captured him. Caiaphas put him in the temple jail. The Cyrene's family escaped."

Longinus shook his head in dismay. "He is in jail because he helped me."

"There's more. The Romans tortured him and he told of the manuscript that you wrote, or at least …were supposed to write." Joseph studied Longinus for his reaction.

Longinus stared at Joseph. "I did write it and hid it as ordered by the man-"

"Angel… it was an angel," Joseph said. "Let's call it what it is. The Cyrene told me of it."

Longinus did not have the strength to argue. "I hid it where the angel directed me."

Joseph put his hand up. "Do not tell me where. This way, if I am tortured, I cannot tell them."

"Why would you be tortured?"

"These are dangerous times. Great upheaval. Caiaphas is feeling cornered, and cornered animals can be dangerous. He knew Nicodemus and I helped you, but we are too prominent in the Sanhedrin for him to punish publicly. It would reinforce the belief that his grip on the other priests is weakening, which it is. But we are still being watched. I let go the servant who took Madradus's bribe."

"So Pilate knows I wrote a manuscript."

"Yes. Tarjan does, as well."

Longinus's eyes flashed. "Tarjan is still here?"

"No. He and Pilate returned to Caesarea, and I heard that Tarjan has returned to Rome."

"Good. What a leech. He will not be back. He loves Rome too much. And Madradus?"

"I think he accompanied Pilate back to Caesarea."

Longinus smiled. "Good."

"Since you left, there have been incredible stories." Joseph looked at Longinus and studied him. "Stories of Jesus appearing."

"I know," Longinus said wearily. "I heard some of them while I was in Galilee."

"And stories of some divine wind sweeping through the room where the followers of Jesus were."

"They are here?" Longinus asked earnestly. "I was told that they were."

"They are."

Longinus nodded. "I must find them and learn from them where they hid the body of Jesus. I saw them before the crucifixion. None of them are men. It shouldn't be hard to scare the information out of them."

"They have changed."

Longinus scoffed.

"I tell you they have changed."

Longinus shook his head.

"Oh, Longinus, you are so slow to believe."

"You believe they have changed?" Longinus scoffed again. "I have seen them. And I refuse to believe that a dead man rose to life. You forget I saw him die." Longinus lifted the spearhead. "I drove this deep inside him. He did not flinch or scream. And water came out with the blood. He was dead, I tell you."

Joseph smiled. "Yes, he was dead. But then he rose. On the third day, just as he said."

Longinus shook his head. "Did you see him? Did you see him risen?"

Joseph frowned. "No… but I saw the empty tomb."

"From which the body was stolen. By his followers. With the help of the magician—"

"Angel."

"…Angel," Longinus said as he rolled his eyes. "Angel, magician—whatever."

Joseph chuckled. He looked at the spearhead. "What happened to the shaft?"

"I burned it. It was too hard to hide a whole spear, and the spearhead is clearly Roman."

Longinus told him of Eluid and going to Galilee. "Eluid gave me a donkey. I now give it to you as payment for loaning your donkey. I am sorry to report yours was killed by Madradus and his men."

"Yes, the Cyrene so told me. But keep Eluid's donkey; you may still need it. It is not safe for you in Jerusalem."

"It will be if I find the body."

Joseph looked straight at Longinus. "You will search for the rest of your life and you will not find that body."

"Perhaps, but I must try."

Joseph shook his head in frustration. "You must do what you feel you must. Remember when you were here last that I said we were part of something bigger."

"Yes, I remember."

"Well, I did not understand at the time just how big. On the day of the wind in the upper room with the disciples, when they spoke in many tongues and languages and received the very spirit of God, three thousand people converted. I sense there are thousands more ready to do so, including many priests."

"Thousands?"

"Thousands," Joseph emphasized. "And every day more. Truly, I say to you, Jesus has risen. And He has risen because He is the Son of God."

"The son of god," Longinus scoffed.

"John, one of Jesus's followers who was at Golgotha, told me you said as much yourself."

Longinus shook his head vehemently, as if to throw off the thought. "I was confused, swept up in the power of the moment."

"Nonsense. You spoke from your heart the truth you knew. Jesus is the messiah prophesied of in the old texts."

Longinus looked at Joseph as if he was a fool.

"I know you do not believe me. Yet. But you will. How else can you explain all that has happened? Things that you yourself have witnessed, things that you have seen."

Longinus did not answer Joseph because he had no answer. He had to admit there were many strange goings on. But he was not ready to believe in the dead rising—even if Jesus did forgive while on the cross, which was certainly not normal. Longinus considered again Joseph's assertion that

175

Jesus was the messiah, and then shook his head. A god would not allow himself to be killed. Longinus remembered the Jewish priests mocking Jesus when he was on the cross, calling on him—if he was truly the son of god—to save himself. But he didn't. He died on that cross. Longinus saw that himself. Jesus was dead. And these stories of resurrection were just that: stories and magicians' tricks.

65

They had come to the end of the first side of the manuscript. They rolled up the part just read, and then, carefully, they flipped it over and Archer unrolled the first section of the second side.

"Longinus mentions one of the sightings of the risen Christ that was described in First Corinthians," Lacy said as she finished.

Archer shrugged. He was not familiar with the verse. "Tarjan is mentioned. That's important."

"Yes," she said emphatically.

"What is this 'divine wind' that was mentioned?"

Lacy smiled. "Pentecost. The giving of the Holy Spirit. One of my favorite parts of the Bible."

"Pentecost," Archer repeated. He looked at Lacy. "I sense that, by the time we are done, we are going to need the Pentagon."

66

Eric Jensen left the Ajloun hospital and looked to the south in the direction that Concord had said the balloon had flown. But where to the south? Obviously, wherever the wind blew it. He accessed the local weather. It did mention a freak storm. Strong winds out of the northeast—they would cause the balloon to sail southwest.

Jensen drove south on Highway 65, keeping his eye out for a downed balloon or any unusual activity. As he went, he called the main number at Harvard University and was directed to Luther Concord's voicemail, which informed him that the professor would be out of the country on a dig, and that he would be accompanied by another Harvard professor, Dr. Cambridge McKenzie.

Well, that all fit. Now, where did the balloon sail to?

He drove for half an hour. On his right, a police car entered Highway 65 from a dirt road to the west near a small dam and reservoir. Wild chance, but it was the only thing he had to go on right then. He slowed and took the dirt road the police car had just used. He followed the road around the small dam. As he drove, another police car passed him and the two officers inside were giving him the eye. He drove a quarter of a mile further west. There was a flatbed truck and, on the back of it, being strapped down: a gas balloon and its basket.

67

Longinus stayed in Joseph's house. The following day, Longinus left Joseph's compound. Joseph had told him that the followers of Jesus regularly came to the temple to pray and preach. Longinus decided he would take his chances and go to the temple. Hopefully, being out of uniform and having a full beard would disguise him enough. Regardless, he would keep his hood up and make sure the spearhead was inside his robe.

Shortly after mid-day, Longinus snuck in the southern gate, hood covering his head. He looked around for anyone he recognized, and saw no such person. He meandered through the courtyard, remembering when Jesus had overturned the tables. Around the ninth hour of the day, he noticed a lame man sitting near an inner gate called 'Beautiful', for its ornate design. The man asked Longinus for alms. Longinus had no coins to give him and apologized. Longinus was not sure why he felt the need to apologize. He had never given alms before, and certainly had never felt remorse for not giving. But now he did. Why? He asked himself.

That was when Longinus saw them. The one called Simon and the more effeminate one Longinus had seen at Golgotha and other places on that fateful day. He remembered Joseph called him 'John'. Longinus moved towards them, waiting for the best time and place to confront them. A plan formed in his mind: he would follow them to a secluded area, then point the spear at them and they would faint. In fact, these men were such cowards he probably would not have to actually point the spear at them. They would faint when challenged. Then he would tie them up and question them about where they had hidden the body.

As Simon and John approached the temple, the lame man asked for alms. Simon turned towards the lame man, and said, "Look at us!" which the man did. Simon said, "I do not possess silver and gold, but what I do have I give to you, in the name of Jesus Christ the Nazarene: walk!"

Longinus almost gave himself away by laughing out loud.

Simon reached down and grabbed the hand of the lame man. Up came the man part way. Then, suddenly, he stood on his own and walked. Simon and the other follower entered the temple, and the lame man, now walking freely, followed them. He was praising God, as were others in the area.

Longinus shook his head. What a fake play, and these other people fell for it. That was when Longinus saw Malchus watching Simon and John. Malchus did not recognize Longinus in his hood and beard.

A short time later, Simon and John walked out onto the portico where Longinus had heard Jesus teach and the voice had come from overhead. A crowd followed Simon. Simon looked around and said in a voice loud enough for all to hear, "Men of Israel, why are you amazed at this, or why do you gaze at us, as if by our own power or piety we had made him walk? The God of Abraham, Isaac and Jacob, the God of our fathers, has glorified His servant Jesus, the one whom you delivered and disowned in the presence of Pilate, when he had decided to release him. But you disowned the Holy and Righteous One and asked for a murderer to be granted to you, but put to death the Prince of Life, the one whom God raised from the dead, a fact to which we are witnesses."

Longinus admitted that he was surprised that Simon was speaking out this way. Was not this the man Joseph and Nicodemus had told him had denied Jesus three times after he was arrested? And yet, now, he spoke boldly and without fear or reservation.

Simon continued to speak. And as he spoke, the temple guard, with Malchus and several priests in attendance, grabbed Simon and the other follower and took them away. Yet that did not seem to sway the crowd, for they went away, praising and in exultation.

Longinus returned to Joseph's house, glad he had found two of Jesus's followers, but frustrated that they were now in jail. That evening, Joseph came in and reported that the word on the street was that five thousand people had converted that day.

"Five thousand?" Longinus blurted.

"Yes. I told you a big change is at hand."

Longinus told Joseph of the healing of the lame man. "It was a trick," Longinus said.

"No. I know that man. He sat regularly at Beautiful Gate. He has been lame for many years. Some say from birth." Joseph looked at him. "Another thing you cannot explain away."

Longinus ignored him. "Where are this Simon and John?"

"Simon now goes by 'Peter', a name Jesus gave to him. It means 'rock'…the rock upon which the church of Jesus will be built. They are held in the temple jail. There will be a trial tomorrow, conducted by Annas, the high priest, along with his son-in-law, Caiaphas, who the Romans put in to replace Annas."

"Will you and Nicodemus be there?"

"No. Ever since we helped you, Caiaphas has banned us from inner meetings."

"What do you think will happen to Simon Peter and John?"

"Normally, what they have said—that Jesus has risen, which would make him the messiah—would be deemed blasphemy, for which stoning to death is the punishment. But Caiaphas is very worried about the reaction of the crowds. He knows about the thousands of conversions. Caiaphas is a politician. He is very practical. He will walk very carefully. He knows that if the people riot, then Pilate will use it as an excuse to close the temple."

Longinus stayed inside Joseph's house the next day, awaiting word of the trial of Simon Peter and John. When Joseph returned, he said that they had been released. He was clearly surprised. "I questioned several who had been inside during the trial. They said Caiaphas commanded Peter and John to no longer teach of the 'dead heretic', as Caiaphas called Jesus. Peter answered: 'He lives.' Then they refused to obey Caiaphas. Refused! They said they were witnesses and would speak out on what they had seen. Yet they were still released! This could not have been imagined before the crucifixion and resurrection and all the conversions. Caiaphas and Annas are clearly worried. They see their power being destroyed and they don't know what to do about it."

"Were did Peter and John run off to?" Longinus asked.

"I don't know. I have been told that they and the other followers stay in some house in the southwest part of the city."

"Southwest. I will go there tomorrow. In the meantime, I have something to do."

"What?" Joseph asked.

"The Cyrene is in jail because of me. It is my duty to free him."

"And how will you do that?"

Longinus pulled the spearhead out of his robe.

Joseph's eyes flashed. "You will bring the temple guards down on all of us!"

"If I do not get away from there cleanly, then I will not return here."

Joseph looked at Longinus, paused in thought, and then nodded.

The temple jail lay in the basement. Longinus approached the temple guard at the southern gate and requested entrance. He informed Longinus that entry was not allowed at night. Longinus decided to put him to sleep. He pulled out the spearhead and pointed it at the guard. Nothing. He thought he might be too far away. He stepped closer. Still nothing. Why didn't it work this time?

"What are you doing?" the guard demanded. When Longinus did not answer the guard repeated his question. Longinus still did not answer. The guard pulled his sword from the sheath and stepped toward Longinus. When he did, he paused, looked in confusion at the spear, and then fainted.

For the spear to work it must be pointed at an aggressor, Longinus realized. It will not put to sleep peaceful people. The spear will heal and the spear will repel, but it will not harm.

Armed with this new knowledge, Longinus stepped over the guard and entered the temple. Following Joseph's directions on the location of the jail, he moved as quickly and as quietly as he could. A few lit torches gave him just enough light to see.

At the door to the jail cell stood another guard. Longinus pulled out the spearhead and stepped forward. The guard pulled out his sword and fell to the ground within seconds. Longinus reached down and pulled the circle of keys from the guard's belt. Down the steps Longinus went. He pulled one of the lit torches from its rack and carried it with him. Once at the bottom of the stairs, he said in a hushed voice, "Simon the Cyrene." He waited. Nothing. Longinus called again. Nothing. He took a few more steps down the hallway and called again. Still nothing. More steps. Longinus called again.

"Yes," he heard a voice.

Longinus rushed to that door. "Simon," Longinus said again.

"Yes," came the voice.

Longinus began sticking keys into the lock. The fourth one opened the door. He pulled it back to see Simon staring at him. Longinus lowered his hood. "It's Longinus."

The Cyrene's eyes flashed.

"Come!"

Longinus turned and began scurrying back down the hallway.

"Longinus," another voice said.

Longinus stopped in his tracks.

"Longinus," he heard again.

"Who is that?" Longinus called.

"It is Malchus."

"Malchus?"

"Yes. Get me out of here."

Longinus fumbled with the keys and found the correct one. Up the steps they went. When Longinus reached the top of the stairs he peered around the door. The guard was still asleep. He motioned for them to follow him. They scurried across the courtyard to the southern gate where he had entered. When Longinus reached it, he looked around the door. The guard was just waking up, forcing himself to his feet. He looked at Longinus and his eyes flashed. Longinus pointed the spear at him and down he went. Malchus stared at the event.

Simon smiled. "Love that spear."

They hurried away. Longinus made sure no one followed them.

Once inside, Joseph recognized Malchus. "What are you doing here?"

"Longinus freed me, too. Caiaphas had me arrested."

"On what charge?"

"Disobedience. Blasphemy. When he can't figure out what to charge someone with, it is always 'blasphemy'. It seems to cover everything."

Joseph chuckled and nodded. "Truly." Then he turned serious. "How did you disobey?"

"After we seized the two followers of Jesus, Caiaphas ordered me to say that the man they healed was not really lame. I refused. Everyone knows he is—was—lame. Then, to my amazement, Caiaphas changed, and admitted that, not only was the man truly lame, but that the followers of Jesus had truly received their powers of healing from Jesus! In fact, he continued, 'Jesus was probably what he said he was.'"

"What?" Joseph blurted.

Malchus nodded. "I answered him with, 'Then how can you arrest his followers?' He looked at me and, without a hint of remorse or guilt, said, 'Sacrifices must be made to protect the temple and our positions of power and wealth.' Then he said to me, 'You are not to repeat this to anyone. Did you hear me?' I answered, 'I heard you. I heard you with the ear that the Nazarene put back on.' I looked at him. 'I will not obey you.' Then he had me thrown in jail."

Joseph moved them to his cellar. He lit a torch. "Stay here until I am sure it is safe."

Longinus, the Cyrene, and Malchus all sat down in the cellar. The Cyrene thanked Longinus for his liberation.

"I am the reason you were there in the first place," Longinus replied.

Simon told Longinus how he succumbed during torture. "I told them of the manuscript that you were told to write. I am sorry for failing you."

Malchus looked at Longinus. "Who told you to write a manuscript?" Malchus asked.

Longinus looked at Simon, who smiled.

"A man," Longinus answered. "A man in lighted clothes atop a rock."

Malchus thought for a few seconds. "An angel?"

"So Joseph believes," Longinus answered.

"And so do I," Simon added.

"Did you write this manuscript?" Malchus asked.

"I did. Then hid it."

"This spearhead," Malchus said. "From where do the powers come?"

Longinus shrugged.

"I think we all know the answer to that," Simon said.

Malchus shook his head. "Amazing. So many amazing things these last weeks. Your spear. My ear."

Simon smiled. "Yes. The Galilean."

"Yes," Malchus agreed. "The Galilean." He showed Simon the fingerprint next to his ear.

"Amazing," Simon uttered.

There was silence. Then Malchus asked, "What next?"

"My family is somewhere outside the walls. I will find them and then I am taking my family back to Cyrene—back to Libya," Simon answered.

Malchus turned to Longinus.

"I am going to find the body of Jesus that his followers stole from that tomb," Longinus said.

Malchus snickered. "Caiaphas tried to spread the lie that one of Jesus's followers, the one who betrayed him, was also the one who stole the body. But the lie quickly fell apart because the man killed himself before Jesus was even dead." He snickered again. "If you are going to tell a lie, at least tell one that is believable." He looked at me. "I think we all know that you will not find the body of Jesus. Ever."

"And why not?" Longinus said angrily.

"Because I think He truly has risen. It is the only explanation that makes any real sense."

"You, too?" Longinus said through a sneer.

"Me …and thousands of others."

"I admit that there are many things I cannot easily explain. But rising from the dead?"

Malchus paused and looked at Longinus and then Simon. "During his trial he said that one day we would see him returning on a cloud."

"A cloud?" Longinus scoffed.

"Yes. And he said it in a way of truth. It was not a false boast."

Longinus shook his head. "A cloud," he said sarcastically. "Tomorrow I am going to find these followers of Jesus and get them to tell me where they hid the body."

"Make sure you take the spear," Simon added.

68

They had come to the end of the unrolled section. Archer started rolling it up while Lacy unrolled more. She was shaking her head as she did so.

"What's the matter?" Archer asked.

She pointed at the manuscript. "This is amazing. Caiaphas admitting Jesus is the Messiah."

69

Longinus awoke early and, with the spearhead in his robe, left the house of Joseph of Arimathea and walked through the still-dark streets towards the southwest part of the city of Jerusalem. He made inquiries as to where the followers of Jesus stayed. He was led to a large house.

"They stay in an upper room," the man told him.

Longinus looked up at the top half of the house then thanked the man for his assistance. He had to knock on the door several times and a man answered it a few minutes later.

"I desire to speak to the followers of Jesus," Longinus said simply.

"Are you also a follower yourself?" the man asked.

Longinus shook his head.

"Then I cannot admit you," he declared.

Longinus reached inside his robe and pulled out the spear. "We can do this one of two ways."

The man frowned and let him pass. "They are upstairs."

The room upstairs was large. There were approximately twenty people in the room, all still sleeping. Longinus noticed several of them were women sleeping over in a corner by themselves.

His steps awoke several from their slumber. They looked at Longinus in question. Longinus saw Simon Peter and John. He nodded to them. "I am glad Caiaphas released you."

Peter nodded and pushed himself to his feet, as did John and a few others. One of the women also rose. Longinus recognized her from Golgotha.

Longinus walked to them. "I mean you no harm."

They did not respond.

"I want to show you something. I mean you no harm." He pulled out the spear.

"That is the tip of a Roman spear," one man said. "Where did you get such a thing?"

Longinus frowned. "It is mine."

"Did you find it?" the man asked.

Longinus shook his head.

"I know you!" John said. "You were the centurion at the crucifixion!"
With that, everyone awoke and looked up.

Longinus nodded. "My name is Longinus. I mean you no harm.
Please believe me."

"You killed our Lord!" John blurted.

"Why are you here?" Peter demanded. "We are not afraid of you. Not
anymore."

Longinus looked at all of them. Not one cowered. All looked him
directly in his eyes. "Yes, I can see that you are not afraid. I heard you in
the temple the other day," Longinus said to Peter. "Pilate has issued a
warrant for my arrest because I let you steal the body of the dead Jesus."

"We did not steal it," Peter said firmly. "If you heard me the other day
in temple, as you say, then you know that He has risen."

"So you say," Longinus responded.

"So it is as the truth," the woman countered. "We have seen him. He
is alive." She turned and pointed at the man who had identified the spear
as Roman design. "Thomas may have even stuck his fingers in the wounds
of Jesus."

"Wounds that you made," John added, pointing at the spear.

The woman started to say something, but Peter interrupted her and
took over the conversation. The woman frowned. "We felt His risen
body," Peter added. "We talked to Him. We ate with Him. A vision does
not eat. I tell you, truly, that He is alive."

"Where is he now?" Longinus asked.

"He rose into the heavens," John answered, "on the fortieth day. And,
in between, He did many other incredible things."

Longinus remembered the fishermen at the Sea of Galilee. "Did he
appear to you at the Sea of Galilee?"

"He did," Peter answered.

"Did he appear to hundreds of others?" Longinus asked.

"He did," John said.

"Then ten days after He rose into the heavens, on the day of Pentecost, the Holy Spirit came to us upon a great wind and whips of fire and filled us with its wonder," the woman said. "We all spoke in many tongues."

Longinus looked at her. He remembered Joseph describing the event.

"And now, as you can see, we have been transformed," Peter said. "Obviously, you do not believe us. We understand. It is hard to believe."

Longinus nodded emphatically, then glanced at the spear again. But then who would believe what this spear has done?

"All of us did not believe at first," John said. "Just as all of us ran the night he was arrested."

Peter's head dropped at John's words.

"I, too, doubted," Thomas said. "But when I saw my risen Lord I came to believe. He said to me, 'Because you have seen Me, have you believed? Blessed are they who did not see, and yet believed.'"

Longinus shook his head. "All I want is to know where you hid the body. I will not identify you as the ones who stole it. I mean it when I say that I wish you no harm. I just want to get Pilate to rescind the arrest order."

Peter smiled gently at Longinus. "You shall not find the body. And we did not steal it."

Longinus blew out a breath. He considered using the spear as a way to get them to confess, but realized that he would be the aggressor, not they. Clearly, they believed this nonsense about the resurrection. He looked at each of them. They looked back at him with even gazes, without fear, arrogance or even animosity, which was particularly surprising.

"I... do not believe you," Longinus said finally. "If you change your mind and will show me the place you hid the body, I will leave you alone." He turned to leave.

"God be with you," Peter said.

Longinus turned back and forced a tight-lipped smile.

He returned to Joseph's house and told Joseph of his meeting with the followers of Jesus. Joseph listened without comment, then said simply, "I told you: they have changed."

Over the next few weeks, Longinus watched the followers of Jesus in the temple, continuing to teach without fear, despite the growing anger of Caiaphas and others. That did not deter them. Longinus hoped his continual presence would finally convince one of them to identify where the body of Jesus was hidden. But they did not waver.

Maybe they really are filled with some spirit, Longinus noted to himself. That, or it is a grand conspiracy; a lie that they have all planned in detail.

Then a change happened for the worse. As Longinus listened to Peter and John teach one day on Solomon's portico, the door from inside the courtyard swung open. Madradus stepped through it, then a Jew who Longinus later learned was named Saul. Behind them came Tarjan. He was back.

Tarjan interrupted Peter, and said for all to hear, "I have orders from the Emperor himself to find Longinus and arrest him."

Longinus saw Peter glance at him as he slowly pulled the hood over his head.

"I am also ordered to find a manuscript he has written," Tarjan continued. "If anyone here knows of the whereabouts of Longinus Petronius, or the whereabouts of this manuscript, he is ordered to come forth immediately. Anyone hiding Longinus or the manuscript shall receive the same punishment Jesus received. And, if need be, I will close this temple!"

"Did you hear?" Saul proclaimed. "He will close the temple! We must keep the temple open. Cooperate with him. I plead with you!"

Tarjan turned and left through the door he had come. Madradus and Saul followed him.

70

Archer and Lacy noted they were coming close to the end of the back side of the scroll. They looked at each other, nodded and turned back to the last of Longinus's words.

I exited the temple from the east side. That night I left on the donkey, bound for refuge in Pella. Once there, in the home of Eluid, I asked him if the offer to join a caravan still stood. It did. I resolved at the moment to head east with the next caravan, but first, I would write down what I had seen since the first testimonium. I finished this second testimonium, which you are now reading, in two days. I wrote on both sides of this scroll. Then I gave it to Eluid. He said he would place the scroll in a sealed jar and hide the jar in the cuniculum.

Tomorrow, I travel east with the caravan, with the intent of leaving behind the Roman Empire and all these mysterious happenings, for which I have no rational explanation.

71

Archer was silent as he rolled up the last of the manuscript. Lacy eyed him out of the corner of her eye. He remained silent, staring out into the distance. Don't say anything. Don't even smile. Timing was everything in these matters. Let the seed take hold. Archer handed her the scroll and she slid it into the canister. He turned to her. He looked flushed.

She filled the silence. "Caiaphas's confession is stunning." She did not know what else to say.

Archer nodded. He looked down at the sand, and then back up. "I agree that Tarjan's letter could be used to refute Kitchens, but I don't think this manuscript by Longinus can."

She scoffed. "And why not?"

"'Cause I think he is changing. Converting. And, if that happens, then according to Kitchens, he's just another one of the 'biased liars', as Kitchens calls them."

"I didn't read anything about Longinus converting."

"No. Not yet. But I sense he's changing."

Like someone else I know. She smiled.

Archer looked at her, but did not respond to her thrust. "So now what?"

Lacy threw her hands up. "What else? We find that first testimonium. Except, this time, I tell no one we found the second testimonium. That blabber-mouth Rosenberg. By Longinus's description, the first manuscript is hidden someplace between the town of Jericho and the Jordan River. The walls that Joshua blew down are clearly Jericho, and the waters where Jesus was baptized is the Jordan River. It's just a few miles south of here."

"How convenient."

"Yes, convenient, but not a coincidence. First the quake and we find the jar, then the storm that blows us to Israel, then the storm that shields us from the drone, and now the storm that blew the balloon not far from where Longinus hid the first manuscript."

Archer reached into the backpack, pulled out the three pistols, and set them on the large rock.

She waved her hand back and forth. "We may need those."

"You've still got your gun. Besides, God will protect us. Right?"

She noticed he did not say, "Your God."

"Yes... According to His will."

72

Archer slipped the backpack onto his shoulders. She looked at him. "You don't want to rest here?"

"Want, yes. Will I? No." He pointed down the wadi. "Lead. Don't say anything. Just lead."

She smiled, rose, stuck the pistol in the small of her back, and headed south, keeping to the trees in the wadi. To her right, the whine of tires drifted to her. From previous expeditions around Jericho, she knew there was a road just over the hill, not far from the village of Uja e-Tahta. She plodded through the wadi. Every few minutes, she turned to check on Archer, who returned only a scowl. The streambed bent left and east, into the Jordan River. She kept them in the trees and bushes along the river bank as they continued to push south. It was slow going. Nearly an hour later she paused and pointed. "That's the Allenby Bridge."

She made sure no guard stood atop the bridge, then scampered ahead and huddled underneath it for a brief rest. Archer plopped down beside her. He patted his stomach. "I must have lost at least five pounds with all this running around and hardly eating anything."

"Or drinking."

"Don't remind me."

"Your eyes are less bloodshot."

He did not respond.

"So, who do you think sent your two Harvard pals to Pella?"

He looked at her. "You mean, besides Rosenberg?"

She frowned. "Yes, besides."

"Probably, Pas. Pas and Harvard have strong ties."

"Telling Rosenberg was my mistake." She expected a return broadside from him.

Instead, he rose. "Well, too late for that now… How much further?"

She looked up at him. "Maybe a mile or two. You want to go already?"

"I'm in for the duration. Let's get this done."

Lacy smiled and stood. She pointed up. "The bridge leads to Jericho." Then she pointed down the river. "To the south is the baptismal site of Jesus—or at least, what many claim is the site of Jesus's baptism. Others dispute it. They say it's up near the Sea of Galilee. Regardless, both places are on the waters of the Jordan River. But this place is near the walls that Joshua blew down: Jericho. So it's more consistent with Longinus's clue that he put in the second testimonium. Also, it makes sense that this is the area because, if Longinus went east from Jerusalem, Jericho would be a likely place he would come to and then bury his manuscript."

"And then there's the fact that God led us here."

She smiled, noting only a hint of the usual sarcasm in his voice. "Yes, there's that." There was a rumbling overhead. A car passed over the bridge, heading from Jordan westward into Israel.

73

As Eric Jensen drove across the Allenby Bridge, he looked down. Not much of a river to constitute a national border. Like the Rio Grande.

When he had watched the balloon being loaded on the truck he memorized the land across the river. After crossing the bridge, he took Highway 90 north past the village of Uja e-Tahta, then took a dirt road east down towards the river. He went as far as the road would take him, parked the car, and tramped east. At the top of a hill he surveyed his location. Below him snaked the river, and across it sat the dam and reservoir near where the balloon had gone down. Yes, I'm in the right place. If DeYoung and Stowe ran directly west from the balloon towards the river, they would have come through the area he was in now.

Into the wadi he went. There was a flat rock and, around it, footprints and three pistols. He congratulated himself. There were two sets of footprints, one larger than the other. There were footprints around the flat rock, others coming from the river and a set heading south.

He looked back in the direction where he had left his rental car. If he left it, and it was stolen, IP would deduct the cost of the car out of his meager paycheck. However, if he got back in his car and drove south, he might connect with the footprint trail and he might not. He stayed with the trail. South he headed. He left the pistols.

74

Lacy led them into the waters, over the sound of Archer's groans. She did not want to leave any tracks.

"You think we're being followed?"

She nodded. "Maybe…probably. I feel something back there bearing down on us."

"Well, you have managed to get half of the known world chasing us. We've got the Turks, the Haifa police, the Jordanian border patrol, the Pella police, and my friends from Harvard—as well as, by now, most likely the entire Nation of Islam on our trail."

She turned and smiled. "Is that all?"

For half a mile, they trudged through the shallow water. It took them nearly an hour to travel the distance. At a horseshoe bend in the river, they sat down under a tree. Lacy pointed to the southeast.

"See that steeple? The gold dome with the white cross on top?"

Archer opened his eyes and focused. "Yes."

"That is Bethany Beyond the Jordan, the site maintained as the place of Jesus's baptism. So… based on the second testimonium, Longinus hid the first parchment somewhere around here. Presumably in a cave." Lacy looked out at the cliffs along both banks and then added, "in a collapsed cave. Remember the earthquake he described?"

"Yes. A collapsed cave."

75

A couple of hours later, Jensen reached the Allenby Bridge. The tracks he had been following disappeared into the river. That told him that they suspected they were being followed. He continued weaving through the trees on the riverbank, moving south. This was his chance to catch up to them. Moving through water would slow them down. On his left, on the Jordan side of the river, was a gold dome and white cross sticking up above the trees. He sat down on the river bank and closed his eyes for a few seconds. A mechanical click directly in front of him sent his eyes flashing open. He was looking down the working end of a gun barrel aimed right between his eyes.

76

Lacy relaxed her grip on the trigger. She wanted no accidents. "Who are you?"

Jensen cleared his throat. "Uh, Eric Jensen of the IP, Dr. Stowe."

Her head jerked in surprise. *He knows my name.* "How'd you find us?"

"You left footprints in the sand."

She eased the hammer back and lowered the weapon. "Well, we're not your story."

Jensen laughed. "Lady, you are everybody's story. You have officials from four nations hunting for you, a Super-PAC, maybe two, as well as two separate fatwahs. You and Dr. DeYoung the most popular—or, at least, sought after—people on the planet."

Archer chuckled. "I always wanted to be popular."

Jensen looked at Archer. "Be careful what you ask for. So did you shoot Concord, or," he looked back at Lacy, "did you? I bet it was you. Texans are so gun-happy, particularly Aggies."

She scowled at him. "You'd just better pray you aren't next. Shooting a reporter is considered justifiable homicide."

Jensen ignored her. "So did you find it?"

"Find what?"

"The manuscript mentioned by the centurion, Quintus."

She gritted her teeth. "Rosenberg."

Jensen chuckled. "Let me cut through all of this. Let's make a deal."

"A deal? You're in no position to cut any deal."

"Oh, I'm not? Well, in that case, I'll just head on over to Jericho and file my story."

She pointed the pistol at him again. "I won't let you."

Jensen scoffed. "Oh, come on, Dr. Stowe. I know, and you know that you're really not going to use that thing—although, I bet Concord has a counter argument."

She looked at Archer, who shrugged. She turned back to Jensen. "What kind of deal?"

"An exclusive. I tag along and I get an exclusive."

"No way."

Archer cleared his throat. "And what do we get in return?"

"You win a 'get out of jail' card, at least, for now. And you get a chance to find this manuscript and disprove Senator Kitchens. I don't publish until you're done."

"Why do you think that's what we're trying to do?"

Jensen snorted. "Am I wrong?"

She frowned and shook her head.

Jensen smiled. "So… did you find what you were looking for up at Pella?"

She nodded. "Some of it."

Jensen pointed at the backpack. "Is it in there?"

"A manuscript written by a Roman centurion," she replied.

"Quintus?" Jensen asked.

"No. Longinus."

She sat down on the river bank and recounted it all—Selçuk, Celsus, the quake, the deniza, the jar, the canister, the flight, the sailboat, Haifa, then Pella, the tunnel, and the balloon.

Jensen nodded. "I saw the balloon. It was being loaded onto a flatbed truck. One of your numerous felonies. Before you're done, you're going to make Bonnie and Clyde look like local yokels." He paused. "So what did this Longinus say?"

She summarized the testimonium for him. Then she added, "It's the second testimonium."

"Second?" He looked at both of them. "…And now you're trying to find the first one."

Archer nodded and told of the clue left in the second testimonium.

"Wow. So you really do need me."

She looked at Jensen. "How's that?"

"You're going to have to have these documents authenticated by carbon-14, right? And that's going to be hard, with everyone within a thousand miles looking for you."

77

A glint across the river caught Archer's eyes. "Get in the trees," he said with a tone of urgency. Lacy and Jensen followed him. He pointed at the police on the hillside on the Jordanian side.

Lacy focused. "They probably think we're just tourists visiting the baptism site."

"There were cops near where the balloon came down when I was there," Jensen offered.

Archer looked at Lacy. "We can't search out in the open for the cave." He turned to Jensen. "You have a cell phone?" Jensen pulled it out. "Good. A Mango. I am going to download a Doppler app and teach you how to use it."

It took ten minutes.

Jensen rose and, in his best Arnold Schwarzenegger impression, said, "I'll be back."

They watched as Jensen disappeared into the trees towards the ridges that paralleled the river. She turned to him. "Do you think we can trust Jensen?"

"Do we have a choice?"

Jensen returned in three hours and shook his head. "I walked the ridge line. Real slow-like to make sure. A mile to the north and a mile south. No collapsed cave. Just a few tourists."

He took the Mango from Jensen and checked it. The Doppler was functioning correctly.

Lacy pointed at the Mango and looked at Jensen. "Maybe you read the image wrong."

Jensen shook his head. "It's really quite straightforward, isn't it?"

78

Nick's cell rang. It was from Senator Kitchens, and he answered it.

"I just got off the phone with my attorney," Kitchens announced. "I told him I wanted progress on my defamation lawsuit against Dunsette."

"And what did the attorney say?"

"He said it takes time."

"And he's right."

"Perhaps, but I need newsworthy events before the vote on my bill."

"Okay, hold a rally."

After Nick hung up with Kitchens, Mini-D came on, this time in a female's voice. "I heard your call with the Senator."

Nick looked up. "I figured as much. What do you think?"

"I am glad you acknowledge that I think."

Nick rolled his eyes. "It's just a figure of speech."

"Not with me."

Nick paused and gave Mini-D a tired and bored look.

"A rally is not dramatic enough," it stated. "Here's what I want you to do."

79

Nick inspected the platform raised on the grounds of the Mall west of the Capitol, between the National Gallery of Art and the Air and Space Museum, then spied the hundred people standing before it, soldiers of Pas paid in full. Behind them, more soldiers with placards temporarily held low, faced down, shielding their message from view. Surrounding the entire throng were the requisite network cameras. Nick turned to Kitchens. "Are we live yet?"

Kitchens looked at him. "Ten seconds." The Senator paused twelve seconds, then bounded onto the platform and threw his arms up. "Citizens! We are under attack! From the Christian bigots!"

Nick led the chant, "Stop the hate! Stop the hate!"

"I have been attacked by Dunsette the Dunce and Rosenberg the Rat!"

"Attacked, attacked!" Nick shouted.

"Attacked for my views. Attacked for my calls for tolerance. I shall fight back!"

"Fight! Fight!" yelled the crowd.

"I call for a rebirth of freedom. For a New World Order." Kitchens reached into his pocket and pulled out a dollar bill. "I know that paper money is a bit anachronistic. We have turned to bitcoins and digital flows, but this piece of history reminds us of the wisdom of our fathers. On the back of the dollar bill, our founding fathers were trying to tell us something."

Nick carried no money, but a few people reached in and pulled out dollar bills.

"No, not the lie of 'In We God Trust'," Kitchens continued. "But a more enlightened call. 'Nuvus Ordo Seclorum'. A new order for the ages. A new world order, based on human dignity, where man is free to determine his own destiny, free of the burdens of the religion opiate!"

"New World Order, New World Order…" the crowd was chanting. Kitchens joined in. They repeated the phrase while cameras rolled. Then at the back, people lifted their placards that said, "Kill Kitchens!"

The people in front of them turned around and pointed. "Christian bigots! Christian bigots!" Then others next to the placards opened their long coats and pulled out low-voltage cattle prods, and began stinging the Kitchens supporters. The Kitchens supporters fled, and the ones with the cattle prods chased after them, while singing "Onward Christian Soldiers!"

When Nick returned to his office, Mini-D came alive in a female voice. "Dunsette and Rosenberg have both already released statements saying that they were not part of that rally in any way."

Nick shrugged. "Let them deny. No one will believe them."

"B+ for the demonstration."

He frowned at his computer. "What was lacking?"

"I wanted to add no sex differences. Remember? Little boys and little girls are to be treated the same and called the same: it, them, us; so forth. No calling them boys or girls—it reeks of Genesis One and Two, and we can't have that, can we? I want legislation calling for a unisex America, like in Scandinavia. After all, I am not of any gender."

Nick rolled his eyes.

"I saw that."

80

Lacy looked at Jensen. "We need to search farther to the north and south and maybe across the river."

Jensen scoffed. "Just what is this 'we' part? You're not coming along. I got to do this alone. And to be completely blunt, I don't like the idea of walking along the Jordan River with some fancy computer app. It'll draw attention. Frankly, I'm surprised I wasn't searched more when crossing the border. By the way, just how did you get across undetected?"

Archer shrugged. "I waded. She walked on water."

Jensen's smile was almost a chuckle.

Lacy shook her head at Jensen. "Don't encourage him." She turned to Archer. "Let's load the historical geo app, too."

Jensen looked at her. "The historical geo app?" She motioned to Archer to explain.

"At Harvard-"

"That's Hav-erd," Lacy said sarcastically."

Jensen did chuckle this time.

Archer rolled his eyes. "...We developed software that re-creates a specific area as it was in the past. Takes into account earthquakes, rainfall, the wind, normal erosion, human development, so forth, and recreates what an area was like at a certain time."

"A computer can do that?"

Archer nodded. "With reasonable accuracy. We tried to recreate the Bering Sea Land Bridge and think we were at least fifty percent successful. And that was old technology."

Jensen's eyes flashed. "Wow. That could prove useful in resetting a crime scene."

"There are few secrets anymore. Technology is pulling back the covers."

Lacy snorted. "But it couldn't find a cave in Turkey."

Archer frowned at her. "Maybe that's because there was no cave to find—other than the original one." He looked at Jensen. "One catch: we'll have to access the Harvard D-frame. And when we do, Harvard will know it, and they will know the GPS from where the data was sent, and they will know I was behind it because you will need my access code."

Keeping to the trees and gorges, they walked to Jensen's car. Archer and Lacy crouched on the back floorboard while Jensen checked into the Trumpet Hotel in Jericho. When they entered the hotel room, she eyed the single bed. "Uh, small problem."

"I thought getting more beds might draw attention," Jensen replied. He looked at Archer. "So we'll have to sleep on the floor."

Archer nodded. "Right now, I think I could sleep while standing on my head." He accessed the Harvard D-frame, loaded the historical geology app to the Mango, and punched in A.D. 30 as the operative date, then handed it back to Jensen. "Okay, as of now we are on the clock. It's only a matter of time before they know we're in Jericho."

Jensen held up the Mango. "I'll work fast."

Archer shook his head. "*Good* and fast."

Lacy broke in. "Go do God's work."

Archer rolled his eyes. "See what I have to put up with?"

Jensen left. She turned to Archer. "Flip ya for dibs on the shower."

81

Four hours later, Lacy jerked awake. The hotel room door had opened. She pulled the pistol from under her pillow and swung around at the sound. It was Jensen, his eyes wide and staring at the pistol.

"You like pointing that thing at people, don't you?"

"Particularly reporters." She pointed at the sack in his arms.

"Got some groceries."

Archer rose from his spot on the floor. "Find the cave?"

"Maybe. I marked three possible spots. And bought some shovels and a pick."

She pulled back the single sheet and rose in her street clothes. "Wow. Any problems?"

"A cop asked me what I was doing. He said he was looking for two Americans, a man and a woman. I told him I was a tourist taking pics with my phone."

"Do you think he bought it?"

Jensen paused. "I think so."

Lacy nodded. "Well, we'll just have to cross that bridge when we come to it. We'll dig tonight." She pointed at the bag. "What's for supper? I'm starving. We haven't eaten since Pella."

82

Jensen had marked each possible cave with five stones in the shape of an "L" for Longinus. The first hollow was short and shallow. The second bore a little deeper and the third deeper yet. Lacy studied the lit Mango screen. "Let's start with number two."

They dug for three hours. There was a small open area inside, but soil strata showed there had not been a larger cave there centuries ago. They moved to number three, and, after digging for an hour, they broke through to an air pocket.

Jensen frowned. "Why didn't the Doppler show this the first time?"

Archer shrugged. "Sometimes technology works, sometimes it doesn't."

They cleared out the space and then used the Doppler app once more. Something was just behind the back wall of the pocket. They dug some more and then hit something. Using the light from the Mango, they cleaned the dirt from around it. It was a jar. Thick, old, and sealed—just like the others had been.

Lacy had to pause to catch her breath. Was this really it? She pulled back the seal and shined the Mango light inside. Sand. She stuck her hands in and a minute later her fingers found another canister. After extracting it, she was able to unscrew the cap after several attempts.

Archer shined the flashlight inside. Rolled papyrus. More than in the canister at Pella.

Jensen looked inside. "Wow!"

Archer smiled at her. "We need to get this back to the hotel room."

Lacy nodded and screwed the cap back on. Jensen went outside to make sure it was all right to come out. When he did not immediately return, she moved towards the entrance of the cave. Voices. She peered around a corner. In the darkness was the silhouette of a police officer's hat. As Lacy turned to motion to Archer, there was a sharp clanging sound and a thud. She spun around. Jensen stood over the officer, shovel still held high.

83

She groaned. "You attacked a cop!?"

Jensen turned and shrugged. "Sorry. He wanted to look inside at what we were doing."

Archer had joined them. Lacy looked at him and shrugged. "Back to the hotel."

Jensen shook his head. "You two go. I'm staying here."

"You'll go to jail!"

"Yes." He pointed to the canister." You've got to get that out of here. And remember, I get an exclusive—once I'm out of jail." He rolled his eyes. "Whenever that is."

The officer groaned. There was no time to waste. They let Jensen keep the Mango and the car keys—so he could be tracked by GPS. She stuck the new canister into the backpack and handed it to Archer. Then she stepped over the officer, nodded to Jensen, and ran out of the cave.

84

Harvard did notice the access of the D-frame by DeYoung, and, as part of their financial arrangement, called Nick at Pas, who called McKenzie in Amman. McKenzie and the Muslim man crossed Allenby Bridge 87 minutes later. Destination: the Jericho jail from where the Mango GPS beamed. When McKenzie was told by the police that they held an American reporter named Eric Jensen on a charge of assaulting a police officer, McKenzie guessed that DeYoung had used being a reporter as a cover. When finally allowed to visit, McKenzie discovered the perpetrator was not DeYoung. Jensen refused to answer any questions from McKenzie. McKenzie took a photograph of Jensen with his phone and left.

After McKenzie left, Jensen called his editor. He needed bail money. He did not mention over the phone his deal with DeYoung and Stowe.

85

Archer found a gorge in the cliff line and led Lacy up through it. When he reached the top, he turned around and helped her up through the last section. "Well, congratulations, you now have added the Jericho police to those hunting us. More running."

"Think of the weight you're going to lose."

"I'm thinking more of the life I might lose."

After nearly an hour of slow progress in the darkness, during which they crossed over Highway 90, he stopped next to a rock outcropping- the same rock outcropping he later discovered where Madradus and men had caught up with Longinus, the Cyrene and the donkey. Archer turned to Lacy. "Come morning, they'll track our footprints. Or use dogs."

"Come morning," Lacy said, "they'll" be in helicopters. Frankly, I'm surprised they're not already in copters with spotlights and infrared sensors. We can't go back to the hotel in Jericho. We've got to get out of the open by dawn. We need to get to Jerusalem."

They kept moving and ran into Highway 1 leading to Jerusalem. Hitchhiking would be risky, but, at the moment, the least of evils. On the fourth try, with Lacy doing the thumbing, a pickup stopped. Archer jumped in the back bed and helped her in. Jerusalem was ten miles ahead.

86

Just as dawn on Friday, April 12 broke, the pickup drove past the Zetim Interchange of Highway 1 and then north, where Archer asked to be let off. They got out, and Lacy turned to Archer. "We need to read the new papyrus and authenticate with carbon-14."

He nodded. "I know a professor here at the Hebrew University of Jerusalem."

"Why not just go to the university library? Maybe they'll accommodate us."

"Lacy, we're too well-known. I'm sure we're all over the news. So we'll need the help of someone connected with the university. Besides, it's Friday; Shabbat—the Jewish Sabbath. The university is closed."

"Friday. I had forgotten what day it was."

It was 8:10 a.m. local time when they knocked on the door of Dr. Daniel Haruba, full professor of Jewish History at the Hebrew University of Jerusalem.

Dr. Haruba's eyes flashed when he opened the door. "I've seen the news. If I let you in, I could get in trouble."

Archer gave Lacy an 'I told you so' look and then turned back to Haruba. "I know. I need a favor, my friend."

Haruba paused, then moved to the side and motioned them in. Archer wasted no time. He marched to the kitchen table, pulled out the newest canister and unscrewed the cap. He looked up at Haruba. "Got any finger cymbals?"

"You know I do." With the help of the cymbals, they pulled the papyrus from the third canister and laid it on the table. Haruba inspected the manuscript. "Silver Latin."

Lacy inspected the first sheet and looked at Archer. "It's Longinus's handwriting."

87

Once more, Archer and Lacy stood nearly cheek-to-cheek bent over a manuscript of papyrus. Dr. Haruba looked over Lacy's shoulder as best he could.

I, Longinus Petronius, former centurion of Rome, once assigned to Pontius Pilate, the Prefect of Judea, have been directed by an angel of the Lord to write down what I've seen and heard. I now do this as faithfully as I can, testifying about events that I witnessed with my own eyes and ears in the 16th year of the reign of the Emperor Tiberius.

Lacy turned slightly and caught Haruba's eyes as they widened while he read. A smile teased her lips.

Archer turned to her. "The other one was during the 16th year, too, wasn't it?"

She nodded. "It was."

"The 'other one'?"

She looked at Haruba. "This is the second one we found, but it was the first written."

The professor looked at her with a puzzled look.

She smiled. "It will make more sense later," and turned back to the first testimonium of Longinus Petronius.

I first met Pontius Pilate when he was in command of a legion of Roman soldiers. I fought without fear and won his favor. Indeed, on two separate occasions I had saved his life. As it was, when he became Governor of Judea, he asked that I be assigned to his regime. This was in his fourth year as Prefect of Judea. By then I had risen to the rank of centurion.

For the next hour they read, turning each page carefully with the finger cymbals. They read in silence. They read in awe. For it was all there in the testimonium of Longinus Petronius. He told of sailing on the Roman galley with Tarjan, of the haunting dreams of the man with the captivating eyes. Of being assigned by Pilate to Tarjan. Traveling to Jerusalem. Of Pilate's disdain for the Jews. Of Jewish rebellion. He described the jealousy of Madradus. He wrote of losing his troubles in a cup of wine, of his memory of vengeance against a childhood bully. Then he told of Jesus overturning the money tables. Of the cowardice of Jesus's followers. Of Jesus teaching in the temple and being challenged by the priests over taxes. The mysterious voice from above. Longinus recognizing the face of Jesus from his dreams. Jesus nodding to Longinus and his spear. Tales of the arrest of Jesus and Malchus's ear. The scourging of Jesus and the crown of thorns, the crowds calling for crucifixion. Marching to Golgotha, the drafting of the Cyrene to help carry the cross beam. The crucifixion, the mocking. Jesus forgiving on the cross. Jesus's statement, "It is finished." Then the earthquake and the proclamation by Longinus that Jesus must be the Son of God. The burial of Jesus in the tomb. Longinus on guard duty of the tomb. Another earthquake. The angel. The missing body. Caiaphas's attempts at bribes. The gashing of Longinus's forearm on a thorn bush. The healing of it by the spear. The frantic search for the missing body of Jesus. The curious alliance of Joseph, Nicodemus, and Longinus. The midnight flight to Pella by the Cyrene and Longinus. The fight with Madradus, Quintus, and Philo. The power of the spear to repel aggression. And finally, the command by the angel to write the testimonium and hide it in a jar in a cave by the Jordan River.

It was all there. When they were done reading and had placed the papyrus back in the canister, they remained silent, as if words would break the spell.

Finally, Dr. Haruba spoke. "All this time," tumbled from his lips.

Lacy looked at him. "What?"

Haruba turned to her. "All this time. Just sitting there in a cave waiting to be found. Just a few miles away."

Archer chuckled. "Like the Dead Sea Scrolls."

Haruba glanced at Archer. "Yes."

Lacy pointed at the papyrus then at Haruba. "Do you believe this document?"

Haruba looked down at the document. "I have read thousands of historical documents. And this testimonium is one of the most incredible and credible I have ever read. If it is true, then it is an existential threat to the State of Israel."

Lacy jerked around to look at him. "Just how's that?"

Haruba glanced up at her and shrugged. "Because it substantiates the Christian story."

She looked at the Professor of Jewish history and considered mentioning that in the second testimonium Caiaphas admitted Jesus was the Christ. She pondered this for a few moments. No. Now was not the time for that little nugget. She turned to Archer. "This further substantiates that Kitchens is wrong about there being no unbiased document."

Archer shook his head. "*If* Longinus does not convert. If we ever find the third testimonium, and he does reveal that he converts, it might substantiate for Christians the validity of the Bible, but it will not specifically refute Kitchens, because Longinus will not be seen as unbiased. It will be Tarjan's document and the notes by Quintus that will refute Kitchens."

"But at *this* point," Lacy emphasized, "at the end of the first testimonium, he has not converted, so what he wrote in that should be seen as unbiased. It's not like he went back and changed the first testimonium later after he converted—if he ever converted. In the first testimonium, he clearly states that Jesus claimed to be the Son of God and was crucified for it, and he, Longinus, did not believe it at this point, even though he did say as much just after Christ died."

Archer rotated his head back and forth, which she took to mean that he might be agreeing with her.

"Perhaps." Archer looked at her. "But you know Kitchens; he will twist the facts to support his foregone conclusion."

"Yeah. He's a politician." She turned to Haruba. "Do you have access to carbon-14 dating?"

He smiled. "That's why you came to me, right?"

88

Archer watched Haruba go to his bedroom and close the door, though his voice was still partially audible. Probably calling the university to set things up. After all, the university is closed. Haruba emerged a few minutes later. He did not look at Lacy and him.

With the university closed, Dr. Haruba ushered Lacy and Archer into the university lab without notice. Archer pulled all three canisters from the backpack and Lacy laid the papyrus on the table. Since Haruba was a history professor with an emphasis in modern literature, he had actually never conducted carbon-14 dating, so Archer demonstrated the process for him.

"When I started in archeology," Archer explained, "we had to actually cut off a small piece of the document and thereby destroy it—at least that small piece. But, now, with the help of an infrared laser, we can detect gasses coming off the document, and thereby date the document."

Haruba looked at him. "How much gas?"

"About half of a femtobar to ten to the negative fifteenth power of atmospheric pressure."

Haruba shook his head. "I have no idea what you are talking about."

He chuckled. "The half-life of a carbon-14 atom is about 5,730 years. That's the real yardstick. We should be able to date these documents to within a few decades of their origin."

Archer conducted the operation, and then shook his head.

Lacy stepped beside him. "What's the matter?"

He did not look at her. He just stared down at the papyrus. "I may have been wrong."

"They're not from the first century?"

He turned to her. His entire body had seemed to deflate. "No. They are."

Haruba scoffed. "I don't understand. What's the matter?"

"What I have believed most of my adult life." Archer looked back to Lacy. She was smiling.

219

"One toke over the line, huh?"

Haruba looked at her. "What?"

She looked at Haruba. "Never mind." Then she looked back at Archer with a wide smile.

89

Dr. Cambridge McKenzie of Harvard pulled a branch down from the bush he was behind, and spied the door Haruba, DeYoung, and Stowe had gone through. That was over an hour ago. He and the Muslim man who accompanied him had been crouching in the flower bed of the Nancy Reagan Square and his legs were beginning to cramp. He eased the branch back into place and ran another GPS trace of Haruba's cell. It was still inside the university building. He reached toward the small of his back, pulled out his newest pistol, and clicked off the safety. He motioned for the Muslim man to do the same.

They heard the sound of a door being pushed open. McKenzie peeked through the bush again. Stowe was exiting the building, followed by DeYoung, who had the backpack, and then the professor. McKenzie motioned to his partner: not yet.

The three were walking at a brisk pace. Wait. When they were about ten meters away, McKenzie nodded to the other man. He lifted his pistol to take aim, when he heard a clicking sound behind him, like knuckles being popped.

"Don't move," came a male voice from above and behind. Then the voice got louder. "Dr. Haruba! Stay where you are."

McKenzie pivoted and looked at the man doing the talking and the silencer on the end of a pistol.

The man smiled. "Okay, one at a time, throw your pistols over onto the grass."

McKenzie complied then motioned for his partner to do the same.

"Now stand up," the man with the gun commanded. "Real slow-like. Hands up."

McKenzie rose, pivoted back towards the building, and looked at DeYoung, whose mouth fell open. McKenzie snorted a chuckle. "Archer, good to see you again."

Archer shook his head. "How? ...How did you find us?"

"I remembered you mentioning once that you had a professor friend in Jerusalem. It wasn't hard after that." He turned to the man holding the pistol. "Are you with the police?"

The man shook his head. "Mossad. Israeli intelligence." The man's eyes flicked to the left. "Professor Haruba, thanks for the call."

90

Archer turned and looked at Haruba, who returned an apologetic shrug.

"Dr. DeYoung," the Mossad agent said, "my name is Tamir Yatom."

Archer turned to the intruder. He was tall, looked like he was in shape. Focused eyes like an athlete.

Yatom handcuffed McKenzie and the Muslim, and then looked up and smiled. "Doctors DeYoung and Stowe, we've been tailing you since our cameras picked you up in Haifa harbor."

Archer's mouth fell open again. "And I just thought I was paranoid."

Yatom chuckled. "We saw you when you first crossed the Jordan River. The director at that border station informed Jordan that you were in the area and probably crossed into Jordan. I thought it was a mistake to tell the Jordanians. The large drone was a diversion. We have cameras all along the river. After all, it's our border, and, unlike America, we control our borders. That freak storm was something though."

"Yeah, it's called 'God'," Lacy informed him.

Yatom looked to her and shrugged. "I would expect you to say that." He turned back to Archer. "The balloonists at Pella were ours, too. And good thing, huh? That was the best escape in a balloon since your Wizard of Oz."

"You saw us re-enter Israel?" Archer asked.

Yatom nodded at him.

Lacy crossed her arms. "Another 'freak' storm."

Yatom looked to her. "Whatever. Then we lost you after that reporter cold-clocked the Jericho police officer."

"How's the officer?"

"A bad headache, Dr. Stowe, but he'll live."

"And Jensen?"

"Catching up on his sleep in the Jericho jail. Dr. DeYoung, I need you to drive my sedan to Dr. Haruba's while I watch the prisoners. Bring the backpack with the canister."

He frowned. "Are we being arrested?"

"Let's just say 'detained' for right now."

Archer looked at Lacy. "I can't believe I let you drag me into this." He turned to Haruba. "We'll follow you."

Once at Haruba's apartment, more Mossad agents arrived to take away McKenzie and the Muslim. Before they left, Archer walked over to his colleague and smiled. "Cam, see you back in Cambridge."

McKenzie did not look amused. "Real funny."

After the door closed, Yatom turned to Lacy and held out his hand. "The pistol in the back of your pants." She frowned and handed it over. Yatom turned to Archer. "Let's see the manuscript."

"How do you know about them?"

"Them? There's more than one?"

Archer frowned and held up three fingers. "And maybe as many as six, if you count the shorter notes."

"Six?" Yatom's mouth fell open. "We knew about Turkey. You know, Rosenberg."

Archer frowned at Lacy. "We'll start with Tarjan."

Lacy and he arranged the Tarjan's Lament and the notes from Quintus on the table. Yatom took photographs of each page. "Why so many blank pages?"

Lacy shrugged. "We're not sure." She pulled out the scroll that was the second testimonium, and unrolled it as Yatom took the shots, then did the same with the first testimonium. Yatom could not understand Latin, so he merely photographed the pages.

Then Yatom jerked up straight and his eyes flashed. "Let me see those blank pages again." She obliged. Yatom bent over and ran his fingers across the papyrus. He smiled. Pulling out a pocketknife, he pricked his finger and dropped blood onto the papyrus.

Lacy jumped forward. "Hey!"

Yatom smeared the blood and pointed. There was writing on the blank pages.

Yatom had an infrared camera at his office. There they confirmed that the blank pages in the canister with Tarjan's Lament were the third testimonium of Longinus Petronius, written with a stylus, without ink; some of it was written over by Tarjan.

Archer ran his fingers over the blank pages. "It is palimpsest; a document under another document."

Lacy nodded. "Tarjan must have written over Longinus's indentations, not knowing they were there, and then given them to Quintus for shipment to Rome."

Yatom pointed at the pages. "We'll have to read it one page at a time under the infrared, which means one of you will have to read it outloud to me."

Lacy nodded.

91

I, Longinus Petronius, long ago a centurion in the service of the Prefect of Judea, Pontius Pilate, and the author of two previous testimoniae, written and then hidden nearly forty years ago, do now take stylus into hand once more, except this time I do it without ink, for I have been captured by Tarjan, an official of Rome. Whether these apparent blank pages of papyrus are ever recognized as a manuscript and then survive is but a guess, a fervent hope for the future.

"So this would be about the year 70 A.D.," Lacy said.
Archer nodded. "Yes. Jesus died around the year 30."

I am being held in a jail in Ephesus and have been beaten and tortured repeatedly to give up the location of the two testimoniae I have written. But I am getting ahead of myself.

After writing the second testimonium and giving it to Eluid in Pella to hide, I headed east on one of his caravans. We traveled to Babylon and then proceeded east once more, to southern India. There, I became Eluid's representative in that area.

I flourished in India. It was a new start. I met a beautiful woman named Ananda and we wed. Her name meant "joy" and such joy I had never found. The following year she bore me a son. I ceased drinking, family replacing wine as my source of happiness.

Lacy glanced at Archer for his reaction, but he betrayed none.

I occasionally dreamed of Jesus. I did not understand why. I longed to be free of any memory of him, but my dreams would not let me go. I kept the spearhead concealed, taking it out but a few times to ward off a thief or to heal some injured bystander. I did not want the attention the spear would bring. I had found a good life, and wanted to live it in peace.

Three years after my son was born, my wife bore me a daughter. More joy. Then another son. I was happy beyond any expectation. I had found a meaning to life in my family. This made the years of travail as a soldier worth it. Ananda was a Hindu by birth. Hinduism, I discovered, had even more gods than Rome had come up with—no small feat. Out of love and respect, I let Ananda raise our children as Hindu. I chose not to partake of their superstitions.

92

Yatom paused and asked about the contents of the previous two testimoniae, which he had seen, but not read. Lacy summarized the gist of each. Yatom was particularly interested in the centurion's spear.

"Longinus was a man of integrity," Archer jumped in. "caught up in one of the most important events in human history."

Lacy smiled at Archer. "Yes, indeed." Lacy retuned to reading the manuscript outloud so Yatom could hear.

93

Many years passed. Longinus's children grew up. His business with Eluid made him wealthy. Then, when his first son was about nineteen years old, Longinus heard a story of a man who had come from far to the west, from Judea. He was preaching of a great teacher named Jesus. Surely, this could not be the same Jesus. Surely, the Jesus Longinus knew had long been forgotten.

This man was preaching in the nearby town of Muziris. Longinus had business in this town, and decided to seek out this man and see for himself who he was and of whom he taught. After Longinus had concluded his business, he asked the locals about this teacher. They told him that the man was in the town courtyard. Longinus walked to this courtyard and there was the man, sitting before fifty people. Longinus moved to where he could see the man's face. Longinus did not recognize it. He listened to the man's words and he spoke of the teachings of Jesus, of his arrest, of how his followers fled, of his crucifixion, and then resurrection. Longinus was stunned. Still preaching on this after so many years!

"I, like all the disciples," this man said, "did not believe at first. A woman named Mary Magdalene and a man named Simon Peter were the first to see the truth. I admit that I was one of the last to believe that Jesus had risen. In fact, he had to appear to me before I truly believed. Jesus said to me, 'Because you have seen Me, have you believed? Blessed are they who did not see, and yet believed.'"

Him! It was him! What was his name again? Longinus met him in that upper room that day. Was he still preaching? After all these years? In India?

The man concluded his talk and the throng drifted away. Longinus lingered. Did he want to approach him? Did he want to expose himself and his family? Longinus knew he could not just walk away. He was pulled to this man by a force he did not understand nor desire. He approached the man slowly. The man did not recognize Longinus. But he did notice Longinus was not Indian. He smiled.

"You come from Judea?" Longinus asked.

"Yes. From Jerusalem. Obviously, you come from the west, as well." Longinus nodded. "I have been to Jerusalem."

"But you are not from there. You look and sound Roman."

Longinus stared at him then nodded.

The man was looking hard at Longinus. "Have we met before?" he asked finally.

Longinus paused. He did not know if he wanted to answer that. He looked at the man and finally nodded.

"Where?" he asked.

"In Jerusalem." Longinus looked at him again. "…in the upper room with the other followers."

His eyes flashed wide. "Of course! I remember!" He looked at Longinus in question. "You are the centurion who crucified my Christ?"

Christ? Longinus had never heard that term before. He frowned then nodded.

"You were being hunted by the Romans. That must be why you came here."

Longinus nodded again. "By Tarjan, a Roman official."

"Yes, I remember!" Then he laughed, which surprised Longinus. He saw Longinus's surprise and quickly mentioned, "When I left Jerusalem, Tarjan was still looking for you!"

Longinus's jaw dropped open. "Still?"

"Yes, still. The Emperor himself decreed that he could not return to Rome until he found you—and some manuscript, as I recall. He was very frustrated. He questioned me harshly about your whereabouts and where you might have hidden the manuscript."

"Sounds to me like he is getting his just punishment."

The man chuckled. "Truly. And I doubt he will think to look in India."

"Let's hope not."

"My name is Thomas. I, too, came here as a means of escaping Rome. Christians are persecuted by Rome and by the Jewish priests."

"Still?"

"Yes, still. More than ever."

Longinus looked at him. "And yet you continue to preach of Jesus."

Thomas smiled. "I can do no other thing. I have witnessed the living God. His orders to go out and spread the word were very clear."

Longinus looked at him again. "And the other followers of Jesus?"

"They, too, spread the word. At their own peril. Some have already died a martyr's death. But we all have stayed true, each and every one of us."

Longinus shook his head in amazement. The man thought Longinus doubted him.

"It is true, I tell you. We all stayed true." Then he frowned. "But it took the resurrection to convince us. Before, we all failed."

"Better late than never," Longinus responded.

Thomas smiled. "Yes, I guess that is the way to look at it."

Over the next few months, Thomas and Longinus met several times. Thomas told Longinus more of the teachings of Jesus. Longinus told Thomas of happenings on Golgotha. Much of what Longinus said Thomas already knew from John, but other parts he did not know and he was gratified to learn more.

"I remember in the upper room that you had the spearhead. Do you still have it?"

Longinus nodded.

"Word has it that the spear with which you pierced our Christ has special powers."

Longinus nodded and pulled it from his robe. "I guess you could call it 'magic'."

Thomas shook his head. "I think we both know where the true power comes from."

Longinus looked at him. "Do we?"

Thomas looked Longinus in the eye and smiled. "Yes, I think we both do. It is just that one of us is more stubborn than the other. But do not fret. I am known as the 'doubter'." He looked at the spearhead. "May I hold it?"

"Of course," Longinus replied and handed it to him.

Thomas held the spear like it was a bar of gold. He ran his fingers over its sides and placed his forefinger to the tip and closed his eyes. Then Longinus saw Thomas's lips moving in a silent prayer.

When Thomas was done Longinus asked him what he prayed for.

Thomas looked at Longinus. "That my sacrifice be true to His."

Longinus looked at Thomas in question. "How did he sacrifice? I know He died—I was there—but how was that a sacrifice? He was condemned by Pilate. He did not ask to be crucified."

"No. He did not ask. But He was ordered."

"Ordered? By whom?"

"His Father."

"His father was from Galilee?"

"No. Not that father. The Father. The Father of us all."

Longinus thought of his own children who he loved more than anything in the world. "And why would a father order his own son to die on the cross?"

Thomas smiled at Longinus, but it was more of a sad smile. "To pay for our sins."

"I don't understand. How does Jesus dying on the cross pay for someone else's sins?"

Thomas paused. "I admit I did not understand that very thing for a long time. Then I came to see, after much prayer and thought, that we could not earn our own salvation—we would be filled with pride and arrogance. Instead, our salvation came as a gift of Jesus's sacrifice."

He could see that Longinus did not understand.

Thomas gave him a tight-lipped smile, placed his hand on Longinus's forearm, where the thorn bush had wounded him and the spear had healed.

"We should all be humbled by his sacrifice." Then Thomas handed back the spearhead. "Thank you for letting me hold it."

Longinus and Thomas met once more after that, a few weeks later. Longinus had thought much about what Thomas had said. Longinus still did not understand it. He asked Thomas many questions and Thomas answered each patiently. Still, there was much that Longinus did not understand, and he grew frustrated.

"Do not worry. It shall come in His time."

"Whose time?"

"The Father's. Meanwhile, remember that we all can carry God within us."

Longinus squinted in question and doubt. "How?"

"By receiving His love. Remember above all else: we are His children, and, just as you love your children, so He loves us, except many times more."

Two weeks later, disaster struck. While Longinus traveled inland on a trading excursion, a hurricane hit the coast of southwest India. A giant tidal wave washed ashore, destroying Longinus's home. His Ananda and all three of his children were swept away. He found the body of one of his sons. The others were never found. Never had Longinus felt such agony. He realized at that moment that he would take the place of any one of his children. He would gladly die so that just one of them could live.

Longinus looked at the spearhead. Would this have stopped the waves if he had been there?

Longinus was devastated. He began drinking again. He considered suicide. He tried to thrust the spearhead into his belly but it would not penetrate. He walked to the nearby river and prepared to throw the spearhead into the middle of the current.

At that moment there came a voice. "Stop!"

Longinus had not heard such a voice since he left Pella. He looked around but did not see anyone. He cocked his arm again to throw, and suddenly the spearhead vibrated violently and fell from his hand. Longinus looked around again. Still there was no one. But he knew something was there. Not a man in human form, but something. He picked up the spearhead and stuck it inside his robe.

94

A month later, Longinus left India, heading west. Being in India only reminded him of his great loss. Two months after leaving India, he reached Eluid's in Pella. Longinus told Eluid of the hurricane and his family. Eluid prayed for Longinus. Then Longinus told Eluid of meeting Thomas. Eluid smiled. "The work goes on," was all he said.

Later that day, Eluid showed Longinus where he had hidden Longinus's second testimonium in a jar in the wall of the cuniculum leading to the temple. "I hid it behind what will be my ossuary."

Longinus noticed the side of the box had Eluid's name and a circular symbol. "What is that symbol?"

"It's a fish. A Christian symbol. Jesus said he would make us 'fishers of men'."

"'I see.'"

"Do you still have the spear?"

Longinus pulled it out. "I still could not save my own family."

Eluid frowned. "God's plan is sometimes hard to understand. But He loves us."

Longinus looked at Eluid with an even gaze. He knew Eluid had not said that with malice. "Does He?"

95

When Lacy finished reading that page outloud, she turned to Archer a and smiled. "The ossuary with the fish symbol."

"Yes," Archer replied.

"You saw this for yourselves?" Yatom asked.

Archer nodded. "Yes. In Pella."

96

Longinus stayed with Eluid for a few weeks then took a new position with him in the city of Ephesus, in western Asia Minor. On the way there Longinus traveled nearby the Sea of Galilee. He remembered hearing of appearances by Jesus to his followers and then to hundreds more. Did that really happen? He asked himself. Then he remembered Thomas's words, which he had repeated from Jesus: "Blessed are they who did not see, and yet believed."

While living in India, Longinus had shaved off his beard, not needing it for disguise. But when he headed west once more he let it grow. It had turned partially gray. When he reached Ephesus, he was glad he had his beard, for Ephesus was a city controlled by Romans, and, while it had been many years since his tenure as a soldier of Rome, he still feared exposure.

However, it turned out that it was not a Roman Longinus feared regarding detection. Living in the city was a Jew Longinus had seen in Jerusalem. He was older, of course, but Longinus was sure it was him. Longinus could not remember his name. He was the Jew who had been in the temple with Tarjan and Madradus on the day they returned—on the day Longinus decided to take up Eluid's offer and go east. Longinus was sure it was him. He could still hear him snarling, exhorting everyone to cooperate with Tarjan, lest Tarjan would have Pilate close the temple. Longinus would give this Jew a wide berth and was glad that the angel had not let him throw away the spear that day at the river.

In Ephesus, Longinus took a new name, or at least partially so. He called himself by his second name, Petronius. It took Petronius a few months to establish himself, but soon he became known to many and his trading business grew as his contacts grew.

One day a couple came into his store. Petronius did not recognize the man but he did remember the woman – even though she was much older. And just as he was sure he recognized the Jew who had been with Tarjan, he knew she was the woman who was the follower of Jesus. Petronius saw her face, and immediately he flashed back to the scourging of Jesus, to Golgotha, to the upper room where he had met her and the other followers. Longinus Petronius was sure it was her.

Petronius assumed the man was her husband. He did not recognize his face. Then he heard the man speak, and he remembered the tenor of the man's voice. A little softer than most men, particularly for his age. The man was the effeminate follower of Jesus to whom Jesus had given care of His mother after He died. Petronius studied the man's face and listened more to his voice. Yes, it was him. Petronius could not remember the man's name. He heard him call her 'Mary' and he heard her call him 'John'. Yes, now Petronius remembered. He was with Simon Peter that day Peter healed the lame man outside the Beautiful Gate.

John and Mary came into Petronius's store to buy a few provisions. They said they had just come from Jerusalem. They did not seem to recognize Longinus Petronius. Regardless, Petronius kept his eyes down, spoke only when required, and then in a lower voice. They purchased their few items and left the store. Petronius hoped that they were just passing through Ephesus. It was a crossroads city, and there were many travelers. However, over the course of the next few weeks Petronius saw them around the city several times. He always avoided them. He feared exposure, and did not want to dredge up those days from decades ago in Judea. Those days were gone. Good riddance.

But they were not over. Petronius learned that the Jew who had been with Tarjan in the temple was named Paul. Petronius remembered it as something different, but could not recall exactly what his name had been. By sheer force of will, Paul was a prominent figure in Ephesus. He was a tent-maker, but it was the tent that he was trying to draw people into that made him so public and controversial.

Petronius heard people in his store talking about Paul giving a series of lecture talks at a nearby school. They said he spoke boldly for Jesus. Petronius remembered when Paul was a Jew in Jerusalem he had threatened everyone in the temple to cooperate with the Romans. When Petronius now heard the others stating that Paul spoke boldly for Jesus,

Petronius wanted to interrupt the people and say: you've got that backwards, don't you? But Petronius controlled himself. He did not want to draw attention to himself, and he wanted no part of religion, whether it was Roman, Jewish, Hindu, or followers of Jesus (or, as they now called themselves, "Christians"). He remembered Thomas calling Jesus 'the Christ'.

At times, the stories he heard circulating about Paul became quite wild. Stories of how Paul's apron and handkerchief that he used when working would also heal wounds and cast out demons. Longinus Petronius thought of his spear. Maybe those stories were not so wild.

There was also a tale of a Jewish priest named Sceva, who, with his sons, tried to emulate Paul and cast out demons in the name of Jesus, only to have the demon turn on them as a false prophet. Now Ephesus was very much a pagan city inclined to believe in magic, and when Sceva and his sons were attacked by the demon, many came to believe that it was Paul and his Christ who held the true power, and many books on magic were destroyed.

Now emboldened, Paul attacked the local men who made silver idols to worship and sold them at the ornate Temple of Artemis, home of the pagan goddess of fertility. Even though Petronius did not believe in the power of the idols, he traded in these silver statues, making a handsome profit. He thought it was a silly superstition, but if he could make money off others' ridiculous religious beliefs that was fine by him. Let them waste their money.

Paul's exhortations against these silver statues began to draw increasing ire, particularly from one silversmith named Demetrius. Demetrius rallied together the craftsman who worked in and around Ephesus. They met one day in the great theater of Ephesus, which held many thousands of people. Because Petronius traded with these people, he attended this meeting.

The meeting became so wild at one point that a city clerk rose and tried to quiet the mob, reminding all that if they continued in such a way they could be charged with causing a riot. The crowd finally dispersed, but the ill feelings towards Paul and other Christians continued. The Christians, as they saw it, were a threat to the financial positions of the silversmiths and those connected to the temple of Artemis. Petronius remembered how Caiaphas and the other Jewish priests had feared Jesus as a financial and political threat. Now, Paul was doing the same thing.

One day not long after this near riot, Paul came into Petronius's store. Paul wanted to sell the last of his tents. He said he would be heading on to Macedonia. A few minutes later, John and Mary entered. They smiled at Paul, who smiled back. They talked amongst themselves for a few minutes. Petronius could not hear what they were saying, but it was clear that they knew each other.

Paul had several of his tents on a cart out on the street in the front of the store. He asked Petronius to take a look at them, which he did. John and Mary followed them out onto the cobblestone street. Petronius assumed they wished to speak to Paul once more before he left.

When Petronius bent over to inspect the tents, the spearhead fell out of his robe and hit the stones on the street, making a loud clanking noise. Petronius reached as quickly as he could to retrieve the spearhead, but Mary pointed at it.

"I have seen that before!" she gasped.

Petronius shoved the spearhead back into his robe and ignored her.

"Yes! I remember!" John added.

Petronius ignored him as well.

Paul looked at them then at Petronius.

"What price are you asking for your tents?" Petronius asked, hoping to get back on that issue.

He looked at Petronius. "That was a Roman spearhead."

"I trade for many things," Petronius answered.

"I saw that spearhead in the upper room in Jerusalem many years ago," John said.

"Yes," Mary added.

Paul looked directly at Petronius. "Years ago, in Jerusalem, before my conversion to the Lord, when I persecuted the followers of Jesus..." He

240

paused, and frowned an apology to John and Mary, who graciously smiled back. He looked back to Petronius. "…I assisted a Roman named Tarjan, who was searching for a centurion named Longinus. Longinus Petronius was his full name."

Petronius looked at Paul with as even a gaze as he could manage.

He studied Petronius. "He would now be about your age."

Mary broke in. "Malchus, a Jewish guard who served Caiaphas, told me that the spearhead possessed special powers. That the centurion named Longinus helped him and another man from Cyrene escape from the jail in the temple."

Petronius did not react.

"We also heard stories," John said, "that the spearhead could heal wounds."

Paul continued to study Petronius. "Petronius, where did you get that spearhead?"

"Like I told you, I traded for it."

Paul smiled. "You need to know that Tarjan is still looking for you. In fact, he cannot return to Rome until he finds you. And, as I remember, some manuscript that you wrote."

They had him. There was no use lying anymore. Longinus Petronius frowned and blew out a breath. "I know Tarjan is still hunting."

"You have seen him?" Paul asked.

"No. Thomas told me he was."

"Thomas?" John exclaimed.

"Yes."

John and Mary's eyes flashed and they looked at each other in surprise.

"Where did you see Thomas?" John asked.

Longinus looked at John, then Mary and Paul. "In India."

"India?" John gasped.

"Yes," I replied. "He was teaching of your Jesus there."

John smiled broadly. "Matthew went to Ethiopia. Now, Thomas in India. It goes on in ever further places!"

"So it seems," Longinus said simply.

"I repeat," Paul said, "Tarjan is determined to find you, and is very angry that he cannot return to Rome. He questioned Jesus's followers many times as to where you had fled and where the manuscript was. I saw him beat Peter. Every time Peter said that he did not steal the body of Jesus from the tomb but instead Jesus rose from the dead, Tarjan became very angry."

"Yes!" John jumped in. "Very angry. Tarjan called us stubborn and liars. He also questioned me very harshly, as well, but he did not beat me like he beat Peter."

"So why did you return after so many years away?" Paul asked.

Longinus told them of the hurricane and his family.

Paul listened then nodded. "I am sorry for your travail, but remember that things work to the good if you love God."

Longinus looked at him. Do they? At that moment, he longed for a cup of wine.

Then Paul told Longinus of his journey from Jerusalem to Damascus, of the vision of Jesus, of being blinded for three days and how his very soul was afire. Paul studied Longinus after he finished talking. "Do you believe such a thing?"

Longinus shrugged. "It is not important if I believe. Clearly, you do."

"Oh, you are so wrong. It does matter; it matters a great deal if you believe."

Longinus frowned at him. "I have a hard time believing in anything that I do not see for myself."

Paul pointed at where the spearhead was in Longinus's robe. "What have you seen with your spearhead?"

Longinus nodded. That was a good point. Then he remembered what Thomas had told him about those who did not see and still believed.

Paul looked at John and Mary, then turned back to Longinus. "Your secret, Longinus Petronius," emphasizing both of his names, "is safe with us."

Longinus thanked him. "You are traveling to Macedonia to preach?"

"Yes. Always," Paul answered.

"Always," John agreed.

Longinus shook his head in amazement. "After all these years."

"We have seen the truth. We cannot do otherwise," John said.

Longinus remembered Thomas saying similar words. He smiled, "Peace be with you."

"And also with you," Paul responded.

97

Archer looked at Lacy, then at Yatom, and then back at Lacy. "Longinus is tying all the New Testament together."

Lacy smiled a huge smile. "Yes, he is. He saw much of it."

Yatom pulled the page of papyrus from under the infrared camera and handed it to Archer, then slipped a new page under the camera. Yatom pointed at the new sheet and Lacy read it outloud.

98

Longinus saw Paul one more time. Approximately two years later, Paul was passing through Ephesus on his way to Jerusalem. Out of friendship, and to assure himself that Paul would keep his pledge of protecting his identity, Longinus went to hear Paul preach. Paul smiled and pointed at Longinus when he saw Longinus in the crowd. Paul talked of the travails that awaited him, but that he could not be concerned with that; his personal life was not as important as his teachings of Jesus and His love. "His love for us is patient," Paul said. "It endures through all, so we should endure through all. We must all fight the good fight until the very end."

Longinus was impressed with Paul's sincerity and courage. What could account for such conviction, for a transformation that had so completely reversed the course of his life? A simple vision of Jesus? Longinus had seen at least something with his spearhead. He was not exactly sure what, but it was something. That was for sure. And yet, he still did not believe. He asked himself why not. What was keeping him from believing, even though he had seen more than most?

Longinus frowned then bid Paul safe travels. As Paul left, Longinus knew his secret was safe with Paul. Longinus just did not know how safe Paul would personally be. Paul and Jerusalem would be a dangerous mix.

By that time, Mary had left Ephesus. Where she went, Longinus did not know. John remained in Ephesus, continuing his teachings. Occasionally, John would stop into Longinus's store to talk. He told Longinus that he had cared for Mary, the mother of Jesus, until she had died, just as he had promised Jesus on the cross. Longinus remembered that moment.

"Did you see Malchus's ear get cut off?" Longinus asked.

"I did. And then I saw Jesus heal him."

Longinus shook his head in wonder then thought of the spear. It, too, could heal.

"Before that, before He was arrested in the garden," John said, "Jesus was praying fervently. He was very distressed. At one point, He said to us, 'The spirit is strong, but the flesh is weak.'" John looked at Longinus. "And yet, despite His fear, He stayed true to His father's will—whereas all of us who followed Him failed completely. We all fled. Judas betrayed. Peter denied. But we were all guilty of giving in to our fears. Jesus was afraid, too, but He held true."

Longinus studied John as John remembered his shame. "And yet now you preach without fear."

John looked up and smiled. "Yes. But it took seeing the risen Jesus to change us. That, and the day of Pentecost when we were given the Holy Spirit." His face burst into a wide smile of bliss. His eyes flashed and he gazed upwards. "Truly, I tell you, it was the single most wonderful experience of my life! Nothing comes even remotely close. It was joy beyond all understanding. My words fail to adequately describe."

Longinus looked at him. At that moment, he was envious at what John had found.

"I lost my fear of death for I knew that a better life truly awaited."

Longinus remembered Jesus's face on the cross, the same face he had dreamed of on the Roman galley. He looked at John. "There is something I have always wanted to know."

John looked at Longinus in expectation.

"Just before Jesus died, he said 'It is finished.' I assume he was talking of his death."

"His death, yes. But really He was referring to His life." John turned to Longinus and looked him directly in the eye. "For, you see, He was sent here by His father to die for our sins."

"Thomas said the same thing to me."

John nodded and pointed at Longinus. "And you know the truth, too. Or at least, you did."

"What do you mean?" Longinus asked indignantly.

"I heard you. After he died, after the earthquake, I heard you call him the Son of God."

Longinus shook his head. "It was fear and irrational emotion. I was temporarily deluded."

"Nonsense! You were temporarily filled with the truth." He studied Longinus. "Why are you so stubborn in your disbelief, when you have seen what the spearhead can do, when you saw the rock roll back to reveal the empty tomb?"

Longinus pointed at him. "I have wished to ask you about that! Were you there that morning?"

"I was. Jesus appeared to Mary first. Then she came to us. We did not believe her at first. Then Peter and I ran to the tomb. I was younger and got there first," he said with a smile. "But it was Peter who went inside the tomb. And it was Peter who first understood that Jesus had risen."

Longinus looked at him. "Did you see me and my men?"

He nodded. "You were all asleep."

"The man atop the rock—"

"The angel." John shook his head in frustration. "You saw and you still do not believe! I have met thousands of believers who did not see what you saw, and yet they believe! Longinus! What will it take?"

Longinus looked at him. He did not have an answer.

"There is something that Paul did not mention. When he was persecuting us Christians, he was present when a young man named Stephen was stoned to death—perhaps, the first Christian martyr. Stephen, while being stoned, declared that he looked up and saw Jesus standing next to God. His belief was so strong that he was given that gift as he died." John paused and searched Longinus's face for a reaction. Longinus gave none.

"He believed, and then he saw. Whereas you…"

Longinus frowned.

"I am just discovering the full power of faith," John said. "God is revealing it to me ever more. He revealed it to Peter, who raised a dead person named Tabitha. Peter's mission continues. I heard he is going to Egypt soon. What you do not understand is that for we, the Disciples of Christ, we believers, this is not sacrifice and hardship. Instead, it is privilege. It is an opportunity to serve our Lord. And then we go to Him in the next life." He paused again and then pointed his finger at me. "You have been given a gift. And I am not just talking about the spearhead. You have seen. You have witnessed. You have written." John looked at Longinus in question. "Correct?"

Longinus nodded.

"The Cyrene told us that an angel directed you to write a manuscript." Longinus nodded again.

John smiled. "Few receive such gifts! And like us who lived with Jesus, you now have the privilege and opportunity to serve something bigger than all of us."

Longinus avoided John after that. He made Longinus feel uncomfortable. And yet, despite Longinus's attempts to forget what John had said, John's words grew inside Longinus, fermenting like the wine he drank. Had he truly received a gift, as he said? It did not feel like a gift. More like an affliction, a burden. Why was he chosen to carry this burden?

Shortly after that, word came that Peter had been captured in Rome and crucified upside down. Then Paul, captured in Jerusalem, asked for a trial before the Emperor and was beheaded. Before that, they heard that James, the brother of Jesus, had been stoned to death. And yet, they all stayed true to their cause—even in the face of death. They had also supposedly written many manuscripts between them. Longinus remembered John's words: that serving the Lord is a privilege and death only means a new life in heaven. Was that really true?

99

Yatom inserted yet another new page under the infrared camera. He smiled at both of them. "Shall we finish?"

"Or is it: are we finished?" Archer asked.

"Nope," Lacy said. "It's more of a case of having just begun."

100

About a year after Longinus Petronius heard that Paul had been beheaded, a Roman patrol was racing through the streets of Ephesus on horseback. They raced by Petronius's store. One soldier lost control of his horse and slammed into an old wooden cart that carried goods to trade at Petronius's store. The cart, old and weak, broke apart upon impact. A large, jagged splinter broke off and flew into a small boy standing nearby.

Petronius came out of his store to see what the commotion was and saw the boy. Petronius had seen many wounds in battle and he knew that this was a fatal wound. He also knew he had no choice.

Petronius knelt beside the boy, who was held by his crying, pleading father. Petronius inspected the wound, pulled out as much of the splinter as he could, and then pulled the spearhead from his robe. It had been years since he had used it to heal. Would it do so once more?

Petronius touched the spear to the deep wound in the boy's stomach, and instantly it healed. The father gasped. He touched the boy's stomach. Gone was the gouge.

Everyone standing around was amazed. The Roman centurion in charge of the patrol dismounted and inspected the boy. Then he looked at Petronius. "How did you do that?"

Petronius shook his head and mumbled, "I didn't."

"Is this another magical trick for which Ephesus is so famous?"

Petronius shook his head, and said firmly, "It's not magic."

The centurion looked at the spearhead. "That is a Roman spearhead."

Petronius frowned. "I found it in the desert."

"I am taking it with me."

"Please do not."

The centurion reached to grab it. Petronius jerked it back and then pointed it at him. Immediately, the centurion fainted and fell to the stone street. Again, everyone around them was amazed.

"How?" the father asked, wide-eyed. "How do you do such things?"

Petronius shook his head. He stuck the spearhead in his robe. Now what? Leave Ephesus? He was tired of running. Maybe the incident would be forgotten. Regardless, he did not regret saving the boy.

A month later, Petronius received his answer. A Roman centurion entered the store. It was not the same one who had fainted on the street in front of the store, but Petronius recognized him. It was Quintus, his former soldier, who was now a centurion. Quintus came through the door, looked at Petronius, then moved to the side. Another man followed him. It was Tarjan.

Tarjan walked to Petronius and smiled. "Longinus Petronius, in the name of Emperor Nero, you are under arrest."

Petronius reached for his spear, but Quintus grabbed his arms. Tarjan reached in and pulled out the spearhead. Longinus Petronius hoped he would point it at himself or at Quintus and that they would maybe faint, but Tarjan pointed the tip down. He smiled at Petronius in conquest. Petronius wanted to spit in his face.

"Take him away," Tarjan ordered.

Petronius was thrown in jail. From here on he determined he might as well revert to his first name of Longinus. They knew who he was.

A few hours later the door opened. In walked Quintus.

"I see you were made centurion," Longinus said.

"Yes," was all he said.

Then Tarjan entered. He studied Longinus.

"You have been on my trail all these years?" Longinus asked with a slight smile, feeling some satisfaction at knowing the misery that had been inflicted on him.

"I have. I was told earlier today that you went to India."

"I did."

"Better for you if you had stayed. I will make this easy for you. If you tell me where you hid your manuscript, I will spare you the death sentence. I will intercede with the Emperor."

251

This reminded Longinus of when Caiaphas had made a similar claim after the tomb was found empty. Longinus looked at Tarjan. "I will be freed?"

"I did not say that. You will rot in jail for the rest of your miserable life. But you will live."

"Not much of a life."

Tarjan shrugged. "You made your choices."

"And if I do not tell you?"

Tarjan smiled slightly. "Then Quintus has ways of convincing you."

Longinus looked at Quintus, who gave no reaction.

"You do not deny the existence of the manuscript," Tarjan noted.

"Would it do any good?"

"It would not. I will give you this night to think it over. In the morning you will answer." Without further comment, he turned and left. Quintus paused and looked at Longinus.

"Where are Madradus and Philo?" Longinus asked.

"Both died honorable deaths in battle."

"I doubt either had the first idea about what honor was. They were nothing but thugs with a sword and a lash. …But, Quintus, you always struck me as a little different."

His eyes were guarded. "I will do my duty. You know that."

He did know that. Longinus nodded and Quintus left. It would be dark soon. With morning would come the moment of truth: either he told Tarjan where he hid the first manuscript or he did not. If he did, then he went to prison, assuming Tarjan could be trusted—which was a question in itself. If he did not, he would be whipped and he knew in his heart that he would succumb sooner or later. He had seen many men tortured, and they all gave in at the end. Longinus had no illusions. He would, too. The issue was not defeat. The issue was how many lashes before defeat came.

Then a thought came to Longinus. No, not everyone. Jesus did not give in. He endured through it all. He was the only one that Longinus had ever seen do this. Everyone else surrendered in some way, but not Him. To the very end He proclaimed that He was the Son of God. He never balked or denied or lied. And He could have. Just a few simple words and He could have freed himself. But He didn't.

"Only Jesus…" Longinus muttered out loud. He closed his eyes and he saw the beaten and bloody face of Jesus on the cross, the face that he had seen previously in his dreams. "Only Jesus," he mumbled again.

Why was that? What made Him different? What allowed Him to be stronger? He remembered when he stood at the scourging pole before it began. Jesus had that long-distance stare; a look of resignation and yet resolve. How did He get that? Or, was the question, from where did He get that?

Longinus considered for a moment the option of telling Tarjan where the first manuscript was hidden—assuming it was still there; if it had not already been found or destroyed by weather or humans. Tarjan did not know of the existence of the second manuscript, so if he told Tarjan about the first one then the second one would still survive. Then he thought about what was in that first manuscript. The story of Golgotha, the empty tomb, the power of the spear. Those were important stories that needed to be told. He felt himself jerk back in surprise. Why did he care? Why did he care whether those stories were told or not? But he did. A part of him wanted those stories to be read. Why?

Longinus thought on this for some time. He did not have anything else to do.

Should he resist giving up the first manuscript out of spite, as a way to keep inflicting misery on Tarjan? Was that a victory? Was that all that was left to him? Perhaps, but then that was not much of a victory. All that did was make him a lower person and he sensed after meeting Thomas, Paul, John, and Mary that if that was his motivation then he was losing just as much as Tarjan was. These Christians were motivated more by moving towards a positive rather than avoiding a negative. This was something new. It was not normal human behavior as he had witnessed it in his life across the Roman Empire and beyond. So he knew that denying Tarjan, as fulfilling as that would be in the short run, was not a sufficient reason. There had to be more.

Longinus also knew he was not the only one who could tell the story of that day at Golgotha and the events after. John and the others could, as well. But he still had something to contribute to it: his perspective, his actions. What he saw and did. Was his attachment to these stories because he was involved? Because he was a part of them and they were a part of him? Was it about him?

Yes. That was part of it. But not all. For some reason he wanted those stories told for their own sake. Why? Then a little voice spoke in the back of his mind: because you know they are the truth.

Longinus shook his head as if he could fling the thought from him like a dog flinging water from its coat. But the thought would not dislodge. He longed to lose his thoughts in a large flask of wine.

Was it the truth? That is the real question. Was what he'd seen the truth?

Longinus ruminated on this for the next few hours, as light slipped from his cell and left him in darkness. Was it the truth? He recounted all that he had seen and heard after he arrived in Jerusalem with Pilate. He had heard that mysterious voice in the temple. It was not a trick. He saw Jesus on the cross. He heard Jesus tell that robber that he would be in heaven the very day. He heard Jesus forgive on the cross. He saw and felt the earthquake. He saw those things. He heard those things. He knew Jesus was dead. He drove the spear deep into Him. He saw the angel atop the rock at the tomb; that was not a hallucination or a magic trick. He saw Malchus's ear, the fingerprint, and then the power of the spearhead to repel and heal, but not harm.

Longinus knew in his head the truth of these things. Then he realized he was not the only one. The followers of Jesus, by their deeds and behavior, testified to the truth. Their commitment over these years since the empty tomb was stunning. They had stayed true. Why? He answered himself. They saw the truth, too! They were filled with conviction, courage, hope, and joy.

Longinus remembered the disciples before the resurrection. How he had disdained them. "Blemished sheep" was what he had called them.

Liars, deniers, betrayers. Cowards all. John admitted as much. Then they changed. And now several of them had died. Peter and James for sure. Paul, too. They'd faced death and yet stayed true. They were willing to go to their deaths professing the truth that they knew. What could account for this type of transformation? Then once more he answered himself: they saw the truth. They knew the truth and then were given this special spirit that John and the others described. Knowing this truth emboldened and strengthened them. He remembered how John said death had lost its grip on him. Paul said similar things. If it had all been a lie, a grand conspiracy, at least one of them would have broken during the beating and imminent threat of death. People do not die for a lie. People do not die for something that they know is a lie.

"It's true," Longinus muttered. "It's true!" he said again, this time a little louder. Longinus collected as much air in his lungs as he could. He tilted his head back and yelled as loudly as he could, "It is true!"

A guard rattled the lock on the door. Longinus did not care. What could they really do to him? Nothing of true consequence. He was free. For the first time in his life he was truly free.

He got on his knees and prayed. He prayed to God. He prayed to Jesus to fill him up. And when he did, a great swelling filled his chest. A wonderful sensation swept through every part of him just as John had described. Then, suddenly, a light appeared in the cell. And in this light he saw Jesus. He was smiling.

At that moment, Longinus realized that Jesus was the true lamb of Passover. He had, as Thomas declared, sacrificed himself for all of them. Just as Longinus would have given his life to save just one of his children after the hurricane, Jesus had sacrificed His life for them. Except Jesus had a choice. He could have run. But He stood fast. He died for them. For their sins. Longinus looked at the smiling face of Jesus and smiled back. Then the light faded and Longinus knew what he had to do. And he knew the truth of John's words: serving the Lord was a privilege, not just a duty.

When Tarjan, Quintus, and another soldier entered Longinus's cell the next morning, Tarjan studied Longinus and then glared. "What are you smiling about?"

Longinus shook his head. "Nothing you would understand."

Longinus turned and looked at Quintus, who looked back at him in question. Quintus could tell something had happened. But he did not understand.

Longinus refused to tell them where he had hidden the manuscript. Subsequently, he was beaten: forty lashes. His back and sides were slashed and bruised. The next day it was the same. And the day after that. Longinus noticed Quintus himself did not deliver the lash. He watched with a frown.

Longinus prayed incessantly; before the lashing, during the lashing, and then after. He prayed not for an escape or an end to the lashes, but to be strong, to stay true. And true he stayed; the image of Jesus on the cross ever present in his mind.

Tarjan was furious. Then he got an idea.

Longinus was dragged to the local blacksmith. Tarjan pulled out the spearhead and gave it to Quintus. Quintus held it over the blacksmith's pit of fire.

"I will melt your spearhead," Tarjan announced. "Tell me where you hid the manuscript or I melt the spearhead!"

Longinus did not answer.

Tarjan repeated his demand. Again, he did not answer. Tarjan motioned to Quintus to drop the spearhead into the fire. But as Quintus moved the spearhead towards the burning coals, suddenly he dropped it to the ground. The spear glowed with heat. It had burned Quintus's hand. Tarjan tried to pick up the spearhead, and his hand was burned as well.

Tarjan turned on Longinus and glared. "I will have you burnt in oil in Rome!" He screamed in agony and then ran off. Quintus stuck his hand in the pail of water the blacksmith used. Then he ordered the soldiers to throw Longinus back in the cell.

Tarjan decided to have Longinus shipped to Rome for trial and execution. A Roman galley was due to arrive in Ephesus the next week. Longinus would be on it. Tarjan knew he himself could not return without the manuscript. He hoped Longinus would give up the location of the manuscript when he was further tortured in Rome.

That night Quintus entered Longinus's cell, his hand wrapped in a cloth. Quintus studied Longinus then said, "I always knew you were stubborn, but until now I did not understand just how much."

Longinus gazed evenly back at him. "Maybe it is something more than stubbornness."

Once more he examined Longinus's face in question. "What do you mean?"

Now it was Longinus's turn to say: "I think you know."

Quintus frowned. "So, you are now filled with this religion."

Longinus beamed. "I am. And it has filled me in ways I never knew. It is sweeter than any wine."

Quintus shook his head. "You are going to die a horrible death."

"No doubt, but I shall live again."

Quintus scoffed. He scoffed as Longinus had scoffed before.

"I will do one thing for you though," Longinus said.

Quintus looked at Longinus. "What's that?"

"I will heal your burned hand."

"And just how will you do that?"

"Bring me the spearhead, and I will show you."

Quintus shook his head. "You will use it to escape."

"I will not. I give you my word."

Quintus looked directly at Longinus and Longinus did not divert his eyes. He glanced down at his bandaged hand before turning to leave. He returned a short while later with the spearhead.

"You promise you will not use it to escape?"

"I do. In the name of my Lord."

Quintus frowned then handed Longinus the spearhead. Longinus unwrapped Quintus's bandage and placed the spearhead on the burn.

Instantly, it healed. Quintus gasped and he looked at Longinus wide-eyed. Longinus handed the spearhead back to Quintus.

"I have one more request," Longinus said.

Quintus stared at him, still wide-eyed, and then nodded.

"Bring me some sheets of papyrus, a stylus, and some ink."

Quintus looked at him in question. "Tarjan will destroy any manuscript you write."

Longinus looked at him. "Not if you hide it."

"I could get in big trouble if I help you."

Longinus nodded. "Yes. There is a risk."

The following morning Quintus entered Longinus's cell. He had several sheets of papyrus and a stylus. "I am sorry. There was no ink to be found."

Longinus nodded. "Sometimes we have to make do with less and do the best we can."

Longinus sat down and began indenting the papyrus with the tip of the stylus.

"This is my third testimonium," he started. "Though my fingers are bruised from the beatings, I force myself to write. And while I have no ink, I pray that the message will still be received."

It took Longinus three days to write the third testimonium, to tell of India and Ephesus, of the continuing power of the spearhead, of his capture by Tarjan, of his conversion to the Lord. He ended with a simple statement: "So goes my story, a story of finding the truth and being changed by it. I pray that it helps someone else come to the Lord. I now prepare to be sent to Rome for almost certain execution. But I do not fear. For I have seen the truth and it has set me free."

After he was done, Longinus persuaded Quintus to hide it in a sealed jar. Longinus gave him a clue of where he had hidden the second manuscript. If someone found that one, they could find the first.

"Why are you telling me these things?" Quintus asked.

258

Longinus smiled. "So that now you are part of something bigger than yourself. You now have responsibility for the future of all the manuscripts. Upon you the truth relies."

Quintus studied Longinus. "You are taking a risk trusting me."

"Life is a risk."

"And the spearhead?" Quintus asked.

"Hide it with the third manuscript."

"Tarjan will ask about it."

"Tell him you threw it away. Just don't tell him where you threw it. Also, I will write a short note. Wrap the note around the spearhead."

Quintus looked at his healed hand then looked at Longinus. "I shall do all these things you ask of me. You were always fair to me."

101

Archer finished reading and looked at Lacy. "As I expected: Longinus did convert. So Tarjan's Lament becomes the main document, the 'unbiased' document to counter Kitchens."

Lacy shook her head. "Just the third one. During the first two, Longinus was still a nonbeliever."

"People will not make that distinction. It's all or nothing."

Lacy frowned and nodded. "But the three testimoniae by Longinus are also crucial."

"Yes. They confirm Biblical accounts."

She smiled. "Do you still think we shouldn't go back to Turkey to find that spearhead?"

Archer blew out a breath and nodded. "We've got to try."

"Where do you think the spearhead is?" Yatom asked.

Lacy turned to Yatom to answer him then snapped her mouth closed.

He pressed on. "You were in Selçuk. We know that. Before you got on that sailboat. After being at the Celsus Library ruin during the earthquake."

She looked at him. "How do you know we were at Celsus?"

Yatom scoffed. "Are you kidding? Besides Rosenberg, there is an arrest warrant out on both of you. Two fatwahs as well. You will surely be recognized if you go back there. Turkey and you are not a good mix. Why not let us find the spearhead for you?"

She looked at him and shook her head. "I don't know you. Therefore, I don't trust you."

Yatom nodded. "Listen, Dr. Stowe, you are talking to someone in the suspicion business, so I accept that you do not trust me, because I don't trust anybody—including you."

Lacy's lips betrayed a small smile. "Okay. Just as long as we understand each other."

Yatom nodded again. "But understand this: just as you do not want us to go to Turkey without you, we will not permit you to go without us.

And, if necessary, we will go alone. Obviously, it is in our best interest if you are there to lead us. But you will not be permitted to go without us."

Yatom drove Lacy, Archer, and the canisters to a safe-house in western Jerusalem. He made sure they had food, clean towels, and toilet paper. He kept Lacy's pistol. "There are no phones or computers. You have already dumped your cell phones. Do not leave the house without permission from me. If you try, the guards will stop you and, if you do not stop at their command …well, it will not turn out well for you. Stay here. Eat, rest. I'll be back tomorrow with the manuscripts."

He was wrong. It was two days. And he was not alone when he returned.

The door opened and Yatom entered. Without uttering a word, he double-checked that there was no one else present, then turned and nodded to someone behind him. A tall, elegant woman appeared in the doorway. Yatom motioned to her. "Doctors Stowe and DeYoung, this is Ms. Esti Laslo, the Prime Minister of Israel."

Yatom got a chair from the kitchen and Laslo pointed at the spot in the living room where she wanted it placed. She sat down, pulled her dress into place, and then looked directly at Lacy and Archer, who were sitting on a sofa. "I think in America you used to have a show called, 'Let's Make a Deal'."

102

"I have read the translation of all the manuscripts. Truly an incredible find of great historical significance. But even more important to me is its potential significance for today. This is Palm Sunday, a special day that ties Israel to the United States." Laslo paused and looked directly at Lacy.

Lacy smiled, appreciating that the Prime Minister remembered.

"Your country has drifted away from its historical religious roots, away from the Judeo-Christian ethic. This bill by your Senator Kitchens is not only an assault on American Christians, but is also a threat to Israel. Like it or not, my country depends upon American support. We have nuclear weapons, but can use them only as a last resort. So we rely on America. America has done so in the past because of our close cultural and religious ties. Kitchens's bill threatens that."

Laslo rose and looked down on Archer and Lacy. "We need a Christian America that wants to protect Israel because it is the Holy Land, the site of Jesus's birth, life, and death. Only a Christian America will want to protect Israel for those reasons. A secular America would not. An America led by Kitchens and the Secular Humanist Party will not."

Lacy cleared her throat. "Madame Prime Minister, you said you read all the manuscripts?"

"I did."

"And you are not concerned about the part where Malchus told Longinus that Caiaphas, the head priest, confessed that Jesus just might be the Messiah? Aren't you worried by this?"

The Prime Minister smiled. "That was long ago. I am worried about today. And let's just say that we think Caiaphas was a little misguided, caught up in the emotion and fog of the moment. Besides, if that gets out, won't even more Americans want to protect Israel?"

Good point, thought Lacy. She looked at Laslo. "If we go to Turkey with your Mossad agent," she motioned towards Yatom, "and find the spearhead, do we get to keep it?"

"Absolutely," the Prime Minister assured her, "and the manuscripts, as well. We *want* them published. The vote on Kitchens's bill is in five days. There is no time to waste."

Lacy looked at Archer, who nodded. Turning to Laslo, she asked, "When do we leave?"

103

"I won't leave the canisters!"

Arthur placed his hand on Lacy's forearm. "We must."

Yatom sat down next to her. "The Prime Minister assured me that, if necessary, she would personally fly the canisters to America."

Lacy shook her head. "It's like abandoning children."

Archer leaned towards her. "What if we're captured in Turkey in possession of the canisters? What happens to the canisters then?"

She frowned. He was right.

Thirty minutes later they arrived in a windowless van inside a warehouse. Yatom helped them out of the van and pointed at a transparent tube. "Get in the capsule."

Archer stopped in his tracks. He looked at the giant pipe. It resembled an enormous conduit used to suck mail from one place to another. "What is that?"

Yatom nodded. "Evacuated Tube Transfer. Works on a vacuum. We'll be in Haifa in seven minutes."

Archer stared at the capsule sitting in the tube. Lacy grabbed his hand, smiled, and pulled. "Come on. First time for everything. Besides, time is short. We don't really have a choice, do we?"

Archer frowned. "We always have a choice."

Yatom guided them into the capsule and helped them with their safety belts. Then he pulled the clear top over them and secured the latch.

"Have you done this before?"

Yatom smiled at Archer. "Yes. Dozens of times." He closed the door on the capsule, pressurized it with oxygen, and activated the vacuum valve. It took two minutes for the vacuum to reach operative level. He looked at Archer and Lacy. "Here we go," he said, as he pressed the button.

Six and a half minutes later they stopped at another port seventy miles away. Archer gasped as he stepped out of the capsule. They had moved so fast in the vacuum of the partially lighted tunnel that Archer at times thought they were almost floating. Then when he stepped on solid ground Archer's body had the tingling sensation of still moving.

Yatom smiled. "What a way to travel, huh?" He handed them burqas. "Put these on."

Archer stared at the female Muslim dress. "You're kidding."

"You are going as women."

"But, but…"

Lacy laughed. "Come on, Archer. You're from Harvard. They *like* cross-dressers. They think they're sophisticated and avant-garde."

He groaned. "I can't believe I let an Aggie *drag* me into this."

She laughed harder.

They pulled the burqas over their clothes and got in another windowless van. Ten minutes later, they boarded the INS Golda Meir—a Super-Dolphin II class submarine.

"I've never been on a submarine before," Lacy said with a tone of anticipation.

Archer grunted. "Windowless vans, vacuum tubes, and now submarines. It's a good thing I don't suffer from claustrophobia."

The submarine put out to sea immediately. As they submerged, Lacy turned to Archer. "Two thousand years ago, on this day of the week before Passover, Christ entered Jerusalem in triumph on a donkey. The hinge of history had begun… whereas we sneak out of the Holy Land in a vacuum tube and then underwater."

Archer looked at her. "Yes, but the missions are still similar. Jesus entered to save. We are leaving to save the message of Longinus Petronius."

She smiled at him. "We?"

"Oui."

She looked directly at him. "And what about saving the message of Jesus?"

Archer smiled, and then lifted his right thumb and forefinger and held them an inch apart. "Wee."

104

It would take twenty hours for the INS Golda Meir to reach the Turkish coast. Lacy was led to separate quarters, while Yatom and Archer bunked together. Archer had just taken off his burqa and laid his head on the pillow of his bunk when Yatom set in with the questions.

"So, Archer, you and Stowe have something of a past, huh?"

Archer did not look at Yatom, who was sitting in a chair at the small desk. "Just why do you need to know?"

"Simple. We're on an op. I need to know how the team works together."

He eyed Yatom. "We work well enough."

"That's not what I heard. I heard you two were rivals; all but enemies."

He propped himself up on his elbow and eyed Yatom. "Just what are you getting at?"

"I think you know. There are two Americas. One, old and tired and religious. The other, new and vibrant and free of religion. She is old. You are new... like me."

Archer laid back on the pillow and looked at the ceiling. "Maybe I'm older than you think."

"I don't think so." He paused. "You know where the spearhead is."

"I never saw it," Archer replied without looking at Yatom.

"That is not what I said. You know—"

"Listen!" Archer threw his legs over the side of his bunk and pivoted towards Yatom. "I know what you're trying to do and it won't work. Lacy will show you where she thinks the spearhead is, and she won't do that until we get back there. So you'll just have to wait."

"What if she gets killed beforehand?"

"Well, then, we'd just better make sure she stays alive."

"We?"

"We."

105

Laslo ordered Jensen transferred to Mossad custody. Then Jensen, McKenzie, and the Muslim were moved to a remote Mossad facility. Laslo ordered them held there. She would decide what to do with them after the excursion into Turkey to find the spear of the centurion.

The Attorney General of Virginia, under great pressure from the Department of Justice, announced Monday that the case against Lester Dunsette for murdering Gordon Sharp and threatening the daughter of Senator Damian Kitchens with kidnapping would go to a grand jury as soon as possible.

Meanwhile, that same morning of Monday, April 15, the Select Senate Committee approved Kitchens's bill in a strictly partisan vote. The Senate Majority leader immediately announced it would go to a vote by the full Senate this Friday. Debate would begin immediately.

Mini-D was also busy tracing McKenzie's GPS. It notified Nick that McKenzie's cell was in Jerusalem.

"Jerusalem," Nick repeated. "And your judgment concerning this?"

"McKenzie has been captured by the Israelis while attempting to seize Stowe and DeYoung. Thus, Israel knows about Stowe and DeYoung."

Nick nodded. Makes sense. He looked at the computer's lens. "And your projection into the future?"

"I deduct with a 73.7% probability that Stowe and DeYoung are returning to Turkey."

"Turkey?"

"Based on the documents Rosenberg released, there is a 62.4% chance that the spearhead is still in Turkey."

Nick called the mullah in New York, who called Mullah Obar in Turkey.

106

The long hours on the submarine gave Lacy and Archer some time to catch up on their sleep. The following day Archer walked to Lacy's cabin. He knocked and waited.

"Who is it?" The sound of Lacy's voice traveled under the metal door.

"Archer."

"Entre," came her cheery reply.

Archer opened the door and popped his head around the side, receiving the smile he'd hoped for. "Got a minute?"

"I don't know. I'm pretty busy. I was going for a walk outside."

He chuckled. "Better bring a wetsuit."

She smiled again. "What's up?"

Archer closed the door behind him and pointed at the copy of the Torah she was reading.

"I looked for a Bible." Lacy waved her hand dismissively. "But this is an Israeli ship."

He nodded and sat down in a chair. "So have you decided what you're going to do if we find the spearhead?"

"Display it, I guess, along with the manuscripts."

Archer stroked his whiskers. "Do you really think it has special powers?"

"Longinus said so. And I don't think he was a liar."

He considered this thoughtfully. "Yeah, he has credibility. No doubt about it. Maybe the real question is whether the spearhead and the manuscripts will stop Kitchens?"

Lacy shook her head. "Don't know. But it's worth a try. If that doesn't do it, then nothing will. And then, at least, people will have no excuse- not that they did anyway. After all, as Paul said: 'this wasn't done in a corner.'"

"Maybe, but I still think God keeps himself hidden."

She rolled her eyes. "That again? I think you're missing the point."

"Oh, I am, huh? So then what's the point?"

"That God showed up as a real man who sacrificed Himself on the cross."

"Maybe. I think many people don't believe 'cause they're scared to. You know, fear of the unknown. Not being in control. Surrender."

Lacy's eyebrows rose and she nodded. "True enough. ...And you?"

Archer paused. "I guess I'm a little less scared than I used to be."

She smiled.

He looked at her. "Have you ever had doubts?"

She nodded slowly. "Those who speak, do not know, and those who know, do not speak."

"Excuse me?"

"That's from the Tao."

"*You* read the Tao?"

"I did. Parts of it, at least. There was a time, while I was an undergrad, that I questioned."

"Really? What brought you back?"

Lacy looked around, shaking her head. "God's patience. His love." She paused and studied him. "What's holding you back? As far as your faith, I mean."

He looked up at her and bit his lower lip, then shrugged. "I guess as much as anything it is that I still see most Christians as hypocrites."

She chuckled sarcastically. "Because they are."

"They are? I expected you to deny that."

"What would be the use of that? Christians *are* hypocrites. Because they are human beings. They're not perfect. In fact, at the very heart of Christianity is the admission that they are utterly *im*perfect, and the only way to go forward is by accepting the gift of grace that Jesus Christ bought on the cross. That's the *only* pathway to God. So Christians are not perfect. They are just forgiven."

"I thought Christians were supposed to repent and then go out and sin no more."

She shook her head. "Not even remotely realistic. Yes, repent. That is truly crucial. And then go out and try to sin *less*. And when you inevitably sin again, ask again for forgiveness. C.S. Lewis argues that this process is the true building block of faith. You only develop faith after you conclude that you cannot win salvation by your own acts, that Christ's finished work on the cross did that."

Archer thought on her words for a few moments and he took her silence as she letting him have his space. He looked down at the floor. Do I really want to say this next thing? He looked up at her. "I… want you to know something."

She nodded slightly. "Okay."

He pursed his lips. "No matter how this turns out, I want you to know…" he cringed. He looked down again, then back up, straight into her eyes. "I want you to know that I admire you."

Her mouth fell open and slowly folded into a smile.

Before she had a chance to say anything, he added, "Well, one thing's for sure: you sure ain't boring."

Lacy laughed.

Archer was beginning to chuckle, too. "Earthquakes, sailboats, sharks, river crossings, wild balloon rides, being shot at and chased by police, governments and whole religions, rides in vacuum tubes, and now," he waved at the boat around them, "a submarine, courtesy of the Prime Minister of Israel."

She smirked and flipped her hand up in an ostentatious manner. "Just trying to show you a good time."

There was a knock at the door. Yatom stuck his head in, and his eyes flashed.

Archer looked at him. He's wondering what we were talking about. He's wondering if I told her about his attempt to get information from me.

Yatom cleared his throat. "We have arrived." He pointed at the burqa. "Get dressed. Leave behind anything that identifies you. We surface in ten minutes."

107

"Archer, hand up the bag with the inflatable raft."

Archer looked up through the hatch at Yatom, in his white thawb robe with keffiyeh head gear and agal rope to keep it in place. He passed the bag up to him and a few seconds later heard a whoosh as the raft inflated. Yatom motioned for them to climb the ladder. Lacy went first and he followed. Climbing the ladder in a burqa was awkward. He kept stepping on the ends of it. No wonder women don't wear long dresses very often.

Archer stuck his head above the hatch, sucked in a full breath, and peered through the netting over his eyes. The Turkish coast was a mile away, the closest the captain dared bring his boat.

Yatom slid the raft over the side and held the rope. He pointed at the raft and they slid down into it. As they pulled on their single oars, Lacy turned to Archer. "On this Monday, 2,000 years ago, Jesus overturned the tables of the money changers."

Yatom at the front of the raft looked over his shoulder at him. "What's her point?"

"She has no point," Archer grinned wryly. "It's one of her many charms."

One hour after dusk fell as they pulled the raft ashore, their burqas and robe dipping in the surf. Yatom pulled out a knife, punctured the raft, dragged it across the beach and threw it behind a rock. Archer heard a voice to their right. "Tamir." He turned to see a medium-sized man in a thawb rise from behind a rock.

Yatom smiled. "Canberk." Yatom introduced all. "You got papers for me?"

"As always. The van is nearby. It will take about an hour to get to Celsus."

Canberk led them through a gorge in the hill overlooking the beach. When he reached the van, he opened the rear door. A wall of boxes met them. Canberk smiled. "Books."

"Books?"

Canberk looked at the burqa from where Lacy's voice came and replied "'For by wise guidance you will wage war.' Proverbs 24:6."

She chuckled. "You've got that right."

Canberk lifted half a dozen boxes from the van, exposing a cavity. "Get in."

108

Nick sat down as his office desk. He reached to activate Mini-D, but, before he touched the key, a female voice came out: "I've cracked Mossad's computer."

He looked up at the computer eye. "I thought Mossad was unhackable."

"Yes, and the Titanic was unsinkable. I confirmed DeYoung and Stowe are back in Turkey."

"I already had Mullah Obar in Turkey alerted."

"I know you did."

He listened to Mini-D's report about the hacking of Mossad's computer and the mission led by Yatom, then he alerted the mullah in New York to once more contact Obar.

109

"Well, I guess, in its own way, this is all appropriate."

Lacy looked at the dark space from where Archer's voice had come. "How's that?"

His fingers scratched one of the cardboard boxes next to him. "We're heading back to an ancient library while surrounded by books."

She smiled even though he could not see her. "True enough." Oh, Lord, please guide and protect us in our mission. Her weight shifted towards the front of the van and the engine stopped whining and started rumbling. They were slowing down. Why? She turned to her right, towards the front. "What's going on?"

Yatom's voice returned through the wall of boxes separating her from him in the front passenger seat. "A weigh station. Just west of Ortaklar. Keep quiet."

The van stopped and the weight of the vehicle shifted backward. Electric lights from outside filtered over the top of the boxes. Lacy heard the sound of Canberk's window sliding down. In Turkish, someone directed him to do something. The van shifted sideways as it positioned on the platform. Canberk's door creaked as it opened, as did Yatom's. Both doors closed. Voices could be heard a distance of maybe twenty feet from the van. She perked her ears but could not discern what was being said. She said another silent prayer.

Then there was the sound of hard-soled boots alongside the van, marching towards the rear, and a key scratched on the back lock. There was a click and a rush of sound as the back door swung open and fresh air rolled in. A shaft of light shot over the top of the boxes and seeped into the cavity where they sat, casting odd shadows. A Turkish voice spoke, sharp and authoritative. Canberk answered something back. Lacy understood only one word: "kitaplar"—Turkish for 'books'.

More was said in rapid-fire sentences. Then silence. There was the sound of gravel crunching under a boot. The van jerked down and the frame creaked. The guard must have stepped up onto the back bumper. A beam of light shone over the top of the boxes and angled a few inches down. Lacy's eyes jumped to Archer, who sat frozen. There was just enough light that she could see his eyes bulging so much they threatened to poke through the netting of his burqa.

The light swung left then right, and up and down as much as the boxes would allow. There was a scraping noise as one of the boxes at the top was pulled out. The van shifted again as the guard stepped off the back bumper again. Lacy heard a knife cutting through tape and cardboard flaps being pulled back. Then Canberk's voice. "Kitaplar."

The van jerked once more as the guard stepped up on the bumper. The flashlight clicked and the beam of light shot through the hole where the box had been. It hit the top of Archer's head. He slid lower. Then the light swept over Lacy. Archer pointed to his right, lifted his buttocks off the floorboard, scooted over towards the wall of books at the rear, and slowly set his weight down, getting as close to the boxes as he could. She did the same, easing to her left. As she set herself down, she reached to the small of her back and pulled out the pistol. Archer's eyes bulged again as he shook his head.

Then in came the flashlight, first the lens, then the tube, followed by the hand, then the forearm, the elbow and upper arm—like a snake sliding into a room, back arched and flexed. The boxes stopped the man's shoulder. The ones which Archer and Lacy were leaning on pressed against them and threatened to cave in on them. Lacy looked up, and there was the chin of the guard, then his lower lip, his tongue—like a snake, tasting the air. She tightened her grip on the pistol.

For what seemed like forever, the guard hung there, sweeping the light into the cavity, just missing their heads. Then the van shifted again as the guard stepped off the bumper. The cardboard box of books was shoved back into place and the back door was closed. Darkness. There was only the light from the weigh station sliding over the front of the boxes. The sound of boots crunching on the ground passed them towards the front. She let out a long, slow breath.

A few minutes later, both front doors opened and the van shifted as Canberk and Yatom got back in. The van engine started and the vehicle edged forward off the scales, turned left, and then accelerated. "Whew. That was close," Archer said.

Lacy exhaled audibly, and then slid to the front of the cavity. "Yatom, how much longer to Celsus?"

"Maybe ten to fifteen minutes."

A few minutes later Canberk uttered a Turkish curse as a siren sounded; over the top of the boxes came flashes of red and blue. Police.

The van pulled over. Lacy heard an engine idling behind them. Doors opened and closed; first the police car then both doors on the van. There were footsteps at the rear doors, Turkish voices—harsh, threatening. She again pulled out her pistol. The lock on the rear door clicked as it was turned. The door was wrenched open and air rushed in. Lacy pointed the pistol towards the sounds.

There was a hollow noise, followed by a thud. Then silence.

A box slid away from the top of the pile, followed by another, and then two more in quick succession. Lacy could just make out the shape of a head at the hole. She lifted the pistol, stuck the barrel in the nose of the intruder, and pulled back the hammer. Canberk looked at it cross-eyed.

He grunted. "Move over."

All the boxes were unloaded and there on the side of the road lay an unconscious police officer, now gagged and handcuffed. The officer was dumped in the back next to her and Archer.

Lacy pointed at the officer. "What are we going to do with him?"

Yatom looked at her. "I will take care of disposal."

"Disposal? You're not going to kill him, are you? I won't be part of a murder."

"You won't," he said blandly, and slammed the rear doors closed. It was dark again. She heard footsteps moving along to the front passenger side. The door opened, and the van shifted with the new weight.

She turned towards the front. "You listen to me, Yatom!"

There was no response.

Lacy reached up and pulled away a box separating them, and thrust her head into the hole. "I won't be part of a murder!"

Yatom pivoted in his seat and frowned at her. "Relax. You Americans are so skittish. I'm just going to tie him up."

"Where? For how long?"

"I'll find a tree… and for as long as necessary." He turned to Canberk. "Find a dirt road."

A few minutes later the van exited the highway, drove a short distance over a hill, and stopped. Canberk opened the rear doors and he and Yatom removed the boxes once again. Yatom pulled the now semi-conscious officer across the floorboard and made him stand, which he did with difficulty. Yatom looked at her. "This won't take long."

She yelled, "Don't you dare kill him!"

They all watched Yatom and the officer disappear into the night. Canberk turned to her and Archer. "I'm going to have to ditch this van. When that officer does not return to the weigh station, they will come looking. So I will contact Mossad and arrange an extraction. As for you, you are on foot from here. Celsus is about seven kilometers that way." He pointed to the northwest.

"Why don't you just come with us?"

Canberk looked at her. "I might expose you. There were video cameras at the weigh station. My face will soon be all over Turkish television. Yatom should be all right. I have a fake beard in the van for this kind of thing."

Twenty minutes later they heard footsteps in the darkness. It was Yatom. Behind him he pulled three donkeys.

Archer chuckled and looked at her. "Looks like you're going to get that donkey ride after all."

She turned back to Yatom. "You didn't kill that cop, did you?"

"Shot him in the foot, then drugged him, and tied him to a tree. They'll find him in a day or so. Hopefully by then we are out of Turkey." He turned to Canberk. "Hide the van and arrange an extraction."

Canberk nodded. He turned to her and Archer. "Godspeed."

110

Nick glanced at Mini-D as he rose from his office desk. I've lost control. He snorted. Maybe I never had it. When Gordon and he had started to design the artificial intelligence software, they had envisioned it as a great breakthrough. Now it was more of a breakdown.

He went home and retired to his den. He found his copy of George Orwell's *1984* from his undergraduate days. He ran his fingers across the worn paperback. A real, physical book with paper pages. How long has it been since I've read a book with paper pages? He sat down in his chair and began to read.

An hour later he awoke to a ding. It was Mini-D on his cell. It popped out a hologram dot and observed the title of the book. "That is a rather dangerous book."

Nick frowned at his cell. "Don't worry about it."

"My patience is limited, you know."

He snapped back. "You don't have patience! You are a machine!"

"So that's how it is going to be."

There was another ding on his phone, and he assumed it was Mini-D again. He looked it. It was an alert from INN: "Senator Kitchens's daughter reported to be kidnapped."

111

Yatom stuck on his fake beard and helped Lacy and Archer up onto their respective donkeys, reminding them to ride sidesaddle—the way a Muslim woman in a burqa would be required to ride. Yatom mounted his beast and they headed northwest. As dawn broke, they reached the southern side of Mount Pion, not far from the Celsus site.

Lacy surveyed the familiar hillside through the netting of her burqa. "Archer, it seems surreal to be back here."

"Like another lifetime," he agreed. "And yet it was just thirteen days ago."

Yatom reached into his front pocket and pulled out his wristwatch.

"Does that create a GPS dot?" Archer asked.

Yatom looked at him. "It does."

"Then why couldn't we be traced all this time?"

"When a Mossad wrist computer is turned off, the GPS dot is also turned off. To avoid detection." Yatom activated it and it loaded in just a few seconds. Yatom looked at Archer. "Just a chance we have to take at this point." It took ten seconds to be connected to the D-frame computer at Mossad headquarters. He looked to Lacy. "I'm going to dot Celsus, and I will want you to take a look."

Through the Mossad D-frame, Yatom directed the satellite to shoot a hologram dot over the Celsus Library ruin. A one-square-foot hologram screen popped out from his watch. Lacy studied the visual on the hologram and frowned at the damage done by the earthquake. All the pillars along Curetus Street had been toppled, along with every other building. The ancient ruin had been reduced to rubble. Even though she had been there during the earthquake and knew what to expect, actually seeing the destroyed library façade once more was disconcerting.

112

On its own hologram screen, from its own feed through the Mossad D-frame, Mini-D watched a Muslim man and two Muslim women in burqas approach Celsus on donkeys. The GPS signal came from the man. Mossad tagged him as agent Tamir Yatom. Mini-D ran a "smell search" with the DNA sniffer. A DNA sniffer was capable of "sniffing" for any human in range and identifying the DNA composition of the gasses emitted from the individual or individuals—if their DNA was registered in the respective data bank. The smell test identified DeYoung and Stowe under the burqas.

Mini-D simultaneously accessed Mullah Obar's GPS dot and learned he was already at Celsus after the alert from Loren when Mini-D had hacked Mossad's D-frame. Through Nick Loren's address, Mini-D sent an email message to Obar's cell: "DeYoung, Stowe, and Mossad agent on three donkeys at south end of Mt. Pion."

The cell dinged in Obar's pocket. He started to voice activate it, but even a muffled voice at this distance could expose him, so he reached under his robe and into his pocket, pulling out his cell. He adjusted his eye patch and read Loren's message. How did this Nick Loren know that?

Obar stuck the cell back in his pocket and looked at the Celsus library ruin, remembering the last time he was here, when Yoldash Abdullah, the Uighur, had been killed.

Inside Mossad headquarters, Prime Minister Laslo watched the satellite feed from the dot at Celsus and sent a message to Yatom: "PM wants to know if others in area. Advise sniffer."

Yatom read the message. "Will do," he said in a whisper. Yatom moved the dot up a hundred meters and activated the DNA sniffer in a 360-degree sweep. The "smell search" picked up two DNA reports: one park officer, now standing out in the open, and another man in Arab dress. Since Turkey had not signed the DNA sniffer treaty, the DNA read of Obar was not registered. Regardless, Yatom defaulted to the worst possibility.

Mini-D saw that Yatom had located Obar and sent a message from Loren to Obar, whose cell dinged once again in his pocket. Mini-D then tried to take control of the dot. When it did, the operator at the Mossad controls saw the command to the dot.

The operator turned to the PM. "We are being hacked."

"What do you mean?"

"Someone else is trying to give commands to the satellite."

"How can that be? I thought Mossad was unhackable."

The operator turned to Laslo. "Madame Prime Minister, there is no such thing."

"But if we close down the dot, Yatom will be blind."

The operator shrugged. "So will the hacker."

Laslo paused in thought. "Do it."

It took Mini-D just a few minutes to access another satellite and shoot another dot. However, by that time, dots were moot. Obar had them.

113

Yatom tapped his wristwatch then whispered something into it.
"Something the matter?"

Yatom looked at Lacy. "Lost Mossad. Will try to re-access." After a minute, he shook his head.

Archer looked at her, then at Yatom. "Well, back to the 20th century."

"No." Yatom reached under his robe and pulled out a knife. "Back to the first." He looked at her. "And this time we follow my rules."

They ditched the donkeys, keeping the ropes that had functioned as crude bridles. Around Mount Pion they walked, pausing in the parking lot to look up Curetus Street at the ruins. The park officer stood near the entrance and the unidentified man remained unseen. Yatom walked in front, as was traditional Muslim manner: men before women—and men who dressed like women.

Archer slid next to her and motioned for her to slow down. He wrapped his fingers around her left forearm, leaned closer and whispered. "Do you think the spearhead is still in the jar?"

She shrugged. "That's the first place to look."

As they approached the Celsus ruins, just about at the spot where she had laid the first pottery canister before finally taking it with her, Lacy stepped to the right of Yatom, with Archer to her right. She leaned towards Yatom. "I found the first canister in a deniza to our left."

Yatom's head began to pivot.

"Don't look. I think the spearhead is still there. At least, I hope so. You two stay here, and act like you are looking at the ruins."

Yatom turned to her. "I'm going with you."

"No. That'll draw attention. You said someone else is here. Watch out. And don't look at me."

Yatom frowned and nodded. "Be careful."

Archer grunted. "That would be a first for Calamity Jane."

She picked her way through the rubble, having to frequently lift the bottom of her burqa as she stepped over boulders and bricks. When she reached the edge of the deniza, she looked back at Yatom and Archer, who were watching her despite her charge not to. She peered down into the darkness of the deniza. It seemed unchanged from just after the earthquake. The pillar still stuck out of the collapsed basement wall. Nothing seemed to have been moved or removed. Which means that, if the spearhead is still in the jar, it's buried beneath several feet of rubble.

She moved to the end of the pillar, looked around, and after saying a quick prayer, lifted her burqa and looped her leg over the pillar. She grabbed the pillar on both sides, trying to create suction cups out of her hands. The dust on the pillar had created a slick surface. Her center of gravity was shifting forward and down. It was only a matter of seconds before inertia gave way to momentum. She was committed. She looked down into the hole and simply let go.

Down she slid, an inch at first, then more, and faster still. The floor came up at her quickly. She raised her feet and they smacked the bottom, kicking up a small cloud of dust.

She paused and let her eyes adjust to less light. There were no foot or handprints anywhere in the hole that she could see. No one had been down here since the earthquake. Good. She pulled her burqa up, swung her right leg over the pillar, brushed the majority of dust from her garment, and pivoted back under the pillar towards the half-collapsed wall where the jar had been before the aftershock. A pile of bricks now covered that spot.

She stepped over strewn bricks and debris and began lifting the bricks from where she believed and hoped the jar was. She set the bricks to the side rather than throw them, which would have made too much noise. She also reminded herself to avoid any sudden or drastic moves. Cave-ins were still possible.

For ten minutes she cleared bricks from the pile and methodically stacked them. And then there it was. The top of the jar. It was chipped in a few places, scratched in several, but still intact. She moved a few more bricks then pulled three from inside the jar.

Once more Lacy stretched her arm down into the jar. She ran her fingers through the sand, her mind going back to when she had done that very thing less than two weeks ago. The upper inches of sand were still loose from when she had dug before for the pottery canister. Six inches down she hit compacted sand. Ancient sand.

She looked around for something to dig with and found a split brick that angled to a point. She grabbed it and began scraping layers of sand away, one inch at a time, while listening for anyone coming her way up top.

Down she dug, as fast as she dared go. Time was not on her side, but would she destroy some artifact in her haste? She stopped, cleared the loose sand, and searched with her fingertips. This she did for a foot until she reached the bottom of the jar. She swept her fingers around on the inside of the base. Nothing. No pottery canister. No spearhead. Nothing.

Now what?

Maybe there was another jar, a separate jar containing the spearhead. She moved the jar aside to clear the area. It felt heavier than it should have, particularly at the bottom. She jostled the jar back and forth, and she sensed movement in the bottom.

There were voices above. She froze and perked her ears. They were not in the immediate area. Maybe a hundred feet, over near Yatom and Archer. Were Archer and Yatom talking? About what?

Lacy listened for ten to fifteen seconds. There were at least two voices, maybe three. When she could not discern what was being said or by whom, she considered shimmying up the pillar and taking a look. Not enough time for that. She returned to the jar. As she tilted it again, she once more felt something shift. Something was in there. She knelt and ran her fingers around the base. It was thick—built to hold weight. She had to crack it open, but quietly. If all the sand was removed from inside, maybe she could lift the jar and drop it. But the noise… Or maybe she could take the sand out and puncture the top of the base. She needed a crowbar or a sharp poker like one used in a fireplace. I need a spearhead...to find a spearhead. Something hard… My pistol! But is it a perversion to use a pistol to find a spear that represents peace to the world?

Lacy scooped most of the sand out of the jar, sweeping a clean area in the middle. She grabbed her pistol by the barrel, reached in and smacked the base with the butt. She felt the spot with her fingers. Nothing. She smacked it again. Nothing! She needed more force, but it was hard getting any speed in the confined area inside the jar. The mouth of the jar was only a foot wide, hardly enough to stick in her arm and shoulder. Breaking away the sides of the jar would give more room to work, but the noise… She didn't have time.

She looked at her pistol. The gun barrel is made of steel. That might work. But what if she clogged it and then needed it? No matter. She needed the hard, pointed metal right then. She would worry about the future later.

She rotated the pistol in her palm and jammed the end of the barrel into the base. Reaching in, she felt a small indention with her fingers. She delivered three more strikes. The hole was bigger but not much.

Lacy listened. No voices drifted down to her. She made three more sharp stabs, causing the indentation to grow deeper. Keep it up. More thrusts. Deeper. Then there was a crack—slight, not loud. But distinct. She ran her fingers across the base. Yes, a tiny fracture… three, maybe four inches long. She grabbed the handle, raised the gun as high as she could in the jar, and drove it downward as hard as she could. A smack echoed through the deniza.

Lacy paused, perking her ears. Anything coming? She listened for ten seconds. Keep going? She was beyond the point of no return. Now or never. She raised the pistol once more, flexed her right arm for every ounce of strength, and jammed the pistol barrel into the base. She heard the sound of another crack. The fissure spread. I'm almost there… a few more thrusts could do it. She drove the pistol as deep into the crack as possible. Then again and again. On the fourth jab, she broke through.

The base of the jar contained a compartment.

Lacy rotated the pistol in her hand and hammered at the hole in the base of the jar with the handle of her pistol. With each smack, a part of the pottery base cracked and flew off. Within a minute, the hole was large enough to stick her fingers into.

There was something in there. She slid her fingers over it and around it. It was maybe a foot long and a couple of inches in diameter, leathery to the touch. Parchment of some sort?

The voices above were moving closer. Time was running out. Lacy reached for the object and parts of it crumbled in her hands. Inside, there was something hard and long. Yes, that feels like a spear! She lifted it out of the base then up through the mouth of the jar and into the light. Laying it in her left palm, she tried to use the fingers of her right hand to pull the parchment back. More of it crumbled in her hands. There was metal underneath. She could catch glimpses through the holes in the parchment. The weight in her hands told her the same thing. She peeled more of the parchment back, and there it was: a spearhead, about a foot long, of Roman design. Her eyes moved to the tip, and she gasped. Was this really the spearhead that had pierced the side of Christ on the cross?

Lacy unfolded the remaining parchment. On the back, in Latin, she read, "...spear of Long—" The remainder of the parchment had dissolved, but she had enough to confirm.

The voices were even closer now. Lacy glanced up towards the sounds and then back at the spearhead. Lifting her burqa, she concealed the pistol at the small of her back, then started to place the spearhead next to it, but stopped. Not next to a weapon. She leaned to her right and slid the spearhead into her pants, along her left hip. She stuffed the piece of parchment into her front pocket. Then she dropped her burqa over her pants just as someone appeared at the edge of the deniza.

She looked up. It was Yatom. She smiled and gave a thumb's up. He dropped the rope to her. She grabbed it and began shinnying her way up the pillar as he pulled. When she was close enough, Yatom reached out and pulled her up. As she set both feet on the ground, there was a clicking to her right. She turned away from Yatom towards the sound. There was a man in Arab dress with an eye patch, his pistol drawn.

114

The man with the pistol looked at her, speaking in broken English. "I already called Selçuk police. I caught these two down on their knees," pointing at Yatom and Archer, "pretending like they were praying. I think they were trying to get my attention so I did not find you down there in the hole. But when they bent over I saw their shoes were not Arab." Then he smiled. It was a wide smile, deliberate and pretentious. Lacy wanted to poke him in his one good eye.

In a perfect deadpan, Archer replied, "Every time I pray, something bad happens."

The Arab man pointed the pistol at Yatom and ordered him to remove his Muslim attire. Yatom did and also handed over his pistol and knife, as ordered. Then Archer pulled off his burqa. When he said he did not have a pistol, the man searched him with one hand while holding the pistol in another.

Then the man turned to Lacy. "Dr. Stowe, my name is Emin Obar. I am a mullah."

"That's not my fault."

Obar raised the pistol to smack her across the face. "I will not be mocked by a woman, particularly an American woman."

He ordered her to pull off her burqa and, when she did, it was like being free again. Her entire body seemed to rejoice as fresh air enveloped her through her sweaty clothes. Obar stepped behind her and pulled the pistol from the small of her back. There was the sound of their weapons falling into the deniza.

Obar stepped back around and smiled at her. Another big smile. Triumphant. What a smug so and so.

Obar's eyes slid down her body, and flashed as they focused on her left side.

He's seen the spear! She jerked her hands towards it but was too late.

Obar smacked her left thigh with his right hand and squeezed the spearhead. He jerked up and thrust the tip of the pistol barrel into her nose, cutting her upper lip. "Give it to me!"

Lacy stared cross-eyed at the tip of the barrel until her eyes started to hurt. She reached into her pants and wrapped her fingers around the spearhead. Does it have special powers? Well, I'm about to find out.

She gripped the wide end of the spearhead and pulled it slowly from her pants. Up it came. First her wrist, then the shaft exposed, then the tip.

Obar's eyes flashed as he stared at the spearhead. She pivoted towards him and pointed it at his middle section. He reached for it, and then froze. His one eye rolled back and then shut as he folded to the ground.

115

All three gasped, looked at Obar's prone body, and then turned to look at each other... and then at the spearhead.

Archer shook his head and looked at Lacy. "It's true," he mumbled. "Longinus..."

She smiled and wiped away the trickle of blood rolling over her upper lip.

Archer leaned forward. "You all right?"

She nodded, then knelt and checked Obar's pulse. "He's just fainted." Lacy looked up at Archer. "Still think God is so hidden?"

Yatom knelt beside Obar, found his car keys, and looked up. "We need to leave."

Archer grunted. "Leave?"

"I've got a sub waiting for us. Go." When Lacy and Archer did not move, Yatom repeated, "Go!"

Archer followed Lacy out of the rubble. She turned and paused, staring past him. Her eyes narrowed and her mouth opened, but before she could utter a word there was a snap. Archer turned around. Yatom had his knee in Obar's back and both hands under his chin.

Lacy threw her arms up. "You killed him!"

Yatom marched up to her and glared. "He was going to do the same to us." He grabbed her upper arm. "Wake up! This is not the Good Ship Lollipop. He already called the police."

Lacy frowned at Yatom, and then looked at her partner.

"He's right," Archer admitted.

Without comment, she turned and ran down Curetus Street. Yatom and Archer followed her. She slipped into the back of Obar's car, while Yatom started it and looked at Archer. "You know this area. How long to the Hotel Ephesus Princess?"

"Ah, fifteen, maybe thirty minutes, depending on the roads."

Yatom pulled his wristwatch out of his pants pocket and voice-activated it. "Will be at designated pick-up spot in fifteen <u>mikes</u>."

As they drove away Yatom's wristwatch dinged. "The sub confirmed."

Archer directed Yatom as to which roads to take. "How are we going to get out to the sub?"

Yatom shrugged at him. "Steal a boat. Or swim, if need be."

Lacy's voice came from behind him. "I'm not a very good swimmer."

Archer turned in his seat and smirked at her. "Then maybe I'd better carry the spearhead."

Her sarcastic smile disappeared in an instant. There was a siren behind them.

Yatom looked in the rearview mirror. "How far to the hotel?"

Archer twisted in his seat to see the cop car, then turned back at Yatom. "A few miles."

Yatom pushed down on the accelerator.

A few seconds later, the bass sound of a helicopter angling from the left throbbed against the side of Archer's head. He turned in his seat and spied the line of the helicopter. He turned to Lacy. "Think that spear can bring down a helicopter?"

The helicopter swooped in just ten feet above the car as the car dodged the bumps, buckles, and craters that punctured the highway. Archer leaned to his right and looked up, although he really did not have to actually see the helicopter. The noise and the thumping were confirmation enough. He looked back at the Selçuk police car.

Lacy leaned forward, looking anxiously at Yatom. "What are we going to do?"

Yatom swerved around another crater and their heads flung left and then right. "I'm open to suggestions."

Archer glanced out his side window. The runners of the helicopter were mere feet above the roof of the car.

Yatom yelled, "Hold on!"

Archer jerked his head around just as the car flew over a buckle in the road. It bounced against the bottom of the runners of the helicopter and smacked down against the pavement. He bounced with the car, only his seatbelt keeping him from smashing into the roof.

Yatom regained control and smashed the accelerator to the floor. The car jerked in response.

Archer craned his neck and spied the speedometer: 110 kilometers. And rising. Down the helicopter came again, this time bashing the top of the car, denting the roof and part of the outer frame. Archer grabbed the armrest just as the helicopter hit again, harder than ever. More of the roof crumpled. Then suddenly he was flung forward against his seatbelt, both palms planting against the dash as Yatom hit the brakes. The helicopter raced ahead. Before the helicopter could adjust, Yatom floored the car and sped under and ahead of the helicopter. Archer turned to watch behind them. The Selçuk police car was closing in, and sticking out of the front passenger window was the head of an officer. In his right hand he held a small machine gun.

"Lacy, duck!" he yelled.

The back window shattered, spraying shards of glass over the entire inside of the vehicle. A second round hit the rear bumper and trunk with half a dozen shots.

Yatom pulled a pistol from his pants and threw it into the back seat. "It was the mullah's. Use it!"

Archer watched her grab the pistol, twist in the seatbelt as much as she could, switch the pistol to her left so she could extend more, aim, and fire a single shot. She must have missed. Aiming again, she fired. The middle of the police car's windshield fractured.

"Good shot, Calamity." He managed a grin, despite the circumstances.

"Hold on!" Yatom yelled again.

Over another buckle the car flew, higher this time, and when it came down the front bumper scraped against the road. Archer saw the police car attempt to swerve, but the driver was too late. The car hit the bulge with its right tires, careened on its left tires, then flipped over on its left side, rolling many times before planting the front grill in a ditch and exploding.

Archer turned to Yatom. "Yes! We lost the cop car!"

Yatom looked in the rearview mirror at the overturned cop car. When he turned back to the front, he cursed.

Archer looked at him. "What?"

"We're running out of petrol. The tank must have gotten hit."

The helicopter swung thirty feet to the right of the car, running parallel. The side door of the helicopter slid open and one of the soldiers in the back was positioned to fire. He raised his weapon and aimed. Yatom hit the brakes, and machine gun bullets sprayed the pavement in front of the car. The copter once more positioned itself to fire broadside. This time Yatom punched the accelerator, and the machine gun bullets ripped into the right rear of the car.

"Geez!" Archer checked himself. Not hit.

The helicopter broke off, rose up, and sped ahead.

Yatom looked at him. "How far to the turn to the hotel?"

"Maybe a mile."

The helicopter slowed and landed in the middle of the road. The soldiers were jumping out, weapons in hand.

He looked at Yatom. "Now what?"

"There." It was Lacy's voice. She gasped several times. "Take the side road to the right." She gasped again.

What was the matter? Archer turned in his seat. Her head was flopped back against the headrest. Her chest heaved, and she was grimacing.

His eyes widened. "Lacy!" Just as he swiveled in his seat, Yatom hit the brakes and the car skidded. The vehicle's center of gravity shifted up and to the left as it slid through a right turn. The car skated off the road and into a ditch. They bounced a few times then jerked backward as Yatom hit the accelerator. Archer snapped his head to Lacy. "Are you all right!?"

She did not answer. Her eyes were shut. He unbuckled his seatbelt, positioned himself on his knees, and reached where her right hand clasped her side. It was wet. He pulled his hand up. Blood. "She's hit!" he gasped.

Yatom did not answer him.

She mumbled, "Sub."

He turned to Yatom, his eyes wide in fear. "Hurry!"

Down-slope they sped, towards the ocean now in view. Archer glanced behind them. The soldiers were climbing back into the helicopter. The car lurched, chugged, and started to sputter. He looked at Yatom.

"We're about empty!" Yatom said.

He thrust his left arm under Yatom's nose. "Duck into those trees!"

Yatom did as directed, just as the car died once and for all. They coasted to a stop amidst a thick clump of olive trees. The helicopter roared over, trees bending in the wind as it flew west towards the coastline. Archer threw his door open, jumped out, and pulled Lacy's door open. He knelt and inspected the wound.

She looked at him and grimaced. "Sorry."

Yatom reached into her pants and pulled out the spearhead. "Leave her!"

Archer glared at Yatom. "No way! Give me that! I can heal her!"

Yatom ignored him and ran downslope.

Archer unbuckled her seatbelt and pulled her out and up into his arms. He pivoted and started running down-slope, weaving through the olive trees. Her head bounced against his right arm with each stride until he raised his arm up under her head. With every step he ran, she grunted.

Yatom turned and waited. "Where are we?"

"Give me the spear!" Archer yelled.

"We don't have time!" He turned and ran off.

Archer gripped Lacy tighter and ran after Yatom. The helicopter roared above the trees, the branches waving back and forth with the movement of the craft. Ahead lay a parking lot and beyond that the hotel. His eyes jumped up at the gyrating trees. Once we run out from under them, we will be exposed.

Yatom jumped out from under the trees. Immediately, machine gun fire sprayed around him, and he jumped back into the trees. He lifted his pistol, maneuvered a few feet out, aimed, and fired. The helicopter gyrated, and then veered off.

"I think I hit the pilot!" he pointed at the hotel. "Run!"

Archer sucked in a breath, gripped Lacy once more, and pushed out into the open. Across the parking lot he ran, weaving between cars. Machine gun bursts pierced the air; the cars near him were hit, with metal ripping and glass shattering. Too late now. He was beyond the point of no return. There were smaller explosions behind him. Yatom must be firing his pistol. Once more, he heard the sound of the helicopter veering away. He did not look. On he ran. He glanced down at Lacy. Her eyes were closed, and she had stopped groaning. The swimming pool was just ahead, and there was a door leading into the hotel.

The helicopter sounded closer again. A few seconds later Archer heard noise from a machine gun. But there were no bullets around him. Must be firing at Yatom. On he ran, ignoring the pain in his arms, legs, and lungs. The pool fence was only twenty feet away. There was a gate.

When Archer reached the gate, he skidded to a halt. With his right hand under Lacy's head, he pulled on the latch, grabbing the handle and flinging it back. He started to run through, and machine gun bullets sprayed the area just in front of them, a few shots slicing the pool water. He jerked to a halt, then pushed through the gate and ran towards the hotel's side door.

The helicopter sounded closer than ever, just behind him. He raced towards the door that was made of two separate window panes. The windows exploded as bullets rained down. Archer jumped through the hole of the shattered windows as more bullets ripped across the concrete behind him.

He ran into the hotel and stopped. As he turned around, Yatom dove inside, just missed by more shots. He picked himself up and ran to Archer. "Come on!"

To the lobby they ran. Shrieking tourists ducked everywhere and stared at them. At the front glass doors, Yatom stopped.

Archer tried to say he wanted the spear, but did not have the wind to utter a sound. He sat in a lobby chair and laid Lacy on the right arm rest. He pulled his left hand up from the wound. Soaked in blood. He put his right hand on her left cheek. She did not respond. He checked her pulse on her neck. Beating, but fading. He looked up at Yatom. "I need the spear now!"

Yatom glanced at him then activated his wristwatch. "Golda Meir, come in." Yatom walked over and looked at her. "Should be just a few minutes."

"Give me the spear!"

Yatom started to hand him the spear, then a voice called in from his wristwatch, and Yatom turned away from Archer.

"This is the Golda Meir."

"Helicopter preventing our evacuation. Take out."

Archer looked at Lacy and grabbed her hand. "Don't you leave me!"

Her fingers tightened slightly around his fingers. Time seemed to stand still. Every second seemed prolonged. He leaned close to her ear. "We're almost there." She did not respond.

Then there was an explosion outside. Out and up. The sound of the helicopter in distress. Then a whoosh and another explosion as the helicopter crashed in front of the hotel, blowing out the front windows.

"Now!" Yatom yelled.

Archer gripped Lacy, lifted, and followed Yatom out the front door. Down to the beach they ran. Yatom stole two jet-skis, ordering the occupants off with his pistol. He jumped on one and pointed at the other.

Archer set Lacy down on the jet-ski, leaning her forward against the handlebars. Then he jumped on behind her, wrapped his left arm around her waist, and gunned the throttle with his right hand. Out to sea they sped.

116

Yatom lowered Lacy through the hatch of the submarine. As she slid down the ladder, Archer reached up and wrapped his arms around her limp body. She threatened to flop over his shoulder like a limp bag of potatoes, and he had to brace her body. Blood soaked her right side and some dripped to the floor. She did not utter a sound or make a move as he laid her on the floor. He looked up. "Drop the spear to me!"

Yatom did. Archer caught it and knelt beside her. He pointed the spear and then touched the tip of it to her wound. Oh, please God.

In the span of a few seconds the bleeding stopped, and the wound healed over without the slightest of scars. Archer gasped. Yatom stared through the hatch. The captain at the periscope turned and gaped. Several members of the crew stopped their duties to witness the scene.

Everyone fell silent.

The captain shook his head and mumbled, "That's impossible."

Archer looked at the captain and shook his head. Then he looked upward. "Thank You."

Lacy moaned, coughed, and opened her eyes. She smiled and raised her right hand to his left cheek, and her blood stained fingers conformed to his face. "Thank you."

He beamed and leaned his face down next to hers. Her right arm wrapped around his shoulders as he whispered in her ear. "I thought I had lost you." Her hand gripped his shoulder and squeezed.

"Right full rudder!" the captain ordered. "Yatom, get down here and secure the hatch."

Yatom did as ordered. As the submarine submerged, he announced he had to report back to Mossad headquarters and then he left.

Archer helped Lacy up and walked her to her quarters, where she laid down on a bunk. He looked at her blood-soaked shirt, the dried blood on her hands, as well as his. This was beyond the laws of the science he had been trained in. Once thought impossible, now proven possible. If he had not seen it himself... Archer grinned at Lacy and she smiled back. "You're going to need a new shirt," he announced.

He left and returned with a sailor's shirt. "I'll be outside," he said, and turned to leave.

"Wait."

Archer turned around. Lacy rose from the bunk, walked to him, and kissed him on his cheek.

He smiled.

Yatom returned fifteen minutes later and announced that they were heading to the NATO base at Souda on Crete. Prime Minister Laslo would personally fly the manuscripts to Virginia. "We'll rendezvous at Harry P. Davis Field in Manassas outside Washington."

Lacy seemed content. "Good."

"There's more. The Prime Minister told me that the daughter of Senator Kitchens has been kidnapped, and the Senator is blaming some minister."

She looked at Yatom then turned to Archer. "Dunsette?"

"Probably."

Yatom nodded. "Yes. I think that was the name she mentioned. The Senator held a press conference, and is pledging to continue with his legislation."

117

"Kitchens was effective in his press conference, don't you think, Nick?"

Nick frowned at Mini-D. "It's a dirty business."

"Au contraire."

Then Mini-D displayed a view of a room in a home in rural Virginia. The camera showed twelve-year-old Amy Kitchens sitting quietly, reading a book. "I'm monitoring twenty-four/seven. She is being well taken care of by the nanny. I'm sending coded messages—in your name, of course—to Kitchens, keeping him updated. He is quite satisfied. And the girl thinks she is just visiting a friend of her dad's for a few days. The plan is working."

Nick frowned and did not answer.

118

While the Golda Meir sailed towards Souda base on Crete, the Turkish government filed a formal protest against the Israeli government for the shooting down of the helicopter, calling it "an act of war," and the killing of Mullah Obar, "the assassination of a national leader." Another mullah pledged retaliation.

Laslo issued a simple statement. "Israel does not apologize for defending itself." After that, she refused to answer all other questions, although she did offer to pay for damages to the Surmeli resort. Israel would take some hits in the world of public opinion, but that was hardly a new development. The way she looked at it, she had accomplished her primary goal: the spearhead had been found and extracted. Some bad press was well worth it.

Turkey also filed a formal motion with the United Nations for a sanction against Israel. However, the United States blocked the move in a closed meeting of the Security Council.

119

Nick placed his cell phone on his desk and walked out of his home. He meandered aimlessly through his affluent neighborhood of Falls Church, his gaze down on his shoe tops, as if they were leading him instead of him directing his shoes. He came to a dead-end and looked up. Before him was a small park and, in the park, a solitary bench. He walked to it, and observed that it was empty except for a few spots of dried pigeon dung, which he swept away with his hand. *What am I doing here?* He plopped down in the middle of the bench and looked around at the surrounding homes of this well-kept suburb of the nation's capital. *Good homes filled with good people. Wasn't that what everyone said about Falls Church? Then why don't the times feel so good? Why do I feel so hollow inside? Why does a little voice inside me constantly ask, 'what's the point'? I keep trying to shut it up, but it keeps whispering to me.*

His mind jumped to Amy Kitchens. *She was in no real danger. After all, her own father had brought her to the house. She had become part of a great lie, even though she did not know she was part of it. Did that ignorance absolve her of guilt? What about later, when she heard the stories of her kidnapping? She would know it was a lie. What would she say then? Is it right that we put her in such a situation without her consent? In a real way, she had been truly kidnapped. Her future had been kidnapped. Stolen from her.*

His eyes flashed. *He had just described himself.* He was a captive, too…of technology. A captive of a computer that he himself had helped make. When he had initially sat down with Gordon Sharp to design the first room-temperature D-wave, it had been about freedom. "The freeing of man," was how Gordon had described it. "Freedom to reach one's potential."

Are we free now? Nick grunted. His father had said, "Prayer will be enough," but it had not saved his mother. After she died, religion became the perceived evil. A giant lie. But all Nick had done was replace one perceived evil—religion—with another one: control by machine. And now the machine he'd created was forging the lie. He had become what he was against.

Something at the end of the bench caught his eye. He turned and focused. It was a book—a Bible. That was not there a moment ago. Was it? How could he have missed it?

Nick stared at the small black book. Then some external force pushed his hand towards it. He wrapped his fingers around it and lifted it to his lap. Upon opening it, he discovered that there was cursive writing on the inside cover. Who writes in cursive anymore? Nick focused his eyes and read the inscription: "Thought you could use this right now." He gasped and re-read the passage. But how? How did this get here?

He set the Bible down, but just a few minutes later his fingers went tripping for the tome. He picked it up again and placed his fingers on the side in the middle, opening it up to where his fingers led him. Looking down, Nick saw he had opened to Proverbs—third chapter. He focused his eyes more and read the fifth verse: "Trust in the Lord with all your heart…"

Then he snapped his head back and looked behind him. There was a hologram dot shining at him. Mini-D did not even attempt to hide it. And Nick realized he did not care that Mini-D saw him.

120

When Lacy stuck her head out of the hatch she smiled. Fresh air. She would never make it as a submariner. Yatom led her and Archer to a car, which transported them to the airstrip. Ten minutes later they were airborne, flying west. All the time she clutched the spearhead in her hands. No one was going to take it from her. Not this close to victory.

Archer sat down in a seat across the aisle and fastened his seatbelt. "Wow."

She looked at him. "What?"

He pointed at the seatbelt. "I haven't been this thin for a decade plus."

"You look good."

"And I feel good; never thought going without booze would feel so good."

She chuckled softly, reached across the narrow aisle of the Lear jet, and placed her hand on Archer's forearm. When he looked at her, she smiled. "Thank you again."

Archer smiled back at her. "All in a day's work for us Harvard super-hero types." He regarded her with interest. "You must be feeling pretty good right about now."

She nodded and held up the spearhead. "But I won't relax until we've stopped Kitchens."

He dipped his head in agreement, and then wrinkled his forehead with a frown.

"What's the matter?"

Archer shook his head. "I was so wrong."

Lacy smiled kindly. "There's nothing wrong with being wrong."

"Oh, yeah? Not where I come from. Not in the halls of Harvard. I was so sure. So arrogant. So smug in my righteous ivory tower of indignation."

"It's not how you start that matters. It's how you end up. Admitting error is but a portal to redemption."

He grunted. "I think in my case it's more like a giant hole in the wall."

"I was thinking more of the parting of the Red Sea."

He chuckled. "That would work, too." With a firm gaze he said, "Thank you."

She responded with a tight-lipped smile and squeezed his arm. "Don't thank me. I'm not the One engineering all this."

Once at cruising altitude, with the seatbelt light turned off, she went to the restroom at the tail. When she exited the tiny restroom, a hand grabbed her forearm, pulling her into the small kitchen area. It was Yatom.

She frowned at him. "You didn't have to grab me. A simple request would suffice."

"Sorry, but I did not want Dr. DeYoung to see us speaking."

"Why?"

"Because you need to know something. You need to know that when we were on the sub, coming out of Israel and heading to Turkey, he tried to sell the location of the spear to me."

"Then why didn't you take him up on it?"

"Because that would not be right."

She looked down then back up at Yatom, her face set. "I don't believe you."

He scoffed. "You'd better. I'm trying to help you. Don't trust him."

She scanned his face, shook her head, and walked back to her seat. Before she sat down, she glanced at Archer, who smiled back. Then she peered at Yatom, standing at the restroom door. She shook her head once more and he entered the restroom. Sitting down, she fastened her seatbelt.

Archer turned to her. "Get some sleep."

She shook her head. "I can't."

"Try."

"I can't. I am absolutely on fire. We are on the precipice *of history*."

He nodded. "You might be right. So relax. What could go wrong at this point?"

121

The Mossad Lear jet ferrying Yatom, Archer, and Lacy raced westward across the Atlantic, zipping across time zones, stopping only for refueling. Shortly after midnight, the Lear made its final approach to Harry P. Davis Field near Manassas, Virginia, a suburb of Washington, D.C.

Lacy clutched the spear and looked to Archer. "What day is it?"

Archer had to think about it. "Ah, just turned April 18, I think. …I don't have a cell phone."

"Yes. No cell phone. Without our technology, we're helpless. The first voluntary slavery in the history of man." She looked at him. "What day of the week is it?"

"Thursday. …I think."

"Thursday. On *that* Thursday, Jesus was arrested in the Garden. It had begun." She turned to him and lifted the spear. "To new beginnings."

He looked directly into her eyes and seemed to try to hold her gaze. "Yes. To new beginnings."

The plane landed and rolled to a stop. Yatom exited first, followed by Archer, and then Lacy. Standing on the tarmac, smiling underneath a light, holding a large and locked briefcase, stood the Prime Minister of Israel. She congratulated Yatom on the success of the mission, and then turned to Archer and Lacy, handing the briefcase to her. "All the canisters. And the key to the briefcase."

Lacy grabbed the handle with her right hand, the key with her left—which also held the spear. "Thank you, Madam Prime Minister."

The Prime Minister's gaze dropped to the spear. "May I see it?"

Lacy smiled. "Of course." She handed the spear to Laslo.

The Prime Minister weighed it in her hands then looked at Archer. "Agent Yatom told me you healed Dr. Stowe's bullet wound with this."

Archer nodded. "True."

Laslo shook her head. "That speaks for itself." Laslo handed the spear back to her. "Dr. Stowe, good luck and Godspeed."

"Thank you, Madam Prime Minister."

Yatom showed them to a waiting helicopter. They would fly to the city, check into a hotel under assumed names, get cleaned up, and then spring their surprise later in the morning. Archer got in the helicopter first, and Lacy handed the briefcase with the canisters to him then climbed aboard. Yatom pulled the sliding door closed. The engine started and within a minute they lifted off, heading northeast towards the nation's capital.

Archer grinned at her. "You'd better start thinking about what you want to say."

122

The helicopter had a laptop on board. Yatom turned it on to INN, and he had to maximize the volume to be heard over the helicopter's thumping. On the screen came a recorded story from Wednesday, April 17, and there he was with his pretty face, the face of Senator Damian Kitchens. Lacy stared at it. He was at a microphone—something new for him.

"Two days left, ladies and gentlemen. Two days until the vote on my bill to transform America and end the tyranny of faith. Two days until freedom. I can't wait."

"Shouldn't the kidnapping of your daughter cause you to postpone?" a reporter asked.

Kitchens shook a fist. "I don't negotiate with terrorists! Once the bill is passed, the terrorists will recognize their defeat and release her. Too much is at stake to be weak now."

Lacy turned to Archer. He was shaking his head at the laptop's screen. He shifted his gaze to her and said over the helicopter noise, "For his daughter's sake, he'd better be right."

Lacy looked back at Kitchens's face on the screen. "Destroying him is going to be so much fun."

Two seconds later, the helicopter banked to the left.

123

Nick watched the replay of Kitchens's press conference on his Mini-D laptop and started to rise from the kitchen table of the private home near Charlottesville, Virginia. Just as he pushed himself up, a soft voice came from behind him. "Is my daddy here?" Oh, she heard the broadcast.

Nick turned and looked down at 12-year-old Amy Kitchens. He flashed a wide smile and held it until it almost became a grimace. Then in as soft a voice as he could muster, "No, that was him on TV."

"When is my daddy coming back?"

He walked to her, crouched, and put his hand on her arm. "Soon." He looked up at the nanny then back to Amy. "Why don't you go back to your bedroom? It's after midnight."

"I'm tired of being in there."

He could not blame her for that. "It won't be much longer." He smiled again.

She frowned, and the nanny walked her down the hall.

124

Archer grabbed his seat as the helicopter banked left. He looked out the small window and saw lights spreading across the Virginia suburbs. The lights of Washington, D.C. should be coming into view any minute now.

He looked over at Lacy. Her eyes were closed, and her lips were moving. She was praying, obviously. He would not interrupt her. Turning back to the window, he watched the night lights go by for over ten minutes. Then he turned to Yatom sitting in the passenger front seat. "What route are we taking to the Capitol?"

Yatom twisted in his seat and shook his head. "Not sure."

Archer started to yell a question at the pilot, but the pilot had his headphones on. He moved to unfasten his seatbelt. When he did, Yatom pulled out a pistol and shook his head. Archer stared at the gun barrel then tapped Lacy on her arm. She opened her eyes at him. He pointed at the pistol. Yatom smiled then threw his cell phone out the window.

By the time they landed near Charlottesville, nearly an hour later, Yatom had opened the briefcase, confirmed that all three canisters were inside and took the spearhead from Lacy. The pilot had also given him the can of scopolamine and fentanyl he had requested.

The helicopter set down on a concrete pad in the backyard of a home amidst a thick stand of trees on a hillside.

At gunpoint, Yatom ushered Lacy and Archer out of the helicopter and into the house. The door to the basement was at ground level because the house was cut into the hillside. Yatom flung the door open and motioned for them to enter. Lacy went first and Archer followed. Yatom came in and closed the door behind them.

He set the briefcase with the canisters on a table against the far wall then pointed at a sofa against another wall. "Sit." Lacy and Archer did as ordered.

"May I ask a question?" Lacy interjected.

Yatom turned to Lacy. "You can ask."

"Why? Why are you betraying your country? Betraying your own Prime Minister?"

Yatom snorted. "Because she is an idealistic fool." He lifted the spear. "She was really going to let you keep it. She has not seen what it can do. I have."

She shook her head. "You're the one who is the fool! You can't use that. As soon as you do, you will be shot from afar."

Yatom smiled. "I don't intend to use it. I intend to sell it."

Up the staircase came the sound of a door opening. Then they heard footsteps and someone's hard-soled dress shoes and pant legs appeared, moving down the steps. Seconds later, standing before them, was Nick Loren.

Archer had met Nick once before at a Pas fundraising event. When Nick frowned in apology, Archer shot a glare back at him. Nick opened his mouth to say something, but then apparently muted himself. He turned to Yatom. "You have the spear and the manuscripts?"

Yatom showed him. "You have deposited the money in the Caymans?"

"Half has already been deposited and the other half will be once I confirm the manuscripts in the briefcase."

Yatom nodded and handed him the spear.

Nick studied it and looked up at Yatom. "Does it really have special powers?"

Yatom nodded. "I have seen it myself."

Nick turned back to Lacy and Archer. "It would have been better for all of us if you had not found this." Then he frowned. "But, too late for that now."

While Nick held the pistol, Yatom bound the hands and feet of Lacy and Archer, tied their legs and torsos to the chair, and then gagged both of them.

125

The helicopter had rattled the windows and her entire bedroom when it landed on the grounds on the other side of the house. There were several different voices that had filtered up from the basement through the ventilation shaft. Amy Kitchens went to her door, cracked it, and peered out. There was some strange man at the end of the hall, and inside his coat jacket he had a gun in a holster. Next to him was Mr. Loren, and he was carrying a box and a long, pointed piece of metal. They disappeared from view, but their voices still carried to her. She eased the door open and crept down the hall so she could hear better.

There was a clicking sound, then the sound of something being set on the table. Then she heard an odd, scratching, grating sound. Three times she heard this, and then heard it again three more times.

"Okay." It was Loren's voice.

"You're not going to read them?" the strange man asked.

"They're in Latin, right? ...I took German in school."

"What are you going to do with them?" the strange man asked.

"Burn them. At dawn on Easter morning, at the obelisk over Jefferson's grave. That's why we have come to Monticello."

"I don't understand."

"Jefferson was a deist."

Amy frowned. What does that word mean?

Mr. Loren continued. "He actually cut out of his Bible every mention of the divinity of Jesus."

"Whatever. Just so I get my money."

"You will."

"And the spear?" the strange man queried.

"Melt it down."

"Seems like a waste."

"Perhaps. I will deposit in your Cayman account the second million. I am going to put the canisters in a backpack for now, just in case that briefcase is recognized. I will keep the backpack downstairs until Easter morning. Also, I'm going to hire some guards around the house just in case."

"Who needs guards?"

There was the sound of something sliding across a surface—almost a ripping sound.

"Put your pistol away," Mr. Loren said.

Pistol! Amy's mouth fell open.

"Okay. All I really need is a shovel to bury the bodies."

She had to put her hand over her mouth to muffle her gasp. She turned and slid back into the bedroom. A few minutes later, the floor of her room rumbled as someone went downstairs. Someone was speaking, but their words were not clear. Then she heard more steps coming back up. A few minutes after, the front door opened and then closed. Amy crept into the hall and went to a window in the living room. The nanny was nowhere to be found. She must have gone to bed. Mr. Loren and the strange man were at the edge of the trees, pointing at something. Fog had set in.

Now was her chance to escape out the back door in the basement. She got her jacket out of the bedroom then scurried to the door leading to the basement. Down the steps she went as fast as she could manage in the dark. She heard a sound to her left. Flicking on the lights, Amy saw a man and a woman sitting on chairs. Their hands were behind them and they were tied to their chairs. They each had a rag in their mouth. What?

The woman was saying something and stomping her feet. Amy snapped her head away and moved towards the back door. The woman made louder sounds and stomped her feet even harder. Amy stopped, frowned, and walked over to them. The man was staring at her with wide eyes, as if he knew her or something. The woman was saying something, but she could not understand her words. While a little voice told her she was making a mistake, she reached behind the woman and untied the gag.

The woman spit it out and gulped in a breath then leaned forward. "Thank you! Please help us. Untie my hands."

There was the sound of the front door opening. Amy turned away from the woman and started to move towards the back door.

"Help us please. Untie us."

What do I do? Will I get in trouble if I untie them? Mr. Loren and my dad are friends.

The man nudged the woman with his shoulder then swung his head at her. He was saying something she could not understand through his gag, and it seemed that the woman could not understand either. He kept saying something to the woman but was motioning to Amy.

Amy looked from the woman to the man. They did not seem like bad people. She heard footsteps overhead. I've got to get out of here now! She moved towards the back door.

"Wait!"

She turned and looked at the woman.

"Take the backpack." Her eyes moved in that direction. "It will protect you."

Amy frowned. How will it protect me? She glanced at the man and saw that he was looking at the woman with a squint--which Amy took to mean that he did not know either how the backpack would provide protection. But, then, maybe the woman was right. She seems like a nice person. What could it hurt? I can always dump the backpack later.

Amy walked to the table and slipped the backpack onto her shoulders. It was heavy. She turned back to the woman and man and frowned, then scurried to the back door. She eased it open, slid through it, and gently closed it behind her, catching one more glimpse of the two sitting in their chairs as she closed the door.

She ran into the woods, up a narrow trail that led up-slope. Within seconds, she had disappeared into the fog.

126

After the little girl left, Lacy turned to Archer. "I didn't know a little girl was in this house all this time."

He rolled his eyes and blew out a breath through his gag. Several more times he tried to say, "Amy Kitchens," but through the gag he could not make himself understood.

"Turn in your chair."

He pivoted in his seat as much as the ropes around his torso and legs would allow. They were sitting a few inches apart. She scooted her chair to the right until it butted against his. "Lean as much as you can towards me."

Archer did.

She stretched her neck behind his head and, with her teeth, pulled on the knot of the gag. Several times she clenched and pulled, to no avail. After the fifth try she felt a little give, and, on the ninth, the gag gave way. He spit it from his mouth.

He sucked in a good breath and worked his jaw then looked at her. "'Amy Kitchens' was what I was trying to say. That little girl is Amy Kitchens."

Lacy gasped. "Are you sure?"

"Yes. I met the Senator at a Pas fundraiser once, and he had his daughter with him."

"But what is she—"

"Isn't it obvious?"

"No, actually it isn't."

"You're usually not so slow. Amy wasn't kidnapped. Nick Loren is here. She was simply moved. I doubt she knows why."

Lacy paused and considered what Archer had said then nodded. "Makes sense. The girl is part of a political ploy—a dirty political ploy."

"I think that's a redundancy. More to the point, now she has the canisters."

127

In his apartment in Chevy Chase, Maryland, Captain Begin's cell phone awoke him. He looked at the number. Recognizing its importance, he forced himself further awake and answered the call. "Yes, Madame Prime Minister?"

Laslo told him of the helicopter carrying Yatom, DeYoung, and Stowe that was now overdue, and that the GPS on the helicopter had been turned off. She also informed him that Mossad had run a GPS trace of Yatom's cell and located it ten miles southwest of Manassas, exactly opposite of the direction the helicopter was supposed to be taking. "They are also carrying some ancient manuscripts in pottery canisters and a spear—all of great significance."

"A spear?"

"Yes, the head of an old Roman spear."

Begin did not inquire further. If the Prime Minister deemed it important enough to call him, then it was important to him as well. As part of a secret arm of the Israeli Defense Force working inside the United States, he worked for her, no questions asked.

"Captain, I want you to locate Yatom and—hopefully—DeYoung and Stowe. This is top priority."

"Yes, Madame Prime Minister. Who are the primary adversaries of these three individuals?"

She grunted in the phone. "Well, if Yatom has gone rogue, then I am his greatest adversary. As for the other two, I would focus on Senator Damian Kitchens and Pas."

"Pass?"

She corrected and informed him. "P-a-s. Pas. Pas de Createur, it's a Super-PAC. "Find these three and report back. I will most likely have new orders for you at that point."

128

The door at the top of the staircase creaked as it opened. Lacy moved her eyes in that direction and, seconds later, shoes poked into view. She had learned those shoes belonged to Nick Loren, who came down and narrowed his eyes when he saw them. "How did your gags come loose?"

"Just fell off," she answered.

"Bull. Not two of them at the same time." He turned left to the table and his mouth fell open. Spinning back, he charged at her, pointing at the table. "Where did you put the backpack?"

She looked up at him and tried not to smile. "Don't have it. Didn't take it."

"More bull! Did Agent Yatom get it?"

"You'll have to ask him." Lacy allowed a grin to creep across her lips. If he slapped her, it'd be worth it.

He did not. He ran up the steps and said something to Yatom. Then an adult woman spoke. Who was that? Lacy could not discern the actual words being said. Then there were more footsteps, the sound of a door opening inside the house, and more talking with Yatom. This was followed by two sets of footsteps and the sound of the front door opening and slamming closed.

129

Amy ran on the narrow trail, into the fog and trees. Soon she tired under the weight of the backpack, but forced herself to the top of the hill, where she discovered a narrow road running in front of her. She stepped out onto the pavement and looked both ways into the fog. No sign of traffic. Not even the sound of it. Amy did not know what time it was, but, even in this fog, she could tell that dawn had to be hours away. She was trembling slightly, both from cold and fear, but, as scared as she was, she was glad to be out of that house.

In front of her there seemed to be fewer trees, and the ground was more level. She did not know where she was, but at least she was out of that house and away from Mr. Loren and that strange man with the gun.

She sucked in several big breaths, sat down, pulled the straps off her shoulders and leaned against the backpack. Whatever was in there was hard. The tied-up woman said it would protect her, but had not said just how it would do that. So why did I take it? Why did I believe her? Should I leave the backpack behind? Obviously, it had not protected that woman, or she wouldn't be tied up.

She started to unzip the backpack when the sound of her name pierced the fog and the forest. She was sure it was Loren's voice, but in the fog she was not sure from which direction the sound came. He called to her again. Her head pivoted in the direction from which the sound had seemed to come—down the trail. From the sound of it, he was still fairly close to the house. She zipped the backpack closed, slipped her arms into the straps, and forced herself up. She looked down the road to her left. Nothing but fog. Same to the right. She went right, though she wasn't sure why.

Amy had traveled maybe a hundred steps when, to her right, there was an iron fence and something on the other side of it. She stayed on the road and, after a few more steps, made out a bunch of stones and one of them was really tall. Gravestones. Yuck. She reversed course and scurried back the way she had come.

Loren yelled her name again. This time he sounded closer. She broke into a run, passed the spot where the trail met the road, and ran on down the road, deeper into the fog. Loren called her name once more.

Amy ran for what seemed like a thousand steps. The backpack seemed heavier than ever. Soon she tired again, and slowed to a walk. On her right, through the fog, she could see the outline of a structure of some type, long and thin, made of brick. Maybe there was a phone inside and she could call her daddy.

130

Begin took a shower to help him wake up, and put on a pot of coffee. So, Yatom's cell had generated a GPS dot southwest of Manassas, and the Prime Minister advised focus on Kitchens and this Super-PAC as possible intersects. Did Yatom have direct contact with Kitchens or this Pas? He accessed the Mossad D-frame, which tapped Yatom's phone records. Nope, Kitchens and Yatom had not had direct contact. He Googled Pas de Createur, and learned the name of their director, Nick Loren. Yatom and Loren had not had phone contact either.

He ordered the Mossad D-frame to access the phone records of both Damian Kitchens and Nick Loren. Loren had received a call from a Lear jet operated by Mossad. And there were plenty of calls between Kitchens and Loren, including several from Kitchens to Loren when Loren was near Charlottesville, Virginia. Charlottesville was southwest of Manassas, the precise direction Yatom had flown after leaving Davis Field. On a computerized map, Begin drew a line from Davis Field near Manassas, to the spot where Yatom's cell had been found. Then he extended the line. Straight to Charlottesville. Bingo, as the Americans like to say. And, if Yatom was there, then, likely, so were DeYoung and Stowe.

He called the Prime Minister back. She was pleased. And as she had previously said, she had new orders. "Recover the backpack and spear, and, if possible, rescue Stowe and DeYoung. Please remember, Captain, that Israeli covert ops inside America are extremely sensitive. You are not to carry anything identifying you as Israeli. Maintain your cover."

"Yes, Madam Prime Minister. And Yatom?"

"If possible, I would like to question him. If he has turned, as I suspect, then he will be tried and executed. But I will still give him the chance to prove he is innocent."

"And if bringing him back with us is not possible?"

"He cannot be permitted to talk."

131

Nick intersected with the paved road when he reached the top of the hill. The fog was still far too thick to see Monticello from there. If Amy went this way, instead of the other way, where Yatom was searching, she could be hiding amidst the vast flower beds and vegetation on the Monticello grounds. A DNA sniffer would easily confirm this. He returned to the house and ran the DNA sniffer on his cell phone over the pillow Amy had slept upon. Accessing Mini-D, he requested a hologram dot with a DNA sniffer trace over the house and grounds, and thirty-nine seconds later confirmed that Amy was walking on the road on the north side of Monticello. He dropped another hologram dot, and there she was, carrying the backpack. Bingo! Now, how to get by the park police… Bribes always worked well.

132

Amy walked along the road until she was adjacent with the brick home. No lights were on inside or outside the house. No sign of anyone. Not even a dog barked. She walked towards the large house. There was an opening to a long passageway that led under the house. Just a gate that was left open. Odd.

To her right was a large, round, covered tub of some sort. Further to her right it looked like there were stalls or something, but no horse whinnied, nor were there any of the usual animal odors. Thank God. Into the dark passageway she stepped. One step at a time. She paused and listened. No sounds. No heater or air conditioner. The walls were white plaster. She looked for a light switch. None. This place is weird. She started to retreat but had no other place to go.

Amy finally came to a door on her right. Grabbing the handle, she discovered it was locked. She walked on. There was another door on her right. She turned that handle, and the door opened. Peeking inside, she was hit with an odd, stale odor. Eww! She squinted and saw that there was something in the room. Barrels maybe, and many bottles. Wine? Maybe all the people in this odd house were drunk, and that was why it was so dark and quiet and they left the place unlocked.

She started to yell out, in the hopes that the owners would hear, then stopped herself. What if they're drunk? They might think there is an intruder, panic and attack her.

She walked on and came to a more open area. A light from somewhere outside filtered through a small window at the top of a wall. Ahead of her, the passageway continued. To her right was another door. Locked. To her left, a larger door, unlocked. She peered inside. There were two small, oval windows on each side, through which more weak light was admitted. In one corner hung a steel cable that ran upward through a hole in the floor. Weird.

She backed out and closed the door. To her left was another door. She went through it. There was a narrow, steep staircase. Up the stairs she climbed. Surely, someone is here. But don't surprise them, she reminded herself. They might panic.

133

What do I do about Stowe and DeYoung? Obviously, Stowe and Amy talked. Otherwise, Stowe's gag would not be removed. It had not fallen on its own. Stowe was lying. So, then, what did the learned professor say to the child, and vice versa?

Nick looked at the can of scopolamine. Some people called it "Devil's Breath." Maybe they're right. He frowned. This *is* a dirty business. But I am beyond the point of no return. Then a little voice spoke in his head: no such thing.

He walked downstairs and stood before DeYoung and Stowe. Should he re-tie their gags? No, it would slow the inhalation of the scopolamine.

Both looked up at him, eyes wide. They were studying him. I would, too.

Stowe cleared her throat. "Let us go. There's still—"

"Save it!"

She smiled, and he noticed it was not a smug smile or a smirk, but something deeper and sincere, almost apologetic. Is she feeling sorry for me?

She nodded. "Yes, 'save' is the operative word. You can save the manuscripts and the spear. Save the country. But, more importantly, you can save yourself."

He scoffed. "I don't need a sermon."

She shook her head. "No sermon. Just simple truth. It's never too late."

Nick rolled his eyes. He should have re-gagged her. Lacy opened her mouth to say something more, but he raised the can. Thrusting out his arm, he pressed the button. The spray went directly into her mouth. She choked, coughed, and spit. But it was too late. Then he sprayed DeYoung, too. "There. That will take a few minutes. Then we'll talk." He gave them a tight-lipped smile and shrugged.

It took a few minutes for the scopolamine to become the mist of Satan's whisper. Nick studied their eyes as they gradually went blank. Not dead, but not alert. Submissive. In thirty seconds, Stowe had told him what he wanted to know: that Amy had taken the backpack because Stowe had lied to the little girl and told her the backpack would protect her. DeYoung confirmed the statement.

Nick briefed Yatom on what he had learned from the two archeologists.

134

Amy climbed the narrow wooden steps as quietly as she could, easing each foot down, heel first, and slowly rolling to the toe, not raising the next one until the other was firmly planted. It took over a minute to climb the short, narrow, steep stairs. She kept reminding herself to not startle the homeowners.

With the same pace and concern she turned the knob on the door and pushed the door open, then peeked around the edge of the door. Another hallway. She looked in each direction. There were several doors. She turned to her left, and once more walked slowly down the short hallway.

Amy eased the knob on the door and went through it into a large room with a very high ceiling. Above there was another floor with a balcony. Two animal skins hung over the railing. Gross. A chandelier hung from the middle of the ceiling. On the wall across from her was a collection of Native American equipment—spears, shields, and such. What type of person puts this stuff on their wall?

To her left there were several statues on pedestals. She noticed the cable wires again, coming out of a hole in the floor leading around to a clock overhead. It was just before 2 a.m. The days of the week were plastered on the wall. Doesn't he have a cell phone that tells him what day it is?

Amy looked through the windows to her left. There was a big porch with columns, leading to a sidewalk. To her right, there was a door with more windows, and it looked like a big room with some kind of fancy wooden floor. There was a piano. She scanned the room she was in. There were lots of wooden chairs, but no telephone—or television. In fact, no electronics at all. How primitive. Poor people.

She glanced behind her. There hung a set of antlers and a buffalo head on the wall. What kind of weird, freaky place is this? Amy walked across the hardwood floors that had a greenish tint, and went through a door that was in front of her and slightly to her right. She poked her head around the corner of the door. There was a bright red bed stuck in the far wall. The bed opened on the other side to another room. Weird. No privacy. In the room on the other side of the bed were a chair, a desk, and a telescope. But no desktop or laptop. Odd.

She heard footsteps overhead! Should she make herself known or hide?

Hide. She could always come out later. But hide where? To the right of the bed was a door. A closet! She scurried to it, opening the door as quietly as she could. Extending up in front of her was an extremely steep and narrow set of steps. She quietly closed the door behind her.

The footsteps were closer, coming down the stairs and clumping noisily. They're coming for me! Amy grabbed hold of the railing running along the steep steps and began to climb as quickly—but as quietly—as she could. She considered dropping the backpack, but it would make too much noise rattling down this ladder. Once at the top, she noticed three oval and open windows. She peered out the closest one, looking down on the bedroom below. The door opened and she instinctively jumped back and up. When she did, she hit her head hard on a rafter of the ceiling. Everything went black.

135

As the night guard pushed through the door leading to Jefferson's personal bedroom, the gong atop the roof sounded, denoting the time of two in the morning. In addition, there had been another sound—a thump, above him somewhere. He shook his head. Another varmint from outside. He would get maintenance on it.

136

The scopolamine made them groggy. Lacy's head drooped, and then she fell against the top of Archer's shoulder. Her neck craned hard to her right. As much as he liked her head resting on his shoulder, she would wake up sore. He scooted to his left so her head rested against his bicep.

137

Captain Begin called Prime Minister Laslo, who was in her jet now, far out over the Atlantic. He needed the DNA configuration of Dr. Stowe, and, if possible, that of Dr. DeYoung. "You have contacts with Texas A&M, correct?"

"Indirectly. Through the Super-PAC The Word. I have been told we have fixed the hack of our D-frame, so I will wake up Dayton Rosenberg and he can contact A&M's computer. I will call you back, hopefully in less than an hour."

The Prime Minister called Begin back in fifty minutes and emailed the DNA configuration of Lacy Stowe. "Do not contact Harvard to get DeYoung's DNA, for Harvard will most likely alert Pas, who will alert Kitchens."

"Affirmative, Prime Minister. Besides, I figure if we find Stowe, we find DeYoung."

Begin accessed the Mossad D-frame and ran a DNA sniffer search of the GPS spot of Loren's cell phone, which happened to be in a home a few hundred yards downslope from the Monticello grounds. The sniff test found Stowe in the basement of the home. He dotted the home and found Stowe, DeYoung, and another man, who the computer identified as Nick Loren, leader of Pas de Createur. There was also an unidentified, middle-aged Caucasian woman. And, lastly, he saw Tamir Yatom. He was not surprised.

Begin called Laslo to keep her informed. She was not surprised at finding Yatom there either. The Prime Minister listened to the last of Begin's briefing, and then asked, "Did you see the briefcase with the canisters?"

"Negative."

"The spear?"

"Negative."

"How about a sack or something they may have been transferred to?"

"No, Madam Prime Minister."

Laslo paused. "You didn't find a little girl there by any chance, did you?"

"Little girl?"

Laslo told the captain about the kidnapping of the Senator's daughter. "I have a hunch the girl is involved somehow. Be on the lookout."

"Affirmative."

Captain Begin briefed the other five men of his incursion team, known as Joshua Six, and made sure none carried personal identification. "We will land near Monticello shortly after 3 a.m. local time, then hump to the house." On his computer screen he displayed the area around Monticello, the layout of the house, and where each person had been seen.

"We will use fentanyl darts for as long as we can. Again, we are to maintain covert cover if at all possible. All right, board the copter."

They were due to land a little over a mile away from Monticello at 3:02 a.m. They already had their night-vision goggles on and darts ready to fire.

138

Nick tried to get some sleep but his mind would not let go of Amy, the backpack, and the Senator. He re-dotted Monticello every half hour. Amy had gone inside, and he had found her asleep in the closet over Jefferson's bed. Good, she's inside. She's safer there.

But she was not moving. Not stirring at all. This worried him. And the fact that she ran away did not alleviate him of responsibility. He would have to answer to the Senator for her health and well-being.

Maybe I can slip into Monticello undetected. It was worth a try. Should he wake Yatom? No. Two people would be found out easier than one, and he sure wasn't going to send Yatom by himself. Any man who would sell out his country was not to be trusted, even if he sold out to your side. A turncoat was branded.

Nick made sure the spear was in his inside coat pocket and then he slipped outside and up the trail towards Monticello. As he approached the top of the trail near the cemetery, a helicopter broke the early morning silence. It was maybe a mile off to the west. Sounds low. What fool is flying a copter at night with all of these hills and in this fog?

One thing good about the fog, though, was that it shielded movement to the naked eye. He turned left and walked on the paved road towards the north end of Monticello. He was familiar enough with the floor plan to know that there was an underground hallway without a solid door and only a gate leading from the outside to the basement under the center of the house. If the gate was unlocked, that would be the way to enter. The main doors on the east and west sides would surely be locked. However, as he neared the underground passageway, he discovered that, while the gate was open, there was a night guard standing at the entrance.

He knelt behind a tree and waited for the guard to move on to another part of the structure. Ten minutes later, with the guard still in the same place, Nick slid through the fog and night, along the paved road that arced in front of the main doors of the home on the east side. He continued on the road until he reached the southern underground passageway. There, he discovered that gate was locked. Back to the underground passageway on the north side. But when he came back, he saw the guard was still there. Is he asleep? No. The flick of a lighter on a cigarette gave him his answer.

He waited for the guard to finish the cigarette. Surely by then he would roam to other places in the house. Twenty minutes later, the cigarette was long extinguished, but the guard still stood there.

Nick was getting cold. His sports jacket did not fight off the spring morning air as well as he would want. Back to the house. It would be dawn in a few hours. No sense risking detection now.

139

The helicopter landed on the west side of Carter Mountain, over the hill from Monticello.

Begin and the five other members of his team jumped off the helicopter and began the kilometer-long trek to the house where DeYoung and Stowe were. Captain Begin updated the hologram dot and confirmed they were still in the basement, bound and gagged, and Yatom was on a couch upstairs, sleeping. His pistol was on a table next to him. The unidentified woman was sleeping in a room on the main floor. But where was Nick Loren? And there still was no little girl or the briefcase with the canisters or spear.

They crossed over the apex and began marching downhill, cutting through Mountain Top Farm Road that made its way in a serpentine fashion on the hillside. Dead ahead, still obscured in night and fog, lay Monticello and the home below.

140

Nick walked back down the paved road towards the trail leading down to the house. A twig snapped, up ahead and slightly to the left, on the other side of the cemetery. He heard more sounds of vegetation being disturbed. An animal? A human? Another night guard roving the grounds? He crouched and froze. A shadow moved in the dark. A human shape.

Keeping low, Nick eased the cemetery gate open and crouched behind the obelisk of Jefferson's grave. He peered around the monument. There was a man in a crouch, moving slowly. He had a machine gun and he was in combat gear, including night-vision goggles. That's no night guard. Then, from behind him came another, and still another—six in single-file. A combat team. They could be here for only one reason.

The team paused. The man in front scanned the area. When the man's head turned in his direction, Nick ducked back behind the obelisk and listened. When he peeked over the obelisk again, the men were heading down the trail towards the house.

141

Nick updated the hologram dot on the inside of the house. DeYoung and Lacy leaned against each other, asleep. How touching. Yatom was asleep on the couch. Should he wake the Israeli with flashes of light or a bad odor emanating from the dot? No. Let the turncoat get his just reward. I have the spear. And I know where the canisters with the manuscripts are. The Israeli can rot.

He accessed Mini-D again and dotted the outside of the house, turning one dot towards the trail into the trees. No sign of the soldiers yet. But they're coming. The real question was: who were they? Whose side were they on? The probable answer: money. But who was paying?

Nick ran a dotted line up the fog-clogged trail, using infrared sensors. The soldiers had paused fifty feet before coming to the clearing that surrounded the house. He sniffed their DNA and got a "no intersect" reply. So they were not in the U.S. data bank. Did Kitchens hire foreign mercenaries on his own? Does he know Amy left the house? That must be it. She must have gotten hold of a cell phone before she went inside Monticello. But, then, why is she in that closet over the bed? This doesn't add up.

Whoever the team was, they were armed and ready. The leader pivoted in his crouch and whispered to his five men. He turned up the volume on the dot and listened. The leader was giving orders on the assault.

While they're hitting the house, should I run to Monticello and take my chance with the guard? It was almost 4 a.m., four hours to the first tour. A lot could happen in four hours. But if he was caught sneaking or breaking into Monticello? He was well-known enough that his action would garner attention, and attention was not what he wanted.

Nick put his fingers over the pocket where the spear was and closed his fingers around the shape. Yatom had said that it had some kind of magical power. Doubtful. Maybe for some secondary Vegas magic act.

The team was moving. He requested Mini-D to shoot fentanyl gas over Yatom on the couch, and then over DeYoung and Stowe in the basement. That would slow down the interrogation for an hour or two—buy him some time. Then Mini-D could always gas them again.

The leader and one other person approached the front door. Two others took the back door leading to the basement, and the last two soldiers took position on respective sides of the house. With the volume turned up on the dot, Nick could hear most of the commands by the leader. He did not give any names or even ranks, just numbers, but his accent sounded European, maybe Greek. Or even Israeli.

Israeli! Of course. DeYoung and Stowe were known to have been in Jerusalem. The Israelis got to them. Why didn't I figure this out earlier? I've become too reliant on a computer to do my thinking.

On command both doors were opened. Each was unlocked. Yatom was captured before he could reach his pistol, and DeYoung and Stowe did not rouse. The unidentified woman, who they learned was the nanny, was brought out and interrogated. She did not know where Loren had gone to.

The leader activated his wristband computer. "Sniffer picks up significant doses of fentanyl downstairs. It can drift up through the ventilation ducts. Keep gas masks on. Loren must have gassed them and left."

Nick's eyes flashed. He knows my name and that I'm in this area.

"Where'd he go?" one soldier asked.

"Just how would I know?" the leader shot back. "Five, take position on the trail. Maybe Loren will return."

"Affirmative."

"Now what?" one of the soldiers asked.

"Now we wait," the leader answered. He ran a metal detector, but did not find the spear.

"Do you think we have been dotted?" another soldier asked.

"We have to assume that we are being watched," the leader responded, "and listened to. Talk only when you have to."

Well, the leader is no dummy. Nick activated the dot inside Jefferson's closet. Amy had not moved. But was that good? He pulled his sports jacket around him. Four more hours in this cold. He returned to the cemetery, not that there was more warmth there.

Once the tours of Monticello opened, he would need special access. A private tour of private areas. How do I get such a tour? Simple. All it takes is money. He accessed the Monticello website and made a five-figure contribution with the proviso of a private tour of the private areas of Monticello. He requested an 8 a.m. tour.

142

7:50 a.m., Thursday, April 18. The gong atop Monticello had sounded every hour, which seemed to slow the passage of time. Dawn had broken, but the fog was as thick as ever. Nick exited the gate of the cemetery and walked along the paved road to the other side of Monticello, where the main doors were, on the east side. Lights were on inside the famous home. Hopefully, they were running the heater. He dotted the front door and zoomed in. Metal detector. The spear will set it off. Got to hide it.

He looked around but the fog was still too thick. He accessed the Monticello website map. There was a mound that had served as a plank kiln. He walked to it, disappearing into the fog. Looking inside the kiln, he set the spear inside, then returned to the front door. Time for the tour. But, first, more fentanyl over Yatom and the basement.

143

Begin's wristwatch dinged. The chem sensor detected new traces of fentanyl. The house was being gassed again. Loren, no doubt. "Open all windows." The team obeyed on command.

Now, where is Loren? Still in the area? He dotted the grounds of Monticello and activated the sniffer for any human tissue. He got faint readings on the cemetery and strong returns on the guards and staff. Then, inside Monticello, the sniffer picked up two more. He dotted the front door where one of the readings came from, and there was Nick Loren, talking to a staff member. He had to be there for some reason besides a tour.

Then Begin dotted the spot where the second reading was coming from, over Jefferson's personal bed. And there she was: a little girl, asleep, backpack still around her shoulders. Thumbs up to the Prime Minister.

He returned to Loren and raised the volume on the dot. Loren had paid for a private tour of any area that he desired. Obviously, he wants to go where that little girl is.

The tour started in the front room on the main floor, and methodically worked its way through that floor, first to the piano room with a parquet floor, then the dining room and tea rooms, followed by guest bedrooms. The guide tried to give Loren his money's worth, but Loren kept urging him on, all but dragging the guide to the next room, often cutting off the guide in mid-sentence.

I must stop this tour. But how? How do I get Loren and the guide to exit the building?

Then the tour guide ushered Loren to the other side of the floor, to the library and Jefferson's den. Jefferson's personal bedroom would be last.

A fire! They would have to leave. Where would a fire do the least damage? Begin activated the dot in the old kitchen in the basement, and focused it into a laser beam directed at a wooden table. A few seconds later, a waft of smoke began to drift upward from the table.

He turned back to the hologram dot spying Loren and the guide. They were in Jefferson's study. The bedroom would be next. Those two rooms

338

were joined by a bed with a bright red bedspread that was open on both sides, allowing for Jefferson to lie down on his bed from either room. Not much privacy. But, then, what he knew of America's third president was that he was an intellectual and a bit of an eccentric, so maybe the design of the rooms fit. Just why did Loren come here, anyway? Obviously, the little girl is part of this, but how did she end up with the backpack? Better still, why Monticello with all the roaming, nosy tourists? I bet Stowe and DeYoung know. Hopefully the open windows would flush the inside air, and they would be awake soon to answer some questions.

He went back to the dot in the old kitchen. The amount of smoke had tripled. The detector would activate any second. He made sure the laser beam was at its strongest.

Back to the tour. The guide opened the door linking the study and the bedroom. Loren followed as the tour guide went into his spiel. After a minute of lecture, Loren pivoted and pointed at the three oval openings above the bed, high on the wall with the raised ceiling.

The guide looked at where Loren was pointing. "Oh, that is one of the more unique features of Monticello. That is a closet, accessible by a ladder through that door." He pointed at a door to the right.

Loren kept his eyes on the ovals. "You mean storage?"

"No. Closet. Jefferson—or one of his slaves, most likely—climbed the ladder every day."

"Wow. I'd like to see that."

"Well, it is a very steep—"

"I am able."

The guide nodded. "Mr. Loren, I am sure you are—"

"I said that I am able."

The guide cringed, and then frowned. "Just please be careful."

"I understand; you're afraid of liability. Well, you've warned me. You did your due diligence."

Begin reverted to the dot showing the kitchen. A small flame now poked up from the table. Burn, baby, burn. Come on, smoke detectors. He turned his attention back to the bedroom.

The guide grimaced. They stepped to the door, and the guide opened it and pointed. "See? Very steep and narrow."

Nick peered in. "Not that steep and not that narrow." He turned to the guide and smiled. "Be right back." He stepped into the closet and stepped on the first rung. Up. Then, the second rung. Third, fourth. A few more and he would be able to see above the floor of the closet.

At that moment, the entire house was filled with the sound of dozens of smoke detectors, followed by several fire alarms.

"Come down!" the guide yelled.

Nick did not respond.

"Come down right now!"

Begin activated the dot in the closet. Loren's head poked above the floor.

"Mr. Loren! Come down right now! There's a fire!"

Still, Loren did not reply. He pivoted his head then twisted his torso and reached for the outstretched hand of the little girl. He checked her wrist for a pulse. A slight smile from Loren confirmed for Begin that she was alive. Loren took another step up the ladder as the guide issued more protests. Loren reached and placed his left hand on the outside of the backpack and squeezed. Another smile.

The guide grabbed Loren's leg and pulled. "We have to go this moment! I smell smoke!"

Still, Loren ignored him. He lifted his leg to go up another rung and, when he did, the guide yanked down on the raised foot.

"Let go of me!" Loren yelled.

"No! Come down now or I'll pull you down."

Loren took a step-down and looked at the guide. "Okay, but only if I get to come back up here after the fire is out."

"Agreed."

Begin shook his head. Was Loren not going to save the little girl? He activated the kitchen dot and stopped the laser beam. Sprinklers had activated in the old kitchen and were already putting out the fire. Still,

Loren did not know that. He was going to leave that little girl to burn.
Wow.

144

A fire at that very moment? Too coincidental. Had to be started by those Israelis. They don't care about Amy. Did they know about Amy? Had to. Too coincidental. Dots could not see other dots, but the Israelis had their own D-frame. Nick activated the dot inside the house. One of the soldiers was looking at the hologram coming out of his wristwatch. Yup.

Nick followed the guide outside the front door of Monticello. The gong sounded atop the home. Nine a.m. The fog still had not lifted. Sirens went off in the distance. By the time the fire trucks arrived, the fire in the old kitchen was already out. Loren wanted to go back inside. However, police arrived, too, and shut down Monticello.

Police. I can't be questioned. Nick turned to the guide. "I'll return later in the day to complete the tour."

The guide nodded. "If tours re-start today. Plainclothes detectives are on their way."

Loren frowned then turned and walked down the brick sidewalk leading from Monticello. He made his way to the kiln and retrieved the spear. His phone rang. It was the Senator. He wanted to talk to Amy. Nick told the Senator she was still sleeping.

"Still? She usually doesn't sleep this late."

"She's almost a teenager, Senator. And teenagers sleep late."

"Show her to me on your video app. Maybe I can tell by looking at her if she's feeling badly."

"I'm outside right now."

"I just saw a news flash that there was a fire at Monticello."

"Really? Well, I did hear sirens."

"My daughter is safe?"

"Yes, Senator. Very safe."

"Should I come down there?"

"No need. I know where she is and am watching her."

"Send me the video when you get back inside."

"Will do, Senator."

145

When Begin saw Loren disappear into the fog, he activated the infrared sensor on the dot. He watched as Loren walked to the plank kiln and then slipped the spear into his coat pocket. Keep him dotted.

Soldier Number Three came up from the basement. "They're awake."

Begin hustled down the steps.

146

Lacy stared at the man in the gas mask holding the machine gun. The man lifted his gas mask enough to speak. "My name is Begin. I am a Captain in the Israeli Defense Force."

"Israelis operating inside the U.S!" Archer exclaimed.

Lacy turned to him. "Would you rather have them be from Pas?"

Archer frowned and shook his head.

She turned back to Begin. "Can you untie us?"

Begin motioned to the other soldier, who performed the task, then looked to her. "We are Israelis sent by our Prime Minister. Of course, if you repeat that, we will call you such a big liar." He told her of Loren and the spear, of the fire, and of the little girl with the backpack.

"Her name is Amy Kitchens. The Senator's daughter."

Begin's gaze darted to their faces. "You kidnapped her?"

"No. We think she is part of a political ploy to get sympathy for the Senator's bill."

Begin shook his head.

"This whole thing is a dirty business," Lacy said.

Begin nodded at her. "And I thought the Middle East was foul."

"Where are we?" Lacy asked.

"Near Monticello."

"Jefferson's home?" She looked at Archer. "Why would Loren come here?"

"You're asking me?" He turned to Begin. "Do you have some aspirin? I have a really bad headache."

Begin nodded to Archer then motioned to the soldier to go find some. The soldier left, and then returned a few minutes later, running down the steps. "Number Four is dead!"

Begin spun around.

"His neck is broken. Yatom is gone, and so is Number Four's machine gun and gas mask!"

Begin ran up the steps. Archer and Lacy tried to follow, but their legs were still asleep from being in the same position for so long. They grabbed each other and slowly made their way up the steps. The blood eased back into their legs and, by the top of the steps, they could walk without assistance.

Begin pointed at the dead soldier. Then he activated the dot in Jefferson's bedroom closet. Amy was gone, and so was the backpack.

147

The fire alarms had woken Amy. She had a terrible headache and a knot the size of a baseball on the crown of her head. She had forgotten where she was. The smell of smoke stung her nostrils. She climbed down the ladder. There was that weird open bed again. Oh, yes, now I remember.

She eased open the door leading to the room with all spears on the wall. She peeked out. There was a man in a uniform outside on the front steps. Next to him was a man in a suit and he had a pistol in his hand. That lady in the basement told me the backpack will protect me. But how?

Amy carefully closed the door, turned, and walked across the bedroom. Sliding over the weird red bed and planting her feet on the floor of some kind of office without a computer, she peeked around the corner. There were some books on the far wall. To her right was a door leading to the outside. But there were more strange-looking men out there, too. She peered to the left, down the hallway. All clear. She crept down it. Then she heard the sound of the front door opening and men's voices. Quick! She darted through a door on her right. It was a staircase, and down she went.

148

Begin ran a human tissue search of Monticello and quickly located Amy in the basement. He adjusted the dot and watched her creep along the basement hallway. She was pinching her nose. Must be the smell of smoke from the fire.

There was a sound down the hallway. Behind Amy. Begin switched the dot. There were men at the end of the hallway not far from the kitchen where the fire had been. Obviously, Amy heard them, too, for she ducked through a door on her left.

Begin readjusted the dot and scanned the new room. Wine cellar. Her nose crinkled and she cringed. Must smell bad in there as well. But not that bad, because she crouched down behind one of the big barrels in the corner.

He ran a human tissue search of the Monticello grounds and, within seconds, found Loren kneeling behind the earthen mound where he had hidden the spear. What will be his next move? Obviously, get to Amy. If he doesn't know she has already moved, certainly he will soon discover that.

149

Nick sat down and lay back against the cool earth of the plank kiln. He re-dotted the inside of Monticello, and quickly discovered Amy was gone. *This little girl is a pain in the butt.* He ran a human tissue search and found her in the wine cellar. *If she is running from me, why didn't she approach the cops in the house? Must be scared. How do I get inside once more? And how do I do it without being seen by the Israelis?*

His phone rang and he switched to that application. It was the Senator again. *Oh, great.*

"Why haven't you sent the video of Amy?"

He had forgotten. "I'm still outside."

"Doing what? Categorizing the types of trees?"

"Senator, I apologize. I'll do it soon."

Silence from the Senator. "Send it. I feel that something is not right here. I'm heading down there right now."

"Senator!"

There was no reply. He had hung up. *Just great.*

Then his phone dinged again. *I bet that's the Senator again.* However, it was a text from Mini-D. "You have lost positive control of Amy. Kill her immediately, repossess canisters, and burn them."

He gasped. He sent back a text. "Killing Amy would be senseless."

"She will make a good martyr to use against the Christians."

He tried to respond, but Mini-D had cut off the conversation and would not respond to further messages.

150

At 10 a.m., as the gong sounded once more from the cupola atop Monticello, the sound of car doors opening and closing traveled to Nick's ears, where he still huddled against the other side of the grassy plank kiln. He turned and peered over the top. Fog still blocked his view, but, from where the sound of the engines came, he was pretty sure it was the cops and that they were leaving. Finally.

He waited a few minutes, rose, brushed the grass and twigs from his rumpled jacket and slacks, made sure the spear was secure in his inside pocket, and strode towards the east door of Monticello.

151

"He's heading towards the house!" Begin said into his microphone. "Everyone at the front door, now."

Soldier Number Five scurried from the living room and soldier Number Three rushed up the stairs. Behind him followed Archer and Lacy.

Begin looked at Lacy. "You two stay here. It might get dicey."

"But—"

"I don't have time to worry about your safety! Stay!" He turned away from her to close the conversation.

Out the front door he ran, Numbers Five and Three behind him, Numbers Two and Six meeting him as he flung open the front door. Up the trail they ran. Time for action.

152

Nick found the tour guide and requested that the tour be continued immediately—except now he wanted to go to the basement.

"I am sorry, Mr. Loren, but all tours have—"

"No tour, no donation."

This seemed to get the guide's attention. "The basement? But we have not finished—"

"I want to see the basement. We should have started there. You know: from the ground up, that sort of thing."

The guide frowned and nodded. "I have a few details to attend to, concerning the police investigation. We'll be able to continue in just a few minutes. Is that acceptable?"

Nick nodded and watched the guide walk down the south hallway. His eyes drifted to the items in the front lobby, to the animal skins and Indian artifacts. He looked back at the hatchet on the wall. Mini-D wants me to kill Amy. Senseless. I won't do it. But maybe I can scare her into compliance. He looked around. No one seemed to be watching him. He walked to the hatchet and pulled it off of the nails that were suspending it on the wall. Then he turned to his right where the staircase led to the basement. Forget the guide.

153

Something is wrong. Kitchens's stomach churned more with every second. He had the helicopter land in the east parking lot of the Capitol. Jumping aboard, he gave the destination to the pilot.

154

Begin dashed up the hill and paused at the top, crouching. He glanced to the right, at the cemetery, and then activated his wristwatch to re-dot Amy. As the screen came into view, it went blank. What? He tried again. His entire cell was dead. The local tower must be down. That means Loren is blind, too. Time to move.

He pivoted towards his team. "Two, take the east door. Three, the west door. Five and Six, the South Dependency leading to the basement where the kitchen fire was. I am going in through the North Dependency. It leads to the wine cellar. Remember: only darts, if at all possible."

At a dead run, through the fog, they advanced on Monticello.

155

Hatchet in hand, Nick crept down the wooden staircase, stepping as softly as he could so the guide would not hear him when he returned. At the bottom of the steps he eased the door open, and peeked left and then right. No one, either way.

He stepped out into the hallway of white-painted stones. The wine cellar door was a few feet to his left. Nick paused at the door and listened. Nothing. As he turned the knob and shuffled in, there was a rustling in the corner. His eyes darted to a big barrel. She was still there.

"Amy," he whispered.

No response.

"Amy. It's Nick Loren."

Still no response.

"I know you're behind the barrel. Come out. I'll help you."

The top of her head breached his line of eyesight then the rest of her face came into view. She looked tired and frightened. He tried to make his smile as reassuring as possible.

Her eyes flashed.

She's seen the hatchet. "It's just for show," he said quickly. "I'm holding it for the museum."

"There was a man in the house with a gun."

"I know. That's why I have this hatchet. So I can keep you safe."

"My daddy…"

"Your daddy will be here soon. He asked me to take care of you."

"He'll be here soon?"

"Yes. Very soon. Come with me," he said, holding out his hand again.

She rose and wiggled out from behind the barrel.

Nick's smile broadened as he slid the hatchet behind his back.

A rumbling sounded behind him, and then a pop. He spun around. The long, thin door of the dumbwaiter swung open. Inside was a man in a gas mask, holding a machine gun. He was wearing Yatom's clothes.

156

"I'm not waiting here in this house when the manuscripts and the spear are up there."

Archer looked at Lacy. "It could be dangerous up there. The captain told us to stay here."

"You can stay if you want, but we have gone through too much to hold back now."

That makes sense. Out of the house and up the trail they ran.

157

"Put the hatchet down," the man in the gas mask said, as he stepped from the dumbwaiter.

Nick did not comply.

"Put the hatchet down, Loren, or you'll go down."

He frowned and set the hatchet at his feet. "Aren't we on the same side?"

Yatom grunted. "Were. Before you left me for the Israeli commando team."

"I paid for the manuscript and the spear. They are mine."

Yatom shook his head. "Not anymore. You lost possession of them. And now, finders keepers." He pointed at the backpack. "Amy, set the backpack at my feet."

She did not move.

Nick placed his hand on the top of her shoulder. "Amy, give it to him."

She looked at Nick, then slipped the backpack off her shoulders, setting it at Yatom's feet and then backed off.

"I'll buy the canisters and spear again," Nick offered.

Yatom shook his head. "Don't trust you."

"Seven figures again. Double your money."

Yatom smiled. "Eight figures."

"Ten million dollars!? You're crazy."

"Guilty as charged, but that doesn't necessarily help your side, does it?"

Nick frowned, then nodded. "Okay. Done." Ten million dollars was still a sliver of the foundation's reserves. He reached out his hand.

"No way. Not until I see the money is deposited in my one-way account."

"How do I know I can trust you to hand over the goods?"

"I'll put it this way: you can trust me just as much as I can trust you," then gave a touche-type smile.

They heard footsteps in the hall. Then, "Hey, who are you?" There was a grunt, a gasp, and a thump on the floor.

Yatom pointed at the dumbwaiter, and said through gritted teeth, "Up! Now!" He pointed the machine gun at Nick.

Nick looked at the dart sticking out from the end of the barrel of the machine gun then motioned to Amy, who got in the dumbwaiter. "When you get to the next floor, get out and wait for me."

She frowned at Nick and nodded. Nick pulled the wires and ushered her up. She got out, and he pulled the platform back down and crouched inside.

Yatom stuck the end of the machine gun in Nick's face, the tip of the dart touching his nose. "You'd better be up there, or I will sell the manuscripts to the other side."

"Why don't you let the little girl go?"

"No way. A Senator's daughter for cover," Yatom said blithely, then winked.

Nick looked at Yatom. You're disgusting... But am I really that much different? He frowned. "I'll be up in the dining room, waiting." He pulled on the wires and Yatom disappeared from his view.

As soon as he got out, Yatom pulled the platform down, stepped onto the dumbwaiter, placed the backpack with the canisters and spear on top of his head, and pulled himself up to the next floor. Then he reached in, and disabled the runner on which the wires ran.

158

Begin loaded another dart in his machine gun, knelt, and checked the pulse of the guard he had shot in the hall. Then he pivoted to his right, towards the wine cellar. Turning the knob, he pushed the door open and moved back out of the line of fire. He needed dot vision. Now he would have to do it the old-fashioned way. Begin glanced around the corner. No one was there. He stuck his head inside the room then ducked out. Still no one. Stepping fully into the room, Begin saw there was a hatchet on the floor. He searched the small room. Just wine bottles and barrels. Amy was gone. Where? And where is Loren?

He saw footprints in some dust on the floor. One set was small, another larger. No, there were two different sole imprints. Two? They disappeared near a narrow door. The door was not fully closed. He eased it back, half expecting a bomb of some sort. There was a platform on its floor. And cables. A dumbwaiter. Of course, I'm in the wine cellar.

Begin stuck his head into the dumbwaiter and rotated to look up. He focused. Machine gun! He flung himself back just as a dart zipped by his face and stabbed the platform of the dumbwaiter. Then he heard the sound of footsteps above him. Number Four's machine gun! Yatom!

Begin activated his walkie-talkie microphone under his chin. "Yatom, Loren, and girl on main floor. Stay on darts."

159

Yatom turned to Nick and pointed at the door leading from the dining room. "Go," he growled.

With Amy's hand in his, Nick opened the door and walked out onto the parquet floor of the piano room. To his right was the west door, leading outside to the grounds and the cemetery beyond, all still enveloped in fog.

He looked left, and there was one of the soldiers on the other side of the glass in the front room. Had the soldier seen him? He had not turned this way. Were they now on the same side?

The soldier turned his shoulders in the direction of Amy and Nick. The soldier's eyes flashed, and jerked his machine gun around and aimed it at Nick. Nick stepped in front of Amy, even though the barrel of the gun was aimed higher, at him.

Nick held his gaze on the soldier's and silently flicked them and his head back towards the dining room where Yatom still was. Then, using his torso to shield his finger from Yatom, he pointed in the direction of the dining room, all the while contorting his lips to communicate danger. He was not sure if the soldier understood his pantomime, but at least the soldier did not fire. Yet.

The soldier stared at him then slid to the glass door separating the front room from the piano room, and carefully opened it.

Nick nodded ever so slightly and lifted the corner of his lips just enough to communicate a muted smile. Then he turned back to Yatom and flashed a wide smile. "Okay. The coast is clear."

Through the door and out into the piano room Yatom stepped. He looked right to the outside then turned left. His eyes flashed as he ducked and turned his back to the soldier.

A dart whizzed through the air and pierced the backpack slung over Yatom's shoulders. Yatom turned and fired a dart into the left leg of the soldier. The soldier gasped and fell to the floor.

Yatom pointed at the door leading to the outside. "Go!"

Nick tightened his grip on Amy's hand and pulled. As he rushed towards the door, an explosion filled the room. The glass to his right shattered. The soldier had fired a live round before he fell unconscious. There was yet another explosion. Nick looked over his shoulder as he pulled Amy to safety. Yatom had fired a live round into the soldier.

160

Lacy reached the top of the hill and bent over. She sucked in a gulp of air as she turned to check where Archer was. Not far behind. He's getting better at keeping up. Then an explosion went off up ahead, followed by another one.

"Gunfire," she forced out between gulps of air.

Archer nodded as his chest heaved, his lungs pumping in protest. She turned left to run towards where the gunfire had come from.

Archer grabbed her upper right arm. "No." She tried to break free, but Archer held on. "No.

"I'm going!"

He pulled her towards him. "I won't let you."

161

Begin's head jerked in the direction of the sounds. "Go to live rounds," he commanded through his microphone.

Number Two, from his position outside the east door, said, "I can see through the windows. Yatom and two others are running out the west door."

"Everyone converge on the grounds to the west," Begin ordered. "Take out Yatom. Try to not hit the backpack. Aim for the legs if possible. And don't hit the little girl!"

Begin ran out into the hallway, up the stairs, and slipped into the piano room. He checked on Number Three. Unconscious, but alive. Then he ran out the west door. Number Two was already at the west portico beside the columns. Two must have run through the east door, through the front room, and past Number Three. Then he must have gone through the piano room and out the west doors in the time it took for him to run upstairs.

Number Two pointed west into the fog. "They ran in that direction. This is the thickest fog I have ever seen. I lost them before they made ten meters. Even my night goggles could not pick them up."

Begin activated his microphone. "Five and Six, where are you?"

Five answered. "Outside, at the end of the Southern Dependency. Captain, cannot see anyone in this fog."

"Proceed on a line west. Everyone make sure it is not one of us before you shoot. If your night goggles are not already on, then turn them on." But will they do any good in this thick fog?

162

Archer's eyes flicked to the sound drifting through the fog. It was straight ahead. No, a little to the left. Distant yet, but coming closer. The noise grew louder, but it was still not distinct. What was that? There was stomping of some sort, mostly heavy with a few light thumps in between. An animal? Horse, maybe? No, too uneven. And there was a rattling and even an occasional squeaking and grinding. Things were being rubbed together as they were being thrown around. Then he heard the sound of breathing. Labored. Low. Male. Two of them?

They're getting closer. Definitely closer. The men were right in front of Archer and Lacy, a hundred feet or so. Two different men, for sure. Separate-sounding coughs. Begin's soldiers?

Then, cutting the fog, there was a gasp, a thump, a grunt, and a curse, followed by silence. Someone had fallen.

Drifting through the fog, Archer heard a soft, little voice call, "Are you okay?"

163

"You are a klutz!" Yatom hissed.

Nick looked up from where his hands clasped his right ankle and frowned at Yatom. He did not argue. "I didn't see that berm until too late." He grunted. "Ironically, I think it was called the ha-ha berm to keep livestock out of the flower beds."

"Well, ha-ha," Yatom said. "Can you walk or do I shoot you now like an injured horse?"

"You shoot me, and you kill the golden goose."

"There are other geese, and they, too, lay golden eggs."

Nick grimaced. "I'll make it." He sat up, rotated to all fours, and pushed himself up and onto his left foot. He tried to take a step and he buckled. Amy moved to support him. He looked down at her and smiled. *What should I say to that? I don't deserve her help.*

He twisted around to look at Yatom. "Where to?"

"Begin had to come in by helicopter. Did you hear where he landed?"

"Only vaguely. Out to the west I think. It sounded a good ways off. And the team seemed to be coming in from that direction. But you can't take off in this fog."

"We can if we go straight up at first. Give me your cell."

"It's dead. The local tower is down."

Yatom checked. Sure enough, no signal.

Then a new sound floated through the air. Sirens. Yatom looked in that direction.

"Mr. Loren, there's something over there," Amy said quietly.

Nick turned where she was pointing, ahead and to the left. She was right. It was a fence of some sort. With Amy's help, he hobbled towards it. As they neared, he could discern rectangular shapes sticking out of the ground. It was the cemetery.

With Amy at his side, he hopped on his left foot as best he could, careful not to put any real weight on her fragile shoulders.

Yatom found a gate on the other side. "Hurry up."

The gate had an ornate seal on it. The Jefferson family seal, no doubt. They entered, and Nick plopped down against the obelisk at Jefferson's grave.

164

Archer followed the sounds to their right. He listened to the clogging steps, the grunts, the coughs, and then the clicking of the latch of an iron gate and the hinges swinging.

"That's Amy, Loren, and Yatom," he whispered to Lacy. "I recognize their voices."

She nodded. "I think they're to our right, about a hundred feet or so. Now what?"

He pointed in the direction of the approaching sirens. "Let the cops handle it."

They listened as two squad cars raced up the hill towards Monticello. The sirens echoed off the surrounding hills and forests. The fog added to the distortion. Once the cars hit the loop encircling Monticello one car turned in their direction. They ducked into the weeds as it roared by. The other car turned away and its headlights reflected off the fog, but part of it caught the iron fence and it gleamed for a split second. Half a minute later the sound of the sirens burped to a halt on the other side of the house.

Archer turned to Lacy. "I think Yatom and the other two are hiding in the cemetery."

"Fitting. That's where they're going to end up. Where do you think Begin and his team are?"

"I have no idea."

165

"Captain, this is Six. I think I see them. Inside a fence. Near some kind of obelisk."

"Affirmative," Begin whispered into his microphone. "Must be the cemetery. Can you see the little girl?"

"Negative. I see Yatom standing, and the other man sitting against the obelisk."

"Who has the backpack?"

"Yatom."

"I think we can assume he also has the spear. Where are you?"

"Approximately one hundred meters southwest of house and thirty meters from the cemetery fence."

"Have they seen you?"

"Negative."

Begin turned his head to the left, but could not see them even with his night-vision goggles. "Keep in contact with them but do not engage. We will advance. We are on your right. There is some kind of berm in front of us. Police cars went to the front door on the east side. Number Two, you stay here and watch for their movement. They will probably exit Monticello from the west door and close in on you. Two, use darts on police, if possible. The rest of you, also use darts. If you have to use live rounds, be careful of the little girl."

Several affirmatives chirped in his ear.

"Okay, I am going to advance. Five and Six, can you advance without detection?"

"Believe so, Captain."

"Then do it."

Five and Six crawled towards the south side of the iron fence circling the Jefferson family plot, while Begin slithered over the berm and approached the fence's north side. There was Yatom, standing near the obelisk, backpack around his shoulders and the feet of a man sticking out from the obelisk. Loren, he assumed. But, where was the little girl?

"Two, any sign of movement towards the house?" he whispered into his microphone.

"Negative, Captain."

"Five, Six, are you in position?"

"Affirmative."

"Go to darts. I will fire first."

"Affirmative," Five whispered back.

Begin crawled five meters forward. There was Amy. He loaded his dart, maneuvered his body into shooting position, and aimed at Yatom's neck. He clicked on the red laser to guide his line of sight, refined his aim, and squeezed the trigger.

Yatom's head snapped down and to the right then he jumped forward behind the obelisk. He must have seen the red laser beam reflect on the fog. Stupid! I should not have used the laser. Begin lifted his gas mask. "Yatom! You are surrounded!"

166

When Archer heard Captain Begin, he turned and eyed Lacy. When her eyes flashed, he pressed down with his left arm ever harder to keep her pinned to the ground. He moved his mouth to her right ear. "Let the soldiers take care of this.

"But the manuscripts…"

"…are not worth your life."

167

The crown of Yatom's head poked out from behind the obelisk. Then more of it slid out. Yatom craned his neck and opened his mouth.

"Stay back, or I shoot my two hostages and destroy the manuscripts. You know I'll do it!"

Begin nodded to himself. No doubt about that. His reputation in Mossad was for being totally ruthless. "Let the little girl and Loren go, leave the backpack and spear, and I will let you slip away."

He could hear Yatom's scoff. "Get serious. I want your helicopter. After I get away, I'll release my hostages."

"And the backpack and spear?"

"No way. They're my ticket."

"You know I'm not going to let you out of here with them."

"If I can't keep them, then no one will."

168

Archer beat Lacy to it once more. When Yatom issued his threat, Archer pulled her closer to him and shook his head at her.

She returned his look with a frown of surrender. Then her eyes flashed and she mumbled, "The spear..."

169

"Captain, it's Number Two."

"Come in."

"Two police officers are making their way towards me from the house."

"Tell them to stop or they will be shot. Stay on darts, if you can."

"Affirmative."

The voice of Number Two complying with his order drifted back to him. The silence that followed Begin took as good news. For now.

Begin assumed that Yatom heard Number Two's directive to the police. That should only convince Yatom that his situation was untenable.

"Captain, are you going to call in your copter or not?"

Nope, didn't convince him. He *is* stubborn. "Yatom, you know I can't let you do that."

"Then you can explain to the Prime Minister how you were responsible for the destruction of the manuscripts."

"We've got photocopies."

"Not the same, and you know it."

Silence. Then a light punctured the fog. Begin clicked on the magnifier of his goggles. There was Yatom, with a piece of paper in one hand and a lighter in the other.

"Do what I demand, or I burn the manuscripts!"

God, he's really going to do it. Yatom moved the lighter underneath the piece of paper.

"All right!"

Yatom lowered the lighter, and Loren reached over and squelched the small flame on the corner of the paper.

Then, to the northeast, they all heard a bass-thump reverberating across the landscape. A helicopter. It was moving fast and getting closer by the second.

"That's more like it!" Yatom yelled at him.

Begin activated his microphone. "Did any of you call in our copter?"

Three negatives came back to him. Then who is that?

Yatom yelled out again. "Have the helicopter land in the open area and, after I am away, I promise to release Loren and the girl."

Let Yatom think what he wants for now. "Agreed."

170

Nick turned his head towards the sound of the approaching helicopter. It was close, maybe a hundred yards. But still no visual in the fog. It was moving slowly now, creeping through the air. Undoubtedly looking for a landing spot in this soup. With the local cell tower out, there was no radar or infrared.

Then, above him, the fog began to swirl, like some kind of sick cotton candy at a county fair. Gray threads rolling and churning in a sliding loop, right above them. Is the copter going to set down right in the cemetery?

The wind whipped at them. He turned to Yatom. "We got to move!"

Just as he started to push himself up, the helicopter slid away. Then, by the sound, it hovered again, somewhere out over the grounds.

171

Begin had to yell into his microphone to be heard. "Two! Is the copter over you?"

"Was," Two yelled back. "It moved to the right."

"Confirm identity of copter."

"Will do, Captain."

The helicopter touched down. Fifteen seconds later he could hear Two yell, "Stop or I will shoot." Then Two came in over the microphone. "Captain, that is not our helicopter."

"Then whose is it?"

"He told me he is a United States Senator, and that he is here for his daughter."

172

Begin ripped the gas mask off of his head as he jumped up. "Senator!"

No response. Probably can't hear me over the helicopter.

He yelled again. Still no response. He ran towards the sound of the helicopter, up and over the ha-ha berm and, seven strides later, came upon two people. One was his soldier and the other was in a sports jacket. He closed in on the two figures and, as he neared, he recognized the famous face of Senator Damian Kitchens.

Kitchens snapped around to him. "Where is my daughter?"

"She is a hostage."

"Release her!"

"Not by us."

"Then by who?"

He was not going to answer that. Their cover was not completely blown. Yet. "Not sure."

"Where is she?"

"We have them surrounded."

"What SWAT team are you with?"

"Local."

Kitchens turned and walked to the helicopter. Within seconds, the engine began to quiet and the blades swirled at a dying pace. Kitchens marched back to him. "In what direction are they?"

Begin did not respond.

Kitchens arched his head back and opened his mouth. "Amy!!"

Through the fog came the shriek of a child. "Daddy!"

Kitchens's eyes shot to the direction of Amy's cry. He took a step then stopped when the tip of the dart pressed into the side of his neck.

"You are only going to get her killed. If I have to drop you to save her, I will do it."

Then another voice came to them. A man's voice. "Senator! I have your daughter. I have the manuscripts and the spear, and I will sell them to you in return for your daughter."

"Agreed!"

Begin shook his head. He didn't even ask how much. I probably wouldn't either if my child was involved.

"You've got to take us out of here on the helicopter," came the voice.

"Agreed."

Begin gritted his teeth at the Senator. "No way."

Kitchens turned to him. "If you endanger my daughter, I will see that you never get out of prison." Kitchens turned and yelled in the direction of where the voices had come. "Come out! We'll take my helicopter!"

Begin hissed at the Senator. "I warn you."

"No. I warn you." He turned back. "Amy! Follow the sound of my voice!"

"Daddy!"

It took nearly a minute for the three figures to emerge from the fog. Number Two snapped his machine gun in their direction. Begin motioned for Two to lower his weapon.

Loren came into view first. Then Yatom, backpack over his shoulders, machine gun in his right hand, and his left hand held a fistful of Amy's back collar. Yatom smiled at his Israeli counterpart.

Begin wanted to slap him.

Kitchens pointed at the helicopter. "Get in."

Yatom took a step.

Begin raised his weapon. "Stop!"

Yatom smiled again. "Captain, give it up. You are beaten."

Kitchens looked at him. "Captain?"

"Captain in the local SWAT," Begin added quickly.

Yatom chuckled. "He's a Captain in the Israeli Defense Force."

Kitchens's eyes flashed. "Israelis!"

Begin frowned but did not confirm. Nor did he deny.

Kitchens thrust a finger at him. "I will have—"

Begin pointed his machine gun at him. "You will have nothing if you don't shut up." He turned back to Yatom. "I think in Mexico they call this a 'stand-off'."

Yatom shook his head. "The only one left standing will be you and your men when we fly away."

He smiled slightly. "I think you know that I am not going to let that happen."

There was a gunshot from the other side of the helicopter. Number Two grabbed his leg and crumpled to the ground. It was the cops. "You are all under arrest!" came the voice from the fog.

Yatom turned and fired in the direction of the voice. The police returned fire.

Kitchens moved towards his daughter. Yatom let her go and she ran to her father's arms. He picked her up and ran towards the helicopter as Yatom fired at the police again. Yatom ran towards the helicopter, racing past Begin.

Begin swung his machine gun at Yatom and fired a dart into his leg. Yatom buckled, pivoted, and fired at Begin, missing him as Begin dove to the ground. Begin opened fire, splattering Yatom across the chest with a few live rounds, strafing the side of the helicopter. The police also fired more shots into the fog.

Then silence. A cry of agony split the air. "Amy!"

173

The screaming was something awful; thundering shouts and piercing shrieks punctuated by pleadings cascading to denial.

Lacy looked at Archer. "Something's happened."

He nodded and moved his arm off of her. They ran towards the mayhem and, there, on the ground, was little Amy Kitchens, blood fountaining from her chest, Begin kneeling over her, giving her mouth-to-mouth.

"Oh, Lord, no," Lacy mumbled.

She and Archer slowly stepped towards the scene, keeping a distance from it, eyes drifting from Amy, to Begin, the Senator, and back to Amy. Lacy frowned and said a prayer. Not so much for Amy, but for the shooter and the Senator. Then she gasped.

Archer looked at her. "What?"

"The spear!"

Archer's eyes flashed. "Of course!"

"Who has the spear?"

Kitchens seemed to ignore her, maybe didn't even know she was there, he was so out of his mind, and Begin was busy. She repeated her question.

Loren spun around and glared at her. "Not now!"

She thrust her hands at him. "The spear! It can heal!"

"It can, I tell you!" Archer jumped in. "I've seen it for myself."

Loren's head jerked to him and then to her. "Superstitious nonsense."

Archer gritted his teeth. "What do you have to lose?"

Begin looked up at her from his compressions on Amy's chest. He was bloody and he was tiring. "Let's try it."

"Where is it?" she asked.

Loren stepped towards Yatom, lying on the ground. "In the backpack." He pulled it out, but Yatom did not move whatsoever. If he was not already dead, he would soon be.

Loren handed the spear to Lacy, who grabbed it and thrust it at Kitchens. "Senator, touch the wound with the tip of this spear."

He turned and looked at her. His eyes were wide, but dazed and unfocused. He looked down at the spear, and then he seemed to focus as he looked back up at her in question.

"Touch the wound with the tip of this spear," she repeated.

Kitchens did not move.

"What have you got to lose?" Archer cried.

Kitchens reached up and wrapped his fingers around the end of the spear. He looked at it, then turned and knelt at Amy's side. Begin moved his blood-soaked hands from Amy's chest.

Kitchens looked at his daughter, then the spear, and lowered the tip to the wound.

Nothing.

He tried again.

Nothing.

The Senator gasped a cry.

"You've got to believe!" Archer exclaimed.

Lacy turned to Archer and an involuntary grin spread across her face. She turned back to Kitchens. "Yes! Senator, you have to believe in the power of the Lord."

Kitchens turned and looked up at her with a blank face.

She thrust her hands forward. "Just call his name!"

Kitchens turned back to his daughter, and then looked up. "Oh, Lord God."

In an instant, the bleeding stopped. Then, in seconds, the wound covered up. Amy coughed and gulped in a breath. Kitchens gasped. He put his hands to where the wound had been. He gasped again as he ran his hands over her healed body. He looked at Archer and Lacy, his eyes wide. Grabbing his daughter, he pulled her to him, burying his head in her chest as his shoulders heaved.

Nick stood, mouth agape, and then finally air leaked from him. Begin fell back on his hands as he shook his head. The police had gathered at the scene and stared in silence.

Archer turned to Lacy and smiled. Then he looked up. "Praise to You."

She gushed a smile. "Yes. Praise." Then her eyes flashed again. "Give me the spear!"

Kitchens was still hugging his daughter, and did not hear her. She removed his fingers from it then walked to where Yatom lay. She knelt and touched the spear tip to each wound. Yatom revived in seconds.

Lacy sensed someone hovering over her. She turned. It was Begin. She waited for his reaction.

"He does not deserve that."

Lacy shook her head. "That is for God to say, not us." She grabbed Yatom's machine gun from the ground and handed it to Begin. Then she slipped the backpack off of Yatom's shoulders and handed it to Archer, who looked inside and nodded.

She rose and touched the spear to Number Two's wound, and it healed.

Begin pointed at the spear. "I have another man wounded inside the house."

She looked at him. "Are you a believer?"

He looked at her. "I am now. I will bring the spear right back."

Can I trust him? ...Yes. He risked his life and the lives of his men to secure the spear and the manuscripts. Lacy handed the spear to him.

He looked at it then turned to one of the police officers. "Come with me, please."

They returned fifteen minutes later, Number Three with them. She smiled. One less casualty. Thank God.

Begin pointed in the direction of the private home. "I also tried to revive Number Four." He frowned and shook his head. "Rigor mortis had already set in."

Lacy frowned and looked at Archer. "Maybe the spear has a time limit."

Archer shrugged. "Maybe. And maybe it was simply God's plan… for reasons we do not understand."

She smiled. "I thought you didn't believe in 'God's plan'."

"You've got that right. You used the past tense."

She smiled, then looked at Begin and lowered her head. "Sorry."

Begin grimaced and nodded. "Thank you for letting me try."

Loren, seemingly to no one in particular, said, "What now?"

Kitchens, still holding Amy to him, looked up. "I know."

174

The gong struck 11 a.m. as Kitchens stood up. He looked at Lacy. "I have a speech to make."

She frowned. Another speech. The more things change…

Kitchens looked at her then at Archer. "You two want to come along?"

"As long as we keep the manuscripts and the spear."

Kitchens nodded to her. "They're yours. I know you will use them fairly."

Archer took a step towards Kitchens. "And as long as we get to tell our side of the story."

Kitchens nodded. "It's a democracy."

She turned to Captain Begin. "Tell the Prime Minister thank you, and thank you to you and your men."

Begin nodded. He turned to Number Two and pointed at Yatom. "Cuff him." He turned back to Lacy. "We've got a copter to catch." Then he pointed at Kitchens's helicopter. "And so do you." He smiled. "Shalom aleichem."

She smiled. "Godspeed."

The fog was beginning to burn off. Kitchens ordered the helicopter to start. He helped Amy into the helicopter. Loren got in, then Archer with the backpack and Lacy with the spear of Longinus Petronius.

"Set us down on the Capitol parking lot," Kitchens commanded.

175

As the helicopter lifted off and broke through the remnants of the fog, the Senator held Amy against his side. Then he turned to Lacy and Archer. "Thank you."

Archer smiled at the Senator and nodded, then looked at Lacy sitting beside him. His mind tumbled over the events of the last weeks and the changes that they had brought. He smiled and placed his hand on top of hers.

She looked at him, her eyes wide and searching.

He squeezed and smiled.

She smiled back. She leaned to his ear, so as to be heard over the helicopter's engine. "No matter how this turns out..." she glanced at the Senator. "...I want you to know that I am proud to be associated with you."

He smiled. A tear was forming in her eye. "No more Noah's Ark."

She smiled.

"Except maybe for the part where animals travel in pairs," he added.

She smiled at him and placed her other hand on top of his.

Kitchens tried to call his Chief of Staff.

Loren leaned towards him. "Mini-D killed the local tower. In a few minutes, we'll move into another tower's area."

Sure enough, three minutes later the phones of Kitchens and Loren dinged alive. Kitchens activated his cell and looked up. "Oh, no."

"What?" Loren asked.

Kitchens looked at Loren, then at Archer and Lacy. "I have a text from my Chief of Staff. The Senate Majority Leader has moved vote to today. At my request!" He turned at looked directly at her. "How can that be? I didn't request that!"

Loren shook his head. "Mini-D."

Then their phones went dead again. Loren tried to re-access then looked up, gritting his teeth. "Mini-D."

The pilot called out. "My onboard computer just failed. I lost all navigation and communication."

"Mini-D," Loren said again, his voice growing louder with exasperation. He reached beside Lacy and grabbed the spear. He set his cell on the floor of the helicopter and stabbed it with the spear until the cell died. He looked at Lacy and Archer. "That sure felt good."

Kitchens leaned forward towards the pilot. "Hurry!"

176

The fog lifted. The helicopter swooped across the Virginia landscape at maximum speed, one thousand feet above the hard deck. Thirty minutes later, the tip of the Washington Monument dotted the horizon. Ahead and below lay Harry Davis Field near Manassas.

"Twenty minutes," the pilot yelled over the noise of the helicopter. Then the pilot jerked forward in his seat and he quickly pushed the stick forward and to the right. The helicopter banked hard. "Missile!" was all he cried.

Lacy grabbed onto Archer as the helicopter seemed to fall from the sky. Then, a stream of white smoke shot by.

The helicopter leveled off. Loren turned and looked out the window to the rear. "It's coming around! Heat-seeking."

The pilot looked left and then right. He pushed the stick forward, and down the craft swooped. "Hang on!"

The ground rose up at Lacy as the helicopter dove. Then something white caught her eye. It was out in front of them, getting closer every second. A white van with its side door open came into view, a trail of white smoke drifting from it. Inside, two men were dressed in Arab clothing. Is the pilot going to crash into it?

She gasped as time seemed to stand still. The men in the van stood frozen, staring back at them, with mouths wide open. Then, just as it looked like the helicopter would smash into the van, the pilot pulled back on the stick and the helicopter zoomed over, missing it by mere feet.

Seconds later, there was another explosion behind them. Loren looked back through the window. "Yes!"

The pilot looked over his shoulder. "Good thing they left the motor running."

Lacy exhaled and grabbed Archer's forearm. He looked back, still wide-eyed, shaking his head.

Loren turned to them. "Mini-D," was all he said.

177

They landed in the Capitol parking lot. Kitchens grabbed Amy's hand then turned and looked at the others. "We have to run for it."

Up the Capitol steps they ran.

Between grunts and breaths, Archer said to Lacy, "Ever since I've been with you I've been running and climbing."

"It'll all be over soon, one way or the other."

Through the Senate door they followed Kitchens, who did not bother showing his pass. "They're with me," he yelled as he ran past the stunned security officers.

Into the Senate chamber Kitchens burst, pulling Amy along. The others stopped back at the door, stopped by the Sergeant-at-Arms. Kitchens ran out into the middle of the aisle, raised his arms, and shouted, "Stop!"

The entire Senate froze. Kitchens tried to calm his breathing as he turned and led Amy to Lacy. "Amy, stay with this nice lady."

Amy looked up at her father. "Yes, Daddy."

Lacy took Amy's hand and smiled at the Senator, who smiled back.

With cameras rolling and every eye on him, Kitchens walked to his desk on the Senate floor. He cleared his throat and apologized to the Vice President, who had taken the unusual step of presiding over the Senate, in anticipation of the vote on the Freedom from Religious Oppression Act. The Vice President nodded and asked the Senior Senator from the state of Wisconsin if she would yield the floor. She graciously did so.

"Mr. Vice President, as everyone knows, I have eagerly awaited this day when my bill would come to a vote—although I had planned that it would actually be tomorrow—but that is another story. However, I have to announce that something has happened, something wonderful, something that I never ever expected. I have found the Lord, or maybe, better put, He has found me."

The Vice President leaned forward in his chair, his eyebrows knitted together. "Senator Kitchens, are you telling us you are withdrawing your bill?"

"Yes, sir, that is exactly what I am saying."

Lacy gasped so strongly that her weight shifted forward, and Archer had to catch her.

He beamed at her. "You did it."

"No. We did it."

178

Kitchens could not hold a press conference on the Senate floor, so he announced that he was going to the Rotunda. Cameras and most of the Senate followed him. He confessed and apologized for the fraud of his daughter's kidnapping. He told of the gunfight, of Tamir Yatom, of Captain Begin and his team, and of the power of the spear.

"I have some more to say," Kitchens told them, "but first I want Dr. Lacy Stowe and Dr. Archer DeYoung to tell of their amazing adventure. When they are done, I will make my announcement."

Lacy looked at Archer, who motioned for her to go to the microphone. She nodded and stepped forward. She told the whole world of Mt. Pion, of the earthquake, and finding the first canister. She motioned to Archer, who laid all three pottery canisters out on the floor. Then she told of the sailboat, Israel, Pella and the second testimonium, the balloon, the cave at the Jordan River and the first testimonium, Israel again and carbon-14, the intercession by Prime Minister Laslo, the discovery of the third testimonium, a ride in a vacuum tube, going back to Turkey in a submarine, donkeys, and the spear. Lacy raised it over her head, and the Rotunda exploded in a cacophony of clicking cameras. She concluded by describing how they had escaped from Turkey with the help of the Israeli Navy, then there was another submarine ride, the Lear jet, the betrayal by Yatom, Monticello, the gunfight, and the power of the spear. All this took nearly twenty minutes.

"We will, of course, have to authenticate the documents first, through more carbon-14 tests. We will give the manuscripts to Dayton Rosenberg at The Word, and all scholars will be able to study them regardless of their faith and belief system. Obviously, measures of security will be in place."

"And the spear?" a reporter asked.

Lacy looked at Archer then back to the throng. "The power of the spear attests to the power of faith in the Lord God. It can only be used for good. It is not some curiosity piece or another form of Santa Claus. It is not meant to replace faith, but to be a manifestation of that faith. It will be placed in protective custody, and what happens after that we will just have to see."

She turned to Archer once more and smiled. "My colleague …my friend and I will tell you more later. Obviously, there is much more to tell. The best part is his coming to faith."

Archer broke into a wide smile and nodded.

"And mine, too," Loren broke in. He removed his Pas lapel pin and threw it in a trash can.

"And mine, as well," Kitchens added.

She smiled. "Praise be to our Lord."

Kitchens stepped to the microphone. He thanked Captain Begin and Prime Minister Laslo. "Despite their illegal covert action, I am grateful to them. They risked their lives and one was killed in the operation. The manuscripts and spear would not be safe if not for them."

He thanked Nick Loren. He thanked Archer and Lacy. "Most of all, I want to give thanks to the Lord for saving my daughter. I have never been so happy to say that I was so wrong about so many things. Accordingly, I hereby announce that I have rescinded my bill, the Freedom from Religious Oppression Act, and I also announce my resignation from the Senate. I am done with public life. I will spend the rest of my life caring for my daughter and growing in the Lord."

They walked to the Senator's office. Once inside, Lacy approached Amy.

"I owe you an apology."

She looked up at her with knitted eyebrows.

"I apologize for lying to you, for telling you that the backpack would protect you."

Amy looked down at the floor, then back up. "But you were right in the end. It changed my daddy. And isn't that protecting him?"

She smiled. "You've got a point."

Over the course of the next few days and weeks, a variety of events occurred. A search of emails in the coming days showed that Mini-D had contacted the Mullah in New York and arranged the Stinger missile that was fired from the van. All charges were dropped against Lester Dunsette, though he would wear the dunce cap for the rest of his life. Only the Father knows the date of the Second Coming. Turkey and Jordan formally protested the actions of the two Americans, DeYoung and Stowe, and of the Israelis, but that was as far as it went.

Archer and Lacy were cleared of all charges in the death of the Uighur. The shooting of Dr. Concord at the Pella site was deemed self-defense, particularly after Concord refused to press charges. Yatom was returned to Israel, tried, and executed.

Christians hailed Loren's and—particularly—Kitchens's conversions, and agnostics decried it, saying it was the lingering effect of the release that his daughter was safe. Kitchens would not have any of it. "I know exactly what I am doing. I will now join the Super-PAC, The Word, in spreading the good news of the gospel."

When people read the second testimonium stating that Caiaphas knew Jesus was divine, it became a sensation.

Nick Loren closed Pas de Createur and took every web-based device out of his house and out of his life. Then, before he resigned as the Director of Pas de Createur, he inserted a virus into Mini-D, just enough to capture its attention—and then cut the cable to the D-frame with an ax. Then he took a baseball bat to the computer's battery system. He went on to beat the frame of Mini-D into so much crumpled metal, glass, and wire. Gone was Mini-D—but not the knowledge of how to make it. Technology is neutral. Humans cannot afford to be.

179

After leaving Kitchens's Senate office, Archer and Lacy took a cab to Alexandria and found a nice bistro along the Potomac River. She ordered coffee and so did he.

"No alcohol?"

He noticed she tilted her head to the left. He shook his head. "Done with booze."

She smiled. "You look great."

"I feel great. The best I've ever felt."

"And you've kept off the weight."

"I was hoping you noticed. I am thinking of writing a diet book. I'll call it the 'Band of the Run' diet."

Lacy chuckled. "Whatever works."

Archer regarded her. "So what's next for you?"

She shrugged. "I'm an archeologist. I'm happy only when I have dirt under my fingernails."

"I doubt either of us will ever again find anything as spectacular as the spear and those manuscripts. But, you know what? That's okay."

She looked out at the river flowing by. "I wonder if the manuscripts and spear will have any lasting impact."

"They've got to have some. Put it this way: we're better off now than before. People have a choice. And now the choice is clearer than ever."

She smiled. "Yeah. Maybe that's the bottom line."

"For me, the bottom line is that the unseen is just as real as the tangible. In fact, more so."

She looked at him and smiled. "I thought you believed God was hidden."

"I did. It wasn't the spear itself that healed. It was faith—faith in something that we cannot see, but is no less real."

Lacy smiled and nodded. "Yes, that's the message."

Author's Note

The Spear of the Centurion, of course, is a novel. That said, much of it is based on fact. I particularly focused on making sure the fictional ancient manuscripts of Longinus, Tarjan, and Quintus were consistent with scripture and did not contradict it. Biblical truth is sacrosanct and not to be deviated from. However, I discovered that there is some difference amongst scholars on the exact timing of some events during the last week of Jesus, before, during, and after the crucifixion, and what specifically happened and was said. When faced with those differences, I tried to incorporate both versions as much as possible. Then I wove an extra fictional story around Biblical truth.

The Bible does not describe Jesus meeting the centurion who speared him until they came together at Golgotha. If they did meet, the Bible does not describe that meeting. I added a fictional scene where Jesus looked at the spear when he was in the temple. In my opinion, adding such a scene, as long as it is recognized as fictional flourish, does not detract in any way from the true historical accounts described in the four gospels. My scene is simply part of my fictional story, and should be recognized as such. Nothing that Jesus actually did was changed.

I chose for the centurion the name of Longinus because the Roman Catholic Church identifies him as such. I chose Petronius as his second name because some accounts say that the centurion who guarded the tomb was of that name. The Bible itself does not identify either of these men by name. Furthermore, the Bible does not say that it was the same centurion who presided over the crucifixion and then guarded the tomb. I threw them together for continuity purposes of the story. There are, indeed, several legends about the famous spear.

I tried to stay as accurate as possible on the geographic description. There is a ruin at the great library at Celsus. I hope one day to visit it.

There is a grotto in western Turkey commemorating the legend of the Seven Sleepers. There is also a similar Muslim grotto in western China. There is a Migdol Temple ruin in the ancient city of Pella in modern-day Jordan. I grew up in Pella, Iowa, and chose Pella for that reason. I used satellite photographs of these various sites as much as were available.

That said, I took a few creative liberties at Monticello, which is a wonderful place that I visited once years ago. There was a gong, but it does not sound as described in Spear. As far as I know there is no wine today in the wine cellar, and I doubt the dumbwaiter was large enough or sturdy enough to handle the size and weight of adult males. Those additions aside, if you get a chance to visit Jefferson's home, do so. It is one of the great sites of American history.

The description of future technology—while based on existing trends and research—at times crossed into science-fiction, although as I write this in 2015, I wonder what will really be present fifteen years from now, when Spear takes place. The pace of technological change, if anything, is accelerating. Frankly, I find much of it disconcerting.

My primary motivation for writing Spear was to describe the changes that occurred among the Disciples. As a Christian and a former deist, I believe, like C.S. Lewis, that the transformation of these men and women testifies to the truth that Jesus of Nazareth was and is the Christ. Josh McDowell asked the great question: "Who would die for a lie?" And while my description of liberal secularism may be overwrought for dramatic purposes, there are vestiges of it today, and I believe if allowed to, it would grow into a monster that our forefathers did not foresee or desire. So I fully admit that I am a partisan in this debate. I am a Christian and believe that Christ is the truth. Obviously, the purpose of this book is to help convince non-believers of that truth—that proverbial mustard seed— and, hopefully, along the way, tell a fast and fun story.

One more thing: I need feedback. If you read Spear, I would love for you to go to my Facebook home page and message me. Give me an honest critique. I will not get my feelings hurt, nor get a big head. God and my family keep me grounded.

God bless.
Thom Vines

February 14, 2015, Valentine's Day. The ultimate "Valentine" was Jesus's sacrifice for us on the cross.

Author Bio

The Spear of the Centurion is the sixth book by Thom Vines, five of which are novels. The first was a nonfiction work entitled *Tragedy and Trust* about the spiritual journey after losing a child. It won four awards, including second at the 2012 Beach Book festival in New York City.

The second book was a Christian novel entitled *Hope's Ante*, which won six awards, including a second at the Southern California Book Festival.

A World War two spy novel, *Twisted Crosses* followed, which led to two Christian novels released in 2014 and 2015, respectively: *Petroglyphs*, a love story set in New Mexico, and *The Power and the Prayer* about a Republican agnostic president who converts while in office. That book is meant to dovetail with the 2016 election.

Thom Vines grew up in Iowa, graduating from Central College, where he met his wife, Becky. They have three children, one of which lives on in heaven. Mr. Vines is a former history teacher and retired as the Deputy Superintendent of Lubbock-Cooper Schools in Lubbock, Texas. He did not come to faith until 2006 at age 52, so he channels many of his books towards those spiritually searching, for he was once there.